"MR. MURPHY SKEWERED THE BYWAYS AND BACKWATERS OF FLORIDA . . . LIKE BUGS ON A BOARD."
—Robert Campbell

"*APPARENT WIND* IS INTELLIGENT, FUNNY—AND SCARY, FOR ALL THE RIGHT REASONS."
—*St. Petersburg Times* (Florida)

"A loopy, cynical, romantic caper novel. . . . *APPARENT WIND* is daring and funny and smart, the literary equivalent of a rhinestone flamingo pin worn with a wink. . . . The book and its protagonist, Doom Loomis, are funny, sexy and smart, an alluring combination."
—*Miami Herald*

"An imaginative crime novel that also asks readers to remember the painful environmental price that Florida has paid for its development."
—*Atlanta Journal and Constitution*

"MASTERFUL . . . *APPARENT WIND* IS MUCH MORE THAN AN EXCELLENT CRIME NOVEL. . . . Murphy touches our environmental conscience without preaching. . . . The characters are interesting; their conversations always have a natural feel. Murphy's dry wit and sardonic style often lead to a laugh. . . . MURPHY IS AN IMAGINATIVE AND SKILLED AUTHOR."
—*Palm Beach Post* (Florida)

A Mysterious Book Club Alternate Selection

Books by Dallas Murphy

Apparent Wind
Lover Man

Published by POCKET BOOKS

APPARENT WIND

DALLAS MURPHY

POCKET BOOKS

New York   London   Toronto   Sydney   Tokyo   Singapore

POCKET BOOKS, a division of Simon & Schuster Inc.
1230 Avenue of the Americas, New York, NY 10020

ISBN: 0-671-68554-6

First Pocket Books paperback printing December 1991

10 9 8 7 6 5 4 3 2 1

POCKET and colophon are registered trademarks of
Simon & Schuster Inc.

Cover art by Clarke Tate

Printed in the U.S.A.

For Genie

I am indebted to Marjory Stoneman Douglas and her timeless *The Everglades: River of Grass*. I also wish to thank James Griffith, Reed Haslem, Don & Glen Jones, David Konigsberg, Ken Kurtenbach, Genie Leftwich, Alan Merickel, and Peg Patterson.

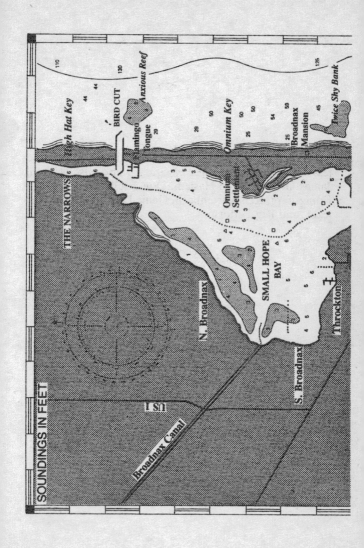

SOUNDINGS IN FEET

THE NARROWS

High Hat Key

BIRD CUT

Flamingo Tongue

Anxious Reef

110
130
125

44

50   50   50   53   54   45

29   26   25   25

Omnium Key

Broadnax Mansion

Twice Shy Bank

6   6   6

3   5

3   5

Omnium Settlement

2

5   5   4   5

6   3

5

6   6

5

N. Broadnax

1   4   3

4

2

SMALL HOPE BAY

5   6   2

2   4   5

3   4   5

6

2

Throckton

S. Broadnax

LT SD

Broadnax Canal

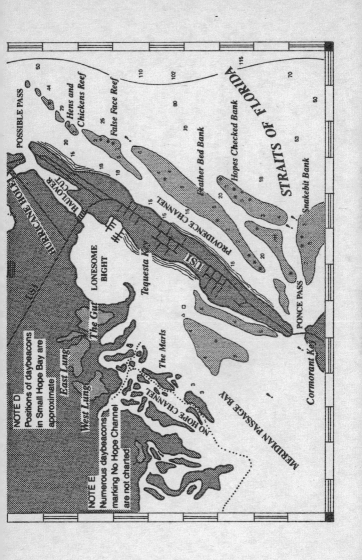

LAND OF OUR FATHERS

HAVING CONDUCTED HIS EVOLUTIONARY BUSINESS WITH unprecedented success, mankind soon changed the face of the earth to suit his own purposes. He began by hunting the giant Pleistocene mammals to extinction, and later, after learning agriculture, he turned the face of the land docile and domestic. But not in south Florida. That region remained a swamp, hostile to human dreams and visions, because it remained submerged.

Juan Ponce de León, the psychopath, discovered Florida on April 2, 1513. Having fallen out of favor with the Spanish authorities in Puerto Rico because he was too crazy, Ponce sailed north in search of gold, since there was nothing like gold to ingratiate a fellow with the powers that be. He found in south Florida a fetid tangle of foliage, insect swarms so dense they cast shadows, reptiles with malicious intent, lurking, and heathen Indians living in a Stone Age state of gracelessness.

Ponce converted the Indians to Catholicism while he shook them down for their gold. They had never heard of gold, since there is no gold, no metals of any kind, in mangrove swamps, which was why the Indians lived in a Stone Age state, but Ponce suspected they were holding out on him. Peeved, Ponce hacked the noses off several hundred Indian faces as examples of the Wrath of God,

1

and left. The indigenous tribes of south Florida vanished forever shortly after their initial contacts with Catholicism.

As events of great moment unfolded to the north, nothing much happened in south Florida for the next 350 years, until the Seminoles arrived. Refugees from the Carolina Creek wars, the Seminoles didn't know any more about living in swamps than Ponce, but they were a great deal more adaptive. As a result they flourished on the abundant fish and game, propagated and multiplied, blackening themselves with charcoal to stave off insects.

Blackened redskins propagating and multiplying within the nation's borders made President Andrew Jackson edgy, so he dispatched federal troops to exterminate them. The troops, however, found this harder to do than Old Hickory had reckoned. Those sneaky heathens didn't stand up and fight like men. Instead, they skulked in the buttonwoods and sniped off the troops as they marched along. Those that ducked heathen missiles were felled by a dozen different diseases. The troops died like monkeys in a hurricane.

The bedraggled survivors brought back tales of a great wetness, more water than land, where one's gun belts and boots mildewed overnight and rotted to goo in a week, where merely walking on the muck caused itchy impetigo shins—the troops were walking because thirty-foot-long crocs had devoured their chargers. It was a dreadful, pestilential place unfit for habitation by decent folks; only Indians could survive in such a place, because they didn't feel misery like white folks did. The decimated brigade staggered north in abject defeat, and Old Hickory called it total victory. Decades passed. Nothing happened in south Florida. Nature held sway.

The Civil War went down with barely a ripple.

However, by 1900 there had arisen in the North a new concept of life—*vacation*—and with it a new concept of land that would alter south Florida forever. After the birth of the vacation, land was no longer viewed as a utilitarian place on which to hunt, gather, farm, or homestead. Land became a parcel, a lot, a unit, a part of a portfolio.

It became real estate.

By 1920, when Prentiss Throckmorton's railroad arrived, south Florida real estate had become too valuable to remain underwater. Here was a tropical climate only two days' travel from February in New York. No longer would one need to brook the impertinent glares of machete-wielding Latin malcontents and rude Negroes to feel the hot glow of sunshine on sallow shoulder blades.

Christ, just imagine what this south Florida land would be worth if it really *were* land.

ORANGE BLOSSOM SPECIAL

DOOM LOOMIS'S LAWYER, A MAN WITH SPAGHETTI SPOTS on his tie and a sardonic set to his jaw, used to say, "A stand-up guy is just another breed of asshole."

Doom couldn't help being a stand-up guy, but he wasn't entirely guileless, either. He pretended to conduct an animated conversation on the pay phone opposite Departure Gate 23 at La Guardia. The 2:17 A.M. flight to Miami was already boarding when Doom spotted the high-heeled Lady in Black clicking down the inclined corridor.

Doom had never seen the Lady in Black before. They had spoken on pay phones. She said she would dress darkly and carry Ozzie's goods, gift-wrapped, in a Channel 13 tote bag. Doom said he would wear a blue serge suit over an open-necked shirt, but he had lied. He intended to look things over before he identified himself. That's why he had chosen this dreadful departure time. He would arrive in Miami about 4:30. Add another two hours' driving time to Omnium Key on Small Hope Bay, and he would get no sleep before his father's funeral. But it was worth it.

At two in the morning he might make the tailers, lurkers, and malefactors before they made him, looking as they would for a chump in a blue serge suit. At the faintest sniff of the untoward, Doom would board his Florida flight like an innocent tourist, and Ozzie could find himself another stand-up guy.

During the closing months of his sentence, Ozzie Mertz prattled unceasingly about the goods he had stashed on the outside. "Just picture it, boys. *Florida*. Sun, surf and turf, sipping piña coladas with a financially untroubled psyche." Ozzie would sigh theatrically, while everybody else groaned with tedium. "But one must remain ever discreet. They will be watching. Discretion—that's the ticket."

"Then shut the fuck up," one or another bored con would suggest. The cons liked Ozzie. He had a warm and generous spirit, but he was stupid.

Approaching, the Lady in Black seemed free of tails, and there seemed to be no suspicious gatherings, no men in clean-up clothes leaning on brooms or knots of guys in pilot uniforms, no thugs trying to look like geeks, south-bound, in Disney World sweatshirts. In fact, there was no one at all.

Then, however, Doom got a look at her face. He barely suppressed a gasp. Her face had been beaten black and swollen. Her right eye was pressed into a visionless slit by inflamed flesh, and her lips were puffed. Glancing neither right nor left, she marched to the waiting area and sat down as planned. She placed her Channel 13 tote bag on the floor between her shoes and waited sullenly.

That did it. Doom hung up the dead phone and headed for the check-in desk. The last of his fellow passengers had already boarded. He watched her out of the corner of his eye as he handed his one-way ticket to the attendant and asked for a window seat. But then he glanced at her again, sitting hunched and sore in the pathetic plastic chair, and Doom melted. His lawyer would have grinned sardonically and shaken his head at human folly if he had seen Doom sit down beside the Lady in Black.

"It's me," he said. "Blue serge suit."

She turned and looked him up and down with distaste. She was probably about Ozzie's age, fifty-five, but it was impossible to tell from the wreckage of her face. "When you see Ozzie, you tell him he owes me," she slurred. Then she stood up and walked away, leaving Ozzie's goods on the floor at Doom's feet.

"We're boarding now, sir," said the flight attendant.

THE VISIONARIES

"LOOK HOW WET IT IS," SAID SHORTSIGHTED VISITORS. "It's a useless old swamp." (Technically, they were incorrect; it was a mangrove forest, a variety of coastal wetland, not a swamp, but nobody cared about that.)

But men of vision reasoned, "If we drained off the water, the stinking swamp would shrivel and die." Evicted fauna would crawl elsewhere or die. So would the insects. So would the colorful birds, and that was a shame, but hell, the man of vision could import even prettier ones from Brazil or somewhere. Once he had the bushes on the run, then he would need to pump the land up above the high-tide surge and rainy-season floods. And there he'd have it, dry land where once there was only water. The man of vision would thus have made himself a parcel of tabula rasa real estate.

It wouldn't be quite that easy, of course. He'd lose twenty percent of his work force to moccasins and malaria and God knows what all. But more labor could always be imported from Alabama or somewhere. Busy uprooting a twelve-thousand-year-old ecosystem for fame and fortune, the man of vision couldn't let human misery stand in the way of new real estate.

Yuletide, 1920, two men of vision—Colonel A. C. Broadnax and the railroad tycoon Prentiss Throckmorton—bobbed serenely at anchor aboard the *Oseola*, Throckmorton's 85-foot motor yacht. Their journey had taken them from Grand Central Station on Throckmorton's own railroad to its terminus at St. Augustine, where they boarded the *Oseola* for the voyage down the Matanzas into the Indian River, with a side jaunt into the Banana River lagoon, thence south in the ocean to Biscayne Bay, which led through Card Sound to Barnes Sound south into Small Hope Bay, a near wilderness at that time.

Colonel A. C. Broadnax and Prentiss Throckmorton were birds of a feather, and that's why neither trusted the other. They lounged side by side in canvas deck chairs on the fantail, arms folded across ample bellies, heels propped on the gleaming mahogany transom. Their feet were beginning to fall asleep due to circulatory impediments. It was sunset, 72 degrees, and buttery light rolled on the serene surface of Small Hope Bay.

"Beautiful, isn't she?" said Prentiss Throckmorton.

"She is that, Throck," replied Colonel Broadnax, "but between ourselves, I wish she'd move more."

"What? Move? Oh. No. Not Delilah. Florida. This spot right here."

"Oh."

"Anyway, how can she move all trussed up like that?"

"I like it when they struggle. And squirm."

Throck was growing weary of this Broadnax. Strictly lower order. Sometimes, however, grand ambition demanded dealing with Neanderthals. A spoonbill called twice from the shallows beneath primeval red mangroves.

"What was that?" the colonel wondered. "An alligator?"

"I don't know. I guess so."

"I understand they can chop a man in twain with one bite. Now that would be a sight to see." Maybe if they remained here long enough some hapless Seminole would go for a wade.

"This spot is known as Small Hope Bay. Of course I'll have to change that. Too defeatist."

"I've got to admit one thing, Throck. We'd be freezing our bollocks off back home."

"Sublime climate. And look at that light. You won't see light like that back home. That light is serene. That's what I'd call it. Serene. Makes a man feel God's in his heaven, all's right with the world."

"It's just that there's an awful lot of water."

"Wet, I don't deny it, Colonel, but suppose there was just enough water to be, well, aquatic without being submerged. Suppose it were just right vis-à-vis water."

Colonel Broadnax wasn't really a colonel, but he had invented the rapid-fire toggle-cam mechanism for machine guns; customarily, a man responsible for so many deaths was accorded honorary military rank. Colonel Broadnax could see it coming. This Prentiss Throckmorton was supposed to be so shrewd, with his gerrymandering and interlocking directorates, but Broadnax wasn't impressed. The man was transparent. Broadnax stretched and yawned to indicate idle interest and said, "Say, Throck, you wouldn't be planning to make yourself a parcel, would you?"

"Funny you should mention it. A man attains a certain station in life where further wealth is no longer the goal. A man yearns to do something great, something that will outlast him. Sennacherib made land in Nineveh. So did Claudius in Italy. There's fine company for a man to keep at the close of his threescore and ten."

"But let me ask you this, Throck. Suppose you made yourself a parcel or two, and nobody wanted to buy it?"

"First you make the land, then you create the demand for it. All a matter of public relations."

"Public relations? What's that?"

Prentiss Throckmorton prided himself on his PR prowess. He had damn near invented the art in his spare time. His luxury hotel in St. Augustine, the Ponce de Leon,

7

proved that. Throck promoted the myth that Ponce explored those shores in search of the Fountain of Youth. He presented Ponce as a rotund and lovable Don Quixote figure on a quest for that which everyone wants, especially aging millionaires, and he dressed his help in cute Ponce suits that he had designed himself in his spare time. Throck had better sense than to name his luxury hotel after a lunatic looking for gold in swamps, who hacked the shit out of raggedy-assed Indians when they couldn't come across.

A sweet breeze wafted in from the sea, riffling the tops of the red mangroves in which perched hundreds of snowy egrets like fluffy Christmas-tree ornaments, and that gave Throck another idea. Instead of letting all those birds fly away when he killed their roosts, he might be able to mount buckshot cannons on boats and shoot down the birds in droves to defray expenses. All he'd need to do was create a new demand for plumed hats through public relations. "What if I leave the technical details to you, A.C.? The machinery and such."

"I'm pretty busy these days, Throck."

"Hypothetically, then. What would you need for a job like that? Rip out the swamp, put up something the right kind of people will like."

"Well, you're talking about a big job. You couldn't just rip up those trees—what do you call those trees?"

"Mangrove trees."

"You couldn't just rip out the mangrove trees. You'd only have yourself an expensive sandbar when you were done. I mean, look how low all these islands are. First gale'd sink you again. No, you'd have to pump up the land, make it higher."

"And how would you do that?" Throck wondered.

"I'd drive steel plates into the bottom, make kind of a corral around the little islands, see? 'Course the corral would be full of water. Then what I'd do is I'd pump the water out of the corral back into the bay. And at the same time I'd be pumping material from the bottom of the bay *into* the corral. Get me?"

"You'd be making land."

"You could make the land any shape you wanted just by the way you configured your steel plates. You could make little heart-shaped islands, you could make them look like alligators, birds, anything."

"What would you want in the way of heavy equipment?"

"I'd want pumps, big gushers with a couple miles of eighteen-inch reinforced rubber hose. As far as the heavy gear, I'd want a couple crawlers, a front-end grabber, rooters, maybe even a blaster if the going got tough. A peatpuller wouldn't hurt. Big job, tearing out a swamp and making something nice."

"How many Negroes would you need?"

"Two thousand to start. You'd lose half of them."

"That many?"

"They'll drop like flies."

"I hadn't considered that."

"You've got to consider everything."

"It's a shame you're so busy. You sound just the man for the job."

Like Claudius and Sennacherib, Prentiss Throckmorton and Colonel Broadnax both recognized that the man who made the land could define the look of it. The land could reflect the values of its maker. Colonel Broadnax was thinking he could make it look like Venice, with canals and gondolas. Or like Morocco, with minarets and eunuchs. First he'd make the land, then decide. After the real work was done and paid for, then he'd figure some way to cut Throck right out of the picture.

Back in his nautically appointed cabin, Colonel Broadnax tied Delilah to the four-poster with brightly colored scarves. She wore only her black stockings and garter belt. Once she was spread-eagled, her sweet pink nipples pointing at the ceiling, A.C. said, "He wants me to do it."

"Do what?" Delilah asked, alarmed.

"Make some land."

"Oh, that," she said, relieved. "Well, sweetie, I'm sure you'll be tip-top at making land."

9

"Would you mind struggling this time? You know, squirm and kick. Money is no object."

SEA BLUE

〰〰〰〰〰

DOOM LOOMIS POSED NO APPARENT THREAT TO SOCIETY. That's why the New York State Penal Authority had agreed to release him three months early so he could attend his father's funeral on Omnium Key. Doom was born on Omnium Key and grew up playing along the shores of Small Hope Bay, but his parents' marriage disintegrated when Doom was ten. Since Doom's father had been a crook, there was no question as to custody. Doom's mother had taken him north to New York, and he hadn't been back to south Florida since. Now Omnium Settlement was sinking, falling inch by inexorable inch back into the oolitic limestone bottom of Small Hope Bay from which Colonel A. C. Broadnax had dredged it sixty-three years before.

Doom's mother was more angry than sad. Her upper lip curled sharply at the corners, an expression vivid in Doom's childhood memory whenever his father had fucked her up again. Even now from inside his ceramic urn, which Marvis Puller gripped between his insteps on the cockpit sole, Doom's father was fucking her up. If it weren't for that last wish of his—that his ashes be distributed over Gulf Stream water—she would be on dry land, not pounding to windward in this treacherous slop. Now her new, her fourth, husband, Norman Futterman, was pleading wordlessly with his eyes, speech gone: "Get me off this boat or kill me quickly."

Doom had only this morning met his stepfather, a self-made meat packer from Wyandanch, Long Island. Norman was the first normal man Doom's mother had ever married. The other three had all been crooks.

Had the decision to sail been left to Captain Bert, this trip to the Gulf Stream would have been postponed for better weather. But Norman couldn't wait. He needed to get back to the packing plant, because, unsupervised, his cutters would embezzle his prime cuts and sell them to up-and-coming Mafia underlings, leaving him hocks and gristle. This boat, a forty-two-foot steel sloop, was Doom's legacy. He had no firm idea how to sail her, but at least she didn't make him feel like Norman, who clung now to Doom's mother's breast like an infant macaque.

Doom was surprised at the violence of *Staggerlee*'s motion. Time after time, hulking rollers bucked her bow, hung her for a moment on the balance of her keel, and then dropped her into the troughs. The wind had been blowing twenty knots with higher gusts from the east for two days. Each year in strong onshore winds, one or more inland tourists were swept from the jetties at Bird Cut to seamen's deaths. Sometimes their bloated bodies washed up on Omnium Beach several days later. Sometimes not.

Doom's father's body had washed up on Omnium Beach. Black, bloated, partly eaten by crabs and fishes, it was found by a strolling florist from Philadelphia who owned a time share on Tequesta Key and who, after seeing what the ocean did to its dead, traded his beachside condo for one in Utah.

Broadnax County sheriff and acting coroner, Lincoln Plotner, ruled the death accidental, by drowning. *Staggerlee* was found at anchor two hundred yards off the beach. Sheriff Plotner concluded that Denny Loomis had anchored for a swim, gotten downcurrent, grown exhausted, and gone under. An open casket was out of the question, he having been a link in the food chain for forty-eight hours.

Norman Futterman wheezed and gagged and made disquieting gurgles with his nasal fluids. "Couldn't we just do it?" he rasped. "We're in the sea. Couldn't we just do it and go home?"

"The man wanted the Gulf Stream," said Marvis Puller. "He's goddamn going to get it."

Staggerlee was stopped nearly dead in her wake by a particularly nasty wave, and Doom's father's pot popped from between Marvis's insteps. It clattered forward on the floor until Doom caught it soccer-style and footed it back to Marvis.

"How much longer, then?" Norman mouthed dryly.

"Good day or two," said Captain Bert. "Why don't you get some sleep?"

"Day or two! Nooo!" For a frightful instant, Norman Futterman envisioned his condition by tomorrow this time and then vomited down the front of his new wife's foul-weather gear.

"Bert, you're still an asshole," she snarled. In a soft voice she said to Norman, "Not two days, darling. He was just kidding." She glared at Bert. "It's more like twenty minutes. Try watching the horizon. Deep breathing." But it was too late for that. His eyes had rolled back in his head. She laid him out against the cabin trunk on the bridge deck and covered him with a blanket as though he were the one to be buried at sea. Heavy spray in fat bullets came regularly over the bow and blew aft into the cockpit. Doom's mother went below.

"I hear you did time," said Captain Bert without moving his lips.

"Uh-huh," answered Doom, hoping Bert would have the good taste to drop it.

"What for?"

"Genocide," said Doom. This old Captain Bert probably was an asshole, but he clearly knew how to handle sailboats. He stood stalwart at the wheel, spinning it deftly away from the waves and back again in the troughs to ease the motion. His hands were like fat hams. Doom would have thought them incapable of deftness. Bert was thinking about dousing the working jib and setting the storm sail. Or maybe no headsail at all.

Marvis Puller had been studying the urn between his feet. He said, "How do we know whose ashes these are?"

"Denny's ashes. Whose do you think?" said Bert.

"Yeah, but how do we know that? We only got the funeral guy's word on it. For all we know, these are brick-ettes from his backyard barbecue."

"Jesus, you are one cynical Negro," said Bert without moving his lips. "I went to school with that boy. He wouldn't bullshit me about Denny's ashes."

Norman suddenly lunged for the rail as if to end his misery in the dark still of the deep. He fell against the lifelines, vomiting. Marvis Puller, averting his eyes, held Norman aboard by the belt.

"Look, you always want to throw up downwind," Bert said.

Doom went below to see his mother.

Down there, the motion felt more random and chaotic than in the cockpit, where one could see oncoming waves and connect them to the lurches and heaves they caused. Below, the violence seemed domestic, not nautical. This was a room, living quarters, with a dining table, beds, a kitchen aft, a toilet up forward—his father had lived here as if in a long, thin house. Of course, domestic violence was nothing new to Doom or his mother. He planted his back against the companionway ladder and waited for his eyes to adjust to the dimness.

His mother, having removed her befouled gear, had curled into the leeward, the low side, berth. Doom heard her crying softly before he actually saw her. From hand-hold to handhold, like an arboreal ancestor, he made his way toward the sound. She looked into his face. She was old, but Doom remembered her young face, when she had taught him to swim in warm waist-deep water at Omnium Beach. The Australian crawl, she had called it.

"I'm leaving this afternoon, Dennis."

"I figured."

She explained that this leaving of hers was more than a return to Wyandanch. Once she shook out the sere contents of that urn, Denny Loomis would no longer be welcome in her memory. She hoped Doom understood.

He assured her he did.

"I haven't been a successful mother."

"Sure you have."

"You wouldn't have gone to prison if I hadn't married all those bums."

"I probably would have anyway."

"I loved your father, Dennis. I never stopped, after all these years, but damn it, he was sixty-six last week, and still working the con!"

"Was he really?"

"Some kind of real estate dodge. 'This will be the one,' he told me. I didn't even ask. He was addicted to law-breaking. Some people are, you know. . . . Prison didn't scar you, did it, Dennis?"

"No, Mom, it was minimum security. Mostly we lived in tents in the woods. Like the Boy Scouts."

"What are you going to do now?"

Doom looked down into her eyes. They were clouded with tears and family regret. Doom blurted out a sob but caught the next one. He had his own history of regret, how could he relieve hers? Doom held her. Her hair smelled old. He was without prospects to make a mother feel proud. And successful.

"You aren't going to write anymore, are you?"

"No, no more writing. Maybe I'll stay around here for a while. I'm curious about the hometown."

"What hometown?"

"Omnium Settlement."

"Omnium's sinking, dear."

"I know. But I have *Staggerlee* for when it gets too deep." Doom tried to smile, but the result felt strictly muscular.

"We sailed all the way to Canada in her. Remember?"

"What? I went? On this boat?"

"You were just a child."

"You, me . . . Dad?"

"We went nonstop all the way to Newfoundland. Your father was a sane, sensitive man at sea."

"Newfoundland? How old was I?"

"You were two? Yes, two."

". . . Where did I sleep?"

"When it was rough, you slept right here, with a lee cloth to keep you cozy—" She giggled tearfully. "I don't want to go all maudlin, but you had a rag monkey you took to bed to make the storms go away. Windy was its name."

"Why didn't you tell me?"

"I thought you remembered. See, I haven't been a successful mother."

"I was two, we left Florida when I was ten—what about the next eight years? I would have remembered sailing when I was eight or nine."

"We never went again. Dennis gave up the sea for suckers. . . . Let's say good-bye down here, alone and out of the wind."

"Good-bye, Mom. Don't worry about me." Good-bye, Windy.

"One other thing, Dennis. Those men up there—Bert and Marvis and the others like them—they'll lie to you about your father. It's in their interests to keep his myth alive."

Back topside, Doom watched the state of the sea. It had changed. Whitecaps were now being blown flat before they could crest, their remains whipped in nervous lines from wave to wave. The low land was nothing more than a smudge astern, call it out of sight. Norman was fetally curled on the bridge deck beneath the blue canvas dodger. There were no obvious signs of life.

"How will we know when we're there?" Doom asked Captain Bert, but the wind took away the answer, and since Bert never moved his lips when he spoke, there was no reading them. Doom clambered around Marvis's feet and his father's pot and stood beside Bert at the wheel to repeat his question.

"By the color. There just ain't no other blue like Gulf Stream blue. You never seen it?"

"A long time ago."

"She's way on out today." This Captain Bert was a seagoing ventriloquist. "Usually she's close in, a mile or two. I'd of thought the east wind would bring her in, but hell, she meanders wherever she wants. You can't ever tell."

Facing dead into the wind, feeling it on both ears equally, Doom had a powerful urge to know—how deep was the water? how hard was the wind blowing? why did the Gulf Stream meander?—concrete things, measurable, provable things. Fuck all dreamy abstraction. "Why don't we put up bigger sails?" *Staggerlee* was carrying a double-reefed main and the tiny blade of a jib. "Wouldn't we go faster?"

"Yep. But we wouldn't like it none. Probably kill Norman."

"Rough?"

"Rough as a cob. Sure, we could shake out a reef, we'd go faster. *Staggerlee* could take it, but we set more sail, the apparent wind's gonna get up over thirty knots."

"Apparent wind? What's apparent wind?"

"Well. . . . You say, what's apparent wind?"

"Yeah."

"See, fact is, sailboats don't sail by the true wind. No, they sail by the apparent wind. . . . Take a tourist standing on the beach, it's blowin', say, ten knots. The tourist is feelin' the true wind. But sailboats ain't standin' on the beach. At least you hope they ain't. Sailboats move, and moving things create their own wind. Stick your hand out the car window doin' sixty—that's apparent wind. 'Course the motorist, he don't give a shit about the wind, because he ain't sailin'. We're sailin'. You take today. Accordin' to this instrument right here, wind's blowin' twenty-four knots, right? Okay, we're sailing *into* the wind at six knots. Therefore, we're actually feeling wind that's blowin' thirty knots. Hell of a difference between twenty-four and thirty knots. Now say we turned completely around and was still doing our six knots—"

"Oh," said Doom, "then we'd feel a wind of only eighteen knots?" You couldn't even depend on the wind being literal. "So it'll be more comfortable going home?"

"Exactly. You want to get subtle about it? Okay. As

the wind speed increases, so does boat speed. When that happens, the apparent wind angle changes right along with wind speed."

"What's wind angle?"

"The angle the wind meets the sails at."

". . . Okay." Nothing was ever simple.

"When the boat goes faster, the angle moves forward. When the boat slows down, the apparent-wind angle moves aft. You want to know something else?"

"Sure, that's why I'm asking."

"This boat ain't the only thing your daddy left you, not by a long shot."

"Shut up, Bert," said Marvis Puller.

"Well, it ain't," Bert petulantly insisted.

"You got no discretion, Bert. You're a cracker hammerhead."

"What's this all about?" Doom demanded.

Marvis sneaked a glance at Norman. Was he listening? Marvis slid aft with the ashes to join Bert and Doom at the wheel. He whispered to Doom, "Could we have lunch or something when we get back?"

"Where we had breakfast?" Doom suggested.

"The Flamingo Tongue Dockside Cafe," Bert specified. He was disappointed. He wanted to be the one to tell, whereas now it would be Marvis, since Marvis was the accountant. "We're in the Stream," he said, nodding at the ocean.

Doom gasped at the sight. The sea had suddenly transformed itself from riled limy green to a soul-deep blue, almost indigo. Long, tapering shafts of sunlight shimmered enticingly down into the abyss. What was down there? Doom recalled seeing while in prison a *National Geographic* special about a pioneering oceanographer named Beebe, who in a primitive submersible rode the Gulf Stream's middle depths for hundreds of miles and saw wondrous things. But on the rec-room TV, the power of that blue to captivate, to lure, was lost. This was the real thing. And the way to see it would be from the inside, like

Beebe, with blue water in three dimensions and his father in particulate suspension.

Doom's mother knew by the change in motion that they had arrived at his father's final resting place. She was already climbing up the companionway ladder. When she was seated in the cockpit, Marvis Puller handed her the pot.

No one spoke. Captain Bert cracked off onto a reach, and the apparent wind dropped. "Does anyone have anything to say?" asked Doom's mother softly. No one did. Without ceremony, she opened the lid and averted her eyes from its contents. "Well, Dennis . . . good-bye." And she shook her ex-husband's ashes over the starboard rail—

"No!" shouted Captain Bert, but it was too late. The wind gusted, caught the ashes, and hurled them aft at twenty knots.

They struck Doom flush in the face, blinding him momentarily. Flecks of gray stuck to his teary cheeks.

"Oh, Dennis!" his mother cried.

"That's okay," said Doom.

"You always want to shake out a man's ashes downwind," explained Bert without moving his lips.

HOME

~~~~~~~~~

"THE SIMPLE FISCAL FACT OF THE MATTER IS THIS: YOU own Omnium Settlement lock, stock, and barrel," pronounced Marvis Puller after he had arranged himself beside Bert in a window booth at the Flamingo Tongue Dockside Cafe. Besides the cook and a waitress, a knot of khaki-clad charter-boat skippers sat at the counter over coffee. A tourist family with snorkeling gear ate fried grouper at another booth. The only other diner was a fat cop who had eyed Doom as he entered.

Staggerlee was the only boat tied up at the docks. Doom had been watching her gentle upturn at bow and stern— nothing had ever seemed so balanced as the shape of his boat. "What do you mean, I own Omnium Settlement?"

"Shh—" Captain Bert had seen someone coming. It was the fat cop.

Broadnax County sheriff Lincoln Plotner slid off his stool, sucked in his gut, and strode across the open floor to where this chip off old Denny Loomis's block sat like a Yankee smart-ass ex-con from the Rotten Apple. You had to be one dubious fucker, you served time in Zoo York, where three pedestrians in five packed felonious intent. It was part of his job to chat up the ex-cons in his county, find out what they had up their sleeves and when they planned to hit the road. Sheriff Plotner wore a gray uniform with a hand-tooled Sam Browne belt that held, just below the bulge of his belly, his handcuffs, Mace sprayer, sap, flashlight, Bowie knife, and .357 Bulldog loaded with dum-dums. His boots were damp from patrolling the ruins of Omnium Settlement.

"What say there, Marvis, Bert?" he asked. Neither replied.

Doom noticed that Sheriff Plotner didn't move his lips either, a county of practicing ventriloquists.

"Why, you must be Denny's boy. Proud to meet you. Sheriff Plotner's the name. Lincoln Plotner. Your daddy and me used to play side by side on the line of scrimmage for the Omnium High Alligators. Salad days on the gridiron. Bert can tell you. By the way, you want to watch your ass out in boats with ole Bert here." Nobody invited him to sit, but he did so anyway, next to Doom. The sheriff stank of something, rotting vegetation or seaweed or something. "Where'd your lovely momma go? I wanted to extend my condolences and fond regards, but she run right off as quick and silent as she come. How's she taking it? I know they been divorced for years, but hell, still must hurt."

"She's fine," said Doom, trying not to move his lips.

"Your momma was some looker in her majorette suit. Right, Bert? Damn right. Buried at sea. Now that ain't precisely kosher, like your momma's new beau might put it. County statutes expressly prohibit burial at sea unless you have a whole raft of clearances, variances, and authorizations."

"We didn't bury him at sea," said Doom. "We distributed his ashes at sea."

"Well, we won't say no more about it. But next time you want to bury your daddy at sea, you give me a jingle first, okay? Just how long you plan to stay in our fair county?"

"That's still up in the air," Doom explained. The sheriff's strange stench was causing Doom's eyes to water, as if they were still full of ashes.

Crooked as hell, Sheriff Plotner determined. Never trust ex-cons who didn't move their lips when they talked. Here was one of those depressed loner types who'd poison your wife and violate your bird dogs unless you kept him under close scrutiny. "Maybe wait a day or two for better weather, have a swim, then hit the road?"

"Maybe."

". . . You look just like your daddy. Anybody ever tell you that? Little sadder, maybe. Dead ringer, otherwise. Right, Bert?" Sheriff Plotner slid out of the booth, the sudden movement throwing off sheets of stink. "Well, I'm off to fight crime. You have a good trip back up north, hear?"

"What was that odor?" Doom asked after the sheriff left in his black-and-white.

"That was Sheriff Plotner," said Bert.

"Yes, but what is it?"

"Nobody knows. He's always stunk like that."

"What do you mean I own Omnium Settlement?"

"You own it," Bert clarified.

Marvis Puller leaned in conspiratorially and said, "There exists a corporate entity called Palmetto Properties. Guess who's president."

"Who?"

"You."

Doom was afraid of that. "Does Palmetto Properties own Omnium Settlement?"

"Yes. But not directly, of course."

This was beginning to sound like one of his father's numbers, all right.

Marvis loved to say things like *corporate entity*. If he had been a WASP, he'd have been dangerous. "You see, your father bought up all the lots in Omnium Settlement as they came available, which was often, since Omnium's sinking. He covered his identity by forming several dummy corporations in which names the land was purchased."

"Where did he get the money?"

"From two principal investors. Have you ever heard of a cracker named Big Al Broadnax?"

"Broadnax? As in the county?"

"The same."

Now they'd arrived in an area Bert knew something about, being a lifelong native of Broadnax County. "Big Al's father dredged out Omnium Settlement back in the twenties, but he didn't do such a hot job, because it's sinking back."

"And now," added Marvis, "Big Al's blocking every effort to dredge it up again."

"Who's the other investor?" Doom asked.

"A corporate entity called Tamarind Financial Group," said Marvis.

"Is it local?"

"Down on Tequesta Key in a place called the Snowy Egret Shopping Center," said Bert.

"What Tamarind Financial really is is a cover for Perfection Park," explained Marvis.

"Perfection Park?"

"Just imagine what Small Hope Bay would be worth if it was dry land and if powerful people wanted to build this big hotel complex for overworked executives."

Doom was beginning to catch on. His father must have got wind of the plans for this Perfection Park and begun

21

to acquire the future site. "Let's get back to how I own Omnium."

"Your father was a master of the fine print," Marvis said as if he were talking about somebody great. "He formed two holding companies, one headed by Big Al, the other by Tamarind Financial. They shared voting control of the dummy corporations that own Omnium—*unless* and to such time as Dennis Loomis should die from any cause whatsoever. In that event, all voting shares revert to Palmetto Properties."

"Which I own."

"Exactly."

Doom considered some of the ramifications of that.

"Bert thinks somebody murdered your father and made it look like an accident."

"Not somebody. Big Al Broadnax."

"But why? It wouldn't be in his interest to do that if my father's death resulted in his loss."

"That's what I been telling him," said Marvis Puller.

"But you don't understand. You ain't from around here. You don't know Big Al. Big Al don't give a shit about fine print in contracts. He don't even give a shit about contracts. Big Al does whatever he wants on Omnium Key, and he wanted your daddy dead, sure as hell."

"But why?"

"For trying to gyp him in the first place!"

It still didn't make keen sense, and that was only another reason why Doom wanted no part of his father's flimflam. He was hoping to find something real in his hometown, not more phony things. "Did you tell Sheriff Plotner about your suspicions?"

"Plotner? That cheap screw rides so deep in Big Al's pocket, he's lint. There's a couple state senators in there with him." Wearing gas masks, Doom hoped. "Why do you think the Army Corps of Engineers ain't been in here to dredge the town back up? Because Big Al don't want it back up. He has other plans!"

"Like Perfection Park?"

"Yep."

"What has that got to do with me?"

"What's it got to do with you!" Captain Bert almost moved his lips with excitement. "Your daddy passed the baton to you!"

"But I don't want batons. I'd be happy to appoint you president of Palmetto Properties. Consider it done."

"Just what kind of son are you, son?"

"Come on, Bert," said Marvis. "You're way out of line here."

"It's okay, I'll answer that. I didn't even know my father. He was a father in name only. And what little I did know about him I didn't like. I like his boat, however. Would you be interested in teaching me how to sail her? For a fee, of course."

SPLENDOR

THE DAY WAS DONE WHEN DOOM FINALLY MOVED aboard *Staggerlee,* his belongings contained with room to spare in the same duffel he had carried from La Guardia. Energy fading with the daylight, Doom watched a loose band of revelers gather at the end of the dock to applaud the sunset over Small Hope Bay. Doom positioned himself behind the big aluminum steering wheel to watch his first Florida sunset in twenty-five years. It was pyrotechnical, yet soft and gentle, the kind that draws retirees, dreamers, searchers, romantics, hedonists, and crazies to Florida at the rate of four thousand per day. When the light had faded to dusk, he would explore his boat from stem to stern for his own education and a place to hide Ozzie's goods, but for now he "steered" dead ahead into the swirls of scarlets and purples burnishing the edges of towering stratocumulus clouds.

Doom Loomis had been charged with and pleaded nolo contendere to fraud, conspiracy to defraud, mail fraud, forgery, and literary mischief. A first offender, he might have got off with a suspended sentence and probation had he agreed to testify against Duncan Feeney, who was still at large. Doom did not so agree, thus prompting his lawyer to opine that stand-up guys were just another breed of asshole.

Doom had been sentenced to five years, commuted to two, at the minimum-security facility in Longfellow, New York, twenty heavily forested miles from the Canadian border. There he was tagged Doom by fellow inmates, a reference to his reading habits and his naturally mournful visage. Except in the dreary depths of winter, Doom spent his sentence maintaining the trails and lean-tos in the Adirondack Park. He went in soft, stiff, and disconsolate; he came out strong and wiry, a trail boss tempered by wilderness rigors, if still disconsolate.

Doom had written *Splendor,* a five-hundred-page psychological saga, which his coconspirators—Duncan Feeney and Professor Goode—attributed to Eleanor Roosevelt. While supposedly researching a new biography of the late First Lady, Feeney and the professor planted Doom's manuscript, typed on a convincing 1948 Olivetti, among her more obscure effects. Then they "discovered" it.

Despite legal hurdles thrown up by the estate, *Splendor* was published to rave reviews both here and abroad. Typical of the English-speaking press was this from the *The New York Times:* ". . . A devastating, spiraling descent into madness. Often funny, always deeply moving, *Splendor* opens a hitherto unknown chapter in the life of a grand American woman that will leave her biographers scurrying to catch up. It is also one damn fine piece of fiction." Even the estate was impressed with the reviews. Hollywood snapped up the option.

Instantly notable, Duncan Feeney and Professor Goode

were invited to appear together on late-night talk shows. Their hosts, waxing earnest, asked them what went through their minds when they realized the enormity of their find. Old Professor Goode appeared fidgety and distracted. Duncan Feeney, however, had a fine TV presence, witty and articulate, urbane yet modest. As a result, he was offered handsome salaries in the medium. He had accepted a position as on-air spokesperson for a Japanese pickup truck manufacturer when the fraud blew up in their faces.

But before it blew, *Splendor* and its "author" Eleanor Roosevelt swept the nation. Her portrait appeared simultaneously on the covers of *Time* and *Newsweek*—"The Eleanor Roosevelt we knew . . . and didn't know." *People* devoted an entire special issue to the "life and loves of Eleanor." Geraldo Rivera hosted a look-alike contest, and all Hollywood was abuzz with rumors as to who would play the Eleanor character. It seemed a perfect role for Goldie Hawn.

Doom had never imagined it would get that big. It was moving like a juggernaut, and watching the outpouring of sentiment from a nation starved for heroes and heroines, Doom felt morose with guilt. So did Professor Goode, who retreated into the swoony pale of Nyquil addiction.

The professor had been essential to the scam because of his impeccable breeding and Ivy League manner, which gained them access to Mrs. Roosevelt's personal effects in the first place, but he had never dreamed that he would find himself lying to Ted Koppel in front of millions.

A natural, Duncan Feeney smiled and called him "Ted." "I can't express to you, Ted, how honored we both are to have discovered *Splendor* for the American people."

The professor, however, was sweating profusely. Then he began to click his dentures, while Duncan bullshitted Ted a mile a minute to keep the camera off his Nyquil-addled associate. But when the professor started humming "Chattanooga Choo-Choo," Duncan knew the jig was up. The professor began to tremble, and like hungry lampreys, the cameras zeroed in on his tormented, twitching face.

Bubbles of saliva inflated and popped in the corners of his mouth.

"It's all subterfuge!" he keened in extreme close-up. "All of it, all stratagems for deceit! All with malice afore-thought!" His head swayed from side to side like a blind piano player's. He fell to his knees and begged forgiveness of Eleanor Roosevelt. "She's suffered enough!" he cried.

Ted turned to glare at Duncan, who at that moment stood for all that was false and cynical in America today. Koppel said in his gravest tones, "How does it feel, Mr. Feeney, to have deceived an entire nation?"

"Great, Ted," Duncan said. Then he bolted for parts unknown.

Doom Loomis turned himself in.

Doom had seen the woman with the movie camera shooting the sunset and paid no attention, but now she was shooting Doom. He picked up his belongings and went below. He peeked out the port. The photographer was boring in on the boat. Not only that, she had an assistant on sound.

The camera person was petite and boyish with black, bobbed hair. Doom could see nothing of her face behind the lens. The sound person was stout and strong with great maternal breasts, powerful thighs, and a determined look on her face. Hit women from Hollywood? They marched straight to *Staggerlee* and knocked on the deck.

Sweating, Doom stashed Ozzie's goods in a wet locker, then stuck his head halfway out the companionway, warily. "Yes?"

"Hello, Mr. Loomis," said the sound person. "We've been looking for you."

"Why?"

"My name is Anne. And this is Anne." Anne handed Doom a card across the lifelines. It said CINÉMA VÉRITÉ. "We want to make a movie about you."

While Doom was in prison the Annes had attracted con-siderable attention with their five-hour documentary about a dispossessed family of six who lived in an abandoned

Jeep Cherokee in the parking lot of a Houston shopping mall. Called *The Midnight Sunbelt,* the Annes explained, it won the coveted Harriet Beecher Stowe Prize for concerned social documentary. And before that, there was *Mom,* an excruciating day-to-day record of Anne's own mother's death from uterine cancer.

"I'm sure they were outstanding. I wish I'd seen them. But I don't think I'm interested. Thank you anyway."

The Annes weren't about to leave it at that. They went on to explain that they had been moved and exhilarated by the pained voice of *Splendor*'s narrator. Often, reading, they had wept. But their sadness was mixed with anger, anger because that voice, which must have been so deeply a part of Eleanor Roosevelt's psyche, had been silenced by sexism and repressive convention during her lifetime.

"We were stunned when it turned out to be a fraud," said Anne.

"Made to feel like chumps for our emotions."

"By ruthless exploiters."

"By scumbags."

However, after gaining some distance from their emotions, they grew fascinated. Ardent artists, brows prematurely furrowed by sensitivity and sincerity, the Annes were fascinated not by the wrenching pathos of Professor Goode or the slippery confidence of Duncan Feeney but by the quiet gloom of the man in handcuffs on "Eyewitness News," the man who actually wrote *Splendor*. *He* was the story here. Thus their documentary on Doom would pose the question: "How could a man write a scorchingly honest portrayal of a woman's sexual awakening and descent into madness, and having done so, how did it change him?"

Doom gave that some thought. He had no idea, but he liked the Annes. And there was this: No one would be likely to murder him for Ozzie's goods, Omnium Settlement, or anything else while he was being filmed. "Please come aboard. Do you plan to follow me around and record my life? Or do you interview me? How does it work?"

"It'll evolve," said Anne.

"Every subject suggests its own means of approach."

"However, we should tell you up front that we're political. That is to say, we believe that everything that happens is political."

"Nothing is apolitical."

"Okay," said Doom. "You wouldn't know how to sail a boat, would you?"

"Gee, no, sorry," said Anne.

"I'm from Indiana," added Anne.

COLONEL A. C. BROADNAX

SEPTEMBER 16, 1926: FROM HIGH ATOP THE SKELETAL frame of the central tower on the nearly completed Oseola Hotel, Colonel A. C. Broadnax surveyed his handiwork below. He wouldn't yet go so far as to say it was good, but it was on its way, and he wouldn't rest until it was perfect.

Actually, the new land looked like hell. The colonel wasn't blind, he recognized that. From his promontory he peered out across a naked expanse of lifeless sun-baked muck, so hard even rainwater wouldn't sink in—it just floated there until it evaporated—and he knew from personal probing that six inches beneath the surface the muck was moist and hot. He had created a giant compost heap. While he recognized that there was no way for the subsurface heat to escape, he was not concerned. It was all part of the process.

Hadn't he already done what his critics said could never be done? He had, through an ingeniously complex system of dikes, dams, and spillways, diverted the natural flow of water west from the ocean and east from the Everglades, thereby draining Small Hope Bay dry. Naturally, in the absence of water, aquatic vegetation died, and he plowed it away. Aquatic animals followed suit; the stench of putrescence hung like a dome over the bay. Step three, the reclamation of desertified bay bottom into attractive real estate, was now proceeding apace, starting with the hotel. The colonel didn't care about the hotel; he was building it only to keep Prentiss Throckmorton, a man of limited vision but limitless capital, on the hook. What Broadnax cared about was the new land. Colonel A. C. Broadnax was not overly alarmed at the puffs of smoke belching up from the cracks in his land like miniature fumaroles.

His work force, housed in tents on the less desirable mainland side of the late bay, had begun to refer to the colonel's creation as Battlefield Bay, because that's what it looked like. The stink of rotting herbage, dead fish, and their own shit, as well as numerous snakebite fatalities, had turned the workers restive and sarcastic. Of course, historically, the proletariat could never be expected to appreciate the shape of an original whole while it was still evolving. The colonel had only begun to fulfill his vision, and he, if no one else, was invigorated.

Next morning, the 17th, he noted that the lifeless muck was actually burning flamelessly, not merely smoldering, beneath the crustal surface. He noticed this because the "land" level had dropped three feet overnight, and the air was dense with black smoke. How could he have known that would happen? No one had ever removed a bay before. In light of this unforeseeable development, he had two options. He could let the muck burn itself away right down to the oolitic limestone bowl below, or he could fight the fire before it grew too hot to approach.

He settled on the latter option, because the former would cost him thousands to truck in fill from the mainland. He exhorted his men out of their tents to do battle with the subterranean blaze. Steadfastly, they refused. When he impugned their masculinity, they began to throw chunks of refuse at him. Unchecked, that insubordination quickly escalated into full-blown mutiny, while the muck fires burned on unopposed.

But then it began to rain.

The colonel exulted in the old Broadnax lucky streak. Ha! Nature was pitching in where Negroes would not. It rained hard all day, eight inches every five hours, and the colonel frolicked with his lieutenants in the downpour. By nightfall the fires were extinguished. A rising east wind then blew the smoke away, and everyone felt refreshed.

But something was wrong. The air began to feel funny on the skin, heavy and hard to breathe. Survivors recalled a strange, pressure-popping sensation in their ears.

Shortly before midnight on the 17th, it struck.

It wasn't like wind at all. It was something wild and remorseless, like incoming artillery. Dreams and visions and the endeavors of man stood no hope in the teeth of its fury. The colonel and his lieutenants drove away in the colonel's Auburn, while the workers, who could not flee, searched for shelter, anything, a mangrove tree, something they could lash themselves to. But the colonel had killed and plowed off all the trees and shrubs within eight miles. There was nothing. Some of the work force burrowed like small mammals into the earth itself, only to drown in their holes. The wind wailed all night, and pieces of the obliterated Oseola Hotel flew before it at killing velocity. Later, many of the dead were found to have been eviscerated by two-by-fours.

Then just as suddenly as it had struck, the wind fell to dead calm. Men crawled out of their pits and pathetic makeshift shelters and gasped at the sight. Nothing was left standing. Destruction was utter. The corpses of their fellows sloshed against their knees. Snakes darted in crazed circles. The Atlantic Ocean had swept over the barrier beach and refilled Small Hope Bay as if Colonel A. C. Broadnax had never existed. Only a single piece of his handiwork remained to outlive him—the fat bulge he had dredged up on the western side of Omnium Key as the site of the Oseola Hotel. In time, Omnium Settlement would arise on that very bulge.

Survivors spoke of a queer, prickly feeling on their skin during the calm, others of a ringing in their ears. Something was still very wrong. An ominous force, dwarfing the affairs of mankind, lurked nearby. That the morning sun shone brightly overhead only enhanced the terrible foreboding, more frightening even than the corpses and the crazy snakes and the hotel debris afloat on Battlefield Bay.

The wind struck again, harder, this time from the west.

The Big Blow of 1926 spelled the end for Colonel A. C. Broadnax and his vision and, temporarily at least, for Florida real estate. Property values plummeted to nil. Smart-ass Yankee wags wrote about suckers who buy Florida real estate "by the gallon." Prentiss Throckmorton, fully diversified, was able to weather the downturn as well as deliver the final killing blow to the Broadnax fortune after he got wind of the colonel's plot to cut him right out of the picture. Nature, of course, had rendered the plot moot, but Prentiss didn't care. It was the principle of the thing.

"I'll smash that perverted climber of a Jew crook beneath my brogans!" he swore to his underlings on the board of directors.

"But, sir," said one underling, "I don't think Broadnax is a Jew."

"Of course he is! What is he, then?"

"A Lutheran."

Prentiss Throckmorton didn't like that one bit—his sainted mother had been a Lutheran—and he glared malevolently at his mouthy underling.

"Of course he might be a Jew *posing* as a Lutheran."

HABITUÉS

NEXT DAY DOOM WAS UP WITH THE DAWN. HE FELT refreshed after his first night aboard, *Staggerlee* rocking maternally at the dock. Doom spent the morning exploring her nooks and crannies, pulling his father's arcane gear from drawers and lockers, examining and replacing it. Below, *Staggerlee* smelled of old wood and damp clothes. Doom ran his fingers over her joinery, the hand-tooled seams and joints in the cherry wood imperceptible to the touch. You didn't have to be a sailor to see she had been built by people who knew the sea and cared about their job. Doom sat at the ship's table in a cozy wraparound banquette and looked about his boat. Vainly, he tried to call up memories of boyhood, the misty coasts of Newfoundland, Windy in his arms. How could he not remember?

Staggerlee had been built in 1950 of steel on the river Clyde in Scotland to a design by John Alden of Boston. She was old-fashioned. Her stout construction, full keel with cutaway forefoot and attached rudder, was the conceptual antithesis of the modern light-displacement, round-bottom racing boat with its skeg keel and separated rudder. Her interior stripped out—pipe berths, propane camp stoves, and port-a-potties—a good racing boat would far outperform *Staggerlee* on any point of sail, "a horizon job," in modern parlance. But when it blew, when the sea got up, *Staggerlee* could continue to sail toward her destination long after a similar-sized racing boat (*Staggerlee* was 42 feet overall, with a 13-foot beam and 6-foot draft) had resorted to survival tactics or retreated to safe harbor. She was built for sea kindliness, not speed, yet her narrow entry, fine turn of bilge, and long waterline gave her a hull speed of seven knots. Even an ex-con trail boss who hadn't been aboard a sailboat since he was a toddler could tell she was a thing of quality and strength.

She was laid out below in traditional sea-boat fashion, frill-less and functional. Her galley, at the foot of the companionway ladder on the port side, was compact, almost tiny, the stove gimballed and guarded by a steel rail to prevent the sea cook from being bucked against it when things turned nasty. On the starboard side, opposite the galley, there was a sit-down navigation desk. Doom could tell that this was a place of serious purpose, but he had certain questions about its design and function. Why, for instance, did the navigator sit facing backward? And what were the purposes of all that obscure apparatus—an SSB radio, loran, compass, barometer, 24-hour clock set to Greenwich Mean Time, indicators of boat and wind speed and apparent wind direction? Toward the bow, where the hull narrowed, there was a head with shower, and forward of that was a vee berth, perfect for lovers. Alone, Doom had decided to sleep in the starboard berth opposite the table.

He noticed a tiny brass handle in the floorboards. He pulled it up, and there were the boat's innards. It seemed to him almost an invasion of privacy, but that's where he hid Ozzie's goods, just forward of the big manual bilge pump.

Doom had no idea how to operate the head, so he used the Flamingo Tongue's rest room. The charter-boat skippers were there again, in a knot at the counter. They fell silent when Doom entered the restaurant and again when he emerged from the john, but he pretended not to notice. The cook was a skinny guy in his late forties. He had a bony face with sharp cheekbones and a little black Latin-lover mustache.

"Good morning," Doom said to him. "Do you have a phone?"

"Sure do, right over there—"

Good, thought Doom, it hung on the wall near the screen door in reasonable privacy. The cute young waitress stopped pouring coffee for the skippers and watched Doom drop his coins. The skippers were watching, too.

A woman answered.

"Hello, this is Mr. Rivera with Florida Power and Light. There's been a billing error, and a credit is due," Doom said, cupping his hand around the receiver and turning his back on the nakedly curious at the counter.

"Oh. . . . Just one minute," said the woman.

Almost immediately Ozzie came on the line, and Doom repeated his Florida Power and Light bullshit.

33

"Well, that's just fine, Mr. Rivera. May I call you right back?"

Doom read him the number and hung up. Doom wished he hadn't gotten entangled with Ozzie and his goods.

"Ain't you Denny's boy?" the cook asked. "You look just like him. Have a cup of coffee? On the house?"

Surprised to hear a friendly voice, Doom sat at the counter two stools south of the skippers. "I'm expecting a call," he said to the cook.

"Sure, sure, anytime at all. Eggs? How 'bout the blue plate breakfast special? Denny was a good friend of mine. All ours. He was in here all the time. This was like his informal office. I'm Archie." Archie actually had tears in his eyes. "Dawn, get Mr. Loomis a cup. This is Dawn, my daughter. She goes up to the college."

College? She looked like a child, untrammeled complexion, blond and blue-eyed, a face glistening with innocence. "How do you do, Dawn?"

"Fine, thank you, Mr. Loomis."

"Most people call me Doom."

"Doom?"

"Yes."

Archie pointed to the skippers. "This here is Billy Houser. That there is Bobby Thorpe. Beside him, you have Arnie Cox and his first mate, Arnie Junior."

They shook Doom's hand with somber condolences, saying things about his father without moving their lips. To Doom, they were indistinguishable in their starched khaki uniforms and nylon-mesh baseball caps advertising tractor-trailer trucks, fishing tackle, and chewing tobacco. They all had enormous hands.

"You was in yesterday with old Captain Bert," stated Billy. Or Bobby.

"Yeah, poor old Bert," said Arnie.

"How so?" asked Doom.

" 'Cause he's stuck on the hill. They pulled his ticket."

"I beg your pardon?"

"Drowned some folks here in Bird Cut, what, six years ago?"

"The Cut can get real nasty when you got a east wind blowin' against a ebb tide. Big seas. You got to be on the ball goin' through Bird Cut in them wind-against-tide situations."

Doom nodded, seaman to seaman. "What happened?"

"Bert was operatin' a drift boat called . . . what the hell was she called?"

"The *Amberjack*," said Arnie.

"Yeah, right, the *Amberjack*. Well, Bert got into trouble, overran the wave ahead, the bow dug in, and the next one caught his stern, rolled him up on the jetty and right on over."

"Sunk like a piano."

"Bunch a Baptists from Alabama drowned."

"Coast Guard jerked his ticket. He's on the hill forever."

"Bert ain't been the same since."

" 'Course, he fucked up bad, real bad."

"Don't talk like that in front of Dawn," said Archie.

"That's okay, Pop, I've heard worse."

"Where?"

"You know who dug old Bert outta his funk?"

"Who?"

"Your daddy."

"Laugh a minute, your daddy was."

He hadn't left Doom laughing, but Doom didn't say so. Doom liked Archie and the gossipy skippers, not to mention Dawn, who he tried not to look at, lest he throb with visible loneliness. "Why aren't there more boats at the docks?" Doom asked. There were thirty vacant slips, *Staggerlee* the only boat present.

"That's because of Big Al Fucking Broadnax," said Arnie.

"Language," cautioned Archie.

"Oops."

"Nobody comes on the Key no more because it's out of the way what with only one bridge and Omnium sinking."

"See," said Bobby or Billy, "Big Al *wants* it to sink so's

he can buy cheap and dredge it back out on his own sweet time, put up some condos for rich Yankees."

"He's just like his old man. That colonel was a prize asshole. Sorry there, Arch."

"It's okay," said Archie. "That's exactly what he was."

"The whole family is, except for the son who died."

"Big Al was to keel over dead as a hammer today, there'd be Mardi Gras tomorrow." Because none of the skippers moved his mouth, it was hard to determine exactly who spoke. Doom thought it might have been Arnie. The words came from his direction.

"How long you plan to stay, Doom?"

"It's kind of up in the air. I'm going to learn how to sail, then I'm going to sea. Maybe to Newfoundland. In the Gulf Stream." Doom couldn't get that Gulf Stream blue out of his mind, and the gratuity he expected from Ozzie might finance the voyage.

"So you gonna live aboard *Staggerlee* in the meantime?"

"Yes."

The phone rang.

"That'll be for me," said Doom.

"Doom? That you, Doom boy?"

"Are you at a public phone, Ozzie?"

"Sweating the old bazookas off in a booth on Route One."

"I've got your goods."

"Oh Doom, that's music to my ears. I'll make it right by you, don't worry. We'll both get nice. Ain't it paradise down here? You're a lucky man to have been born down here. I'd of never left. Hey, you know we're in the same area code. I'm in this sweet-as-you-please subdivision down on Cormorant Key with my honey, Doris. Where are you?"

"I'm not far."

"So great, come over tomorrow. Spend the day. We'll catch us a mess o' snook, like the crackers say, and drink an Igloo cooler."

"Was that Doris I just spoke with?"

"That's her, yeah. You'll love Doris."

"Ozzie, if it's safe for me to visit you there, why are we doing this public-phone song-and-dance?"

"Just because it's fun, Doom boy. I thought you were the big one for the cloak-and-dagger stuff."

"Have you spoken to the Lady in Black?"

". . . Uh, no. Tried. Been trying. No answer."

"Then are you aware somebody beat hell out of her?"

". . . What do you mean?"

"I mean I couldn't tell how old she was from three feet away!"

"Oh, well, she often gets in scrapes. She's kinky, you know the kind I mean. So never mind tomorrow. How about I come on out there and meet you today. Where you located?"

"I need twenty-four hours to think about this, Ozzie."

"Come on, Doom, don't dick me up here."

"I won't. Call me at this number tomorrow nine o'clock."

"Come on, Doom—"

"By the way," Doom said, "the Lady in Black asked me to tell you that you owe her."

OMNIUM SETTLEMENT

DOOM DISCOVERED A CLEVERLY COLLAPSIBLE BICYCLE with tiny wheels and a high seat stowed in *Staggerlee*'s lazaret. Pondering the Ozzie problem and his own future, he pedaled from the dock at Bird Cut toward Omnium Settlement. Before he had pedaled two hundred yards, Doom recognized that he had blundered. He wore no hat. His brain began to fry. The edges of things shimmered, mutated. He made a mental note to buy a hat in his hometown, perhaps a sombrero. He had forgotten the power of this southern sun, but then, he hadn't been beneath it since childhood. The wind had died overnight, and by now, noontime, the Atlantic had fallen slack, lakelike. Nothing moved but heat waves. Doom barely moved, but, being filmed, he tried to make it look good. He mused on the indignity of a fatal heat stroke aboard this funny little bike. He'd slow, waver, then keel over sideways like a comedy act, thunk, dying funny for the cameras. . . .

The Florida peninsula, particularly that necklace of islands at the extreme south, is a geological infant. The world's landmasses had inched into their present positions eons before there ever was a peninsula at the bottom of North America. Dinosaurs had lived and died, mammals had risen to ascendancy, and the first trickle of humanity had crossed the land bridge from Asia while south Florida was still submerged.

Once, the earth was warm, but then it turned cold. Four successive "Ice Ages" followed. Glaciers plodded south, gouging out the Great Lakes and the Mississippi basin, and melting glaciers deposited as rubble such features as Long Island, Cape Cod, and Martha's Vineyard, literally forming anew the eastern half of the continent. While most of the world's water was locked up in ice, sea levels fell, and bumps in the bottom of the shallow sea that had covered the Florida peninsula emerged as dry land. Finally, after the Wisconsin Ice Age, about fifteen thousand years ago, south Florida and the Keys had assumed roughly their present form.

But this was not land in the sense that a Kansas farmer would use the word. There was no soil. Along the eastern rim the land, once the seaward face of a coral reef, emerged as naked limestone. To the west, in the bays, the "islands" were nothing more than shoals and sandbars in the oozy, marly sea bottom. The only aspect this land shared with Kansas farmland was that it wasn't underwater.

No one knows how long the islands baked naked in the

sun before vegetation arrived. Perhaps it was a long time, because not just any plant would do. It is a rare plant able to survive in saltwater. But one can.

The red mangrove.

Though red mangrove forests reach a mature height of thirty feet, the first generation of Florida pioneers reported primeval mangrove forests along the western side of Omnium Key and the shores of Small Hope Bay soaring over a hundred feet tall. Tough prop roots arc out from the central bole to grasp the bottom and eke out whatever nourishment is available in the hostile saline environment. Even before the forest is mature, the maze of prop roots and trunks is impenetrable to man. He can and does destroy the forest with machines, but he cannot walk through it.

Terrestrial trees drop their seeds into the soil, where they germinate and sprout, but that simple strategy for survival would fail in the mangrove's environment, where the seeds would drown in seawater. Instead, the mangrove propagates viviparously, producing its young directly on the parent tree.

The mangroves sprout long seedlings, shaped like miniature torpedoes, which develop into self-sustaining trees. By late summer and early fall, they drop from the parent tree. If the water beneath the parent tree is too deep for the foot-long seedling to touch bottom, it takes to sea, a colonizer in search of a safe haven. The seedling can survive afloat for a year or more. When it fetches up on a shallow sandbank, the seedling begins to grow, sending out rudimentary prop roots first to support, then to stabilize itself. Perhaps five years pass during which the prop roots grow strong enough to withstand the normal storms of autumn, and if a hurricane hasn't blown it away, the tree will have produced other seedlings and dropped them into the water. The process continues, and the naked shoal turns green.

And then something remarkable happens. The mangrove begins to create land. Land building begins when the mangrove sheds its own leaves among the jumble of prop roots. Turtle grass, shells, and other marine debris wash against and are caught with the shed leaves in the prop roots. There the whole mass begins to rot and turn into the unique conglomeration of detritus called muck. Then other trees, the buttonwood and the black mangrove, grow up behind the red mangroves on the now-favorable, less saline environment they have created. The naked shoal has become a forest. Varieties of birds roost in the branches, and oysters congregate on the prop roots, drawing raccoons and other mammals, which in turn attract predators. A new, more complex ecosystem is born. It takes the red mangrove longer to build land than man with his crawlers, grabbers, rooters, blasters, and peat-pullers, but it is better land.

. . . Doom dismounted at the top of Main Street. The Annes pulled up and stopped their production vehicle, a beat-up VW van with no reverse. Doom and the Annes stood on the rise and stared down at what remained of Doom's hometown, which now he owned. Anne shouldered her Arriflex 16 SR 11 Auteur, while Anne donned her Sony ECM 50 sound pack with twin shotgun mikes. In two minutes they were ready to walk.

A fat chain had been dragged across the top of the street and padlocked to deep-driven pipes. A sign hung from the center links: NO TRESPASSING PER ORDER OF BROADNAX COUNTY SHERIFF'S OFFICE. Doom and the Annes stepped over the chain and walked into Omnium Settlement.

The western foot of Main Street slid straight into the tannin-dark water of Small Hope Bay as if it were a boat-launching ramp. There had never been much to Omnium Settlement—the island was only a half mile wide—but now there was less. The seawall was completely submerged, and only the top six inches of the town dock pilings poked through the surface at high tide.

The inundated shoreside buildings—a failed fish co-op, a seafood restaurant with an alfresco patio, and several tourist bungalows—had rotted to rubble, only skeletal frames standing. Farther east up the rise, maximum elevation six feet, the buildings were boarded and shuttered, still intact but just a matter of time. There was a Shell station, brown pelicans perching on the pumps, a mom-and-pop grocery, and two motels, the Tropic Aires and the Little Oseola, each with a scattering of canting cottages named after indigenous waterfowl, a storefront post office, and Cal's Bait and Tackle. Anne panned the street.

What had he expected? Doom knew his town was sinking, knew the sight of it in broad daylight would not inspire cheery expectation, but he hadn't imagined such bereftness. He had thought one could still buy a hat in Omnium Settlement. A skinny black mongrel slunk like a cat across the street and crawled through a crack in the wall of Fred's Hobby Shop on which a vandal had painted in fat brush strokes Die Big Al! The salt air, hot sun, and passing time had leached the life out of everything.

Something skittered in the dry, fallen palm fronds. Doom remembered that sound, reptiles and mammals moving in the vegetation, animal life going about its business in the kind climate. Doom remembered from his jailhouse reading that in the warm places of the world there tend to be great variety of animal species with fewer individuals; in cold places there are vast numbers of individuals, few species. And he managed to remember his own boyhood wonder at the identity of the thing skittering in the palm fronds. Perhaps it was that lizard with the long gray stripes or the chameleon he and his friends used to keep for pets. They'd ride around on your shoulder for a while, turning the same color as your shirt before leaping off and skittering away. Why did he remember reptiles but nothing of his own life?

Wait—Doom remembered Fred's Hobby Shop. Fred's sign had faded to burnt umber, but Doom remembered when it was fire-engine red. He used to spend his allowance here. Fat and jolly, Fred was a beardless Santa Claus with bad teeth.

"Lemme see your hands," Fred would say. "Always wash up before you make a model and always follow the instructions to the letter." To the letter. Doom remem-

41

bered Fred's red, enthusiastic face. Fred had lived upstairs, alone.

The hobby shop was shuttered and gutted, but Doom peeked in anyway—right into a man's grimy, bearded face. Doom leapt back.

The face poked out through the chink. "You a cop?"

"No," said Doom. Anne shot the face.

"I got my family in here, so I'll fight you if necessary."

"That won't be necessary. I'm just looking. I used to live here."

"Yeah? That's what we're trying to do right now."

Doom was afraid of that. Living in the rubble of Fred's Hobby Shop. "I'm sorry to have disturbed you." He started to walk off.

"It's because of the economy."

Doom stopped, turned. "Pardon?"

"We left Wooster because there ain't shit left in Wooster. So we go to Houston. Houston turned bad before we even got there. So we come to Florida, but it's sinking. Where do we go from here? Cuba?"

"Do you need food?"

"I catch fish."

"How many in your family?"

"Seven, counting me and the wife."

"That's a lot of fish."

"Right now we're more worried about cops."

"Why?"

"Because you parked up on the road. They hate that."

In fact, Sheriff Plotner had already spotted the van and a stupid-looking bicycle built for circus midgets. Skateboarders, probably, Mary Jane, death-head earrings, knees intentionally cut out of their jeans. Squalor and ruin always drew in disaffected youth. However, if he went down to roust them, he'd have to alight from his black-and-white. That would cause his heart to go pitter-pat in the heat. Zoo York plates on the van was reason enough to run the youth. Sheriff Plotner believed that the world would be a lot better place if Zoo York just dropped off the continent and drowned in its own sludge. The heat hit his temples like a sap when he dismounted to unlock the chain.

"Are there others living here?" Doom asked.

"Couple families in the motels over there. They come and go. We're what you call a fluid population. We wait for shit to trickle down. You making home movies?"

One day they'd find Sheriff Plotner dead with his tongue lolling on the pavement. He shivered in the air-conditioning, flipped on his flasher and siren, and stomped the gas. Tires spinning, sand flew in rooster tails, and the reinforced bumper knocked cardboard rubble out of the way. Lizards scurried. Once, skateboard vandals had strewn spikes in his path and he nearly careened ass into the drink. Often, however, the full bore and stroke roar was enough to set them running, swimming, sometimes, and he didn't even have to crack a window.

Cameras? People taking pictures? "60 Minutes"? The liberal press, Christ, that's all he needed. Imagine what Mike Wallace would do to Big Al Broadnax on camera after Mike got wind of neo-Okies camping in the town that Big Al helped to kill. Sheriff Plotner skidded to an impressive stop, nearly losing the rear end. It was Denny Loomis's kid—

"What are you doing here?" he demanded without letting in too much heat.

"Looking. I was born here."

"Then I guess you didn't see the sign."

"What sign?"

Crooked as hell, no question about it. "You're in violation even as we speak. So are your lady friends. What are they doing?"

"I think they're making a movie."

"No movie-making without a permit."

"So tell them yourself. They don't work for me."

"Hey, little lady, cut . . . cut now, you hear!"

Cutting for cops wasn't the Annes' style. Anne crouched down and shot the sheriff through the passenger-side window while he twisted left in his seat to keep Anne at his back. "See any skateboarders?"

"Any what?"

"Heavy-metal youth, you know, skateboarding in defiance of statutes."

"I didn't see any."

"See anybody else?"

"Just you."

"There's vagrants living all through here."

Anne tried to shove her shotgun mike through the crack in the sheriff's window. "Now you better cut, missy, or I'll be gettin' out of this car after you, hear?"

"Why don't you help them?" Doom asked.

"Who?"

"The people living here."

". . . Look, I'll let it slip this time because you're new in town, but don't you become a thorn in my side." Sheriff Plotner cracked reverse, roared up the hill, and intentionally ran over Doom's bike.

ROSALIND

THE WHEEL FORK AND DOWN TUBE WERE BENT, THE front rim rippled, a half dozen spokes rent, but the bicycle remained rideable. Doom pedaled a dazed zigzag track to the south end of Omnium Key while the Annes followed, filming. Omnium and its new settlers were not his responsibility. He hadn't caused either to sink. He was just passing through, learning to sail away. Why, then, as he pedaled across Hurricane Hole Creek onto the mainland, did he feel burdened by guilt as well as by a bent bicycle wheel?

Everything changed when he joined Route One on the mainland and turned south. Omnium Key, its single road, was trafficless; Route One in both directions was choked to a crawl. Out-of-state vehicles sweltered cheek by jowl with local pickup trucks. Tourists had to fight this stretch only once, maybe twice in their lives, and the locals hated them for that. Route One traffic turned the locals murderous, impeded in the simplest errand by sunburned rubberneckers. Heat, stress, and natural enmity often erupted in violence. Twice a month, a tourist or a local, depending upon who was the more heavily armed, fell critically injured in traffic fracases. In several instances full-blown riots ensued, no sense to it, motorists venting their testosterone on each other's vehicles. Smoke from burning personal transportation was seen as far away as Homestead.

Faces contorted, drivers honked and screamed and pounded their fists on their dashboards, or on their wives and children. Since each vehicle was hermetically sealed to keep the climate under control, Doom heard no words as he pedaled past the bottlenecks on the crushed coral berm, just a pantomime of crazed rage no less dangerous for its silence. Occasionally, a motorist resenting his progress tried to snap open the passenger door in his path, but Doom outswerved them all. Doom didn't remember this electric pitch of hostility and sweaty violence, but he remembered how to ride a bicycle. A rotten little urchin in a New Jersey car threw a chocolate milk shake at him. He outswerved that as well, deftly shooting the little pecker the bird.

Doom was bound for Tequesta Key, the commercial hub of the northern Keys. Tequesta Key lay only a quarter of a mile south of Omnium Key, but that was across water in Possible Pass. There was no bridge across Possible Pass, just as there was no bridge across Bird Cut at the northern end of Omnium Key. In fact, there was only one bridge to and from Omnium Key. Big Al had seen to that.

He got the idea back in 1968, when he saw how slickly the Republicans kept the Commie rabble away from the democratic process—simply by closing the bridges to Miami Beach. Three bridges would be a lot harder to close than one, should the need arise, so he dynamited the other two. He made it seem the act of terrorists. Seven radical groups claimed responsibility.

Doom followed Route One across the causeway onto Tequesta Key. The Annes were nowhere to be seen, lost back there in the blue pale of exhaust emissions. Doom stopped at the first dive shop on his side of the road: Total Immersion Diving Ltd.

Rosalind Rock had run Total Immersion alone since her husband, Claudius Broadnax, died of an air embolism in sixty feet of water off High Hat Reef. Rosalind suspected suicide. Death by embolism is said to be swift and sure, a painless lapse into permanent sleep. Mostly, embolisms kill the inexperienced or panicky diver who bolts for the surface holding his breath. That diver often arrives there dead because nitrogen and other compressed gas bubbles have expanded under the lessening pressure of ascent. If breathed off through normal exhalation, the bubbles remain harmless. If they are not breathed off, their expansion obstructs oxygen flow to crucial organs like the heart and brain. Yet Claudius Broadnax was not a diver to panic, and he certainly wasn't inexperienced. He had been an advanced instructor for seventeen years, a commercial diver on North Sea oil rigs for five. He had dived to the *Andrea Doria* in 250 feet of cold, dark Atlantic water, and he had dived beneath the Ross Ice Shelf in Antarctica. That kind of diver simply did not blow out his bloodstream by holding his breath on the ascent. No matter what. Claudius Broadnax had been gone three years now, and Rosalind continued to grieve.

Doom found her bent from the waist, her back to him, so that the stretchy black spandex bathing suit gripped her parts gleefully. She was doing something mechanical with a motor, but Doom didn't even think to notice what, because her thighs didn't touch at the top. The sight of her bent like that made him ache with loneliness. Her legs were long and sinewy. She wore no shoes, and the effort of her task caused her toes to curl and uncurl spasmodically against the naked concrete floor.

Doom moaned softly. Perhaps prison *had* scarred him.

Did she hear him or did she by some subtler sense feel his covetous presence? She snapped upright and spun to face him. There was alarm in her brown eyes. Doom was sorry.

"Can I help you?"

She had sharp, intelligent eyes. She wore her hair short, combed straight back, accentuating her long, slim neck. Her upper jaw was too narrow, causing her confined front teeth to overlap. Doom was sorry he couldn't look longer at her face, but her nipples, erect from effort and air-conditioning, poked lovingly against her tiny black top. Doom waged a rigorous campaign against his own eyes, which with a will of their own tended to address her nipples directly. Just like the average ex-con.

"I'd like to buy some scuba diving equipment. I'd like to see the Gulf Stream."

"Are you certified?"

"I beg your pardon?"

"I can't sell you life-support gear unless you're certified. It's against the law." And didn't he look just the type to go drown himself on his first dive? "I can sell you masks, fins, snorkels, like that, but not tanks or regulators."

All Doom knew about scuba diving he had learned from Jacques Cousteau reruns on the rec-room TV, locked and mounted halfway up the wall at Longfellow. "How about hats?" He pointed to Total Immersion T-shirts and base-ball caps displayed on a pegboard over her head.

"Hats are fine," she smiled. The skin at the corners of her eyes crinkled. Her tan was dark and thorough, but her sunglasses had left a paler mask around her eyes.

"I'll take the red one, please. And the red T-shirt, please. How do I become certified?"

"You need to take lessons. I have a class starting next week. If you're going to be in town that long."

"I live here now. In Omnium."

"Omnium?"

"I live on my boat."

"You're a sailor, huh?" He didn't look like the average boat bum who came and went along these shores.

47

"Well, not yet. I'm learning."

"What sort of boat do you have?"

"A forty-footer named *Staggerlee*."

"Oh. You're Denny Loomis's son."

"Guilty."

"I heard you were in town. My name's Rosalind Rock."

Rosalind Rock. Wow. "How do you do? I'm Doom. I mean, that's what people call me."

She could see why.

"Could I take private lessons? I mean alone?"

". . . Sure. When would you like to start?"

TAMARIND FINANCIAL

MASK, FINS, SNORKEL, AND TEXTBOOK IN HIS BENT BIKE basket, Doom Loomis pedaled north on Route One feeling happy expectation for the first time since his release. He was taking private diving lessons from *Rosalind Rock*. Even now he wore her hat and shirt. There was a kind of intimacy in that. But happiness didn't last long in the angry traffic. It soon turned back to uneasiness, then plain fear. The motorists despised his relative ease of movement and wanted him dead.

The sun had done something depressing to the shit-burger joints, cheesy motels, seashell shops, and drive-up banks. It had cooked away their franchise facades and burnished their plastic signs, leaving dilapidation and gloom. Shadowless white light made this strip seem a place conducive to neurosis and heedless violence. Low-tide smells mingled incongruously with overheated exhaust. The dense traffic, which should have brought business to local merchants, only discouraged it, because tourists and other itinerants dared not leave the line for fear of never regaining it.

Then he spotted it. The Snowy Egret Shopping Plaza. Wasn't that where Bert and Marvis said this Tamarind Financial front was supposed to be? Some traffic-crazed passerby hurled a full can of Bud Lite at him from a metal-flake purple pickup truck as he stopped beside the road and dismounted, but the missile whizzed harmlessly over-head, striking the thirty-foot-tall red neon snowy egret, taking out its legs with a flash and a tinkle. What was the point of stopping at all? His father's flimflam had nothing whatever to do with him. Why mess with it? Why not pedal out of this hell? Why not let it ride?

The squat stucco building housed Moultrie's Western Auto on the ground floor, white sidewalls piled in a pyr-amid twenty feet high at the point. A Jack LaLanne Health Spa, a dangerous-looking sports bar called the Dugout, Rose o' Sharon's Salon de Beauté, Dixie Drugs, and the Tamarind Financial Group shared the second floor, its balcony fronted by a wrought-iron railing decorated with snowy egrets, now bent and rusted into abstractions. The hot asphalt parking lot stuck to his shoes as Doom rolled his bike around back to the stairs.

A clean-cut young man in a sweaty seersucker suit hur-ried down them. He could barely keep pace with his pump-ing knees. Doom stepped aside for him. He carried a heavy cardboard box in his arms. He didn't even glance at Doom as he blew past and loaded the box into the rear of a parked van already stuffed to overflowing with boxes. "Tamarind Financial" was scrawled on each box in magic marker. Then the clean-cut young man bolted back up the stairs two at a time and disappeared into an office. Doom decided to observe this activity unseen. He retreated behind the fender of a red Dodge truck, rubber objects and a faded high school graduation tassel dangling from the rearview mirror. Doom watched the clean-cut young man dash up and down twice more with boxes. This young man was clearly absquatulating.

Just then a burly cracker with a peeking beer gut

emerged, pumped and pissed, from the Jack LaLanne. He was considering stopping in at the Dugout and kicking the tar out of anybody over sixty-five. Fucking silverhairs made this state lousy, entitled to a tax break and free major med. What was he entitled to? He was entitled to jack shit. If he kicked butt for it. He froze when he got a load of Doom down there in a red cap lurking beside his truck. Fucking Yankees made this state lousy. "Hey!" he bellowed over the bent egret rail. "The fuck are you doin' to my Ram!"

"Your what?"

"My truck! My four-by-four! Yer dickin' with my personal transportation!" His countenance glowed red with rage, an open wound with facial features.

Obviously insane, Doom recognized, wheeling his bike away from the Ram. That put Doom out in the open.

Sputtering, spitting, the cracker charged down the steps. Doom looked around for a weapon. Slap him senseless with his flippers? Doom mounted up, ready to flee, but the crazed cracker didn't attack, at least not yet. Instead, he made for his Ram, counted hubcaps, examined the hood and fenders for a nick or any Yankee treachery that would make homicide justifiable in the eyes of the law. A tattoo on his bicep said "I like Eich."

The clean-cut young man hustled down the steps with a VCR in his arms. Several tapes bounced around on top of the machine. He froze when he spotted Doom astride his bent-to-hell bike. "Holy shit!" the young man exclaimed. "You look just like him!"

"I kung-fu your spine out, you dick with my Dodge!"

"He was my father."

"So what do you want from me?"

"Nothing much. A chat."

"Then you better be a fast pedaler."

"I'd like to discuss the plans for Perfection Park."

"Oh, swell, come back tomorrow and we'll have a nice long chat over brunch."

"But you seem to be moving today."

The clean-cut young man didn't answer. He loaded the VCR into the back of the van and braced it in place.

"Is the scam about to blow in your face?" Doom asked. This guy was perfect sucker bait, with his choirboy complexion and seersucker suit. He'd make the saps feel secure in the promise of affluence and a beautiful future, even as he picked them clean as last week's road kill. "My father's schemes often blew in his face."

"Now you tell me."

"Is Perfection Park real or is it sucker bait?"

"For all I know, somebody greased your old man. On the other hand, maybe he ain't *muerto*, maybe it's all a put-up job. Maybe he's just supposed to seem dead for reasons nobody bothered to tell me. Maybe this crazy cracker over there with love in his eyes is another part of the show, just like maybe you're part of the show. Swell bike, though."

Doom could see his point. It was hard really to know a thing, particularly one of his father's things.

"Yankee faggot!"

Then the bomb detonated.

The blast was contained largely within the four walls of the Tamarind Financial Group, but a part of its force vented through the open door and the plate-glass window. Both, shredded, flew out over the parking lot. Several iron egrets blew clean over Ye Olde English Fish and Chips Pub, a quarter mile away. The sultry air filled with debris, spinning and jinking and fluttering in the stark sunlight. The concussion blew the clean-cut young man right off his feet. Doom, too, found himself supine, though he didn't recognize it until he tried to run.

Instantaneously, the Tamarind Financial Group had become a gaping black obscenity in the Snowy Egret's side. Doom rolled under the van when flying pieces of the Group began to clatter down on him and to stick fast in the molten asphalt. From there, Doom watched the clean-cut young man crawl in babbling circles, stuff bouncing off his back.

The young man visualized gory parts of his person pirouetting in the air, then dropping back to earth, where in no time the sun would bake them crusty.

"Hey, Daddy, what's that on the windshield?"

"Gee, son, I don't know. . . . Jumping Jesus, it's a *nose!*"

He crawled into the van and started the engine. He began to babble in a pinched whine. As soon as he found a forward gear he'd drive to Sweden, New Zealand, somewhere they didn't do this kind of shit. Doom rolled out from under the van. Before it lurched away, he lifted the VCR and the tapes from the back.

Discord and hysteria reigned. Shoppers and merchants alike poured out onto the balcony, gathered in groups on the parking lot, shoes sinking, jabbering and whimpering, trying to find some sense in the smoke of chaos.

A passing EMS unit pulled into the parking lot with lights flashing. Here seemed to be authority. They'd make sense of this, tell people what they should do. A hush fell over the crowd. The white-uniformed driver, a stethoscope draped around his neck, swung down from the driver's seat without taking his eyes off the site of the blast. "Jesus," he said. "Rocket attack. I've seen incoming before. Up near the Imperial City. Tet. How many dead?"

The fat cracker clutched his face and sobbed at all the shit still raining down on his freshly painted Ram.

No one noticed Doom wobble off with the tapes in his bicycle basket, the VCR under his arm.

PERFECTION PARK

DOOM FOUND MARVIS PULLER SITTING ON THE concrete seawall at Bird Cut throwing a plug into the flood tide, which was squeezing tons of seawater through the narrow inlet at nearly ten knots.

Marvis Puller loved to fish and wouldn't have minded if, when his time came, he dropped dead with his rig in hand. Marvis was a CPA who had given thirty-five years to his one-man firm in a Harlem storefront. He had contributed to the community by helping his neighbors muddle through the white man's economy, and he was proud of that. Marvis had been reasonably honest in those days.

He and his wife Matilde, from Martinique, had raised two sons, neither of whom went to jail or played in the NBA. That lovingly done, Marvis and Matilde culled their belongings, piled them aboard a U-Haul, and headed for the Sunshine State, where you could fish till the cows came home. But Matilde, loading aluminum lawn chairs into the trunk, dropped dead on the sun-soft asphalt parking lot at the Spoonbill Mall not two weeks after they had crossed the Georgia state line, cheering. Marvis lost all interest in fish, and honesty seemed a sucker's game if that was the return you got, a dead wife. He had holed up in a rotten little Tequesta Key motel with forty-five-watt bulbs in the lamps, and there he waited to join Matilde until Denny Loomis, a keen eye for undervalued talent, occupied Marvis's mind with real estate whoop-de-dos, thus reviving his will to live and to fish.

"Check out my new rig," he said. "Top-of-the-line Orvis Fishflex 4000. Try a cast? Big snook come cruisin' through the Cut. They're tusslers, snook. Good eating too. You get crevalle jacks through here, but they ain't great eating in my book." Marvis arced his lure out over the rushing water and plopped it two feet from the seawall on the High Hat Key side. He was beginning to talk like Bert and the skippers. "What happened to you? You look like you been rolling around in a parking lot."

Two Hispanic families were food-fishing nearby, so Doom said it softly: "Somebody blew up Tamarind Financial."

"What!"

"Shh. I just came from there. Do you have a VCR?"

"Huh? A VCR?"

"A TV would do."

"Bert has a VCR. Blew *up?*"

Doom turned to the Hispanic families. "Would you folks like a VCR?"

The father squinted suspiciously. "How much?"

"Nothing."

"What's the catch, mister?"

Captain Bert lived alone in the Briny Breezes Trailer Park up on the Manatee Narrows, from where he could watch the boat traffic come and go. Bert had spent his life at sea. He joined the Merchant Marine on the same day he graduated from Omnium High. His first ship was torpedoed out from under him during the murderous battles of Convoys SC.122 and HX.229. He was one of four survivors from a crew of forty-two. After the war he built a Starling Burgess–designed sloop and sailed her alone through the Caribbean and two hundred miles up the Orinoco River before she was stolen by pirates. Beached, Bert signed on aboard a banana boat bound for Curaçao, but it sunk en route from general lack of seaworthiness. Returning to Florida, he worked as a rigger, a mast builder, a commercial sword-fisherman, and stone crabber before he assumed command of the *Amberjack,* which he sank in Bird Cut.

"I told you!" he said. "I told you Big Al would stop at nothing! Blew it the hell up!"

"We don't want to leap to a lot of conclusions," said Doom.

Bert's Apache Airstream Double-wide felt like a boat inside, except for the vinyl Barcalounger, the deep shag wall-to-wall, and the imitation cut-glass chandelier Doom had to duck under. Bert pulled the breakfast nook stools in front of the TV. "Here, Marvis, you can have the Barcalounger." Marvis loved the Barcalounger.

What was he doing there, Doom asked himself, if he didn't mean to get involved? He should have been studying his scuba diving text for tomorrow's first lesson or practicing his tacking and jibing and splicing the main brace.

He'd already had his timbers shivered, in town barely thirty-six hours. Bert, Marvis, and Doom gathered around the TV:

A slavering fellow with a vacant look in his eye and a dong as long as an Orvis Fishflex 4000 advanced limbo-style on a naked butt of undetermined sex—

"That's not exactly what I was hoping for," said Doom.

"I saw this one," said Bert. "Pretty good."

"Let's see the next one."

A German shepherd ate kibble in a kitchen as a naked woman in purple mules entered, began to stroke the dog's flanks, and moan. Is that all he had for his trouble, a fuck-film library? Or was *this* Perfection Park? Bert was interested in the purple mules.

"Come on, Skipper."

Skipper. Bert's eyes lit up. He ejected the dog fancier and inserted the last selection—

Jimmy Buffett sang "Tequila Sunrise." An aerial view of Omnium Key and Small Hope Bay swelled to fill the screen, followed by some artsy split-screen video foolishness before the credits rolled. One Bernard Renfrew was cited as producer/director. Then a voice-over said, "Come with us now to a place not quite of this world, in short, a perfect place."

Doom recognized that voice. He had heard it on the telephone every Christmas and birthday, even those he spent in prison. And there was the man himself onscreen, standing on Omnium Beach, smiling charmingly at the camera. After a few bars of paradise music, the title appeared:

Perfection Park

Denny Loomis wore a blue blazer, gray pants with a white belt, and a snappy red ascot. Hands in pants pockets, he strolled barefooted and said chattily, "Experience Florida as Ponce de León experienced it, but without the wilderness inconveniences." Denny chuckled amiably, a man you could put your trust in, a regular guy who looked you right in the eye as he lied. "While we can't guarantee the Fountain of Youth, we can offer the next best thing—a self-contained, climate-controlled, insect-free, ergodynamically designed *total* environment where the harried executive can unwind as he and his family reforge that lost bond with the natural world. That, then, is the concept of Perfection Park. Let's turn now to the specifics of execution and actualization."

A schematic drawing of Small Hope Bay and Omnium Key appeared, features labeled. In voice-over Denny Loomis said, "In order to live up to its name, Perfection Park will require certain alterations to the in situ geography." While Doom watched incredulously, his dead father explained that Small Hope Bay would have to be drained before it could be perfected.

"The northern entrance at the Manatee Narrows will be plugged and a spillway inserted to control the water flow into what will then be renamed Perfection Bay. Bird Cut will be blocked by a seawall and sand filled in behind to preserve the integrity of the beach. Those two engineering feats accomplished, the natural, if torpid, southern flow will drain the bay in about ten days." Computer graphics showed this happening, then Denny Loomis with a straight face said, "Why spend investor capital for a job nature will do for free?" This narrator was a good fellow, you could tell, he would treat your capital investments as though they were his own. A kind of footnote flashed on and off almost before it could be read: "Environmental Impact Study to Come."

Once the bay drained itself, the southern terminus would be plugged to prohibit back flow and to adjust outflow during rainy seasons. "Now actualization may commence," intoned Denny Loomis.

More schematic drawings appeared. They showed an artistic scattering of sweet little islets built on poured-concrete foundations, each islet to be named after an indigenous water bird, which would be flown in from Brazil. For privacy to commune with nature, there would be only one bungalow per islet. Once the islets were complete, landscaped with genuine tropical vegetation, and once the bungalows were built, Perfection Bay would be refilled to a controlled depth simply by opening the spillway at Manatee Narrows, "thus letting," said Denny Loomis, "nature take its course."

Launches festooned with garlands, fresh daily, would ferry unwinding executives and their families to and from the beach and the main dining, recreational, and entertainment facilities, which would be located on the current site of Omnium Settlement.

"Before we go," said Doom's father, affecting a JFK persona, strolling the beach, "we have a confession to make. The concept for Perfection Park is not entirely original with us. In fact, ours is a time-honored concept. Back in 1927, the pioneering Florida developer and visionary, Colonel A. C. Broadnax, undertook a similar project. However, his dream faltered with his premature death in 1930. We intend, therefore, to name the main dining and recreational facility the Colonel Broadnax Hall of Flowers. Who says we can't learn from history?" Big toothy smile and a wave. "So long now, from paradise in the making."

Captain Bert, Marvis Puller, and Doom Loomis sat in silence. Doom excused himself and went to the head to wash the tears from his eyes. When he returned, he recognized that Bert and Marvis had also been crying, but presumably for different reasons. They hadn't had Denny Loomis for a father. "Who is this Bernard Renfrew?" Doom asked when he had his voice under control.

"He worked at Tamarind Financial," said Marvis.

"What does he look like? A Young Republican?"

"Yeah, a real white guy."

"Denny sure looked great, didn't he?" asked Bert quietly.

"He sure did," Marvis agreed.

BIG AL BROADNAX

BIG AL, COLONEL A. C. BROADNAX'S AGED AND INFIRM only son, felt like shit today. His lackey, Lucas, had wheeled him into the central courtyard of his Greco-Moorish mansion and parked him in his favorite thinking spot beneath the leafy hydrangea. It, like the poincianas, sapodillas, guavas, cattleya orchids, viburnums, pyracanthas, saw palmettos, mangoes, pomegranates, and air plants, was artificial. But none was made of plastic—only hicks would have plastic plants. These were made of silk by Italian master craftsmen. It took a doctor of botany to tell the difference. Real plants were pains in the ass; they attracted deer flies, dog flies, yellow flies, sand flies, and mosquitoes. Silk plants needed only occasional dusting by lackeys. Big Al sat weary, constipated, and sad. The ghost of a breeze riffled the leaves overhead.

There was, however, one bright spot on Big Al's horizon. Perfection Park. Big Al loved Perfection Park. Goddamn right his old man thought of it first, the grand artificer thwarted by nature and Negroes. So Big Al had no intention of letting those Tamarind hicks make crucial conceptual decisions while he remained obscure, a silent partner. Perfection Park made his loins tingle with forgotten ardor. Only thing he wasn't wild about was that name. It wanted subtlety. Only hicks liked things blatant. He'd give that name some thought.

There was something nagging at Big Al's mind, and that was that crooked bastard Denny Loomis's son lurking around town, the funeral now three days old. Denny Loomis had been up to something sneaky, and now his jailbird son was picking up the standard. Sheriff Plotner had offered to run the punk on a technicality, but Big Al preferred to take a wait-and-see stance. He hadn't dredged his family's ruined fortune up from the muck by being impetuous. First he'd find out what this Loomis punk was up to, and then he'd crush his ass like an armadillo on the interstate.

"Lucas!" Big Al called.

Lucas Hogaboom weighed in at 285 stark naked, which must have been a fearful sight. He was an ex-biker-doper-sex-offender who had served Big Al ever since Sheriff Plotner caught him red-handed exposing himself to Catholic-school girls down on Tequesta Key and offered him a choice: be subservient or be castrated.

"I want you to put a tail on that punk Loomis."

"You got it, sir. I'll get Binx and Ridly."

"I don't care who you get. Get somebody good. No dope fiends."

"You got it, sir."

"Is there any word on these Tamarind Financial punks, just who the fuck they are—were?"

"Not yet, sir, but your Jews are working on it."

"Tell them hurry the fuck up, what's taking them so long, there's faster Jews where they come from."

"You got it, sir."

Big Al loved to see large men bow and scrape to him in his wheelchair. "And you be careful, Lucas. This punk is from New York, so he's armed to the teeth." Speaking of which, Big Al reminded himself to get Lucas's teeth fixed. They were the sort of choppers you'd see in ancient mummy museums.

"Me too," grinned Lucas brownly.

"You too, what?"

"Armed. To the teeth."

"That's all well and good, Lucas, but never, *never* be impetuous. Just remember you can kill more flies with honey than with—what? I forget."

". . . Kerosene?"

"Whatever. Just bear it in mind."

"You got it, sir," said Lucas. Did the old dinosaur fuck even so much as *thank* him for blowing up the shopping center? No, he did not. One day, Lucas determined, he would shoot this ancient asshole in the back of the neck while wheeling him to the john for a futile try at a shit.

SAFETY FIRST

"BLEW UP!" ANNE COULDN'T BELIEVE THE ROTTEN luck. "While you were standing there?"

Anne couldn't believe it either. "And where were we?"

"Stuck in traffic."

Doom and the Annes sat in *Staggerlee*'s cockpit drinking coffee at dawn the next day. Doom studied a navigation chart of the area. For local color Anne shot some brown pelicans standing on the dock pilings waiting for a handout, but her heart wasn't in it. "We need a new production vehicle."

"We didn't know it would be like this."

"This congested."

"It's worse than the FDR Drive."

"We can't just sit sweltering."

"In stasis."

"How about a motorcycle?"

"My brother was killed on a motorcycle."

"How about a bicycle built for two?"

"Would you mind if I went about my business alone today?" Doom asked after he had picked a likely-looking place on the chart. He had already committed one felony—grand theft VCR—and then there were Ozzie's hot goods. To handle them with prior knowledge constituted accessory after the fact as well as conspiracy to transport stolen goods. To commit felonies on film constituted stupidity. Then there was his first diving lesson, scheduled for ten o'clock. He'd be nervous enough without having to explain the Annes to Rosalind.

Indeed, the Annes did mind. "It constitutes censorship," said Anne.

"Maybe this film about me isn't such a good idea. I'll be leaving soon, anyway."

"Oh, so you're just going to sail away when your hometown really needs you?" said Anne.

"What can I do?"

"Those people in the hobby shop need you."

"This sounds like editorial comment to me. What happened to cinéma vérité? I thought you filmed reality, not formed it. Besides, how do you figure they're my responsibility?"

"Ownership implies responsibility."

". . . Ownership?"

"You own Omnium Settlement, don't you?"

"How do you know that?"

"We do our research."

"Our deep background."

"Who told you, Bert or Marvis?"

"Bert and Marvis."

Maybe there wasn't even time to try to begin a relationship with Rosalind.

"He's right, Anne. About the editorializing."

"I know it."

"We're trying to mold events politically."

"To fit our worldview."

"We mustn't."

"I know it."

"We felt censored."

"It was reflexive."

"The fact is," said Doom, "I met a woman. My diving instructor. I'd like to get to know her before—well, before I get into *Splendor* and the movie."

"A woman?"

"That's different."

"Why didn't you say so?"

"It's true, ours can be a disruptive medium."

"Sometimes I wish we were poets."

"With yellow notepads."

The Annes seemed glum now. Doom hadn't meant to precipitate a crisis of artistic faith, but time felt short.

"That's the gink," said Ridly.

"Where?" asked Binx.

"Right there—getting off that yacht—heading up the dock—that gink."

"The sad-looking gink?"

"Do you see any other gink besides the sad-looking gink?"

Binx and Ridly sat in the parking lot aboard an idling (for the air-conditioning) Toyota. The smoke of controlled substance hung around their heads like Newfoundland fog. A passerby, like Doom, if he had looked, which he didn't, couldn't have seen into the back seat. Still, Binx lit another spliff and puff-puffed. He giggled over something obscure.

Ridly, on the other hand, felt bitter, aggrieved. "I should be an engineer," he said. "A consulting engineer for a prestigious aerospace concern, two grand a day plus expenses. Instead I'm running errands for the likes of Lucas Hogaboom."

"My brother Glen was spacey."

"What?"

"Spacey. My brother Glen."

"I should be a securities analyst. Buy short, sell long, eat sushis for lunch with high rollers."

"The gink's goin' into the Flamingo Tongue."

"No shit."

"Hey, Ridly, what's sushis?"

"Raw fish."

"My brother Glen used to eat raw fish."

Ridly sighed.

"It got so's it was embarrassing. You'd go into a bank or someplace had an aquarium for decoration, and there'd be Glen—grabbin' around in the water, plastic deep-sea divers, treasure chests opening and closing, till he caught one. Ate it wigglin' in his fist. He said Siamese fighting fish was the best eatin'."

"Jesus," Ridly muttered. A man seeking advancement didn't find it following guys for Lucas Hogaboom and smoking dope with Binx Bukowski, listening to stories about his brother Glen, who probably didn't even exist. "Do you *have* a brother Glen?"

"It's hard to say."

"What's so hard? You either do or you don't."

"I might. That's all I can say for sure."

The skippers were in their places drinking coffee at the counter, Archie and Dawn behind it. The Flamingo Tongue seemed to Doom a venerable, unchanging place in a fast-flowing tide of mutability. The skippers pivoted on their stools in unison and nodded genially. Doom used the john—it said Buoys for men, Gulls for women—and when he emerged Dawn was pouring him a cup while Archie set a paper place mat and utensils next to the skippers. Doom seemed to be a figure of slightly dangerous fascination to the Flamingo Tongue regulars, and he liked that.

"Could you tell me how to operate a marine head?"

The faintest breeze of a smile wafted over the skippers' faces—a line like that didn't come along every morning of the world. "Now that's an important thing to know, you live on a boat," said Arnie.

"I guess you know how to take a shit?"

"There are other words, Bobby," said Archie.

"I was just wondering at what point to begin the lesson, Arch. So now I know." To Doom, Bobby said, "You got to have that valve *up* while you do your business. Then you put it down to flush. And *then* you put that little valve back up. Pump, pump, pump her dry. Don't go away unless that valve's *up*. Got it?"

"Yes."

"You could sink your boat you leave that valve open."

"Remember Donny Potts?"

"Guy who's paralyzed?"

"Paralyzed?"

"Yeah, Donny went to bed one night fine, next morning he woke up paralyzed."

"I didn't know he was paralyzed."

"Stiff as a nacho chip."

"Well, before he got paralyzed, Donny sunk his boat like that."

"Left the valve down?"

"Yep. Down."

"Donny had a drinking problem."

"Donny didn't have no problem drinking. His problem was stoppin'." The skippers giggled without moving their mouths.

Archie turned somber. "Damn if that isn't exactly what your daddy used to do. Sit right there drinking coffee, listening to their dumb stories."

The phone rang.

"That'll be for me," said Doom.

"Okay, Doom boy, any decade now'd be fine," said Ozzie.

"Do you have a boat?"

"A boat? Doris has a boat. Is this going to get weird?"

"Discretion—that's the ticket, Ozzie."

"Look, Doom, a thousand bucks cash to meet me in the parking lot of the Seven-fucking-Eleven on Cormorant Key. Next door to the bottle refund center."

Doom refused, going on to outline his more prudent plan.

After Doom had hung up on Ozzie's protests, Archie said, "I forgot to tell you, Doom. A couple guys were in here asking for you."

A wave of fear churned the coffee in his stomach. Doom was kidding himself, and he knew it. That was what frightened him most. This sanguine torpor, this vaguely hopeful lassitude. Maybe it was the sun. He was totally vulnerable to assault by strangers with unknown motives, no matter what precautions he devised, and he had devised none. And now Bert and Marvis were shooting off their mouths

about how he owned Omnium Settlement. Still, he stayed.
"What did they look like?"

"Yankees," said Billy.

"Might of been a Jew," said Arnie.

"What did you tell them?" Doom asked Archie.

"Well, he—the one might have been a Jew—said you invited him down for a vacation. He said he was an old pal of yours."

"Then you told him where to find me?"

"Yes . . . I hope that's okay." Doom's expression seemed to say it wasn't.

"What did the other one look like?" Doom asked.

"Old codger. Sat down in that booth over there and fell flat asleep."

"Alzheimer's," pronounced Archie. "You see a lot of that down here."

"Geezer starts wipin' his teeth and brushin' his ass—next stop's the home."

"That's where Donny Potts ended up."

"The home?"

"Yep. The home for paralyzed geezers."

Back at the dock, Doom discovered that some vandal had chucked his bicycle into the water. He could see it down there on the bottom. Colorful little fish pecked at it. That's another thing Doom remembered about childhood—there were always colorful fish visible in the water, doing what evolution had determined them to do, right before one's eyes.

Doom called a cab. "Total Immersion Diving on Tequesta Key, please."

TOTAL IMMERSION

Doom had read the text from cover to cover. It made common sense to him, except for Boyle's Law relating to the inverse variation between the pressure and volume of a gas at a stable temperature. He hoped Rosalind wouldn't quiz him on that, making him feel like a moron. He further hoped she'd wear the same tiny spandex suit. Her thighs didn't touch at the top.

Doom was freezing in the over-air-conditioned cab. Its driver wore a woolen sweater and down vest. . . . Doom's imagination traveled from Rosalind's curling toes and flexing ankles, over her rippling, muscular calves and soft, sensitive thighs, up, up to her bulging blah, blah, blah. "The Con's Hymn." Doom struggled to turn his rampaging thoughts back to Boyle and his Law.

"Pardon me," said the driver in the rearview mirror, "what is your stand on the dumping of plutonium wastes in the world's oceans?"

What was this guy's angle? . . . "I'm all for it," said Doom suspiciously.

"Me too." And that was all the driver said for the rest of the traffic-bound trip.

She was wearing a wet suit!

Thin, tight two-tone yellow-and-black neoprene gripped her wondrous body from neck to ankles. The suit was unzipped to mid-chest, and Doom tried not to obsess on the peekaboo inner edges of her breasts nestling hauntingly beneath the rubber. Doom tried not to look. His knees began to twitter.

"I have a practice pool out back," she said, leading him

through the workroom, past racks of tanks, disassembled regulators, and a compressor. Even now, far to the north, Longfellow cons were calling up fantasies similar to Rosalind Rock's rubber-sheathed bottom leading them to a limpid pool in a sultry climate with rustling palm fronds. "You'll need a suit," she said without turning to him. "Pool's a little chilly."

Did Boyle make mention of rubber pressure on a beautiful butt when the temperature is highly unstable after a deuce in the slammer?

She had seen nervous first-time students before, but this guy was a wreck. He could barely walk for wobbly knees. She shifted through a rack of wet suits until she found a reasonable fit and held it up to Doom's body. He was glad he had been in the pen and gotten in shape. "You can change in there."

Doom wondered whether a gentleman wore his bathing costume beneath his wet suit. Rosalind, it appeared, wore nothing beneath hers, so Doom decided not to. He slithered in naked, and the constriction felt good. Carefully, he zipped it up the front.

The practice pool was surrounded for privacy by a wooden slat fence and overhung by banyan trees. Fifteen feet square and equally deep, it had a broad step at the shallow end, and that's where Rosalind stood, water lapping the mystical top of her suit. Pieces of equipment— masks, fins, regulators with stout black hoses, buoyancy compensators, scuba tanks, gauges, and arcana Doom couldn't identify. Her practiced fingers mated a two-stage regulator to an aluminum eighty and screwed it tight, then slowly opened the valve. Highly compressed air hissed through the first stage, causing the hoses to pulse and lift.

Rosalind tested the equipment by taking two deep breaths. "Did you read the first three chapters?"

"Yes. I read the whole book."

"Really? Did you understand it?"

"I'm a tad hazy on Boyle's Law."

"That's okay, it's the concept that counts." Pedagogically, Rosalind had these lessons down cold, so she studied

Doom's gray eyes as she spoke. She explained that unlike in other sports, the diver is wholly dependent on mechanical devices for life support—breathing, in other words. That's why, in order to ensure safety, they had to talk first about danger. She stressed that danger from sea life, overblown by *Jaws*-like exploitation, was minimal to nonexistent. Pressure, however, was a clear and present danger.

From the text, Doom had grasped the general concept. Seawater, all water, has weight. Even air has weight. At sea level, organisms experience a pressure—weight—of 14.7 pounds per square inch, or one "atmosphere." Each 33 feet of descent in seawater adds another atmosphere to the total, or absolute, pressure. Thus, at 100 feet the diver experiences absolute pressure three times that at sea level. "Okay, so what?" she asked. "Why does the diver need to think about pressure?"

"Because pressure causes physiological changes," Doom answered. Look at her eyes, clear, alert, flashing, and look at her overlapped front teeth. A woman like this was bound to be married or otherwise unavailable to an ex-con with limited prospects.

There are two types of pressure effects to be considered—those that occur on the descent when pressure increases and the far more serious ones that occur on the ascent when pressure decreases. Doom and Rosalind discussed them both, together. She could see his brain functioning, a rare thing in men in her experience since Claudius died of the effect of decreased pressure on the ascent. She thought of Claudius while Doom recited the cause and prevention of squeezes on descent; pneumothorax, the bends, and air embolisms on the ascent.

She remembered Claudius talking about these things, the strength and assurance in his body as he stood before the class. The depth of his sadness, not then apparent to her, a nervous student, made him even more compelling when she experienced it later. They had had only five years together before, barely forty, the sadness overcame him. She still felt guilty that she couldn't save him somehow.

"Are you all right?"

"Yes, fine," she said.

"Should I come back another time?"

"No, please, I'm fine. Tell me about the bends."

"It's caused by inert gases such as nitrogen—air is seventy-eight percent nitrogen—which go into solution in the bloodstream under pressure at depth. When you ascend and the pressure lessens, the dissolved gases try to get back out through the blood and the lungs. If the pressure lessens too quickly, the unloading process falls behind and the swelling bubbles obstruct blood flow. But the nice thing about the bends seems to be that partial gases go into solution in the bloodstream at a predictable rate for a given depth, so the bends is entirely avoidable by not going too deep or staying too long."

"You've never done this before?"

"I just read the book."

"Did you write *Splendor*?"

Doom's heart sank. . . . "Guilty."

"I saw you on the news in handcuffs. I loved that book."

"You did?"

"Yes. Naturally, I felt like a fool."

"I'm sorry."

"Did you go to jail?"

"Minimum security."

"I never understood the point of writing a terrific book and then putting Eleanor Roosevelt's name to it. That seems absurd."

"I fell in with a pretty absurd crowd."

"Are you going straight?"

"Yes. Are you married?"

"No. I was, but my husband died." She decided not to mention at this time that he died scuba diving.

"I'm sorry. Was that why you got sad?"

"Yes. Will you autograph my copy?"

" 'To Rosalind Rock, best wishes from Eleanor.' Something like that?"

Rosalind giggled. Okay. So far so good. "Shall we get wet?"

GENIUS

BACK AT THE BOAT, DOOM DONNED MASK, FINS, AND snorkel, intending to retrieve his bicycle from the bottom. He clambered fin-footed over the lifelines, regained his balance, and stepped into the drink off *Staggerlee*'s port side. When his splash bubbles surfaced and dissipated, he saw the bottom of his boat for the first time. Doom had skimmed enough of his father's copy of *Skeene's Elements of Yacht Design* to know vaguely the elements he was looking at—a strong, full keel for directional stability, cutaway forefoot to enhance maneuverability, keel-attached rudder for safety, full buttocks for buoyancy in a following sea, moderate beam to damp the tendency to pitch. He floated in her element, watching for a long time, imagining her bottom in a seaway, bowling along romantically at her optimum angle of heel, kicking waves aside, centers of effort and lateral resistance equalized, himself and Rosalind arm in arm at the wheel. He ran his hand along her sweet bilge curve and slowly swam the curve forward toward the bicycle off *Staggerlee*'s bow. The bicycle was gone.

A flash of silver caught his eye near the bow. Something big had shot from the shade beneath the dock. Doom looked for it, whatever it was. Behind him! He spun clumsily and came face-to-face with a five-foot-long barracuda. . . . What a face it was. Long jaws tapered to a nasty point, and snaggled teeth, the front ones pointing straight ahead like thrusting weapons, glinted in the sunlit water. The fish hung motionless except for a flickering pectoral fin. Then its heavily armed jaws began to operate slowly and deliberately as if warming up to chew off Doom's thigh.

His heart pounded. There would be no escape from this toothy projectile. It could swim faster than the human eye could follow. It would sever his leg at the hip so cleanly he'd not miss it until he tried to swim away. Then Doom's own blood would make the creature crazy. He had heard about those feeding frenzies. Doom risked a quick glance topside. The Annes were filming him in the water. Billows of blood and offal would make the national news. "Simpleton eaten by fishes beneath his own boat." The Annes couldn't see the barracuda because of its natural camouflage, black on top, silver below. He could scream and flail the water for help—and depth charges—or die in manly, stoic silence.

But the fish didn't move, just hung there, watching, jawing the water. Hadn't Rosalind told him he had nothing to fear from the denizens? But what if this were a rogue, a psycho piscis?

Doom retreated aft to *Staggerlee*'s rudder post. The barracuda followed as if attached to Doom by rope. Doom could hardly draw enough air through his snorkel to maintain consciousness. The fish stopped five feet away and trained its cold, flat eye on its prey. Still it did not attack. . . .

Maybe it was just curious. Was that too romantic, curiosity in fish? Doom swam tensely toward it, and now it retreated, keeping the same five feet between them. Doom's fear faded. This thing was beautiful, if you really looked. He had heard somewhere that cautious swimmers shouldn't wear shiny objects in the water because barracuda might mistake the flashing for prey and strike. But this creature didn't grow so huge confusing wedding rings with food. Breath came easier. He watched for nearly an hour, and the barracuda watched Doom back. This fish seemed a marvel of evolution. Doom wondered if the fish felt the same way about him. Probably not.

"Ahoy, Captain Ahab, it is I, Fishmeal—" a man called from the dock. Doom recognized the voice, but the caller couldn't see Doom in the water. He could hide there beneath the bilge, pretend to be out, but that would only forestall the inevitable. The barracuda vanished. Doom didn't blame it. If Doom could swim like that, he would have vanished, too.

Duncan Feeney stood on the dock grinning from behind his woolly black beard, which ascended nearly to his eye sockets before the follicles petered out. Professor Goode stood beside him, wavering like a sailor in a force-9 blow.

"Hello, Professor," said Doom when he had climbed up the dock ladder.

"How have you been keeping, Dennis?" said the professor.

"Fine, Professor. Prison wasn't an unhealthy experience."

"You do seem fit. Quite the aquanaut." Professor Goode had gotten off with a suspended sentence because the judge concluded that a prison term would kill him; besides, no judge interested in public life could sentence an old man that pathetic to prison with the media watching. "I've been attending to my critical works. Currently, I'm parsing Crashaw and the Metaphysicals. Perhaps you'd peruse the first draft."

"I'd be honored, Professor." Doom felt sad to see the professor so close to death.

"We've been searching for you, Jacques," said Duncan, "but we never thought to look in the drink."

"You could have just left me alone."

"But I have an idea."

"No more ideas, Duncan."

Duncan and Doom sat around the ship's table while Professor Goode, limp on Nyquil, fell asleep on the starboard settee.

"This is a fine craft, Dennis. Whose is it?"

"Mine. My father left it to me when he died."

"Are you going to sell it?"

"I'm going to sea in it."

"Are you aware that we're being filmed?"

"Yes."

72

"This is a movie?"

"Yes."

"Is it cast?"

"It's not that kind of movie."

"What kind is it, Dennis?"

"A documentary. Call me Doom."

"*Call Me Doom*. Very interesting. What's it about?"

"I mean, I want you to call me Doom. For example, say, 'Good-bye, Doom.' "

"Jailhouse moniker? Christ, I wish I'd taken the fall. It's hell being a man on the run. Identityless. That's why I raised this beard. Like it?"

"How's the professor been?"

"Great, never better, mind like a steel trap. He's behind my idea one hundred percent."

"He looks like hell, Duncan."

"It's okay, he's a deconstructionist."

"You haven't been taking care of him."

"You haven't been taking care of him, either."

"I've been in jail, Duncan. That was part of the deal, that you take care of the professor."

"Wait. Is this a documentary you're making? Is it? Beautiful! Aren't you going to introduce me to the artists, Dennis? Doom?"

"This is Anne, and this is Anne."

"Easy to remember. How do you do, Anne? Anne? I'm Duncan Feeney. The Eleanor Roosevelt concept was mine. I conceived it. That's what I do. Conceive." Duncan smiled his charming smile. "Let me put my new conception in succinct terms: Lady Bird."

"Lady Bird . . . Johnson?" asked Anne on sound.

"Pre-cisely, Anne."

"Duncan, you're not suggesting I write a book by Lady Bird Johnson."

"You're the only writer who could."

"You belong in a home, Duncan."

"I'm disappointed, Doom. I thought you of all people would grasp the implications and ramifications here. I bet the Annes grasp the ramifications. Don't they?"

"No."

"Maybe it's the climate. You're probably thinking the hitch in my concept is that coming from us, of *Splendor* fame, people will think it's just another fraud."

"Of course I'm thinking that."

"Ah, but that's precisely the point!"

"What is?"

"That they *know* it's a fraud! Consider the aesthetic principle at work here. They'll know it's a phony, but they'll pretend it isn't in order to participate!"

"What?"

"Just like theater! We don't believe that Hamlet actually stabbed his mother behind the arras. Whoever the fuck he stabbed. We *pretend* we do in order to be astonished. The willing suspension of disbelief!"

Professor Goode moaned in his sleep and began to paw at his face as if arachnids were marching on it.

"Now then, you add in the element of a documentary of the whole process, and there you have another layer of aesthetic ramifications. Documentaries by definition record truth!" Duncan's eyes looked like two burnt holes in an army blanket. "Only this one won't. Get it? Do you see the utter originality of that? I told you it was genius. What do you say?"

"I say no."

"Come on, Doom, Lady Bird won't fly without you."

"I landed in jail because of *Splendor*. Remember?"

"Yeah, but you just said it wasn't such a bad experience. Besides, they won't put you in jail for this one."

"They'll only pretend to put me in jail?"

"Just think about it, the levels of irony and the manipulation of the medium for aesthetic purpose—let them work on you for a while."

"I'm sick of irony, and I don't want to write anymore. I spent two years on the trail, and I had a lot of time to think."

"What trail?"

"I want something real. I don't want any more phony things."

"Well, I'm frankly disappointed to hear that Dennis Loomis has caved in to middle-class pressures. The professor will be devastated."

"Look at him, Duncan, he's devastated now. Is he really writing about Crashaw?"

"Of course not. He's a Nyquil freak. Let me be frank, Doom. The professor has his heart set on Lady Bird. In his state I personally think the disappointment will take years off his life. Please, Doom."

"Everything is different now, Duncan. I'm different now."

"I'm desperate, Doom. I *need* something! It's hell out there!"

"I'm sorry, Duncan."

Duncan began to sob. His shoulders bounced with it. "Excuse me, Doom. Pardon me, Anne. Could we cut, Anne? I'd like to cut now."

But the Annes never cut. That was the whole point of cinéma vérité. They filmed Duncan sobbing.

"I've tried, Doom! We're dying out there in the world!"

Doom watched him cry for a while, watched the professor in troubled sleep slap his toes together, the soles and uppers on both shoes separated, and then Doom melted.

"Look, Duncan, there are some things happening here. I can't go into them right now, but I might need you and the professor. Maybe I can find you a place to stay for a while."

"Have you got something going down?"

"No, nothing like that."

"Big bucks?"

"Naw."

"It's not cheap keeping an old man. He needed a double root canal and a triple bypass."

"I might be coming into some money soon."

"Yeah? Really? Soon? How soon?"

"I don't know just when."

"We're with you, Doom. Whatever's coming down, you can count on us, no questions asked."

"Nothing's coming down."

". . . You realize that this boat is worth a bundolo, don't you, Doom? I have a keen eye for boats."

"You still don't get it, Duncan. I don't want to sell this boat. This boat is the best thing that's happened to me in years. I live here. This is *home*."

"Okay, Jesus, it was just a thought."

That night Bert, Doom, and Marvis Puller went sailing. They sailed out ten miles into the Atlantic on a broad reach and back on a fetch. Then they practiced setting and dousing the spinnaker. When they returned, Doom read a library book about the Gulf Stream. It said that the Stream carries a volume of water one hundred times greater than all the world's rivers combined.

OZZIE'S GOODS

NEXT MORNING, TWO HOURS BEFORE DAWN, DOOM USED *Staggerlee*'s own head, left the valve *up*, then ate breakfast at the Flamingo Tongue. Dawn was indeed making eyes at him while she poured his coffee.

"Yesterday I saw a big barracuda right under the dock," said Doom.

"Must be old Smiley," said Arnie.

"Smiley?"

"Yep, that 'cuda's been down there long as I can remember. I used to see that fish when I was a kid catchin' bait for Able Munger. Remember Able?"

"He was a total asshole."

"Arnie—" cautioned Archie with a nod at Dawn.

Dawn rolled her eyes at Doom.

"He was a anal orifice."

"Fully puckered."

"Man used to drop dead fish on you off the bridge as you come through the Cut." This, of course, was in the days before Big Al Broadnax had the bridge over Bird Cut blown up. "You got some big-time Yankee TV type on board's gonna tip you fifty bucks, you don't want Able Munger droppin' six-pound rock hinds on his head."

Doom estimated that the skippers were in their sixties. If they saw Smiley when they were kids, then that made Smiley fifty years old, maybe more. Was that possible, or were they pulling Doom's leg? He made a mental note to read a barracuda book.

"Old Smiley won't touch lures, cut bait, live bait, nothin'. One wily fish."

It was still dark when Doom, Marvis, and Captain Bert cast off *Staggerlee*'s dock lines and motored out through Bird Cut into the ocean. The tide was slack. A plume of tannin-brown bay water fanned out a mile to seaward. When the tide turned, the ocean would return the bay's water and add some of its own. Then a plume of clear seawater would fan out into Small Hope Bay. Four times in twenty-four hours the ocean and the bay exchanged fluids like active lovers.

Doom asked for the wheel, and Bert gave it over. Doom had given the Ozzie problem some thought. He had cut out the bottom of a gallon gas can, put Ozzie's gift-wrapped goods inside, and taped the bottom back on. His plan was this: in Doris's boat, Ozzie would anchor as close as he could to Buoy Number 41 marking the entrance to No Hope Channel, which led through a maze of low mangrove islets, shoals, and sandbars called the Marls. Doom explained to Ozzie that Number 41 was a flashing 2.5-second green light, visible for five nautical miles, which according to the chart was situated four miles northwest of Ponce Pass on a bearing of 280 degrees magnetic. "You can't miss it, Ozzie."

"What, I gotta be Horatio Hornblower to get my goods?" Ozzie had responded. "How 'bout we just meet at a stoplight on land?"

No, Doom was adamant. He'd been lax long enough, and now he was thinking. Ozzie was supposed to wait at Number 41, pretending to fish. When he saw *Staggerlee*, he was to hail her and say he was running low on fuel, and Doom would pass him the gas can of goods. Ozzie would take his goods out of the can, put Doom's gratuity in, and return the can. There were, however, some holes in the plan. For instance, he'd have to tell Bert the purpose of the trip before in good conscience Doom could enlist his help. Marvis wanted to come along for the ride, so Doom had to tell him too. Marvis and Bert had big mouths.

Captain Bert went forward to the mast and set the mainsail. Doom killed the engine. Then Bert set the number-one genoa. The twelve-knot breeze from the east meant that *Staggerlee* could sail to Ponce Pass on a gentle beam reach. Sails trimmed and drawing, the wheel came alive in Doom's hands, and his Ozzie-anxiety vanished for the moment. He was sailing his own boat. The false-dawn wind felt soft and moist on his face. He pulled the bill of his Total Immersion cap close over his eyes for concentration and listened to what his boat was telling him.

"You need a proper course to steer. Always plot yourself a course, no matter what," Bert cautioned.

"I'm steering 165 degrees magnetic. I plotted it last night. Off Possible Pass, we turn onto a heading of 225 degrees."

"Hey, I thought you didn't know anything."

"I've been reading my father's books. There's only about a four-degree variation around here, but I took that into consideration."

"You're a fast reader."

"I don't need much sleep."

According to the speed log, they were making a steady six knots. Bird Cut south to Ponce Pass was a distance of 9.5 nautical miles. Thus, Doom calculated, if they maintained a VMG of six knots, they'd arrive at the pass in eighty-five minutes. Plus another three miles from Ponce Pass to the No Hope Channel marker—according to

Doom's father's Weems & Plath nautical slide rule, they would meet Ozzie's boat at 0615.

"Bert and Marvis," said Doom in a gentle voice, "I appreciate you helping me sail, but you mustn't ever mention this trip to anyone."

"Goes without saying," said Marvis.

"My lips are sealed," said Bert.

"That's great. But, well, you did tell the Annes that I own Omnium Settlement."

"See, Bert, I told you he'd be pissed."

"I'm not pissed—"

"Hell, Marvis, you told them, too."

"Only after you already shot your mouth off."

Bert was embarrassed. "They told me all about their cinema verity business. . . . I'm sorry, I got all excited." His shoulders sagged.

Doom felt the weather helm tug the bow to port. Spots of glowing phosphorescence tumbled in *Staggerlee*'s quarter wave; she felt strong, steadfast, and ready for the open ocean. He didn't want Captain Bert to brood, so he called him Skipper and asked him sail-trim questions, soaking up the concepts.

The curve of the sun had topped the horizon when they turned to enter Ponce Pass between Tequesta and Cormorant Keys. The double-dogleg channel was deep enough, but one had to stay in it. Pelicans walked on the edges. Doom grasped the concept of red-right-returning, but he grew confused in the twists and turns.

"Watch it, watch it. Port, port—"

"Take over," said Doom, trying to sound calm, but his heart was racing.

"That's okay," said Bert, grateful that it was Doom's turn to be embarrassed. "Ponce's always been kinda tricky." Once through, Bert pointed almost dead ahead. "There it is. That's the place."

Doom broke out his father's binoculars and looked over the bow. "I've got it, and there's a small boat just to the south of the buoy." It was an olive-drab aluminum skiff with an outboard, but nobody was aboard. A fishing rod hung over the stern, its monofilament line shining in the new sun.

The breeze had gone light in the lee of the Keys, and *Staggerlee* ghosted toward the skiff. Doom panned his binocs 360 degrees. A big Hatteras Sportfisherman with pudgy white tourists sitting on the transom headed for the pass, outbound. A drift boat like the one Bert had sunk in Bird Cut was also making for the pass from the west. Not another boat was in sight. But how many were out of sight?

Sailboats are slow, even the fastest of them, which *Staggerlee* was not. It was taking a maddeningly long time to reach the skiff. And where the hell was Ozzie? Bert leaned down and turned on the engine. "Let's get the jib down so we can see what we're doing."

Marvis released the halyard and Doom pulled the limp sail down on deck. From the bow pulpit he trained his binoculars on the gently bobbing skiff. Nothing moved aboard. Was he sailing into a setup? Doom looked carefully from one little islet to the next. He saw nothing but a pair of great blue herons pecking fingerlings in the shallows, so he turned his gaze back to the skiff.

Staggerlee was drawing close now, and still the skiff seemed empty, yet the fishing rod hanging over the stern suggested otherwise. Doom climbed to the top rail of the bow pulpit and got his first glimpse of Ozzie—a set of bunioned toes wearing green rubber thongs. Doom's initial thought had Ozzie sunbathing, but on a rational level Doom knew that that notion was ridiculous. No one lay flat on the skillet bottom of an aluminum boat to take the Florida sun.

Staggerlee passed the skiff close aboard the port side. The bell buoy clanged on starboard. From his elevated stance, Doom watched Ozzie's face pass below, but the sight took a while to fix itself in Doom's mind, by which time the skiff had slipped aft to the cockpit. Bert and Marvis were hanging over the side to see. Doom watched their jaws fall slack and their eyes go round.

Ozzie's face was purple and bloated. His tongue protruded, swollen to the size of a rotten peach. The fishing line ran from the rod tip in a bight back to Ozzie's neck, around which the wire leader was wrapped a dozen times and knotted. At the end of the wire hung a two-inch-long lure shaped and painted like a bait fish. This was deeply imbedded by the treble hooks in Ozzie's left cheek. Doris's boat leaked. Ozzie lay on his back in four inches of water, arms and legs sloshing indolently. The bloat of his face had eradicated his features. Blood had flowed from his ears, but it had dried brown and crusty. His black eyes, protruding like a pug's, stared straight up.

Doom nearly fell fleeing aft when Bert shoved the throttle forward. The main jibed over accidentally, but nobody noticed. Doom flopped on the cockpit seat and trembled. No one spoke. The leaky death boat was already a hundred yards astern, fading. Think, Doom told himself, panic later. Then the main jibed back and everybody jumped as if at a gunshot. *Think*. Was there anything to connect Doom to Ozzie?

Doris! No doubt Ozzie had told her he was off to get his goods from that stand-up imbecile Doom Loomis. "We've got to get out of here as quickly as possible," he said. No shit?

Bert was already trying to shove the throttle through the stop. Doom would have preferred it if this narrowing channel to which they had committed themselves had had some name other than No Hope.

Mangroves closed in around them as the channel narrowed even further. Two boats *Staggerlee*'s size could barely pass beam to beam without scratching their topsides. And what if somebody had noticed *Staggerlee* as she passed close to the skiff and then ran like hell? "Is there a way out of this channel without going back past Ozzie?"

"I know a place we might be able to bounce across if we wait for the tide." Now Bert was articulating like a Shakespearean soliloquist.

"Then what?"

"When?"

"After we bounce across."

"Then we can join the main channel, head south to Cormorant Key, and out to sea that way."

Doom took Ozzie's gas can below and cut it open with his father's rigging knife. Poor, stupid Ozzie. "Discretion, that's the ticket." Feeling like a grave robber, Doom tore the wrapping paper off Ozzie's goods. The paper was decorated with yellow smile faces. Inside was a shoe box bulging at the corners. Doom sawed off the tape.

The box was packed full of banded thousand-dollar bills. Even their smell was overwhelming. Doom counted a dozen stacks before he stopped and held them up in the companionway for Bert and Marvis to see, but their eyes were glazed over.

Arms folded, the Annes were waiting angrily when *Staggerlee* returned to the dock. They knew they had been stood up intentionally, but they did not reprimand Doom. They had intended to, but they refrained when they recognized that something was badly wrong. Their anger turned to curiosity, watching Marvis and Bert, glum, distracted looks on their faces, scurry off without a hello or good-bye.

"We went for a sailing lesson," Doom lied lamely.

"We can't go on like this," said Anne.

"I know it."

"It's not productive."

"It's counterproductive."

"I'm sorry."

"A waste of time."

"Why don't you tell us what's going on?"

"We don't make any judgments."

"Would you like to meet Rosalind? We're going diving tomorrow."

That was a start.

SENNACHERIB BROADNAX

BIG AL'S ONLY SURVIVING SON, SENNACHERIB, WHOM everyone called Snack, sat in a palmetto-frond duck blind and lit another spliff, but it did him little good, blurring things. He hadn't seen a merganser in days. It was about 105 degrees in the duck blind, way the fuck and gone west of Dragoon's Hammock, and he was feeling crazy. His old man was "disappointed" in him again after another arrest, his fifth in as many years, for speeding, reckless endangerment, and possession of a controlled substance, to wit, the best domestic doo-dah the arresting officers had ever ingested. This time they nabbed him up in Corkscrew County, so Sheriff Plotner couldn't put in the fix for the old man, and anyway Snack almost hoped he'd have to do some time. Of course, no Broadnax would ever land on the chain gang spearing Dixie cups and stiff condoms along the berm, but Snack would have felt safer in the Corkscrew County slammer than he did at home.

The old man was trying to kill him. Hadn't Big Al called him a terminal disappointment? Terminal. Hadn't Big Al sent Snack to "check out" Tamarind Financial at the Snowy Egret?

"What do you mean, check it out?" It all seemed suspiciously vague to Snack. And his father had been up to something fishy for several months now. The evidence was clear.

"What do you *think* I mean! I mean check it out. I wouldn't bother you, son, I know you have important things to do, such as riding your motorcycle like a common nigger, and, hell, I'd do it myself—except I'm in a fucking *wheelchair!* I raised you, you ingrate mutt! What did your slut of a mother do? She did rat shit! *I* raised you, and this is the thanks I get—"

Snack had barely parked his bike before the entire Tamarind place blew to smithereens. If he hadn't been stuck in Yankee traffic on Route One, he might well have been inside—checking it out—when the joint went up. Had that been Big Al's intent right along? Maybe not primarily, maybe he just tried to kill two birds with one bomb. Wasn't he always talking about cutting overhead?

Sennacherib's brother Claudius had always been a severely troubled individual, with his dark moods and morbid dreams. Once, in this very duck blind, just ten years earlier, when Snack was sixteen, Claudius had said he suffered from what his shrink called a pre-Oedipal fear of infanticide. That had sounded to Snack like the load of Yankee guru bullshit you'd hear in Zoo York City. But then he got to thinking about it, about his own childhood fears.

He recalled most vividly those evenings—it always seemed to be hurricane season, raining—when his father would light yellow candles and gather Claudius and Sennacherib before him on the hook rug to tell them stories about their dead grandfather, Colonel A. C. Broadnax. Snack didn't remember the gist of the stories, but he remembered his ensuing dreams. In them, the colonel stood thirty feet tall, white-bearded and severe, like one of those prophets from Bible study, or like John Brown, whose body lies a-molderin' in the grave. He waved a huge sword in circles above his head and swore oaths at Nature herself as if he had the power to smite her if she pissed him off.

"He's watching us right now, from heaven," Big Al would tell his sons. "He sees everything you do, and when you do bad, the colonel gets mad and wants to smote you." Snack and Claudius had had an older brother who died before adolescence. Maybe his own grandfather had smoted him. Maybe that's what Claudius's shrink meant by fear of infanticide.

Snack missed his brother, and it didn't help to think that Claudius had killed himself by holding his breath on ascent, as Rosalind believed. Sometimes out of a clear sky Snack would burst right out sobbing. That's what he was doing up in Corkscrew County—120 on his 850 Norton Commander, sobbing.

He and Claudius had built this duck blind back in junior high, and even now, sitting in it, he felt like sobbing, but instead he decided to straighten up, have a shower, and visit Rosalind. She always liked it when people had feelings and talked openly about them. Snack believed that if he had had a woman like Rosalind, he sure as shit wouldn't have killed himself, no matter what had happened when he was a kid.

INDIGENOUS CREATURES

ROSALIND ROCK LIVED IN RUSTIC ISOLATION. HER UN-painted stucco ranch house sat atop cinder-block stilts in the pine-and-hammock forest far to the west of Small Hope Bay, beyond the sweep of low-slung pastel subdivisions with heavy security at the gates, beyond the last of the malls and the sun-baked golf-course condos, each hole named after an indigenous water bird. Here on the limestone ridge, elevation six feet, the works of man petered out not from lack of technology or potential profit but because the forest was protected within the boundaries of Dragoon's Hammock State Park. Rosalind told Doom that her grandmother lived out in the Hammock in isolation even more rustic than Rosalind's. Her grandmother's name was Lisa Up-the-Grove.

They had made two dives that morning in shallow water, and Doom loved it. "You might be a natural," Rosalind had told him.

"Could we go out and see the Gulf Stream now?" Doom asked. The sea was glass-flat, alluring in the sun.

Deep diving this soon in the curriculum was risky practice, seldom done, but she said yes. This Doom was strange. Strange men were not unknown to Rosalind. She recognized her attraction to the weird, troubled, damaged, and homeless. Yet she loved the wonder in Doom's eyes after his first dive in the ocean and again, later, when he told her about the barracuda beneath his dock. Of course, maybe he only seemed nice, his gentle manner a different feather on the same old lure, and he'd prove to be another crazy in search of vulnerable women to damage.

Rosalind had anchored in ninety feet of water over the seaward edge of Hens and Chickens Reef. While the Annes shot from the bow, Doom and Rosalind suited up and climbed over the transom onto the boarding platform, where Rosalind stood studying the current. Here the water was as clear as an Adirondack winter night. The Gulf Stream, the blue god.

"Nervous?"

"Yes."

"Frightened?"

"No."

"Would you like to have lunch at my place after?"

"Did you say Lisa Up-the-Grove?"

"She's mostly Seminole. She lives a few miles from me." Rosalind came from a long (for Florida) line of misfits, refugees, rustics, and Indians who wanted nothing so much as to be left alone, which, of course, they weren't.

Rosalind's great-grandfather Caleb Rock deserted the Union Army after the carnage of First Manassas. Sensing that his commanding officers were ready to do it again, Caleb lit out for the wilderness. His first stop was Meridian Passage Bay, not far from the Marls, where Ozzie Mertz would be murdered 127 years later. Caleb lived off the land and the water. Having been before the war a cooper's apprentice from Braintree, Massachusetts, Caleb had no wilderness survival skill, but such was the fecundity of the place that none was required. He'd settled on a protein factory. Fish, each in their season, literally clogged the bays and backwaters. They could be scooped up by hand. Game of all kinds nearly committed suicide in Caleb's cooking pot.

In time Caleb himself turned feral. He made everything he needed. Clothes were no problem, since much of the year he went naked, blackening his body with charcoal to repel insects. At first he avoided his fellows for fear of being recognized as a deserter, but years passed, and he stopped worrying. Still, from habit, he shunned white settlements. His beard grew to nipple length.

However, Christmas Eves, passing, made him sad and lonely out in the glades, sloughs, and mangrove islands. At last he scraped the mildew off his black wool suit, plugged the moth holes, and sailed to Hopeful Town on Cormorant Key to share the season with Christians. There he met Rose Up-the-Grove, a non-Christian. She returned with him to Meridian Passage Bay, where she gave birth to a daughter, who died before she could be named, and to a son, Mobley, who lived.

Mobley Rock loved the Florida wilderness as much as his mother and father did, but by the time of his majority, south Florida was changing fast. Visionaries had stepped in, declared war on the wilderness. Initially, they had planned to drain the entire Everglades to make vast riches from agriculture, but that didn't work for lack of technical know-how and soil nitrates, so the visionaries tempered their ambitions and just drained off the edges to make vast riches in real estate.

Mobley married Lisa, Rosalind's grandmother, another member of the loosely related Up-the-Grove family, and settled on the family homestead. One day developers visited the Rocks to tell them they were in violation and had to move on. The developers waved legal paper to prove it. Mobley demurred. The developers made rash threats. When the developers' bodies were found moldering in the slough, Mobley and Lisa lit out for Lostman's River in the still-unexplored Ten Thousand Islands.

There the Rocks tried this and that to get by. Lisa trapped and planted, and Mobley ran rum up from Cuba. But now change rushed in. The land boom was raging. Throckmorton's railroad, pressing southward, ran all the way to Jupiter, then to Miami. Someone was building a luxury hotel on the beach at Omnium Key. Visionaries drained tract after tract, scraped off the vegetation, laid out towns which they named after indigenous waterfowl, built structures, roads, and only then set about drawing the suckers down.

Florida was settled backward, first the towns, then the residents. Nobody thought about civics, sewerage, schools, medical facilities, or courts, let alone parks and libraries. That same year, 1925, Mobley disappeared on a run from Havana. Neither his boat nor his body was ever found, and he never knew that Lisa was pregnant with Rosalind's father.

Rosalind's story stopped abruptly there. She fell silent, concentrating on her driving.

"You didn't have a happy childhood?" Doom asked.

"Does anyone? Did you?"

"No."

"I was thinking about my father. He split when I was a little girl. Lisa raised me. My father died a while back. We had just started writing."

"What about your mother?"

"She split, too."

"With your father?"

"No."

"Is she alive?"

"No."

"I see."

"What do you see?"

"Just history. I think history's important. For instance, my father was a crook."

"All his life?"

"Except when he was at sea."

"Where they goin'?" wondered Binx, following a discreet two hundred yards behind Rosalind's truck. "We're already out here west of Jesus. Maybe I better twist one."

Ridly didn't care where they were going or whether they ever came back. This was a grotty gig at best, following some gink off to get laid, a man of Ridly's unfettered potential. "Maybe I should take up golf. A lot of business gets done on the links." He passed the bulging spliff back to Binx. "Man with a five handicap'd shoot right to the top, teaching the fat cats how to follow through."

"My brother Glen took up golf once. 'Course, he was handicapped to begin with."

Ridly had heard that the water hazards in south Florida were dense with alligators. Fat cats probably made the underlings fetch their miscues. Fuck golf, decided Ridly.

"Look," said Binx, "they're turning off."

"Then turn off."

"Cops." Binx was looking in the rearview mirror.

Ridly spun in his seat to see. Sure enough. "Keep going, don't turn."

Binx and Ridly kept going, Binx watching the cop in the mirror. "He stopped. The cop stopped at the turnoff. What's he doin'?"

Rosalind turned south off the paved road onto twin ruts through the woods. Sharp limestone outcroppings poked up through the humus. Bark like alligator hide, the pines climbed a hundred feet or more into unobstructed sunlight. Their boles were fire-blackened. Out here fire was as essential to the ecology as water. Doom tried not to look at Rosalind's breasts bouncing in the potholes. Her pocked "driveway" was three miles long. Doom's eye muscles hurt when it was done.

She parked her Jeep in the house clearing, and when she alighted, three blond Labs bounded out of a moonvine patch to circle her, yelping with joy. Animals appeared from all directions. Rangy, feral cats trotted from the palmettos to entwine their flanks around Rosalind's naked legs, something Doom would have loved to do. Twin goats came from under the house, and a short donkey followed the cats out of the palmettos. A raccoon with three legs peered down from a slash-pine branch, and something with a strange ringed tail crept along a higher branch.

"What's *that?*"

"That's a slow loris. It's a variety of lemur from India and Sri Lanka. The dogs woke him up. He's nocturnal. You'll see tonight how slow he moves, like he's underwater."

Tonight? Did that mean—? "How did he get here?"

"There used to be a dirty little tourist-trap zoo down the road a ways. The scumbag who owned it went belly-up and just released his animals into the woods. Birds too. We have bananaquits, scarlet racemes, cockatiels. Oh, and there's a couple howler monkeys and a marmoset. Lisa and I feed them and fix them up as best we can."

Rosalind and Lisa Up-the-Grove had also tended a pair of baboons until a cracker stopped his 4×4 out on Dragoon's Hammock Highway and shot them both dead for the hell of it. Lisa had recognized the truck and laid for it next time by. She shot the cab full of bullet holes, but miraculously, the driver escaped with minor injuries, which depressed Lisa. Sheriff Plotner arrested the cracker for destruction of private property and hunting baboons on state land without a permit. Sheriff Plotner also had Up-the-Groves in his family tree.

Doom was awed by the wildness of the scene, its exotic smells and sounds and unfucked-with quality. Eyes, some with oddly shaped pupils, peered from the trees and the bushes, from under the house and on the roof. Remove house, Jeep, road, bathing suits, and Doom and Rosalind might be an Upper Pleistocene couple watching joyfully the diversity and variety of their world.

So far so good, Rosalind smiled to herself. His face didn't change much, still mainly morose, but the wonder was apparent in his eyes. This was the crucial, often terminal, point in her relationships with men since Claudius died. She was careful always to bring them out here before things progressed too far. If her prospective lover walked gingerly on his toes to protect his Weejuns, bitched about the wet heat, worried about snakes, or, conversely, if he started prattling about murdering animals with hand-loaded ammo, the new romance would wither to acquaint-anceship. "Want to see some alligators?"

"You have alligators?"

"They're about the only indigenous creatures around here now."

Doom, the dogs, and the cats followed Rosalind around behind the house, down a sandy path toward a stand of hog cabbage and pop ash above which bald cypresses towered.

"Watch out for snakes," she said. "We should be wearing shoes."

"You don't have any pull with the snakes?"

They came upon a muddy depression, like a large cow-pasture pond, in the forest floor. Rosalind told him it had been dug by alligators perhaps a hundred years ago. Clots of duckweed smeared the tannin-dark water, and at first Doom noticed no alligators. He stepped down onto the muddy bank, crisscrossed with tail-swish marks, for a closer look. Primordial ooze squished sensually between his toes. Suddenly he saw noses and round black eyes pop the surface. Were they watching or smelling the approach of Homo sapiens?

"Will they charge?"

"No. I've seen the big males come roaring up the bank to chase the dogs, but it's just show. Crocodiles tend to be aggressive, but American alligators are pretty slow and docile."

"How many are there?"

"Eleven. It's hot today. That's why they're in the water." Rosalind explained that reptiles, alligators partic-ularly, aren't the loutish, primitive creatures that humans in their mammalian snobbishness depict. "Alligator me-tabolisms are so efficient, they only need four or five square meals a year."

"A *year?*"

"Yeah, we're gas guzzlers by comparison. Here they come."

Wakes spread in little vees behind their snouts, and the

black surface roiled with languid tail strokes. Rosalind touched Doom's shoulder as a sign to move back, and he didn't need to be told twice, six-hundred-pound gators snaking his way. The Labs dropped their forequarters and put their chins between their paws like playful puppies hoping for a good chase. A ten-foot-long bull ambled up the bank and peered at them. The dogs, hyperactive mammalians, spun in excited circles. Doom thought he saw curiosity, not menace, in their movements.

"Look at the babies!" exclaimed Doom.

Quarter-scale miniatures of their elders, the babies hung back, half in, half out of the water, waiting to see. Nine adults slithered to the crest of the bank, where they perched motionlessly, jaws agape.

"Maybe I can get them to bellow for you," Rosalind said, preparing herself for something, firmly planting her bare feet in the sand. "I can't always do it. Jim can get them to bellow every time."

Jim? Who's Jim? "Who's Jim?"

"He's a friend of mine from the university. He's a crocodilian expert."

Aww, shit, thought Doom. He wouldn't stand a chance against a crocodilian expert.

Rosalind cupped her hands around her mouth and began to squeak high in her throat. The trilling squeaks became deep guttural grunts, one after another, her abdominal muscles pulsing with each grunt, and she ended the call with a sound like a French horn at its lowest register. She stopped and waited. The alligators watched silently for a while, their faces fixed in dreamy smiles.

It began with the big bull. He puffed out the soft skin under his chin and switched his tail back and forth in the mud. The others, one by one, imitated him. Then they began to bellow and rumble in unison. Several slapped their heads on the ground, and the sound of their bellowing, rumbling, and slapping echoed around the pines.

Doom was astonished, even as he was a little worried about this Jim person. "Why do they do that?" Doom asked when they had stopped.

"There's a lot of theories, but nobody knows for sure. Sometimes they do it when an airplane goes over, sometimes for no apparent reason at all. Maybe just for fun."

The dogs heard another sound, stopped spinning, and listened. When they began to bark, Rosalind told them to shut up so she could hear, too. Doom listened. Even the alligators seemed to listen. A powerful engine was approaching.

As Doom, Rosalind, and the Labs came around the rear of the house, a gangly man in his twenties was dismounting from his coal-black Norton Commander. He wore black leathers but no helmet. The young man's hair was pulled abruptly back from his forehead and tied with a colorful roller-skate lace into a ponytail. His nose was long, and it came to a fine feminine point. His smile, at Rosalind, vanished when he spotted Doom.

"Hi, Snack," said Rosalind.

Snack pointed at Doom and said, "Hey, I seen this guy—"

"This is Doom Loomis," said Rosalind. "Doom, this is Snack Broadnax."

"Where did you see me?"

"At the Snowy Egret—right before it blew!"

"Blew?" asked Rosalind. "You mean that gas leak?" News of the explosion had of course made the front page, where Sheriff Plotner was quoted as saying that it looked "like a gas leak, plain and simple."

"Gas leak, bullshit, plain and simple. And this guy was *there!*"

"You must have been there, too," Doom pointed out.

"Yep, I was, but I didn't swipe nothin' out the guy's van." He turned to Rosalind: "But this sharpie did."

"What's going on here?" Rosalind demanded.

Doom explained that the place that blew up, Tamarind Financial Group, was probably a front for Perfection Park.

"What the hell is Perfection Park?"

"Could we talk about it later?"

"I think we better talk about it now."

Doom explained the Perfection Park proposal, and Rosalind's face went red with outrage. "Don't worry, it's just some fraud my father cooked up."

"What have you got to do with it?"

Doom thought it unwise to tell her he owned the proposed site of the Colonel A. C. Broadnax Hall of Flowers at this particular time. "Nothing," he said.

"Bullshit! Loomis was hooked up with my old man somehow."

"That's right, he was trying to swindle him, but now my father's dead, so why don't we just forget it."

"Yeah, well, I protect my sister-in-law from sharpies like you."

"Never mind that," said Rosalind. "Does your father mean to build Perfection Park?"

"Well . . . I don't know. He talks a lot about it."

"Then he must be stopped," Rosalind declared.

Snack said, "Stopped? . . . I don't think anybody's ever stopped my old man. From anything."

"Snack, your father is a fucking lunatic."

Snack blinked twice, slowly, like a loris at dawn. "Do you really think so?"

"Just look what he did to your brother!"

". . . Yeah."

GATORS

"BOTH OF THEM?" SAID BIG AL BROADNAX. "THIS PUNK Loomis and my own flesh and blood, Sennacherib?"

"Yep, out at the Rock place. I saw them just now," said Sheriff Plotner, hat in hand. His gray shirt was dark with sweat. It was hotter in this phony silk garden than out in the pineys. He still had sand spurs and other prickly shit in his pants cuffs from skulking around out there, spying on his own kin. He couldn't tell if this old fart appreciated it or not.

"What were they doing?"

"Talking."

"About what?"

"I don't know."

Plotting, probably. Against him. His last surviving issue, a turncoat to the Broadnax name, openly plotting with this punk Loomis. "Is this punk Loomis porking Claudius's wife?"

"Not while I was watchin'."

"I'll evict her," pronounced Big Al.

"Ah, well now, sir, we'd have a problem with that."

"Why?"

"Because you don't own it."

"Don't own what?"

"Her land."

"I gave that lot to Claudius for Christmas or some such stinking day."

"No, sir, that land's been in the Rock family since pioneer days."

"Don't talk to me about pioneer days! *Me!* I was a fucking pioneer!"

"Yes, sir, I know it—"

"Then I'll tell my Jews to buy the land and pioneer that slut's cunny right off it!"

"Can't do that, sir."

"Why not!"

"She donated it to the state."

Now, there was a difficult concept for Big Al to grasp. Donated? Nobody donated land. Land was all a man had in this life. Claudius had always been a rebel—marrying a crazy recluse like this *Cross Creek* cunt proved that— but Big Al always thought he could tame Claudius down. Now Claudius was dead, and Sennacherib had left him, too, gone over to the opposition, as good as dead. It was damn near more than a man could bear. "Let's arrest her."

"What for?" the sheriff asked.

"That's your department—think! . . . She keeps alligators, don't she?"

"She's got a whole raft of animals out there."

"Well, ain't that illegal?"

"What?"

"Keeping fucking alligators!"

"Sure, if she had them in a zoo, that would be one thing. Can't do that without permits and authorizations. But she don't. It's just there happens to be a gator slough on her premises. See, in the eyes of the law it's all a matter of enclosure. There ain't none." The old fart didn't have an appreciative bone in his entire wasted body. Just like the Denny Loomis murder. He, Sheriff Plotner, didn't get so much as a thank-you-kindly for covering it up.

Alligators? Alligators gave Big Al an idea. "Send Lucas in on your way out, Sheriff." Plotner stunk bad enough to wilt silk hydrangeas.

SEX AND DEATH

PRISON HAD NOT SCARRED DOOM LOOMIS!

Afterward, naked, Rosalind slipped like a con's epiphany out from under the mosquito netting and walked to a wicker rocking chair beneath the big rear window. Doom peered through the net, not missing a wiggle in her lanky stride across the room. Rosalind's house had no internal walls, so from the bed Doom could see diffuse theatrical moonlight fall over her body. But Rosalind had something on her mind.

"I liked that," Rosalind said evenly, crossing her legs.

"Me too," said Doom, putting it mildly.

"And I like you. I'd like to get to know you better, but we need to talk."

"Perfection Park?"

"Yes."

Doom joined her, and they sat in twin rockers. Rosalind pivoted hers for knee-to-knee talking. Doom felt like covering himself, perhaps with the lacy white doily from the rocker arm. Women were lucky in that respect—they didn't go all fleshy and vulnerable after.

"If you're planning to profit from it, then I don't want you under my mosquito netting ever again."

"I want nothing to do with Perfection Park."

"But I feel you have something to do with it."

He had no choice but to explain his father's fine-print prowess and how at his father's death from any cause, Doom acquired control of the dummy corporations that collectively owned Omnium Settlement. "Anyway, Perfection Park is nothing but a dog-and-pony show my father put together to bilk Big Al Broadnax out of his investment money. It's smoke. I'll show you the video. It's ridiculous."

"So wait, your father stole Omnium Settlement from Big Al and willed it to you?"

"Basically."

"Doom, that means—that means Big Al killed your father!"

"We shouldn't leap to a lot of conclusions—"

"He drowned, right? Accidentally?"

"Right."

"According to who?"

"Sheriff Plotner." Doom could see it coming—

"Big Al owns Plotner!"

The evening's lovely interlude was taking a turn for the depressing. "Would you be interested in a sailing trip? We could go to the Bahamas . . . or maybe Newfoundland."

"Newfoundland?"

"I don't want any more phony things, Rosalind. I'd like to stick to real things."

"Doom, I know Big Al. I was married to his son! Big Al is going to do this thing. It's in his rotten genes. He's going to make Perfection Park, and he'll stop at nothing."

"He's old, and these things take time. Maybe he'll show good taste and have a massive brain hemorrhage."

"Big Al means to ruin Small Hope Bay. You own something wonderful—you have responsibilities."

"But Rosalind, I don't really own Omnium. It's all a cheap con. I'm sure you do know Big Al, but you don't know my father."

"So you're not going to do anything?"

How could he refuse her, naked, ardent? "I could make a few calls. Maybe I could at least find out who's behind Tamarind Financial. But it'll be my father. Would you be interested in doing that again?"

Next morning Rosalind packed a picnic, and they went to meet Lisa out in her grove. On the way they stopped at the slough to watch crocodilians greet the new day. Doom put his arm around Rosalind's shoulders while she identified each alligator by name and natural history, as one by one they slithered into the warmth of the sun. This was the real thing. This was what he had hoped for.

Doom and Rosalind drove on sandy ruts deep into the forest. The trip felt exciting to Doom, like a small expedition into the unknown. Two hours of bumpy motoring in first gear and another hour of hot walking brought them to Dragoon's Hammock.

There the environment changed dramatically. The sunny, open forest of slash pines and palmetto thickets gave way in the course of a dozen strides to a seemingly impenetrable riot of vegetation. Rosalind showed him the way in. Live oaks festooned with air plants, poisonwood, tropical bustics, mastics, and gumbo-limbos reached greedily for the sunlight, while smaller trees—velvetseed, tetrazygia, wild coffee—flourished in the shade. Stout liana vines entwined them all. This environment was so foreign to Doom that he didn't know how to observe it. This was not like the evergreen and hardwood forests of the North that Doom had come to know in prison. This was Tarzanesque jungle, moist, dark, and mysterious, in which

Doom's sense of the whole was obscured by the close quarters. He sought, instead, to notice details. He and Rosalind watched a yellow tree snail, *Liguus fasciatus ornatus,* climb a royal-palm trunk, leaving a silvery wake glistening behind.

They arrived at Lisa Up-the-Grove's front step before Doom even saw her house. Actually, it was a shack, assembled decades before, seemingly from found lumber, stuck up on cypress-log stilts as if the rigors of pioneer times still obtained.

"Lisa—" called Rosalind. Something avian cawed and cackled in response. "My father was born in this house. During the rainy season Lisa lives with me, but this is her home. Lisa's weird." Doom and Rosalind sat together in a wooden swing on Lisa Up-the-Grove's screened porch and ate their picnic lunch, but Lisa didn't return. Slapping bloody mosquitoes, they took a nature tour of the hammock, but still Lisa did not return.

"Are you worried?" Doom asked.

"No. But she is an eighty-year-old woman. I've sort of reconciled myself to finding her dead out here one day."

They headed back to Rosalind's house, but before they saw the house, first Rosalind, then Doom, knew that something was wrong. In place of the familiar barks, caws, mews, clucks, and screeches, there was only silence. One of the Labs, Elsie, slunk like a cat along the rut.

Rosalind stiffened.

The other two dogs hunkered side by side in the palmettos, but the cats remained in deep cover.

"Look—" said Doom. A tiny woman in a long, colorful dress stood at the edge of the alligator slough, her back to Rosalind's approaching Jeep. A moment later the tiny woman heard the motor, spun, and leveled a handgun at the windshield.

Doom ducked behind the dash, but Rosalind jumped down and ran to her grandmother. Doom unfolded himself and followed her to the edge of the slough. . . .

Blood mixed with duckweed undulated on the black water. Rosalind moaned deep in her chest. Like the leavings of a dreadful feast, naked alligator carcasses ringed the pool. The only skin remaining on their bodies was in pathetic patches on their feet just above the claws.

"They killed them all," said Lisa Up-the-Grove, and Doom saw her face for the first time. It was a mass of wrinkles, like a sun-withered apple. Tears ran a zigzag course down her folded cheeks. Rosalind hugged her close, then ran for her house.

Doom squelched down the bank. There were eleven corpses, including the yearlings, lying in bloody pools where they had been skinned. Doom recalled their shimmers and bellows when Rosalind had called them yesterday. This morning he had begun to learn to understand them as individuals, and now in death they were indistinguishable one from the other, except the babies. Each alligator had a blue-black bullet hole between its eyes. Why hadn't the alligators hidden from their assassins by submerging in the opaque water? Maybe they had been domesticated just enough to come when called. And what kind of dirty fucks had done this thing?

Doom decided then and there to show them no mercy. Blood on his shoes, he climbed back to the crest of the slough.

"One of the rat bastards got snakebit," said Lisa. A soft young voice came from this leathery woman, and her eyes, though teary, were bright and sharp.

"How do you know?"

Wordlessly, she led Doom around the slough and near the rim pointed to a dead rattlesnake seven feet long, fat as a drainpipe. There was a bloody stump instead of a head.

"You're not from around here," Lisa pointed out.

"I was born here, but I've been away a long time. My name is Doom Loomis."

"I knew your daddy. He was a crook."

"I never knew him."

"You best be good to my granddaughter. I'm in the right mood to shoot men." And she jiggled the gun in her right hand.

"Don't worry, Mrs. Up-the-Grove, I will. Would a man die from a bite like that?"

"Might. Might not. Maybe nobody got bit at all. Maybe they just killed it because killing's what they was here for."

When Doom returned to the house, he found Rosalind curled in bed with a ball of fur pressed to her heart. It was alive. "What's that?" he asked.

"A bush baby."

He held Rosalind and her bush baby for a long time while she cried. "Rosalind," he said when it was almost dark. "I have an idea. We might be able to get the name of one of the killers." After Doom explained his idea, he asked what they'd do if it worked.

"Shoot the scum."

"Okay. . . ." Did she mean that or was it the grief talking? Lisa Up-the-Grove looked ready to shoot reptile killers, in which case there would be trouble. Perhaps it was time to summon sociopathic assistance. "Can I call New Jersey from your phone?"

"What's in New Jersey?"

"Longnecker's in New Jersey."

A woman answered in New Jersey.

"Hello," said Doom, "this is David Dietz calling from *Adirondack Life* magazine. Your subscription is about to expire."

"Oh," said the woman, sorry to hear that Adirondack bullshit. "Just a minute." She shouted "Longnecker!" in Doom's ear.

Doom spoke to Longnecker in code, and the only bit of it that made any sense to Rosalind was "Omnium Key, Florida."

Well, Doom figured, while he was making covert calls, he might as well check on the roots of this Tamarind Financial front, so he called Whittelsey Dowd, a white-collar criminal still incarcerated at Longfellow. Whittelsey Dowd was an inside trader, stock manipulator, and breacher of fiduciary duty and, therefore, a perfect resource for Doom, who again talked in code. "Tamarind Financial on Tequesta Key, Florida" was the only phrase that made a lick of sense to Rosalind, listening. After that he called Duncan and the professor to set things in motion for tomorrow.

There he went again, thinking like a crook, like his father. So much for real things. When he hung up, Doom found Rosalind standing beside her bed, staring at him. Lisa Up-the-Grove stared at him, too, from the back door.

"I'd like to invite you both to spend the night with me on *Staggerlee*," he said.

LONGNECKER AND HOLLY

POSING AS TOURISTS FROM SUBURBAN NEW JERSEY, Longnecker and Holly motored south on the Sunshine State Parkway past the Ocala interchange. Longnecker drove, fiddling disconcertingly with the radio, while Holly stared out the window at endless, ordered orange groves and thought this the most tedious landscape she had ever laid eyes on.

"Bible thumpers and hardscrabble nail knockers! Christ Jesu! I want *jazz!* Where's the *jazz*? Where's the hard bop? I wanna hear some Cleanhead Vinson!"

"Get real," said Holly.

Their bumper sticker said HAVE YOU HUGGED YOUR KID TODAY?

Longnecker listened to a weather report for the northern Rockies as if it made a difference to his life, then said, "That Doom Loomis, he's one stand-up hombre."

"So you mentioned." Holly, frankly, had heard quite enough about this Doom Loomis character, about how Longnecker would still be languishing in Longfellow if Doom hadn't let him escape into the forest while out on the trail patching lean-tos. Doom had known Longnecker was plotting a bust-out. Doom had seen him depoting supplies on the trail to Lake Tear of the Clouds. Doom had even tried to talk him out of it.

"Look," Doom had reasoned, "it's not so bad here. We have fresh air, exercise, nature. If you bolt now, you'll be a fugitive for the rest of your life, a man on the run."

"But Doom, that's the only time I'm really happy."

"When?"

"When I'm on the run."

"Oh. . . . That's different."

As trail boss, Doom was in charge, and rules clearly stipulated that he had to rat on Longnecker. Longnecker's escape cost Doom a month in lockup. There were even some scary threats about transferring Doom to the hardtime lockup at Dannemora, where they'd keep him naked in the dark, pissing in a galvanized bucket, until he told them where Longnecker went. Doom didn't particularly mind the Longfellow lockup. He read *Murphy, Malone Dies, The Unnameable*, and *Watt*, in that order. He emerged mentally adroit, if more disconsolate, and a figure of respect, a stand-up guy, among inmates and correction officers alike. And that's why now Longnecker and Holly were headed for someplace called Omnium Key, because Doom Loomis was one stand-up guy. Holly knew all about it. What the hell kind of moniker was Doom anyhow?

Holly had begun to enjoy Upper Saddle River, New Jersey. Her life there seemed clear and cheery, not like life underground at all. Certainly not like when Longnecker was a fresh fugitive and they had holed up like a couple of chipmunks in a leaky yurt outside Broken Leg, New Hampshire, freezing their tits off. After that winter, their new Upper Saddle River neighbors seemed exotic to Holly, contributing as they did to the GNP in three-piece suits. Sometimes at night she wished she had taken up with a contributor, a man with ties to the community, but she always landed with Longneckers, men who never fit in.

It wasn't as if Longnecker didn't try. He had made several touching attempts to fit in. He had stolen this Range

Rover from the Bergen Mall parking lot because it was the car of choice in Upper Saddle River.

Holly's new friend, Phoebe, had even hinted around about sponsoring them for membership in the Upper Saddle River Golf & Tennis Club, which insiders called the Saddle. Holly found it difficult to visualize Longnecker in knickers, putting, but the concept of a country club appealed, tranquillity, green canvas umbrellas to block reality and the afternoon sun, and now that life might be gone before it really got started. Longnecker was speeding off to do something crazy with this stand-up weirdo in Florida, a state she had always detested, where no doubt she'd find herself in the center of a weirdo jamboree. Holly often suspected it was the scars of a Catholic upbringing that had left her susceptible to Longneckers. Look at him, steering with his knees at seventy while rolling a duber the size of a tampon.

"One pays this kind of bread for personal transportation, one expects to get an FM radio."

"You know, Longnecker, it didn't sound so bad to me at Longfellow," said Holly petulantly, and he looked at her as if she had suggested they sign up for the Saddle and shoot golf. "Longnecker," she ventured again after what seemed about four days in the orange groves, "will you promise me one thing?"

"You name it."

"Promise me you won't blow anything up."

"Sure, babe. Got to pee?"

"Yes."

"Let's stop and buy some tourist trash, maybe a Stuckey's Praline Loaf."

"Longnecker?"

"Yeah, babe?"

"If you don't intend to blow anything up, why do we have all this dynamite aboard?"

"Traction."

CRIME WAVE

LEAVING ROSALIND AND LISA ASLEEP IN THE FORWARD cabin, Doom got up at dawn, pulled on shorts and his Total Immersion T-shirt, and headed for the Flamingo Tongue. He hadn't exactly decided to call Doris, but he was leaning that way. She deserved at least some of that money, yet contacting her would be a reckless act. The police were probably talking to her right now; even a stupid cop could trace Ozzie's death boat back to her.

There were three newspapers in racks outside the restaurant, two locals and the Miami *Herald*. It didn't make the *Herald*'s front page, but the other two blared:

ANOTHER CORMORANT KEY KILLING!

. . . Another? Doom's knees went soft, reading,

> Doris Florian, 62, was found strangled to death in her home at 3156 West Anhinga Dr. last night. This followed by twelve hours the murder of Oswald Mertz, who was found strangled in Ms. Florian's boat near No Hope Channel.
>
> Police found Ms. Florian's body when they traced the boat registration to her address. Neighbors reported that Mr. Mertz moved in with Ms. Florian about six months ago and that they were "a nice, quiet couple." Police are searching for a connection in the killings.

"Getting to be just like Miama," observed Arnie without moving his lips.

"It's the drugs," said Bobby.

"It's the Yankees," said Billy.

"It's the liberals," said Arnie.

Dawn was making eyes at Doom.

Then wafts of stink began to swirl about the Flamingo Tongue. Knowing the source, Doom didn't look up from his newspaper.

"Fret not, boys," called theatrical Sheriff Plotner, the screen door banging shut behind him. "I got these killings in the bag." He squatted on a stool next to poor Arnie Junior. "In the ba-ag."

Dawn poured him a cup of coffee to go but did not tarry in the area.

"Why, hey there, Mr. Loomis. You boys know Denny Loomis's son? You must feel right at home, what with all the killings." Nobody answered, but Sheriff Plotner didn't give a shit. "I'll let you boys in on a little police secret, you swear it don't leave this room. Ever. Both victims was . . . strangled."

"Hell, Lincoln, it says that right in the paper," Arnie pointed out.

"No it don't. Where?"

Arnie Junior excused himself to go outside for a breath of fresh air.

"Damn if I didn't tell those hacks *off the record*. Well, then, I'll tell you something else. Mertz and the Florian woman—they both lived together in the same house!" Sheriff Plotner was ebullient. "I been waitin' thirty years for a clean-cut killing. I crack this one, you boys'll be watching me on Ted Koppel."

Dawn was bagging the sheriff's coffee at the far end of the counter. Doom felt as if he might throw up from the combination of stink and fear. Sooner or later this compost heap would trip over the fact that Doom and Ozzie did time together at Longfellow. It wouldn't prove anything, but it would provide the dreaded first connection. And then there was the talkative team of Bert and Marvis to worry about. Doom had made some reckless mistakes, but now that would have to change.

With his coffee, the sheriff wafted out the door to fight crime and appear on Yankee TV.

"Ole Lincoln Plotner don't get to smell no better as the years go by."

"I don't mind the smell, just it gets in my eyes."

"Ever smelt a dead shark?"

"Naw, I think it's more vegetable in stink. Like muck."

"Remember Platehead Johnson?"

"Got hit in the noggin by a torpedo?"

"Right. You'd fish with ole Platehead in the sun, bored, not catchin' nothin', he'd say, 'G'won, touch it.' You'd touch it and the damn thing'd burn your fingers like Archie's griddle."

"What made you think of Platehead?"

"Somethin' about the way Plotner stinks."

"Platehead stink?"

"No."

The phone rang. Archie went to get it. He summoned Doom. "It's collect," said Archie.

Doom laid twenty bucks on the counter.

"Greetings from Longfellow U.," said Whittelsey Dowd. "Spanish Eddie sends his best, likewise Ralph and the Hat." Doom and Dowd didn't have much in common except that they liked to watch nature documentaries on the rec-room TV. "When I get out," Whittelsey Dowd used to say, "I'm going to buy a llama."

"Why a llama?" Doom asked.

"I've always liked llamas." Whittelsey was serving a nickel for stock manipulation, insider trading, and general white-collar criminality. His family had come over on the *Mayflower,* so he felt behooved to disgrace the name. "How's life in the sunny South?"

"I'm living on a boat."

"The cons will love to hear that. 'Wild Kingdom' is coming on this afternoon, but these dorks want to watch the Dolphins play some other lummoxes. We're freezing our seeds off, wondering if winter will ever end. Women?"

"There are two aboard right now."

"Two! Naked?"

"Oh, sure."

Dowd groaned longingly. "Do they have all-over tans?"

"Most everybody does down here. Have you got something already?"

"Your guy loves the cover of darkness," said Dowd. "This Tamarind Financial Group was buried tit-deep under paper. TFG is a wholly owned subsid of Telco Finance based in Orlando, Florida. Telco's part of a conglomerate called Celestial Real Estate, Inc. Celestial's headquartered in L.A., but Celestial's a subsid of the Tendine Corp., and Tendine's nothing but a post office box in Wilmington, Delaware. It goes on like that. Want more?"

"If it's important."

"How would I know what's important? You didn't tell me anything, you just gave me directions, and I followed them at no small exertion to myself."

"What can I send you, Whit?"

"Oh, the usual."

"What kind?"

"The gamut." Porn was currency at Longfellow, a kind of dirty bearer bond.

"It's on the way."

"Have you ever heard of Donald Sikes?"

"The tycoon?"

"He's a developer. Owns half of Manhattan, among other cities and municipalities. That's who lurks at the bottom of Tamarind Financial Group."

"Donald Sikes?"

"What's going on down there, Doom?"

"I don't know."

"Come on, Doom, I'm in stir. Entertain me!"

"I don't, honest."

"If you're going after Donny Sikes, forget it. Man's a recluse. He doesn't even show up for grand juries."

"I'm not going after him."

"Look, Doom, I'm out of here in six and a half months. You could use a crook like me. I have resources. I wouldn't make a move against Donny Sikes without my resources. Please, Doom, I *need* something!"

"Okay, you're on." It sounded to Doom as if Whittelsey was about to cry.

"Really?"

"Sure, call me when you get out."

"I will, Doom, you can count on me. Six months, nineteen days." Whittelsey Dowd hung up and returned to the rec room to tell the cons, who were staring at the TV with stupefied looks on their faces, that Doom Loomis was going after Donny Sikes. The gridiron was bathed in Miami sunshine, but back at Longfellow it was already pitch-dark. The red aerobeacon atop Kempshall Mountain twenty miles away was blinking forlornly. Whittelsey's news arrived like a spice-scented trade wind. The rec-room cons cheered. That Doom Loomis, he was still one stand-up hombre. Whittelsey Dowd sat down in a broken plastic chair and choked back a gob of regret. The effort hurt him deep in his chest.

When Doom returned to the counter, the skippers were still remembering Platehead Johnson, about how his plate got struck by lightning up around Jupiter somewhere.

"He just wasn't the same old Platehead after that."

The phone rang again. Dowd was calling back. "I almost forgot the coincidence. Remember Ozzie Mertz?"

". . . Sure."

"Well, that's who Ozzie embezzled from. Donald Sikes."

ENVIRONMENTAL PROTECTION

"I DON'T BELIEVE FOR ONE SECOND THIS HAS ANYTHING to do with alligators," Duncan stated flatly from behind the wheel of the subcompact Doom had rented. "He's up to something. I can see it on his face. The man is up to something funny, and he's holding out on us. I hate that."

"He's standing us our accommodations," said Professor Goode.

"Accommodations? It's a trailer park. I expected never to wind up in a trailer park."

"I rather like it."

"Of course you like it. There's not a soul under a hundred and eight. You probably feel like a graduate assistant. And another thing. Where is he getting the bread?"

"At some point, Duncan, events will force you to fall back on your own resources. Then where will you be?"

"Fucked and banjaxed."

"Wait, stop. That was the place."

Duncan braked. "How could that be the place? It looks like a dead diner."

"Nevertheless, it's on the list. Dr. Conklin."

In fact it used to be a diner called Goodhue's Alligator Eats. The letters had been removed from the sign, but the sun had burnished forever their imprint into the metal case.

"Christ, look at the dump. I wouldn't buy a cheeseburger from Dr. Conklin," said Duncan, backing into the weedy limestone parking lot. There was a drive-up window around the back.

Duncan and the professor had visited ten doctors since morning, and the list was growing short. They might need to extend the radius out to twenty miles around Dragoon's Hammock, and the fucking air-conditioning was busted.

Goodhue's Alligator Eats had failed because few hungry tourists ventured this far west of the beach, and there weren't enough locals ready to eat twice at Goodhue's. Doctor Conklin was failing for similar reasons, but he didn't care. He and Helga were having fun. She chained him, arms up, under a ceiling joist in what used to be, and still looked like, Goodhue's kitchen. Helga was wearing his favorite black garter belt, stockings, and underwire bra with nipple cutouts. She opened his pants and with the toe of her black kid boot lowered them down around his ankles.

"You were a very naughty fuckface, and now I'm going to punish you severely." She drew a horse crop from the top of her slithery boot.

"Oh, no, no, please don't punish me, please, please— Helga, what was that? Did you hear something?"

"Like what?"

"A patient?"

"I doubt it. I'll check." Helga pulled on her lab coat.

"Good afternoon," Duncan said to Helga, "I'm Agent Armbrister of the DEP and this is my associate, Professor Crashaw, from the Tropical Serpent Research Center. We'd like to talk to Dr. Conklin, please. Won't take a minute of his valuable time."

Wordlessly, Helga returned to the kitchen, where the doctor hung. After a while he appeared, wearing green plaid slacks, white loafers, no socks, and a starched white shirt with a stethoscope draped around the collar.

"I must protest," said the doctor. "I paid my debt to society, and I resent being hounded by the DEA."

"Not the DEA," said Duncan, "the DEP. The Department of Environmental Protection."

"Oh. That's different."

"We're researching the frequency of snakebite injuries in the region, specifically those due to rattlesnake bites." Duncan was growing bored with Doom's spiel.

"Funny you should mention it. I had a remarkable one just yesterday."

"You did?"

"Was it yesterday? Or Monday? Well, recently. It was a nasty one."

"How so, Doctor?" asked the professor.

"My patient had this snake head the size of a small smoked ham stuck to his calf. I thought it was a sick joke at first, then I realized it wasn't and I about tossed the old cookies."

"You mean the fangs—?"

"Sunk to the hilts."

111

"Did your patient survive?" Duncan pretended to take notes.

"Walked in under his own steam, walked out the same way. Took it with him."

"What?"

"The head. Carried the damn thing out by the fangs like it was his lunch box."

"How do you account for that, Doctor?" the professor asked.

"Insane, I guess."

"I mean his condition. Did the snake not bite him?"

"Bite him? It pumped in enough venom to paralyze a rugby team. You see, my patient was enormous. That's how he was able to—wait a minute. He didn't die, did he? Look, I can't be held responsible for his death—"

"I'm sure your procedures were deft and timely."

"Oh, why thank you very much, Professor."

"What was your patient's name?" Duncan asked.

"Oh, well, now, you see, I'm not at liberty to disclose—"

"Doctor Conklin, the DEP, the DEA, the IRS are all under the same aegis. An uncooperative reputation with one is the same for all," Duncan pointed out.

". . . Well, in the interests of our fragile environment, my patient's name was—what? It's on the tip of my tongue. . . . I'll consult my nurse, if you'll excuse me—"

The big snakebite victim's name was Lucas Hogaboom.

FU AND FRIENDS

DONALD SIKES? . . . DONALD SIKES OWNED TAMARIND Financial. That changed everything. . . . Didn't it? And what about Ozzie? Dead because he wronged Donny Sikes? Doris, too? Naw, just one of those coincidences you hear so much about.

Doom sat in *Staggerlee*'s cockpit and tried to delude himself. He read the New Revised Edition of *The Annapolis Book of Seamanship*, but he couldn't concentrate on the rules of the road, buoyage, or marlinespike seamanship, so he looked at the pictures. He couldn't concentrate on anything except the gathering clouds of responsibility. Embarkation with Rosalind for Newfoundland seemed a fantasy to him now. He wondered what Smiley was doing and decided to go see.

Doom collected his snorkeling gear from the lazaret, pulled on his mask, and leaving his fins behind, stepped over the lifelines into the water. It felt cool and calming compared to life topside. When his splash bubbles cleared, he searched for Smiley. Doom always felt an instant of fear jumping in, as if Smiley might mistake his sudden arrival for a threat and reflexively lash out, yet empirically Doom knew the fish was far too comfortable in its evolutionary design to fear sudden visitors.

But where was Smiley? Behind. Hanging with perfect buoyancy three feet beneath the surface. Languidly sculling its pectoral fins to maintain station. Doom visited almost daily, and he wondered whether Smiley recognized him. If so, did he have any feelings about Doom's presence? Did fish feel? Mammals did. Dogs and cats obviously had feelings. Doom's beloved boyhood dog had feelings. With a stab of sadness Doom remembered Joey dreaming, running, and whining in his sleep, and he remembered the look in old, sick Joey's eyes when at the end the vet inserted the needle. His wise eyes, cataract clouded, had said, Yes, I know it's time to go, farewell. Smiley's big black eyes followed Doom's every move. One day perhaps Smiley would let Doom touch its flanks, feel its streamlined power, and if so that would denote trust, a feeling.

Doom approached the fish. Gently, slowly, Doom put out his hand, open as though showing a strange dog his goodwill before petting its head. There was still two feet between his hand and Smiley's flank. Before Doom had closed that distance three inches, Smiley vanished, there one instant, away the next. Doom felt the ghostly wash of its tail in the water, but he saw nothing of its actual leaving. By now Doom knew where to find the fish after it vanished. Behind. And there it was, three feet from Doom's heels, working its snaggly jaws to propel water across its gills.

Doom wondered if Smiley lived alone under the dock, and if so, was that how he wanted it? Solitary, a meditative existence. Perhaps Smiley was occasionally visited by an old female for a quick submarine assignation. For all Doom knew, Smiley was a female—probably took an experienced ichthyologist to sex a barracuda—but Doom preferred to think of Smiley as a lonely male adrift in a world not of his own making, lurking under a dock. Doom watched the fish for an hour, and the fish watched Doom, both motionless, a kind of communication across the gulf of evolution that Doom always found instructive and satisfying. He hoped Smiley did, too.

When Doom hauled himself up the rope ladder over *Staggerlee*'s stern, he found two assholes watching him from the dock. Hairy-legged, both sported plaid Bermudas. One was short and rotund with a stupid grin on his face, and the other, older, taller, fitter, wore a droopy Fu Manchu mustache that entirely covered his upper lip, hairs curling over it into his mouth. The two assholes peered at Doom across the lifelines. Doom pretended not to notice them. He sat down, dripping, in the cockpit and picked up his seamanship book, pretending to be absorbed in an explanation of anchoring technique.

"Police officers," said the one with the Fu Manchu.

A great roll of fat spilled obscenely over the other asshole's belt.

"You're gonna have to come with us."

"You're arresting me?"

"Ain't that what I said?" asked Fu, and his friend giggled, gut twitching.

"Not exactly, no."

"We're arresting you."

"On what charge?"

"Real estate fraud."

"I'll need to see some ID."

"What?"

"Badges," Doom clarified, trying to cover the fear churning in his bowels.

The porky asshole looked to Fu, who nodded, then drew up his paunch with both hands so Doom could see the handle of the nickel-plated revolver stuck in his belt. With an ugly heave Porky replaced his paunch. He had flat, cloudy eyes, like a day-old dead fish.

"I got a badge, too," said Fu. "Only mine's bigger. Makes a teeny hole going in. Going out makes a hole you could put your head in without getting blood on your ears." Fu had read that line in a Mickey Spillane novel during Spanish class back in high school when he was a young, aspiring thug and since then always looked for an opportunity to haul it out. The porcine asshole chortled at the boss's wit, teeth brown and broken.

Fu's real name was Roger Vespucci. Roger Vespucci's sainted mama used to tell him he was directly related to Amerigo Vespucci, Christopher Columbus's navigator to whom "this whole stinkin' country owe its name." Once, in show-and-tell, Roger told the entire seventh-grade class about his noteworthy ancestor, only to have a rotten little four-eyed egghead say that Amerigo Vespucci didn't discover dick, that Amerigo wasn't even *aboard* for any of Columbus's four voyages to the New World and that the only reason they named America after a bullshitter like Vespucci was because he kissed ass in the Spanish court. Tears ran down Roger's face in front of everyone. He could still remember the heat of their tracks.

He bided his time until one day, mysteriously, a ten-pound chunk of roofing tile dropped on four-eyes's noggin while he was playing steal-the-bacon, leaving him without the speech function.

"Forget it, I'm not going anywhere with you two assholes."

A sallow tourist and his gawky, gangly son fished from

the end of the dock. A knot of disaffected youth, the knees sliced out of their jeans, passed a joint in and around a ruined pickup truck. These were merely the nearest witnesses. Surely the assholes wouldn't try anything now. Doom scrawled something across the title page of his seamanship book and closed the book on his pen. Then he scanned the cockpit for weapons with which to repel boarders. There was a twelve-gauge flare launcher, but that was in the gear locker below. There were two stout winch handles within reach, in pockets port and starboard near the bridge deck.

The fat guy made to board *Staggerlee*.

"You, Porky, get off this vessel!"

Porky stepped back and looked to Roger Vespucci for further instructions. Something was wrong here. Up in Detroit you pull heat on a gink, he lies down and flies right.

Then Doom heard the marine engine approaching from aft. A short skiff with white topsides and two hulking outboards slipped up beside *Staggerlee*. A skinny kid with a bouncing Adam's apple stood at the helm—and Doom was surrounded. Now both dockside thugs were coming over the rail with malicious intent. Doom dove for the portside winch handle—

Porky caught his toe in the lifeline and fell hard to the deck on his hands and knees—directly in front of Doom. So he took the opportunity to clout Porky midspine with the hefty steel winch handle. Porky screamed and twitched and spasmed. Doom swung the handle in a sweeping rearward arc to get the boatman coming over the port rail. Had it landed, the blow would have staved in the boy's brainpan, but he remained aboard his boat, out of range.

Doom continued the arc on around, hoping to clock Fu, but he bobbed and weaved away. Deftly, between swings, Fu sapped Doom above the ear with a cowhide-covered chunk of lead.

At first Doom didn't think he was hurt, even though the blow sounded so very loud inside his head. Doom kept swinging—maybe he'd find some bone—but the world seemed odd, cloudy, distant, and inexplicable. Doom was staring at the bottom of the cockpit, the floor—called the "sole" on boats, he distinctly remembered reading in the nautical-terminology chapter. And then there was that shiny little drain grate in the forward corner. He had never noticed that grate before. Wasn't it a lovely touch of craftsmanship that the screw heads in its outer flange were perfectly aligned? One's appreciation of a thing is often enhanced by getting really close to it. Porky, supine on the seat, moaned in Doom's ear.

Roger Vespucci drew Doom's hands behind his back and cuffed them there. He clicked another pair of handcuffs around Doom's ankles. Doom felt very comfortable and thought he might rest for a while before he started hitting at the assholes again. He made a mental note to read a definitive treatise on cockpit drain grates.

"I'm paralyzed! Paralyzed, I tell you!" keened Porky.

Just look at the morons and nincompoops Roger Vespucci was saddled with. Can't even snatch a lone, largely unarmed individual without incident. And now a small crowd was collecting on the dock.

"Police. We're police officers. This man is fifth on the ten-most-wanted list," said Roger Vespucci.

"I'm gonna kill him! I'm gonna kill—!" Porky gave out a moan when he tried to move, stabbing pain coursing all the way down the backs of his thighs.

Look at him there like a dying elephant seal. And then there was that drooling inbred cracker cretin standing in his boat like an audience. "Hey, Byron, you mind helping us *pull this guy aboard!* I don't mean to bother you."

"I'll kill him!" Porky repeated.

"Forget it, you aren't going to kill him."

"Aww, please let me kill him!"

"Hey, dickbrain Byron, will you get over here and *help!*"

"My boat'll drift away."

"Tie it off!"

"Can I kick him?" Porky wanted to know.

"Okay, if you can get up and help, you can kick him." Like dealing with fifth-graders.

Porky wheezed as he got to his feet in sections. He kicked Doom in the ribs, but it seemed to hurt Porky more than Doom.

A murmur ran through the crowd, and Roger Vespucci heard the phrase "police brutality" more than once. It was high time to get in the wind before this developed into a nasty incident with real cops.

Doom could see but couldn't move as Fu and Byron loaded him, loglike, aboard the skiff. Somebody slid him into the cuddy cabin, where his head fetched up against the forward bulkhead. After a time he came to recognize the motion—the skiff was banging through ocean swells at full throttle.

"Lemme kick him again."

"COPS!"

ROSALIND RENTED DOCK SPACE FROM PONCE'S PLACE, a sunburned blue stucco, gone-to-seed motel, where guests seldom spent an entire night. Ponce's Place would have been bulldozed into oblivion a decade ago to make way for whatever the market would bear were it not for the deep-water dockage out back. Down here, latter-day Ponce de Leóns come in search of deep-water dockage, more precious than gold. Sociopaths on Jet Skis swerve heedlessly around the marina. The live-aboards wear earplugs.

Rosalind pushed four full scuba tanks in a shopping cart through the motel grounds to her boat, loaded them aboard, and strapped them into the amidships rack with bungee cord. The inbred handyman brazenly leered at Rosalind's ass and thighs as she strained at the load. Had she glanced in his direction, the inbred handyman would have made obscene gestures with his swimming-pool skimmer.

Rosalind was ready to go, but Doom was late. He had never been late before. He always arrived early to help lug tanks. . . . There was no reason for alarm; Doom might have been delayed in traffic. Happens all the time. Why did she feel sick with fear?

She walked back to the dive shop where her grandmother was waiting and phoned the Flamingo Tongue. Dawn answered.

"Hi, Dawn, this is Rosalind. Is Doom there?"

"Uh, well, no, he isn't. . . . He got arrested," said Dawn.

"Arrested? When?"

"This morning. They came and took him from his boat."

"Who did?"

"Well, the police, I guess."

"Sheriff Plotner?"

"No, he's here right now—stinking up the place."

Rosalind hung up. "Come on, Lisa, we've got to go—somebody kidnapped Doom!"

"Gotta shoot those kinds. It's the only way to reason with them," said Lisa Up-the-Grove.

Rosalind fired up her engines as Lisa cast off fore and aft spring lines, and together they motored slowly, obeying as few did the no-wake regulations, until they cleared Possible Pass. Then Rosalind shoved the throttle forward to the stop. A short wind-against-current chop made the going lumpy, but Rosalind didn't slow down until, twenty-five minutes later, they entered Bird Cut on a slack tide and rafted up beside *Staggerlee*.

Anne-on-camera was filming Anne-on-sound as she talked to the fisherman and his son at the end of the dock.

"They arrested him all right," said the father.

"They hit him in the head," said the gawky son, "then they kicked him when he was down."

"He resisted arrest," said the father.

"He did not."

"Sure he did. He hit the fat one with a club."

119

Rosalind broke in. "What did it say on the police car?" Anne spun to shoot Rosalind's frightened face. "Did it say Broadnax County or what?"

"There wasn't no car. They took him off in a boat," the son replied. The father didn't really want to get involved.

"A boat?" Rosalind noticed the seamanship book lying on the cockpit sole at her feet. When she picked it up, the book fell open to the title page. Doom's pen dropped out.

She saw: "Cops!" scrawled in bold black ink . . . in quotation marks. Why quotation marks? She thought of the skinless alligator corpses she and Lisa had just buried, flies buzzing, with help from her neighbor's backhoe. Why did they take him off in a boat? . . . Why quotation marks?

"What did it say on the boat?" she asked the son, still hanging around enjoying having his picture taken.

"Nothin'."

Rosalind marched straight to the Flamingo Tongue. She smelled him before she saw him sitting in a booth scouring his plate with a crust of bread. She decided to try polite reason. "May I have a word with you, Sheriff?"

"Why, it's Rosalind. Always a pleasure to see kin." He looked her up and down, but not in the way of kinfolk. "Have a seat."

But Rosalind couldn't handle sitting without toxic-waste-disposal gear. "Did your office arrest Doom Loomis?"

"No, but that story's been flyin' up and down this dock all afternoon. Let me tell you something, honey. Cons just ain't like our kind. It's a well-known fact of penology—cons only serve time for five percent of their crimes. Now, you take a New York con like this Loomis, there's no tellin' the number of felonies he perpetrated. They nabbed him for another one, that's all."

"They took him off in an unmarked boat. Isn't that a tad unusual?"

"Maybe he did a marine felony."

"You know what I think? I think Big Al Broadnax had him kidnapped."

120

"Whoa! Now, hold your tongue there. That's your late husband's daddy you're slandering."

"I just want you to know I know it. *We* know it! And you're his stooge—we know that too!"

"Here now, you just keep your voice down, little lady."

"And you tell Big Al that if he harms Doom, I'll find my own cops—I mean real cops!"

Sheriff Plotner sputtered with humiliation and confusion. By now the skippers had pivoted on their stools to watch; Dawn, wiping the counter, had stopped in mid-swipe, and Archie stood slack-jawed. Worse, however, was the fact that he didn't know anything about any snatch on Doom Loomis. "Take it from me, little lady, you go messin' around with cons, it'll break your heart."

But the screen door had already banged shut behind Rosalind. Sheriff Plotner hurried after her into the heat that, he knew, would one day kill him.

WEIRDO JAMBOREE

UNAWARE THAT A FLAMINGO TONGUE WAS A VARIETY of seashell, Holly visualized a blunt, black, stubby, wrinkled organ, and the thought of eating one caused her gorge to climb. Longnecker cut his way out of the Range Rover, having tied the door shut with twine after demolishing it against a toll station up near Yeehaw Junction on the Sunshine State Parkway.

"That's a sailboat over there," he said. "Maybe that's the *Staggerlee*."

Maybe Holly had been wrong. This looked to be a very classy yacht. In fact, it was kind of pretty around there, all that shiny turquoise water, the big sky and white light.

She and Longnecker strolled out on the dock just as a long-legged, barefoot woman in brown shorts and a T-shirt ran past them from the Flamingo Tongue. She seemed to be weeping, and she seemed to be heading for the same sailboat as they.

"I hope Doom ain't alienating the ladies," said Longnecker.

"Psst!" hissed Holly. "Cop!"

"Where!"

"Coming up behind us!"

"Don't panic, keep walking. We're tourists from Upper Saddle River, and we're going fishing."

"But we don't have any poles."

"Now you listen to me, missy, don't be going 'round making accusations you can't support. . . . Hear?"

"He's talking to the tall chick. He didn't even notice us!" Holly hissed.

"Just keep walking."

The weeping woman climbed aboard the boat called *Staggerlee*, but Longnecker and Holly kept right on going to the end of the dock, where they peered into the clear water as if reconnoitering a fishing spot. In fact, fish were visible. Several ballyhoo, like miniature sailfish, circled on the surface, and a school of sergeant majors and a small sheepshead poked around the barnacle-encrusted piling. Longnecker glanced back covertly under his arm and, breathing easier, watched the fat cop climb into his black-and-white, which Longnecker had failed to spot parked behind a big green dumpster, and drive away. He felt giddy with relief, even as he reprimanded himself for lack of vigilance. Maybe it was the heat.

Holly said, "I've always wanted to go snorkeling."

They walked back to *Staggerlee*, and Longnecker quietly called Doom's name, but instead of a stand-up guy, a big-eyed motion picture camera came up the companionway. Longnecker recoiled and scurried out of range. The weeping woman emerged behind the camera person. Then Anne-on-sound climbed up, and she was followed by an ancient Indian woman with leather skin.

"Who are you?" Rosalind asked Holly.

"I'm Holly. That was Longnecker. We were invited by a guy named Doom Loomis. Longnecker doesn't like to have his picture taken. It's a religious thing with him."

That naturally fascinated the Annes, even if they didn't believe it.

Rosalind introduced herself, then the Annes. "The Annes are making a documentary about Doom. And this is my grandmother, Lisa Up-the-Grove."

Two Annes and an Up-the-Grove. A whole boatload of weirdos if ever Holly saw one.

A sob overcame Rosalind.

"Oh, honey, what's wrong?" asked Holly.

"He's gone! They took him!"

"Took him! Who took him!" demanded Longnecker.

"Kidnapped him!"

"Then they're dead meat," assured Longnecker.

Lisa Up-the-Grove looked Longnecker up and down. Longnecker was rail thin. He wore pointy cowboy boots, tight jeans, and a Hawaiian shirt with black-beaked macaws roosting in bright green banana plants. Lisa nodded her approval. He didn't look like a dangerous man, but there was something deep in his spirit that reflected from his eyes. He was a bad fellow, and Lisa Up-the-Grove was glad. She nodded, setting the turkey skin beneath her jaw bouncing.

Dawn shouted "Rosalind!" from halfway up the dock. "I have a phone call for Doom—"

Rosalind trotted up the dock to take it.

The flush of success wasn't a familiar flush for Professor Goode, and he felt disappointed that Doom wasn't available to take his call and to congratulate him.

"This is Rosalind Rock. May I take a message?"

"Oh, Rosalind. Doom has spoken very highly of you. This is Professor Goode calling."

"Hello, Professor. He spoke highly of you too."

"You don't say?"

"Do you have news?"

"Actually, I do, yes. I have a chap bitten by a rattlesnake

yesterday, the day in question. Apparently a large chap."
The professor was sweating profusely in his roadside phone
booth. "His name is Lucas Hogaboom."

"Lucas!"

"Do you know him, my dear?"

"He's Big Al Broadnax's right nut!"

"Oh yes, I see—"

Back at the boat, Rosalind spit the name Lucas
Hogaboom.

"He's trash," said Lisa Up-the-Grove.

"Big Al Broadnax killed our alligators!" said Rosalind.
"And I bet you he's the one who took Doom! Oh,
Grandma, if he did that, I'll—"

"I know, sweetie, it's the only way to teach 'em."

Alligators? What alligators? Holly wondered. She had
a childhood aversion to reptiles.

"Grandma," said Rosalind, "I'm going to see Big Al
and try to reason with him."

"Reason with Big Al?"

"I'll go with you," Longnecker said. "I love rationality."

Anne held her camera languidly, dangling it by the pistol
grip, but she was only pretending not to shoot. She didn't
miss an image, and Anne didn't miss a sound.

"Now, Longnecker," Holly cautioned, "don't go off
half-cocked—"

"Don't worry, we're just going to reason with this Big
Al fuck."

"Do you have your mustache?"

Longnecker patted his breast pocket.

"What about your wig?"

TALKIN' TURKEY

THE AIR-CONDITIONING UNIT HAD BARELY KICKED IN BY
the time Sheriff Plotner reached the Broadnax compound,
broken Coke bottles imbedded in the outer perimeter
walls, three miles south of Omnium Town on the Atlantic
Ocean. Now that the opportunity for true crime-busting
greatness and Yankee TV coverage had arisen, the sheriff
couldn't go suppressing any further capital felonies by an
old fart who'd lost his grip on reality.

Sheriff Plotner waved at Fidel, who guarded the elaborate wrought-iron gate. One of the good Cubans. He
roared up the raked-pebble drive through the stand of
banyan trees and careened to a halt before the sprawling
Greco-Moorish compound. Wing Li, the obsequious butler, tried to stay ahead of the noisome sheriff as he showed
him into the stifling phony garden in the center courtyard.
Fucking gooks.

Big Al Broadnax still hadn't had a shit, and he felt like
he was sitting on a sharpened pool cue. Maybe it was time
to hire himself a new sheriff, since this uppity slop bucket
thought he could have audience any old time he pleased.

"Sorry to bust in on you, Mr. Broadnax, but we have
ourselves a problem here," said the sheriff after the gook
departed.

"Yeah, what?"

"Well, sir, under the present circumstances, I can't go
around covering up no more felonies—'specially if I don't
know about them beforehand."

"Just what the puke are you talking about?"

Lowering his voice to a whisper, Sheriff Plotner said: "Felonies."

"What felonies!"

"Well, felonies like snatching Denny Loomis's boy. In broad daylight. With violence."

"What? Are you drunk! I didn't do that, you cobstopper! Why would I do that? If I wanted to do that, I'd have you go and arrest the punk!"

". . . You didn't do it?"

"No. Somebody snatched the punk?"

"Uhh . . . yeah, I guess—"

"Great, glad to hear it. Will that be all, Sheriff?"

"Uh, well, yes—no. Can I ask you a question? It's kind of important."

"What?"

"You killed Denny Loomis, didn't you?"

"Denny Loomis?" Big Al's black eyes flashed, and he stared suspiciously at Sheriff Plotner. "Denny Loomis drowned, didn't he?"

"Well, actually . . . no."

"No?"

"He was strangled."

"No!"

"You didn't do, uh, do it?"

"If I'd wanted him done in, you know what I'd do? I'd have you arrest the punk, then I'd have you shoot him trying to escape. That way there it'd be legal. Why do you think I keep you in office, Sheriff?"

Panic in one relentless wave after another swept over the sheriff's body. Had he covered up a capital crime for a perfect stranger? A man didn't make it on Ted Koppel by doing that.

KINFOLK

~~~~~~~~~

BIG AL BUILT HIS GRECO-MOORISH MANSION ON THE
Atlantic, completing construction on the precise day in
September marking the fiftieth anniversary of the Big
Blow, fifty years from family disaster to this, the most
opulent, showy, and overblown Greco-Moorish mansion
south of West Palm Beach.

"Gee, it's been a long time, Rosalind," said Fidel at the
gate. The driver of the car wore a long black wig attached
to a Mets cap, but then, it wasn't up to him to make
assumptions about Rosalind's friends. Besides, styles
change. "I've missed you."

"Me too, Fidel." She squeezed his hand.

"Go right on in. I'm sure he be happy to see you again."

The crushed cocina-stone driveway, winding around the
gigantic roots of banyan trees, was lined with larger-than-
life marble statues of Colonel A. C. Broadnax. In several
he sat mounted atop rearing cavalry chargers; in others,
of the classical motif, he wore togas and olive-branch
crowns; in a contemplative mood at the top of the driveway, he stood reading from *Plutarch's Lives*. Wing Li
showed Rosalind and Longnecker into the silken garden
after asking Longnecker if he could relieve him of his cap
and curls.

"No, thank you," said Longnecker.

"What in hell are you doing here?" demanded Big Al,
peering sourly at Rosalind, then at Longnecker. "Who is
this man?"

Longnecker was amazed at this crazy garden. The entire
house seemed to have been built around this garden. Yet

all the plants were phony, not a single act of photosynthesis going down in the entire garden. He'd copped a feel of an elephant ear on the way in—it seemed to be made of cloth, satin or something. Plus it was a good 120 degrees in here. That was enough to turn a man's brain the consistency of yogurt. Maybe that's what happened to this Dickensian old fart, sat here in the "garden" until his brains liquefied.

"I'd like to ask you something, Big Al," said Rosalind.

But Big Al didn't wait to hear what. He aimed an accusatory finger at Rosalind. However, his digits were so arthritically gnarled that the finger pointed 90 degrees off line. He said: "You're trying to lead Sennacherib down the garden path!"

"What?"

"Sennacherib! My only son!"

"I know who Sennacherib is!"

"Of course you do! That's my point! You're leading him down the garden path. Just like Claudius!"

"Don't you dare bring Claudius into this! Don't you dare!"

Longnecker wondered when the reasoning was going to begin.

"Don't tell me about Claudius! He was my son!"

"Right. That was his major problem!"

Big Al wheezed with rage and twirled his chair to confront Longnecker. "Just who are you? One of my son's wife's new blow jobs?"

That didn't upset Longnecker. Even before that he was thinking about snapping the old man's neck like a bean pod.

Rosalind collected herself. She said, "Big Al, did you kidnap Denny Loomis's son?"

"What? Ha! So it's true. Somebody kidnapped that punk? Ha! Swell! I hope they kill him! Most do, you know. Most kidnappers kill their victims. Ha!"

Rosalind glared, teeth clenched, a little vein in her neck throbbing. "Are you saying you don't know anything about his disappearance?" she strained.

"I'm saying I'm glad. Glad, I tell you! Glad! He was a punk!"

"Did you send Lucas Hogaboom to murder my alligators?"

"Yes!"

". . . You admit it?"

"Yes!" Big Al shook with glee.

"Why did you do it?"

"Why! Because you're leading Sennacherib down the garden path! Just like Claudius!"

"Then let me tell you something, Big Al—"

Her voice was calm, too calm, thought Longnecker. This woman's eyes were like twin gun muzzles. Longnecker felt right at home.

"—Claudius didn't die in a diving accident. He died diving, but it wasn't an accident. He killed himself."

"Lying slut bitch! May you give birth to gargoyles!"

"We talked about you all the time. You made him crazy."

"Hag! Crone! May God grant your cervix drops out!"

"He killed himself because he had you for a father!"

"Twat bitch!"

Longnecker had always felt an odd sense of relief when reason ceased to obtain, when the limits of codified behavior were breached. It usually didn't take long.

"Lucas! Lucas!" bellowed Big Al, head back, tendons straining, twitching.

Lucas Hogaboom appeared from the far end of the courtyard, beyond the palmetto thicket. He was hobbling fast on his crutches, his enormous right leg swathed in bandages.

"Throw these punks out!"

"You got it, sir."

"Take it slow, Lucas baby. No need for the rough stuff," said Longnecker, a reasonable man. "We're going. I mean, hell, you're one terrifying hombre, even on the sticks. Say, what happened to you anyhow?"

"He got bit by a rattlesnake," said Rosalind, who began to cry with rage and guilt—she had ruined reasoning.

Lucas Hogaboom paused to watch. It made him erect to see pretty women cry.

"Throw them out, you shithead!"

"Was it a big one?" Longnecker asked Lucas. "The snake."

"Yeh, real big."

"Where'd he get you?"

Lucas Hogaboom leaned from the waist, supporting himself on the opposite crutch, and pointed to a spot on the outside of his massive shin, halfway up. "Right chere."

"Right there?"

"Right chere."

And that was precisely where Longnecker kicked him with his pointy cowboy boots.

The scream was chilling, shockingly high-pitched from so big a man. Lucas dropped on the Grecian tile floor, shimmied and twisted like a beached grouper. Screams came in terrible staccato bursts, yet even in agony Lucas struggled to extract his gun, visibly bulging in his pants pocket. So Longnecker stomped once on the back of Lucas's skull, and he stopped shimmying.

"Police! Call the sheriff!" Big Al howled into the air.

Longnecker pushed his Zippo out of his tight jeans, snapped a flame, and touched it to the nearest sapodilla. It went up like a two-year-old Christmas tree. Fire leapt to the adjoining cattleya orchids, and in a flash they too were gone. Destroy the garden in order to liberate it.

"Fire! Fire!"

White-uniformed house staff poured into the garden. They covered their mouths and squealed at the sight of flaming philodendrons.

"Seize him! That's him, there in the ball-cap hair! Seize him, you cunts!" But none was that foolish, what with Longnecker standing, a bad smile on his face, over the supine mass of Lucas Hogaboom. The cooler-headed servants went at the blazing silk with aprons and dish towels. All that remained of the sapodilla, the orchids, and philodendrons were red-hot wire frames, curling into springs as they cooled.

"Let's go, Rosalind," suggested Longnecker. "We'll get no reasoning here."

Hot silken embers wafted on the updrafts, threatening adjoining botanicals.

On the way out Longnecker grabbed the handles on Big Al's chair, spun it around, and wheeled him, screeching and gesticulating, down the long marble hall. "Reason," instructed Longnecker, "implies causality. Without cause and effect, reason don't mean shit. If I learn you hurt my friend Doom Loomis, then that will cause me to come back and reason with you—" Longnecker rocked Big Al back onto his rear wheels and ran him into the wall. That being something he had wanted to do for years, Wing Li watched with suppressed glee.

On the way to the car, Longnecker stiff-armed a militaristic statue of Colonel A. C. Broadnax from its pedestal. Its head broke off and rolled into the bushes. As they drove down the long driveway, Longnecker leaned out the window for a good look at the Greco-Moorish mansion, its points of maximum structural stress where the charges would be most efficacious.

KING DON

〜〜〜〜

HE WAS ABOARD SOME KIND OF MARINE VESSEL, SOME-thing bigger than a boat, he judged from the long, slow rolls, but she wasn't moving. Was she at anchor? She had to be a ship, because boats don't have walk-in laundry rooms.

Doom sat chained by the ankle to the internal frame of a washing machine. This he had determined more by feel than sight, since the portless cubicle was dead dark. He had fitfully languished the night away against a bagful of dirty shirts, pants, and underwear. No one had come to feed or water him since Fu and friends had lugged him aboard unconscious the afternoon before. He had pawed around the laundry in search of water—there had to be water in a laundry room—but his chain snubbed, faucets still out of reach. Thirst and fear kept him awake all night. His ribs throbbed, but he couldn't remember why.

Yet he must have slept, because dreams lingered like sticky substances in his head. Dreams of his father and of his own murder intertwined. His own murderers were just finishing up their morning coffee, smoking a cigarette, then they'd roll the washing machine over the side. Doom would squint for an instant into the unaccustomed sunlight before his two-foot-long tether clattered him over the bulwarks and down, down to where the sea turned as black as the laundry room. The average depth of the Atlantic is two miles. Down there he'd question the old man straight out, both of them being drowning victims, even if they had nothing else in common, "Just why in hell did you steal me my hometown? What was your *motive*? Didn't you know it would get me killed!" Like a barracuda, the old man would hang motionless in the current and watch Doom plunge past; then, wordlessly, he would swim away.

Doom was angry as well as thirsty and frightened. Here he and Rosalind had a thing full of hope, or at least possibility; now some real estate sharp was ready to murder it for money or property. Or something. Doom had never killed, but he considered it. He could kill if killing seemed appropriate and escape possible. He stretched out as far as his chain would allow and located the clean laundry, the sweet-smelling, folded stuff. Systematically, he peed on it all. That done, there was nothing further to do but wait for the inevitable to befall him.

How long did he wait before the door snapped open? There stood Roger Vespucci, a gun in hand but not pointed at Doom, just hanging in Roger's fingers. "I'm gonna put these cuffs on you, son, and I don't want any shit about it."

"What are you going to do?"

"I just told you. Turn around. You're off to see the man."

"What man?"

"A real card. You'll get a kick out of him."

They walked up three decks on a spiral staircase, down a long, carpeted hallway with clipper ships decorating the deep pile, stupid anchor-lamps lighting the way. Doom caught a glimpse of the sea through a tinted window—no land was visible on this side. What side was this? Starboard?

The main saloon, their destination, occupied the entire upper deck aft of the bridge. Smoked floor-to-ceiling windows ringed it panoramically. Doom gaped at the decor, and for an instant suspected it might be an elaborate joke. Sky-blue carpet with swirls of green covered the floor from bulkhead to bulkhead. Doom could barely see his feet for the pile. Crystal strings cascading, Las Vegas–casino chandeliers tinkled above his head as the vessel rolled in the soft swell. Sculpted nymphs peed in a fountain shaped like a giant bivalve shell. There was a black grand piano, an undulating wet bar with a pink Carrara marble top, an entertainment console crammed full of space-age digitals, a big-screen Sony, a CD player, tape deck, tuner, and VCR. The furniture was all of crushed velour in shades of blue and purple, sea shades. Emblazoned in the carpet in three-foot-high green letters was the vessel's name: *King Don*.

"Here, Roger, take those cuffs off Mr. Loomis. What can he do? Nothing. Have you two met, formally, I mean? Roger Vespucci, meet Dennis Loomis."

Roger smirked at Doom.

"Roger, set us up with a couple of piña coladas, if you please. We'll get right down to business." Boyish and grinning, Donald Sikes offered Doom a seat on the sofa. Roger Vespucci exited after unlocking Doom's hands.

Bobby Goldsboro sang "Watching Scotty Grow" on the $12,000 sound system. The pudgy man half-sunken in the blue velour love seat listened for a while. His face was fleshy. He had a child's complexion, creamy and pink. His legs were hairless. "I like old Bobby Goldsboro, don't you?"

"Of course not. What is this, an act? Or are you the asshole you look? Bobby Goldsboro."

"I don't suppose you like Zamfir either? Master of the pan pipes? Naw, you're probably one of those guys who learned culture in the pen—yeah, I did some research on you—they're the worst kind of snobs, cons with pretensions."

"And what about this stupid boat? Whoever heard of chandeliers on a boat? This is the tackiest vessel I've ever seen, and I've been around boats since I was a child. Who designed this boat? The Medellín cartel?"

Donald Sikes burst out laughing. "I like a man who speaks his mind. You know where you stand with a man like that. Sit down, Mr. Loomis."

"I'll stand."

"I like a man who stands," grinned Donald Sikes. "A standing man has nothing to hide. Here, I'll stand, too." A honeydew-melon gut hung over the top of his madras shorts. "Do you know who I am? I'm a rather well-known personality. Donald Sikes is the name."

"Never heard of you."

"Well, I'm reputed to be a man of few words. You won't get a lot of superfluous syllables from Donny Sikes. You sell me your interest in Omnium Settlement for a negotiable price. That's clause one. Under clause two you sail away with full pockets in that snobby little sailboat of yours. Wait. Don't answer yet. I'm ready to sweeten the deal—I'll tell you what really happened to your daddy."

"Okay."

Pat Boone did his rendition of "Maybelline."

"Okay? Just like that?"

"I'm a man of few words."

"You know, I thought so. In fact, I told Roger, 'Don't hurt Dennis Loomis Jr. I think he might be a man of few words.' I might otherwise have told Roger to drop your verbose butt overboard with an anchor-chain necklace."

"What really happened to my father?"

"Big Al Broadnax murdered him."

Doom's knees went rubbery, but he locked them in place and said, "Why?"

"Because your daddy tried to gyp Big Al out of his Perfection Park investment. Don't tell me you don't know about Perfection Park. I mean, that's why you're here—to discuss Perfection Park. And Palmetto Properties."

"I saw the tape."

"Not a bad tape," Donny giggled, squeezing his eyes shut like a little boy trying not to laugh behind the teacher's back, "for hick work. Tape like that wouldn't fly in Gotham, but down here, what difference does it make? Down here somebody'll just blow up your office anyway."

"Was the whole thing your idea?"

Donny nodded vigorously.

"You were after Broadnax?"

Donny was full of glee, head bobbing.

"And you got my father to set the bait?"

"He was a natural. But he tried to pull a fast one on me, on Donny Sikes. I should have known, man of his character, he'd come up with something like this Palmetto Property shuffle, but it doesn't matter, a minor glitch as far as Donny Sikes is concerned. Of course, Broadnax, now, his reaction to getting gypped was a little different. He killed your old man when he found out."

Doom gave it some thought, tried to see the thing as a whole, then said, "Why?"

"Why what?"

"Why bother?"

"Who bother?"

"You."

"Good question! You're thinking why would a man like Donny Sikes, one of the ten richest since the Ice Age, want to skin a senile has-been like Big Al Broadnax?"

"Right."

"And that would be a valid question, all things being equal. But they're not. Equal. This is personal. You're probably wondering what Donny Sikes has against an old fossil like Big Al Broadnax. Ever hear of a man by the name of Prentiss Throckmorton?"

"No."

"Well, you should have. Prentiss Throckmorton was a visionary. A giant. He was the kind of man that made this country great. If it weren't for Mr. Throckmorton's railroad, Florida would still be a festering swamp. He was my grandfather."

"So?"

"So? So Colonel A. C. Broadnax murdered him!"

"You mean Big Al Broadnax?"

"No, not Big Al!" Donny was growing agitated. "Big Al's father!" Donny stamped his little foot, but it vanished silently in the carpet.

"Big Al's father murdered your grandfather?"

"Yes! Gramps! The bastard murdered him!"

"You mean this is a matter of revenge?"

Donny Sikes was going rigid.

"When did this happen, the murder?"

"In 1934. Late summer, almost autumn. Why?"

"How old are you? Forty, forty-five?"

"Forty-six. Why?"

". . . You weren't born then."

"What's that got to do with anything?"

"Nothing."

"You don't seem very upset."

"About what?"

"About Big Al Broadnax killing your old man!"

"My father and I weren't close. Besides, I'm leaving. Isn't that part of the deal?"

Donny wasn't sure if this smart-ass con was condescending to him or not, but he decided what difference did it make? "I have the papers all drawn up." He produced them from a lawyer's litigation bag that lay open at his feet.

Actually, there was only one paper, two copies. It said simply that Doom sold his Palmetto Properties holdings to Donald Sikes for the sum of $50,000. That was clause one. Clause two stipulated Doom's post-deal departure for distant waters. "And if I don't sign?" Doom wondered.

"Then that would constitute breach of contract. A breach of Donny Sikes's contract is one hundred percent fatal. You weren't thinking of breaching our contract, were you?"

"Just curious. Anyway, that's what I wanted from the beginning."

"What was?"

"To sail away. To Newfoundland."

"Freeze your gonads off in Newfoundland, but what's that to Donny Sikes? Nothing."

"It's just that $50,000, well, that's not much compared to the kind of money you'll make off Perfection Park."

"Come on, it's pure profit. You did nothing to earn it. As it is, I'm willing to view fifty grand as an operating expense. What's fifty grand to Donald Sikes? Chicken feed. But much more than that, then I'll feel like I'm getting fucked. In that case I might as well dump you overboard. See how I work? And besides, what makes you think I mean to build this Perfection Park? It's about the stupidest idea I've ever heard. That's why I picked it—because I knew it'd appeal to a moron like Big Al Broadnax. Well, truth be told, it was your father's idea. He seemed to have an acute instinct for what morons would like."

"Okay, Donny, I see how you work." Doom signed, kept his copy, and Donny marched his copy to a little cylindrical safe built into the bulkhead behind a bad oil painting of a clippership under studding sails. He returned to Doom with a bag of banded bills, just like Ozzie's. Apparently Donny had buzzed for a lackey, because Roger showed up without being hailed. "Our business is complete, Roger. Please arrange a boat for Mr. Loomis. And Roger, where were our piña coladas?"

"The blender's on the fritz."

"Fix it. And now, *Doom*, I trust I'll never see your ass again." Donny grinned. "Surprised I know your jailhouse moniker? Knowledge is power. The fact is, I had a friend up in Longfellow by the name of Mertz, Ozzie Mertz. He told me all about you. I even read *Splendor*. Never did understand the point of that scam, but what's that to Donny Sikes? I was saddened to read that my friend Ozzie came to a violent end."

"Uh-huh."

Four young men in khaki uniforms, just like the ones Doom had peed on, ran out the amidship davits and winched the ship's boat twenty-five feet down to the sea. "Is this the entire crew?" Doom asked. "Four?"

"All we need," smirked Roger Vespucci under his Fu Manchu. "Why do you ask?"

"I'm interested in boats," replied Doom.

RED-RIGHT-RETURNING

THE SUN WAS SETTING GLORIOUSLY AS DOOM WADED out of the knee-deep surf where Donny's crewmen discharged him. A half mile out the *King Don* lay at her anchor like a tacky white island. Doom glanced at it over his shoulder as he trudged up the beach to the road. From this slightly elevated vantage point, he could see his own boat at her dock, but he couldn't tell if anyone was aboard. He didn't want to return to a dark and empty boat. The usual knot of tourists and romantic locals had gathered, joints and drinks in hand, at the end of Doom's dock, to watch the wild colors of dying daylight.

There was movement aboard *Staggerlee*. . . . Rosalind! She and the Annes stood in the cockpit while Anne shot the sunset watchers to establish time and place. Rosalind squealed and pointed when she spotted Doom coming over the rise. Doom hopped and raised his arms in the air. Anne's camera whirled in Doom's direction. A lump rose to clog his throat. Rosalind jumped from deck to dock and ran toward him. Doom ran, too—they met in the Flamingo Tongue parking lot beside the green dumpster, where they embraced. They held each other close for a long time. The sunsetters turned from the west and applauded the reunion. Doom waved at them, and they cheered.

Dockside, Doom averted his teary face from the camera lens, but Anne didn't miss a nuance. He wanted to lie down naked with Rosalind, but the boat lacked privacy. "I think I'll fry some eggs," Doom said. "I haven't eaten since . . . when? Day before yesterday?"

"Poor dear. You stretch out. I'll cook something."

She cares, look at her—she cares! Rosalind was too tall for the galley. Stooping, she began to assemble ingredients. Life at that moment felt beautiful to Doom, lying on the starboard settee feeling the sweet feminine stimulation of *Staggerlee*'s rocking, the flood tide lap-lapping around her hull, Rosalind's muscular back rippling. He grinned at the cabin top, and Anne got the grin on film.

"Your snake plan worked great," said Rosalind. "A goon named Lucas Hogaboom butchered our alligators."

"Who's he?"

"Big Al's main lackey. You ought to see him. Pure scum."

"Why would Big Al kill your alligators? How does he stand to gain from that?"

"Big Al isn't a reasonable person."

"Neither is Donald Sikes. That's who snatched me, Donald Sikes," said Doom.

"Donald Sikes? *The* Donald Sikes?"

Doom explained how Donald Sikes fit into the Perfection Park scheme, how in fact he was its architect and how he had hired Doom's father to execute it. "My father came up with Perfection Park itself. I knew it was smoke. Just a rotten little real estate scam to bilk Big Al. But my father was buying up Omnium Settlement with Big Al's money and squirreling away the land in a corporation of his own. Donny Sikes says Big Al killed my father."

"But you don't believe him?"

"Something doesn't wash. My father was swindling Donny Sikes as well as Big Al. But Sikes didn't seem to care. Unless he has a whole different purpose we don't know about. Yet. Have you ever heard of a guy named Throckmorton?"

"Prentiss Throckmorton? Sure, he's a big name in Florida history. He's the guy who built the old railroad. He's one of the idiots who tried to drain the Everglades."

"Donald Sikes is Throckmorton's grandson, and Sikes thinks Big Al's father killed Throckmorton in 1934."

"In 1934?"

"Here, catch—" He tossed her the bag of bills, and she caught it against her body. She gasped as she spilled money out on the cutting board, Anne's camera boring in.

"I sold him Omnium Settlement."

Rosalind's face fell.

"He kept me chained to a washing machine. He had the advantage."

"Oh, thank God he didn't hurt you."

"The other part of the deal is that I get out of town forever. He threatened to kill me if I didn't."

". . . Can I go with you?"

Doom was moved, forgetting totally about the camera. "You'd do that?"

"Yes."

Doom tried to strengthen his voice, get the crack out of it and sound like he knew what he was talking about. "Rosalind, I think they're both too greedy, arrogant, and crazy to go on prospering."

She stopped frying and sat down beside him. "What should we do?" she asked.

"We'll have to take measures, and they won't be pretty. They're both powerful crazies, and if we go after them, we'll have to devote ourselves to it at the expense of other things."

"I know it."

But did she really? "Since they're both nuts, we might be able to set them against each other. But we'll need to wait for Longnecker."

"Longnecker's here."

"He is?"

She told him about their visit to the Broadnax compound.

"You went there to plead for me?"

"Well, yes, but I didn't handle it too well. Longnecker kicked Lucas in the snakebite, set the garden on fire, and ran Big Al's chair into the wall."

"Good, he hasn't changed. Uh, where's your grandmother?"

"She's out at the house, feeding the animals."

"Annes, would you mind excusing us for a minute?"

The Annes didn't mind cutting now that finally they were onto something cinematic, so they smirked and left.

Doom hated to admit that thinking like a criminal excited him, but the evidence was prominent. . . .

Late that night, after Rosalind had fallen asleep, Doom walked up the hill, back across the road, and down to the damp sand at the edge of the ocean. There he sat for an hour in a tight ball, watching the sea's gentle motion, undulating obsidian, and everything seemed to be drifting away on the ebb tide. But then, control of anything, even one's own feelings, was illusory. Thick longing for something vague, something balancing out there on the taut wire of the horizon, clogged his throat.

BLACK CAESAR'S YACHT CLUB

ABOUT DAWN ON THE MORNING OF THEIR DEPARTURE, Doom gathered up his snorkeling gear for a last visit to Smiley, but he had barely pulled on one fin when he saw a teenage boy on the dock. The kid was hoisting Smiley up by a stick stuck through the barracuda's gills and out its mouth. The grinning boy was posing for a picture, which his sallow, fat father was framing with a plastic camera. There wasn't even a caudal-fin flicker of life left in Smiley. That made the anglers feel successful and happy, but it made Doom dangerous.

The anglers had left their rods, heavy, thick things with fancy gold reels and wire line, on the edge of the dock. In a cold rage Doom removed his flippers, climbed onto the dock, and kicked the rods into the water.

"Hey, Dad, that guy just—!"

Doom picked up their big aluminum tackle box, with trembling hands tore it open, and shook the contents—feathers, jigs, spoons, plugs, pliers, hooks, line, and sinkers—into the water. Then he chucked the box in the water.

"Hey, you!" the father yelled. "You—"

"Shut up!" Doom snarled at the father. "Put down that fish," Doom demanded of the son in a level voice.

The father took one look into Doom's eyes, saw in them violent death, and called retreat. "Come on, son—"

"But Dad—"

"Put it down, son."

"Gently," Doom dictated.

Doom heard the father, leaving, explain to his son that some of these crackers would just as soon knife your spleen out as look at you. "It's different down here than home in Detroit."

Doom removed the stick from Smiley's mouth. A finger of blood ran from its gills. The silver had faded from its flesh, turned to opaque gray. Doom picked up the big dead fish by the tail and slid it back into the water. Smiley sank in a fluttering corkscrew motion, a cruel parody of its swimming, and came to rest on its side in the white sand among the objects of its destruction.

Shortly after that *Staggerlee* got under way. A throng had gathered on the dock to wave bon voyage. Archie and Dawn, Billy, Bobby, Arnie, and Arnie Junior were there, and so were Holly, Duncan and the professor, Marvis and Lisa Up-the-Grove. And Rosalind was there. Bert was hiding aboard in the forepeak to lend some covert sailing assistance; so was Longnecker, to lend firepower. Rosalind took the bow line from its cleat, tossed it on the foredeck, and tensely Doom backed his boat away from the dock, into the channel. He felt sad, even if the leaving was phony. Omnium Key had begun to feel like home. Perhaps that's what life held in store for him—intinerancy, a life of departures. He thought of Smiley bobbing back and forth in the tide, picked at by crabs, like his old man.

That same gentle east wind was blowing, and their plan was to take a long starboard tack to the northeast. When they had put a horizon between *Staggerlee* and the *King Don*, whose crew would be watching through the glasses and the radar, they would crack sheets and bear off onto a reach northward. Carysfort Light in sight, they would run back to the coast to enter Card Sound through Angelfish Creek. From there it would be only a three-mile sail into the mangrove backwaters Bert had picked as their hideout. He said it used to be the lair of pirates. . . .

The channel narrowed, tightened down to a stream nearly overgrown by haggard red mangroves. Here and there, they brushed *Staggerlee*'s shrouds and spreaders. Beer cans and plastic soda bottles bobbed among their prop roots. Scum undulated in the wake. Longnecker stood by to fend off. The air was damp and overbearing, the water a milky, typhoid green, devoid of all life but bacteria. Why were the mangrove leaves covered with white dust? What was wrong with this place? Was it the proximity of Route One? Doom could hear traffic but not see it behind the trees. Or had some ecological disaster occurred? Glad to have Bert at the wheel in tight quarters, Doom stood lookout on the bow for flotsam, jetsam, corpses.

Then they rounded a dogleg, and the creek brushed Route One. Actually, this was Old Route One. New Route One, a four-lane highway, crossed Barnes and Card Sounds onto Key Largo ten miles south, leaving Old Route One a lonely loop through the marshes. On a crumbling wedge of limestone, between the creek and the road, perched Black Caesar's Yacht Club. Seeing his new home, Doom felt his resolve fading. He longed to return to Omnium Key and listen to stories at the Flamingo Tongue. The sun slunk behind a stack of stratocumulus, turning the water to black, like festering mucus. A flock of brown pelicans from the healthy world flew overhead in a line astern and disappeared.

Black Caesar's, a two-story paintless frame hotel with a bar and restaurant on the ground floor, had a serious list to starboard, as if its backbone had snapped or the land had sunk beneath it. There were six slips along Caesar's dock. A houseboat had sunk in the first. Its plywood roof remained above water, delaminating in the sun. Slimy dock lines were still attached to the submerged deck. Adjacent to it, a cheap fiberglass sailboat baked, mast and rigging lying along the deck—someone's dead dream of a nautical getaway. A once-handsome wooden motor launch had capsized years before against the dock pilings, one of which had penetrated her topsides. The remaining three slips were empty except for floating garbage.

Bert cleanly entered the slip, and Doom stepped gingerly onto the dock for fear of falling right through it. He made the bow line fast to a splintery piling. Bert rigged fore and aft spring lines. . . . They were home. No little fish played among the pilings. This water was opaque, bereft of life.

"Bucket of blood," pronounced Longnecker, squinting at the lopsided building. He decided to slide another pistol into his belt beneath his Hawaiian shirt, this one painted with volcanoes and frigate birds. Doom wondered if Black Caesar was really black. This didn't look like a good place for harmonious racial interaction.

Bert, Doom, and Longnecker entered the bar from the creek side, but they piled up just inside because it was too dark to walk safely. They stood by vulnerably while their eyes adjusted to sudden night.

Several hard-bitten fuckers at the bar turned to glare at the strangers. The fuckers wore chewing-tobacco caps and were no doubt as heavily armed as Longnecker, who was considering opening fire for the sake of prudence. Pupils dilating, Doom saw no warmth of welcome in Black Caesar's Yacht Club. It stank of stale beer, fish, and urine, not the musty sweet wooden nostalgia of the Flamingo Tongue. A wiry man with a mean face tilted the pinball machine with a kung-fu kick, then glared at it. Six guys in greasy baseball caps sat crammed into a booth watching with unmasked distaste the trio of lost tourists letting in the daylight.

Black Caesar was indeed black. He sat shirtless behind the cash register at the corner of the bar. Black Caesar's upper body looked as if it were assembled from suspension bridge cables and hot rivets.

"Good morning," said Doom congenially. "I'd like dockage space."

"Looks like you already took dockage space."

Bert was tense and jumpy, but Longnecker felt right at home in this menacing environment.

"Did we take someone else's place?"

"Yeah. But he's dead. In a dispute over dock space. Cost you a hunnert."

"A hunnert a month?"

"A night. 'Course, if that don't suit you, there's all kinds of marinas in the region. Take your pick. Some'll rent you Jet Skis or a surfboard, any manner of waterfront tourist shit. They even got shoreside crappers where the little lady can freshen up. 'Course, they'll want to know your name and address, certain personal particulars." Black Caesar spotted a mosquito orbiting his head. His eyes drew a raptorlike bead on it, then in a black blur he clapped it between two leather hands. He flicked away its flat corpse. "Me, I don't ask no questions. I don't give a fuck whether you live or die."

"That kind of indifference never comes cheap," said Doom, handing over three hundred dollars to start his exile.

"Would you gentlemen care for an aperitif?" Black Caesar offered, counting. He had a live one here.

MEETING AT THE SUMMIT

THE MEETING HELD THAT NIGHT BY LAMPLIGHT IN *Staggerlee*'s saloon—Bert and Marvis, Duncan and the professor, Longnecker and Holly were there—had about it a military, a naval, air, Doom reluctantly in command. He hadn't come to Florida to run a conspiracy. An hour before this general gathering, about dark, Rosalind had arrived with Snack Broadnax. During the ride from Omnium Key to Black Caesar's she had presented to Snack the serpentine evidence implicating Big Al in the alligator killings.

Snack was sad, but he tried to cover it with anger, a less vulnerable emotion. Snack used to love sitting on the bank with Rosalind and Lisa Up-the-Grove watching the gators bask in the winter sun. He had helped name them, helped Rosalind take notes on their behavior in an effort to, as Rosalind put it, "more deeply understand their lives"; he had been there when the two babies emerged from their eggs peeping for their mothers. Now they were slaughtered on orders from his old man.

"So okay," growled Snack, "he's an asshole. What do you want me to do about it?"

"We'd like you to spy on him for us," said Doom.

"Fuck you."

"That's all right. I understand."

"He's my own father. He brought me into this world!"

"Your mother helped," Rosalind pointed out.

What was he angry at? Simply that Big Al had killed the alligators or that Doom Loomis had taken Rosalind? Or that now he had to *do* something? Or was it something

146

else entirely, something like fear of infanticide? "I ain't no Abel Cain."

"Thanks anyway, Snack. I know we're asking the impossible, spying on your own father. I'd feel the same way. Could I ask you a question before you go? What were you doing at the Snowy Egret Shopping Plaza on the day Tamarind Financial blew up?"

Snack glared at Doom. "My father sent me," Snack said defiantly.

"Oh."

"What do you mean, oh?"

"Just oh."

"What are you trying to say? You trying to say my old man meant to kill me?"

"Kill you? That never crossed my mind. Why? Do you think he meant to kill you?"

"Hell, no! My own father? Trying to kill me? Besides, I thought we were talking about alligators. I want a drink."

"Sure," said Doom. "What kind would you like?"

"I want a private drink." He climbed up the companionway and headed for Black Caesar's.

"I've missed you," said Doom to Rosalind.

"Me too. This place is horrible."

"I know it. Would you like to make love?"

"Doom, we don't have time. Snack could come back any minute, the others'll be here in a little while—"

"You won't stop liking me, will you?"

"When?"

"When I start doing mean things."

"We'll do them together."

The others straggled in late. They seemed uniformly depressed at the slimy backwater qualities of Black Caesar's Yacht Club. Doom was glad they hadn't seen the place by daylight, when the true extent of its malarial gloom was vivid.

Doom poured tots of his father's Barbadan rum all around, but the Annes demurred, busy setting up their gear in the cramped quarters forward of the settee near the mast step. Then Doom passed all present two thousand dollars in stacks of crisp twenties. "I've come into some money, and I want to share it with you. I'm going to need your help. It could get ugly, and everyone should decide whether or not they want to help. I hope you'll keep the money whether you decide to stay or not."

Topside somewhere window glass shattered. Talk ceased abruptly aboard *Staggerlee*.

A man screamed for help—

"Snack!" said Rosalind.

Doom and the others bolted up the companionway, over the dock into Black Caesar's bar—

Three wiry guys in greasy baseball caps were pummeling Snack Broadnax, who had curled into a tight springboard-diver's tuck on the floor to protect his vitals. Four others cheered on the savagery from bar stools.

"Stop!" Doom shouted, but they didn't. Doom leveled his father's twelve-gauge flare gun at the twinkling Bud Lite sign on the far wall, squeezed his eyes to slits—and fired. He was not disappointed in the effect. With an air-sucking whoosh the meteor left its launcher and instantaneously exploded against the wall. Night became noon. All but Doom recoiled from the smash of phosphorus flying around the bar in vicious smoking tendrils of potential blindness and third-degree burns. The Bud Lite sign was atomized. Men and women from his own party, as well as the opposition, screamed and hit the deck hugging their heads while Doom reloaded. If the opposition turned restive, Doom decided he would fire one into the bottles behind the bar. But if that didn't work, he'd have to start firing at people. Snack crawled away from his huddled assailants to the safe ground around Doom's shoes.

"May I have your attention, please?"

May I have your—? Now *this* was a stand-up guy in action, mused Longnecker.

"I represent certain powerful interests in Tallahassee. For security reasons, I can't be more specific." Small fires crackled near the blackened point of impact, but no one dared move to extinguish them. "I'll be here only a short time, during which I need peace and quiet to conduct my consultations. If you gentlemen leave me and my friends entirely alone, I'll pay you each three hundred dollars upon my departure. Mr. Caesar, I'm holding you personally responsible. If these men bother us, I'll accordion your spine under the raw weight of authority."

Rosalind felt a shiver replace the surging adrenaline. Was Doom really as dangerous as he looked?

"Conversely, if they leave us alone, I'll pay you a bonus of five hundred dollars."

Black Caesar blinked twice. . . . "Belly up, crackers," he called to the crouching regulars. "Drinks on Black Caesar. What we gonna drink to? How 'bout peace on earth and goodwill to Tallahassee?"

Doom pulled Snack to his feet. His face was purple and bloody. Back at the boat, Rosalind tended his wounds while the others, abuzz, looked on. The Annes had to muscle the camera through the crowd.

"What was the fight about?" Doom wanted to know.

"Snook."

"The fish?"

"When's the best time to catch 'em." Snack winced as Rosalind dabbed disinfectant under his eye. Then Snack began to cry. "It was my fault, I started it. . . . I want a home! That's all! Is that too much to ask for?" Rosalind hugged him, an orphan. After a time he collected himself and said, "I'll spy on him under one condition."

"What?" Doom asked.

"That you don't hurt him."

"I don't want to hurt him."

"If you do, I'll get you good."

"Fair enough," said Doom.

AGENTS OF CHANGE

THEY WAITED UNTIL AFTER DARK, AFTER SHERIFF Plotner had finished sucking the marrow out of his Flamingo Tongue blue-plate special. They intercepted him at the green dumpster.

"Sheriff Lincoln Plotner?" Duncan Feeney wore an unseasonable blue wool pin-striped suit.

"Yeah?"

"I'm Agent Armbrister of the FBI." Pointing to Longnecker, in an identical suit, Duncan said, "And this is Agent Peebles. You're under arrest as an accessory after the fact to the murder of Dennis Loomis. You have the right to remain silent so on and so forth."

Sheriff Plotner choked back fried chicken bile. His knees went soggy, and sweat burst forth from his forehead. He forgot to wonder what the FBI was doing in a local murder case or even to ask for ID from the arresting officers. They had to be real—only the FBI would wear wool suits in Florida. Besides, he was guilty as sin, and they had him dead to rights. The best he could hope for would be to escape the indignity of barfing creamed corn on his own spit-shine.

"We have other felonies waiting in line, like misuse of office and filing false documents in a murder case. Whether we lay them on you or not depends entirely on your level of cooperation."

His brain limp, he noticed only in passing that Agent Peebles was cuffing his hands behind his back and relieving him of his Magnum and his Mace. Good-bye, Ted Koppel. Sheriff Plotner squeezed his atrophied abdominals to pre-

vent himself from peeing in his uniform. In the dark, Longnecker couldn't tell if the sheriff was actually weeping as
Duncan Feeney folded him into the backseat of his own
black-and-white. Longnecker had expected trouble, but
this poor guy was a lamb, and Longnecker felt a little sorry
for him. . . . What the hell was that *stink?* Christ, it must
be the stink of cold fear.

Siren and flasher screaming their approach, Duncan did
sixty up Route One, the traffic diving and careening out
of the squad car's path. Duncan had always wanted to
drive like that, without having to become a cop. He could
have become an ambulance driver, but that didn't pay shit,
and fire engines just didn't corner worth a damn.

Sheriff Plotner's head bobbed, and his eyes had gone
blank.

"Hey, buck up, pal," said Longnecker. "We might be
able to fix this." Longnecker opened the side windows.
At this speed, the stink didn't remain long. The sheriff's
body, like a half-filled fuel bladder, sagged right, then left
as Duncan swerved wildly in and out of his lane. Longnecker thought for a moment that the sheriff had died.
Doom wouldn't have liked that.

BABY BEAR

BERT AND MARVIS HAD FOUND AND RENTED THE GOLD-
ilocks and Baby Bear bungalows from the Three Bears
Motel—Mama Bear and Papa Bear bungalows had burned
to the ground after a domestic disturbance—several miles
north of Homestead. Doom grinned lasciviously out the
side of his mouth and told the manager that they were

making a dirty movie. Doom slipped him an extra hundred bucks to take a break.

"Hey, listen, how 'bout I watch?" proposed the manager. "I'll pay a hundred bucks to watch."

"I'm sorry, but watching is prohibited by the International Brotherhood of Pornographers."

Tomato fields, dark and featureless as the night sea, sprawled west all the way to the border of the Everglades National Park. Yet south Florida herself, her land, offers nothing to growers but a site, no nourishment whatever in the marl. Farmers scrape off all native vegetation down to rock, then they truck in real soil from the north. South Florida agribusiness enjoys a one-month monopoly on tomatoes. Picked green by undernourished migrants and shot full of gas, these fruits are built to travel north, where during February no one eats a tomato not reared on utterly infertile Miami Limestone.

Doom was ready in the Baby Bear bungalow. He had typed up the scripts and placed them on music stands. The Annes were busy setting light and sound levels.

"If you agree to help," Doom told the Annes in private, "you'll probably end up with a film you can't show to anyone without landing us all in jail."

"What choice do we have?"

"You have a choice."

"You're going to do this thing with us or without us, right?"

"Yes."

"It's this film or no film."

"Do you think I shouldn't do it?" asked Doom.

"It's not up to us to judge."

"Yes, but what do you think?"

"Politically it's justified."

"Morally it stinks."

Wasn't that just the problem with crime? Doom was troubled by the calculated ruthlessness of his scheme, but what choice did he have? Careful calculation was essential. Anything half-assed would get them arrested. Or killed. And this time, if he was arrested, it wouldn't be Longfellow. This time it would be hard time with sex-starved incorrigibles.

The Annes hung sheets on three sides around the sheriff's chair, then adjusted their light levels accordingly.

Meanwhile, Duncan sped crazily through the night. Duncan was jealous. Wasn't he the conceiver, Doom just the scribe? But hell, the money was good, even if the gig lacked leadership potential. And where was Doom getting the money he was throwing around? Maybe Duncan would find an opportunity to make his own side deal somewhere along the line. He extinguished his flasher and siren and drove sanely through downtown Homestead. It was nine o'clock; everything except the 7-Eleven was locked and dark. He pulled the black-and-white around behind Baby Bear bungalow with the headlights off.

"Where are we?" mouthed the sheriff, a trembling lump on the backseat.

"Never you mind," said Longnecker, guarding the sheriff's crown with his hand as Plotner squirmed out. "You just think about saving your ass. I don't like to say jail's tough on bad cops, but they usually go in farting normally and they come out farting like a slow leak in a tractor tire." Longnecker was ad-libbing now.

Longnecker sat the sheriff sideways in the chair to accommodate his cuffed hands. Doom was glad Rosalind wasn't there to see the fat, weeping figure bedazzled by about 10,000 watts of white light. His thighs were dark with sweat.

"What is that *stink?*" Anne asked Anne in a whisper.

Agents Peebles and Armbrister took their places at the music stands and prepared their interrogation.

The sheriff said something, but the sound didn't make it through the glare.

"What?" asked Duncan.

"Lawyer . . . I want—a lawyer."

"Okay, fine," said Duncan, capping his pen theatrically. "Take him to the Miami lockup. He wants a lawyer. He doesn't want to make a deal."

"Huh? No, please. I do, I do want to make a deal."

"Then just sit and relax. There, that's good. Now, Sheriff, did you or did you not cover up the murder of Dennis Loomis?"

". . . Yes."

"Let the record show that the sheriff admitted to killing Dennis Loomis, then covering it up," said Duncan, the picture of authority.

"No! No, please! I didn't say I *killed* him! I covered it up, I didn't—oh, Jesus!"

"Why did you cover it up if you didn't kill him? Were you working for someone?"

"I—I leaped to conclusions!"

"How so?"

"I thought—I thought Big Al did it!"

"That would be Big Al Broadnax?"

"Yes! Yes, I thought he did it!"

"Are you saying he didn't?"

"Yes. I mean no, he didn't."

"How do you know?"

"I asked him."

"And he's an honest man?"

"No, but I could tell he didn't."

"Would you say Big Al has you in his pocket?"

". . . Yes. Look, I'm sorry, honest. I got—confused!"

"You're doing fine, Sheriff. I'm sure we can work this out."

"You are?"

"Depending on the candor of your answers. Who killed Dennis Loomis?"

"I don't know! I swear on my wife's grave!"

"Do you know one Donald Sikes?"

"The tycoon?"

"He's a developer."

"Well, I've heard of him. Everybody's heard of him, but I never met him or nothing. Please don't make me go to jail—I'll do anything. Anything! What can I tell you? . . . Ah, Tamarind! The Tamarind Financial Group—Big Al blew it up!"

"But we heard that explosion was caused by a gas leak."

"No, no, I covered that up too—for Big Al! Big Al did it!"

"Why did this Big Al blow it up?"

"I don't know. Maybe he thought they were trying to gyp him!"

"How so?"

"I don't know. Big Al ain't . . . ain't entirely right upstairs."

"That should do for now," said Doom from behind the wall of light. Doom didn't want to prolong the agony. He carried a chair into the light and sat beside the sheriff.

"You! What the fuck is this! You faggot! I'll have your ass for—" He looked into the camera. "Duress! This confession took place under duress! I take it all back!"

"You're right, Sheriff, duress. Your confession would never stand up in a court of law, but neither of us wants to go to court. However, seeing your confession on film, people might begin to ask embarrassing questions. The real FBI might even pose a few, and Big Al Broadnax wouldn't be happy, especially about your eagerness to confess his crimes. Reelection would be in doubt."

"So what do you want?"

"Answers, for now. Later I may want direct help. If you help willingly, I might be able to hand you the killer of Ozzie Mertz and Doris Florian. And I might be able to get you out of Big Al's pocket. You see, when this is over, Big Al will be finished."

"You're going up against Big Al?"

"Yes, and so are you. What choice do you have? Tell me about my father's body."

". . . He was strangled. You could see the marks on his throat. You had to look close, because, well, because the crabs had gotten to him pretty bad."

"What was he strangled with?"

"Fish line. Somethin' fine. Wait a minute! Mertz and the Florian broad—they was both strangled, too!"

"That's a keen observation, Sheriff. Why did Big Al send Lucas Hogaboom to kill Rosalind's alligators?"

"What? He did? I didn't know—"

"Come on, Sheriff. I'm a little angry at you about my father. If you piss me off further, I'll sell you right out."

"No, honest, I don't—wait! You and Snack Broadnax was out at the Up-the-Grove place plotting against Big Al. . . . Maybe somebody saw you out there and told Big Al."

"What do you know about the Perfection Park scam?"

"Scam? What do you mean, scam? You mean it was a scam? I didn't know it was a scam."

Doom decided to keep it simple for now. "Sheriff, I want you to stop hassling the people in Omnium Settlement. I want you to allow them to live openly in Fred's Hobby Shop and wherever else they want to live."

"Okay. Big Al won't like it none."

"Sheriff, Big Al is going down."

"I forgot."

"I also want you to arrange a meeting between Big Al and me. And a meeting between Roger Vespucci and Big Al."

"Who's Roger Vespucci?"

"I also want to know what goes on at the Broadnax compound. I want you to spy on him."

". . . Okay."

Doom removed the sheriff's handcuffs and handed them back to him. "When this is over, we'll still need law and order on Omnium Key. I for one would vote for Sheriff Plotner. I think Agents Peebles and Armbrister would too."

The agents agreed it would be a vote well cast.

GRAVESIDE THEATER

HEAVY-HEELED, DOOM MARCHED DOWN THE LONG marble hallway, outdistancing Wing Li, trying to work up some genuine anger. In matters of theater and of bullshit, genuine emotion is always most efficacious. But Doom wasn't prepared for the garden heat—it struck his temples like the clout from Roger Vespucci's sap—nor was he prepared for the elaborate naturalism, density, and sheer size of the vegetation. Longnecker and Rosalind had of course described this place to him, but as a "garden"; instead, it was a riotous jungle. Like those in Dragoon's Hammock, but phony, tropical trees strove skyward as if to compete for sustaining sunlight. Down on the blue-tiled ground, only gloom penetrated the top cover.

Doom was no more prepared for Big Al himself than for Big Al's works. There he sat in his steel wheelchair beneath the spooky spread of a leafy something-or-other. Doom had pictured an old man, an ill one, perhaps even a dying one, but Big Al Broadnax looked like a two-week-old disinterment. The flesh of his face seemed to have melted into the skeleton below. Every long bone in his body was corkscrewed, each joint crepitant. Big Al weighed barely a hundred pounds. His entire person was shrunken and withered like a fallen fruit in the Florida sun. Frankly, Doom was taken aback, his work for real anger wasted. So he went with phony anger—it might pass in the limited light.

"You killed my father, and I demand redress!"

"Stop right there, you punk! Lucas!"

Lucas Hogaboom had been skulking behind a cabbage palm, its fiberglass trunk overgrown in moon vine. He stepped from cover. His leg was cast in plaster, immobilized from hip to ankle. His crutches creaked under their burden.

"Hey, snakeman," Doom waved.

"Beat him! Beat him!" whined Big Al.

Wincing, Lucas advanced, but he was moving as if underwater. Doom had ample time to draw the photograph from the sweat-soggy envelope under his arm and hand it to Big Al, who held it two inches from his nose and squinted:

"Wait!"

Lucas was only too glad to oblige.

"This is my son!"

"Good eye."

"And that—that's the pecker who lit my orchids!"

"He's not a stable individual. No telling what a man like that might do."

In the photograph Snack was tied to the sheriff's chair. Longnecker stood behind the chair and pointed a gun into Snack's ear. "If anything should happen to me, Snack won't be around to rebury you." From somewhere unseen a fountain plashed. "Likewise, if I leave here unsatisfied, Snack goes for a vertical swim." Doom wasn't sure about the patter, but it felt reasonably convincing.

"I didn't kill your stinking father, damn his jism, why's everybody think I killed him! I had no reason, no—what the stink do you call it?—no motive!"

"You had a motive."

"What motive!"

Doom pulled papers from the envelope and carried them toward Big Al.

"Stop right there! Don't come near me," Big Al wheezed. "Lucas, take that from him and bring it to me."

Lucas Hogaboom dragged himself painfully along to serve his master. Doom handed him the papers, and he struggled onward with them.

"What the fuck's this!"

"That's a contract. Clause 47-R says that in the event of my father's death for any cause whatsoever, all lots in Omnium Settlement revert to Palmetto Properties, a company which, upon his death, I control."

Big Al pretended to read, but these days even bold print was a blurry smear; fine print was hopeless. But Big Al didn't let on. "I've never seen this in my whole stinking life!"

"That proves it."

"Proves what!"

"That you killed him."

"How!"

"If you'd known about it, you wouldn't have killed him. It wouldn't have been in your interests to kill him. But not knowing about it, you did. That's precisely why my father inserted Clause 47-R."

"Why!"

"Because he knew it was dangerous doing business with you."

Big Al's head was spinning. A smudge at the bottom of the page looked something like his signature, but he had never heard of Clause 47-R. "Lucas, why the fuck didn't my Jews tell me about Clause 47-B!"

"Uhh . . ."

"Fire my Jews! Fire them all! Get me a whole new Jew crew!"

Lucas hobbled out, grunting in pain.

There were possibilities here, Big Al was thinking. "Say, Mr. Loomis, you wouldn't be interested in selling your interests in this—what did you call it?"

"Palmetto Properties."

"What if I bought Palmetto from you for a fair price, then you let Snack go. Fair? Fair enough, I'd say. What do you say?"

"Why should I help the man who killed my father?"

"Because I didn't kill him! . . . Who told you I did? Did that putrid sheriff tell you?"

"No. Donald Throckmorton told me."

Suddenly Big Al was having trouble breathing. Something the consistency of semen gurgled in his trachea. ". . . Did you say Throckmorton?"

"He goes by the name Donald Sikes, but his real name is Throckmorton."

The very sound of the name Throckmorton caused him cold chills in the pelvic region. "Donald Sikes?"

"He and my father were swindling you in the Perfection Park deal. You didn't know Perfection Park was a phony?"

". . . Of course I knew. Where is he? Throckmorton."

"Is that a porch out there?" It looked like a porch with a heavy marble balustrade, each support sculpted to represent the Venus di Milo. "You can see him from here."

"What!"

Doom slid open the huge plate-glass door. The air—at

ninety-two degrees—felt dry and autumnal compared to that in the garden. Big Al grunted and wheezed as he wheeled himself out onto the patio. The ocean was silvery, its expanse unbroken but for the ungainly bulk of the *King Don* lying to her anchor.

"You mean—?" Big Al's voice cracked.

"That's his boat."

". . . It's cold out here." Big Al wheeled himself as fast as he could back into his den. Doom followed. This man was an arsonist and a murderer of innocent alligators—at least. Then why did Doom feel sorry for him?

"Do you know Don Throckmorton?" Doom asked innocently.

"Who, me? No, I never heard of the—!" Big Al tried to collect himself, to stave off impetuosity. There might be a means of turning things his way. "You have me at a disadvantage. This ain't business we're talking, this is extortion, but let's talk about it like it was business. So would you be interested in a deal for Omnium Settlement, Mr. Loomis?"

"Well, I really hadn't given it much thought."

"You've got to think of everything. Especially if you go kidnapping my beloved son Sennacherib. I could have you eliminated for that." Which Big Al fully intended to do anyway, the brass-balled punk, trying to extort Big Al Broadnax.

"I'll need a hundred thousand dollars. Cheap at twice the price."

"Lucas!"

Lucas, grunting, hobbled back in.

"Get me my checkbook."

"No checks. And I don't take American Express. Cash."

"I ain't got a hundred thousand in cash! Are you nuts! Forty thousand."

"Seventy, cash money."

"Make it fifty, you got a deal."

"No deal. Sixty. My last offer."

"Fifty-five."

"Fifty-seven."

"Done."

"Lucas," said Big Al two minutes after Doom left with the cash.

"Yes, sir."

"Kill him. Then get my money back."

"You got it, sir."

PROFESSOR GOODE

PAPER-STUFFED VALISE IN HAND, PROFESSOR GOODE nimbly strode Black Caesar's dock toward *Staggerlee,* sidestepping holes, rent planks, and exposed nails. It had been years since he had stridden nimbly anywhere, and many years before that since he had done so lecture-bound with a case full of cogent research. He had his old student Dennis Loomis to thank for that.

Professor Goode had made friends and acquaintances at the trailer park. Bert and Marvis were teaching him to fish, and last night he had discussed with Professor Munday, a retired Romantic-poetry specialist from the University of Chicago, the Mt. Snowden episode in *The Prelude.* Their views were highly compatible, although Professor Munday was much more favorably inclined toward "Michael" and the gentle swain poems than was Professor Goode, who had difficulty keeping a straight face when talk turned to gentle swains.

Professor Goode had delicately queried Professor Munday as to why he had chosen life in a tacky trailer park when other more seemly avenues of existence seemed open to him. Professor Munday said that only in truly rootless, disassociated, and self-referencing places like the Briny Breezes Trailer Ranch could one achieve and maintain a firm connection to the dry hole at the spiritual center of American society.

Doom greeted Professor Goode in the cockpit and made to assist him down the companionway ladder, but the professor didn't need help. He was rock solid on his feet, and Doom was glad. The professor seated himself at the table, laid out two pens and a yellow notepad before he assembled his notes. He hadn't done a single hit of Nyquil in three days.

"Would you like some orange juice?" Doom asked.

"Perhaps later, thank you. I thought we'd get down to it straightaway."

Doom sat beside his old professor.

"Shall we begin with Prentiss Throckmorton?"

"Yes, Professor."

Professor Goode cleared his throat, momentarily remembering the old days, thirsty if unrefined young minds, some overflowing into the aisles, to hear Professor Goode parse the "Bower of Bliss" canto in *The Faerie Queene* and thereby be shaken from their iconoclasm. "It could be said that Throck, for that's what his cronies called him, yanked south Florida into the present by the ties of his own railroad. As he walked it farther and farther south, his minions built subdivisions, entire towns, in its wake, and only then did he set about luring residents down. He credits himself as the inventor of what today we call public relations. He was quoted in *The New York Times* of July 18, 1922, saying, 'The public is a rabble meant to be manipulated.' He held bathing-beauty contests, staged publicity stunts with midgets and African wildlife to attract attention to his real estate offerings in south Florida. Throck was inventing the very tools of hucksterism. He is unique in another way: He was murdered."

"Did Broadnax do it?"

"Throck hired Broadnax to build him a luxurious retreat, the centerpiece of which was to be the Oseola Hotel, but Small Hope Bay was in the way, and Broadnax was to remove it. The Oseola was an idea dear to Throck's old heart. Not just another sucker's subdivision, the Oseola was meant to be the site of his retirement. He intended to die there."

"Did Broadnax actually manage to drain Small Hope Bay?"

"Dry. In fact, there are sketchy reports of fires breaking out on what had been under eight feet of water. But Broadnax had his own agenda. Apparently he meant to cut Throck right out of the picture."

"So Broadnax did swindle Throck?"

"He tried, but first there was The Bust. On September 17, 1926, a hurricane struck. The blow obliterated the Oseola and the rest of Broadnax's work. It refilled the bay. The coldest winter on record followed, then in '28 another savage hurricane. And then the stock market collapsed. Broadnax was broke.

"After that—*after* the Oseola was gone, after property values had dropped to zero—after it was all over, Throck got wind of the old plot to swindle him. Throck completely ruined Broadnax. He bought up all Broadnax's creditors and hounded him into ruin."

"So is that when Broadnax murdered him?"

"That's when somebody murdered him. Somebody strangled Throck in the bathtub at his Fifth Avenue mansion."

"Strangled, huh?"

"The killer apparently entered the mansion by shinnying up a drainpipe and forcing a window. Suspicion fell on Colonel Broadnax. Two witnesses placed him in New York at the time of the murder. However, one witness died in a fall from a high window, and the other recanted. There was never a trial. The murder of Prentiss Throckmorton is unsolved to this day. Broadnax himself died penniless a year later, survived by his only son, Aloysius, the present-day Big Al."

"What about the present-day Donny Sikes? How does he fit in?"

"His mother, Abigail, was an illegitimate daughter of Prentiss Throckmorton's. She lived in Throck's mansion and worked for him as a personal secretary, but Throck never claimed her as his own. Probably a class conflict. However, she was generously rewarded in his will."

Doom passed the professor $2,000 in new twenties.

"What is this?"

"That's an additional fee for research. Compliments of Donald Sikes and friends."

"Why, thank you very much, Dennis."

"My pleasure, Professor."

"If I may speak, Dennis—"

"Please do."

"It's about Duncan. Duncan is falling into a funk. The trailer park is no place for a young crook like him. Jail may be the only place for Duncan, but until that day comes, he needs something to boost his waning self-esteem. Frankly, I think young Duncan could present trouble if left unsatisfied. And now, as for yourself."

"Yes, Professor?"

"I think this whole endeavor is bad for you. All this plotting and conspiring and double-dealing—it can only come to a nasty end. A violent end. That's its nature."

"What do you think I ought to do?"

"You don't look well these days. I think you and Rosalind ought to sail away just as quickly as you can."

Doom and Rosalind went sailing that afternoon in Card Sound. Doom practiced upwind helmsmanship, searching for "the groove" about which he'd been reading, trying to feel on his face the lifts and headers as the apparent wind shifted. By dark he understood why all the writers had warned that one can't learn to drive a boat upwind from books. Doom recognized, further, that if his father had not become a professional crook, had remained a sailor, Doom would already know how to steer. He would have understood the effects of the apparent wind on sail and helm.

By dark they returned *Staggerlee* to her befouled berth.

GHOSTS

DONNY SIKES WAS TROUBLED, SITTING IN THE FANTAIL sipping a piña colada, feet propped on the mahogany transom. Things didn't feel right down here. Things went wrong down here. He had had Big Al all set up to take the fall for the murder of Denny Loomis, motive and everything, but that stupid sheriff called it an accidental drowning. How could he miss the fishing line wrapped around Loomis's neck? . . . People down here weren't acting according to the laws of human nature, and Donny Sikes prided himself on his innate understanding of human nature and his ability to manipulate it to his own ends.

So, all right, his initial plan to hang the Loomis murder on Big Al Broadnax didn't work. Sometimes that happens. One has to remain flexible, but why didn't the secondary plan work? You tell a guy, convincingly, that his father's been murdered, you tell the guy the name of the murderer and the murderer's motive, you'd expect that guy to go take a measure of revenge. Human nature. Age-old shit, avenging fathers' murders. Ancient Greeks did it all the time. Comes up even in the Bible. It would have been a beautiful thing to watch—the son of the man whose murder Donny had ordered doing Donny's bidding, then taking the fall for the killing, while Donny, in the clear, sat sipping piña coladas on the poop deck. He never expected Doom to actually sail away as he said he was going to do. People down here weren't as duplicitous as in New York. Could that be it? Or maybe the sun made them lax, torpid, and stupid, ambition-sapped. He'd have to take that into consideration from now on.

Donny felt a surge of relief when Prentiss Throckmorton joined him on the afterdeck. Gramps wore his three-piece Harris tweed suit, the one Donny remembered from childhood, its scratchy feel against his cheek as he cried into the lapel. Gramps would know what to do.

"Would you like a piña colada, Gramps?"

"Quit drinking that gop. It'll rot your brain out," said Gramps. "Nobody wants a drunk for a grandson."

"Yes, sir."

"How many times have I told you that?"

"Many."

"Pour it overboard. All right, then. You know what I think? I think you have a fly in the ointment. The fly's name is Loomis. I mean young Loomis, Doom Loomis. I didn't get to my station in life by being ignorant of human nature. That's what you must learn—human nature. You never did have an adequate understanding of human nature. In addition, you are impetuous. For instance, killing that punk Ozzie Mertz. That was impetuous."

"But he embezzled from me. You always told me if you give an employee an inch, he'll take a mile."

"But I never said kill him. You could have used Mertz. He was ripe for manipulation. And what about Mertz's common-law slut of a wife? You didn't need to have her killed. That was gratuitous. That was overkill. And then there's the strangulation. You could have shot them, the way civilized people do, dumped their carcasses in the swamp."

"But, Gramps, things are different down here."

"Rubbish. Things are the same the world over. Who did the actual killing?"

"A man named Walter Freed."

"A professional?"

"Yes. . . . I did it for you."

"For me?"

"Because old man Broadnax strangled you!" Donny Sikes was about to cry. He hated it when Gramps was hard with him. Gramps was a hard man intrinsically. How else did he get where he got?

"I understand, Donny, you did it for sentiment. Sentiment's all well and good at weddings and funerals, but not in business."

"But Gramps, this isn't business, it's vengeance."

"I know that, but vengeance must always be treated like business. In vengeance there is no room for passion."

Roger Vespucci whipped up another piña colada in the new blender and went to deliver it to the boss, but Roger stopped at the sound of Donny Sikes's voice out on the fantail. Talking to himself again. After his fifth or sixth piña, it would start. Family shit. Donny Sikes figured he was the only guy in the world with a rotten childhood. Roger Vespucci's was no bed of roses, but hell, that was blood under the bridge. He didn't carry on conversations with the deceased. He knew a guy in the pen did that, talked to the dead. Somebody finally offed the guy. Then the guy didn't need to talk long distance.

"So what do you think I should do, Gramps?"

"I've been mulling it over in my brain the last few days, and I think you ought to kill Doom Loomis, then go ahead and build this Perfection Park."

Donny was surprised to hear that. "But Perfection Park was never anything real, nothing but sucker bait to hook Big Al Broadnax."

"I know that. Don't you think I know that? After all, it was my idea. But I've been thinking about it, and Perfection Park sounds like a viable proposition to me. Let's build it. We'll leave something lasting after we're gone, something solid, terra firma. A man reaches his threescore and ten, he wants—"

Roger Vespucci knocked on the bulkhead and said pardon me, sir, piñas.

"Come in, Roger. I want to talk to you."

Roger offered him his piña, but Donny Sikes said no thank you.

". . . No?"

"You have it. Roger, I've been thinking about this Perfection Park business. I'm leaning toward building it."

". . . Really building it?"

"Terra firma."

"I beg your pardon?"

"What?"

"Nothing. Uh, when would you start?"

"Immediately. Let's get some bulldozers in there. Let's clear out the site. Pronto."

"Yes, sir. Uh, boss, a funny thing happened in town today."

"Funny ha-ha, or funny peculiar?"

"I went in to buy a new blender, and this guy comes up to me in the checkout line and says he has a note to you from Sennacherib Broadnax."

"What'd the guy look like?"

"Weird fucker. Wearing this Mets cap with a wig attached to it." Roger took Snack's note from his shirt pocket and handed it to Donny Sikes.

"He wants a meeting, this Sennacherib hick," said Donny after reading Snack's note. "Fine, fine with Donald Sikes. Let's meet." What the hell kind of name was Sennacherib? "Set it up, Roger."

DUNCAN'S ELEMENT

DUNCAN LOVED DECEIT. IT WASN'T THAT DUNCAN WAS a cynic, saying everybody's crooked at bottom, so why should I be honest? He viewed things in a more positive light—he wanted to be more crooked than anybody. That's what he'd hate most about jail. There'd be a lot of guys more crooked than him. Duncan glued his Fu Manchu mustache in place as he approached the guardhouse.

"Yes, sir?" asked the ancient Cuban at the gate.

"Roger Vespucci to see Mr. Broadnax. I'm expected."

Fidel checked his book. "Yes sir, go right on in," and ploddingly he pushed open the ornate iron gate with curlicues at the top. He was out of breath as Duncan motored past him. That's what he gets for a life of honest labor—

Oh, there was big bucks here—motoring along the driveway toward the Greco-Moorish mansion, the calm blue Atlantic for a backyard playground—enough to support a lifetime of leisurely deceit. The imported marble hallway stretched to Daytona Beach, and at least forty Iranian children went blind weaving the rugs. Duncan began to bow and scrape even before he got to the garden, where Big Al sat in his chair beneath a leafy hydrangea. Sheriff Plotner stood nearby, sweating, fidgeting. Duncan smiled at him reassuringly. Don't worry, Duncan is here—watch the old fart's head spin.

"Mr. Broadnax, this is that Roger Vespucci I told you about."

"How do you do, Mr. Broadnax?" said Duncan obsequiously.

"Never ask an old man how he is. He might tell you."

"Yes, sir."

"This is my son, Sennacherib."

Snack seemed to be lurking beneath the bushes. He and Duncan shook hands like strangers. Doom had "released" him only the evening before.

"Now then, Mr. Vespucci, what can I do for you?"

"Well, sir, it's my wife. She needs surgery. Brain surgery. Tumor behind the eye. I'm afraid the prognosis is not good. I've been working two jobs, but I still can't make ends meet. To tell the truth, sir, I'm near the end of my rope. I asked Donald Sikes for a loan, and he said no—"

"No? He said no? The swine." Big Al's lips formed a hideous rictus, exposing brown-rooted teeth in receding gums, and for an instant Duncan didn't make it as a smile. "Sennacherib—"

"Yes, Father?"

"Note this. This is an example of bullshit. A man will go a long way if he learns to distinguish bullshit from

169

nonbullshit. Vespucci? Vespucci? Where did I hear that name before?"

"Amerigus Vespucci," added the sheriff helpfully. "Columbus named America after him. Amerigus—America."

"Amerigo," said Duncan.

"What!" asked Big Al.

"Amerigo, not Amerigus."

"Who gives a fuck! What do you want!"

"Money," said Duncan simply. "You're right, Big Al. May I call you Big Al? All that wife stuff—bullshit. You're a wise man to see through it. I heard you were a wise man. You even look like a wise man. The fact is, me and Donny Sikes ain't close, and I want to sell his ass right out, speaking plainly."

Big Al felt good. He had this Amerigus fellow in the palm of his hand, and now he'd bounce him like a basketball in front of his son, show Sennacherib the kind of man his father was. "I guess you want to sell me something, Mr. Vespucci."

"Information."

Big Al wanted to know how much information and how much it would cost.

"Doom Loomis shills for Donny Sikes. Sikes will send Loomis around to sell you a phony deed to the Perfection Park property. So be careful. That's free information. Want to hear more?"

"Pho—the deed was pho-phony?"

"What? He's been here already?"

"I never laid eyes on the punk! What the hell's his name? Loomis?" Big Al's limbs began to twitch.

"I see you're a little bit behind the times, Big Al. You better get out your purse for this next bit of info. I ain't a greedy man. Give me ten grand, you know, for my poor wife's operation. Cash."

"You tell me, then we'll talk price."

"Okay, Big Al. I'd want a little proof myself. Ready? Donald Sikes has a bomb planted on your property."

"A bomb—?"

"Yep, a big one."

"A big bomb—here?"

"Sort of a chilling thought, huh? A guy who can blow your tits off whenever he feels like it. That's the kind of savage prick you're up against, Big Al."

This guy is a pro, thought Sheriff Plotner, having himself a grand old time reducing Big Al to quivering goo. The sheriff about missed his cue. "Where is it!"

"Now, that's the question, isn't it? Where? Where indeed? Could be under your chair."

"Ten . . . thousand?"

"Cash."

". . . Deal."

"It's not a deal until the jack shows up." Duncan waited, grinning, until the jack showed up. Lucas limped in with it. Then Duncan said, "It's under your gimp van with the hydraulic lift to hoist your ass aboard."

The sheriff waddled out onto the patio, down the marble and cocina-stone steps, at the base of which his black-and-white was parked. A Longnecker special was stowed beneath the front seat in a brown paper bag. Stinging drops of sweat rolled into his eyes as he removed and carried it to Big Al's garage, where he fiddled around for a while, shining his light on the van's underbody, imagining himself actually removing the bomb, a gutsy piece of police work. He could have gotten blown halfway to Bimini, and the old fart wouldn't have appreciated it.

Meanwhile, back in the phony garden, Big Al was thinking things over. He wasn't without clout. He had the law on his side. His son would never respect him if he didn't bring it to bear on this smartass Roger Vespucci with the stupid mustache.

"Here it is," said the sheriff, bearing the bomb gingerly. **"I disarmed it. Little somethin' I learned in advanced antiterrorist school. All wired up to the ignition, real professional, the kind favored by Muslin fundamentalists and Christian Phalangists."**

"Sheriff Plotner, arrest this man in the name of the law!"

Here was a new wrinkle, thought Duncan. "Arrest me? Are you nuts? I just saved your neck—"

"Arrest him for extortion and attempted murder. What else? Arson! He tried to arson me! Go on, slap the cuffs on the punk!"

Sheriff Plotner was getting confused. This wasn't in the script. It must be what Loomis had called on-the-scene improvisation. Sheriff Plotner slapped the cuffs on Duncan Feeney. "Maybe you Yankees don't know about Florida jails. You'll come out farting a whole lot different than you do today."

"Take him away! . . . Unless we can strike a deal."

Here it comes. Duncan felt tingly all over. He loved it when the chumps jumped into the pit of their own accord. "A deal?" said Duncan in a quavery voice.

Big Al winked over his bony shoulder at his son, then turned on Duncan: "You go on back to Mr. Donald Throckmorton Sikes, and do whatever he tells you to do. Catch on? Then you come tell me about it. You just became a spy for Big Al. Either a spy—or an inmate. Take your pick, punk."

"Okay, you win. What about my ten grand?"

"You get it. Nobody can say Big Al Broadnax don't pay his help. Ain't that right, Sheriff Plotner?" The rictus returned to Big Al's face, flushed with victory in clear view of his only surviving son.

"Mission accomplished," said Duncan Feeney back at the boat, bounding down the companionway.

Doom had seen that grin before, back when Feeney told Ted Koppel what an honor it was to have discovered *Splendor* for the American people. At least someone was having fun.

"And here's the take." Duncan slapped a pile of cash on the navigation table, where Doom had taken to sitting while he planned, plotted, and conspired. "Five thousand bucks cash money."

Marvis Puller marked it down in the books.

That night Bert, Doom, and Rosalind went sailing in Biscayne Bay. Under a luminescent moon they practiced setting, jibing, and dousing the starcut spinnaker with

Doom doing the foredeck work—he had just finished reading a spinnaker book—Rosalind on the helm, Bert on halyard, sheets, and guy. No one even mentioned Big Al Broadnax, Donny Sikes, or in any way the matter at hand. They discussed jibing angles that increased the apparent wind speed, which Bert called "hotting up the 'chute," and he showed Doom how to trim the colorful sail to keep a little luff curl in the shoulder. "A well-trimmed 'chute ain't supposed to look good to the naked eye," he said, "twitterin' on the leading edge like it does," and he eased the sheet until the shoulder twittered. "Feel the boat speed pick up?"

Doom felt it. It felt good.

THE HIT

~~~~~~

Lucas Hogaboom met Binx and Ridly at the Dugout in the Snowy Egret Shopping Plaza. Lucas picked out a dark, sticky booth in the back for privacy and room to stretch out his throbbing leg. It was swollen to twice its normal size, and soon it would erupt through the plaster-like molten lava through the earth's crust. He imagined he saw hairline cracks already spiderwebbing the cast. He popped three more hits of Percodan and one codeine, washing them down with a Bud Lite.

"We found him," said Binx. "We followed that chick with the tits, and she led us right to him. That was Ridly's idea—follow the tits—that's what we did, and he was right."

"So where is he?" The pain made Lucas's eyes water. Maybe another codeine.

"You know where Old Route One goes up through Key

Largo? There's a beat-to-shit fish camp up there called Black Caesar's, run by this tough nigger."

"What's the nigger's name?" asked Lucas.

"Black Caesar."

Why did he have to deal with toads, Ridly was asking himself, when he should be president of a forward-looking alternative-energy program that burned barnyard droppings, as a result of which he would win prizes and be invited to speak on the floor of the Senate?

"Okay, boys, here it is. Listen up. I want you to kill Loomis," Lucas Hogaboom ordered.

"Kill . . . him?" said Binx.

"What are you, nuts! Kill him? You didn't take your medication today, you crazy cracker," said Ridly.

"Want me to twist one?" asked Binx. Binx hated discord.

"Five grand apiece," offered Lucas. Actually, Big Al had said ten apiece, but Lucas figured he was owed a brokerage fee.

"Would you get that fucking Pillar of Hercules away from me? Stinks like an armadillo. Thanks. He wants us to kill the gink. Can you believe it, Binx? He thinks this is fucking TV. He thinks he's dealing with Tubbs and Crockett or some assholes. You got to get out of the sun, pal, quick."

"I got some good shit," said Binx.

"Okay, Christ," said Lucas Hogaboom, "you don't wanna do it, just say no."

"No."

"Fine. What about you, Binx?"

"Well, I don't know, Lucas. . . . This whole thing sort of reminds me of my brother Glen."

"Your brother Glen?" asked Lucas.

"Reminds me of the time Glen and me rented a boat and went fishin' up on Lake Okeechobee. We found this spot back in a twisty channel, all kinds of forks and dead ends. We caught us a boatload of largemouth in a half hour. My brother Glen says, 'We gotta mark this spot so's we can come back here.' I said, 'How're we gonna do that,

Glen?' Glen says, 'We'll paint an X in the bottom of the boat when it's directly over the spot.' So I said, 'Glen, you are stupid! . . . How do you know we'll get the same boat?' "

On the TV above the bar, someone said, "It's not just your car, it's your freedom."

Fuck 'em, Lucas would to do it himself. Twenty thousand was big bucks. With that kind of bread he could open himself a little business selling the hides of endangered species. He'd killed a biker in Oakland, California, back in the sixties with no problem. However, that had been an accident. Once he had stabbed a guy in the Winn Dixie frozen-food section, but that guy had pissed him off. Loomis had never pissed him off. The asshole in the Mets cap with the wig—now, *he* pissed Lucas off. Maybe he'd off him too while he was at it. Lucas popped another codeine and washed it down with the dregs of Binx's beer. Sure, he could do it himself. Easy. Just pretend Loomis was an alligator.

BIBLE SCHOOL

THE CAMERA LENS PEERED DOWN AT SNACK FROM THE hole Doom and Marvis had cut in the ceiling. The Annes had run control cable from the camera to the adjacent Goldilocks bungalow, where now they waited with Doom. The lens looked to Snack like a shark's eye. No, more like the eye of an idol, a craven image.

Snack was thumbing through the Gideon Bible while he waited, but he found no solace in its antique language and eccentric characters, a crowd of bearded crazies wandering around the hardscrabble desert waving swords, what did they expect but to get hives and boils and shit dusty stones. Who was that asshole who tied up his son and made to chop off his head because God told him to as a test? Esau? Maybe Big Al thought God told him to blow up his own son in a shopping center. Hell, maybe He did. And who was this guy Gideon? With trembling fingers he twisted a fat one and went out back, where gleeful mosquitoes homed in, to smoke it. Something big moved in the bushes—

"Wha—!"

"It's me," said Doom. "Are you all right?"

"He's late."

"He'll be here."

Snack's sativa massaged the kinks in his neck. "Sure, great. Fine. No shit. . . . I'm scared."

"Then let's forget the whole thing. There are other ways."

"I mean I ain't scared of the guy. I'm scared of fucking up. You're a smart guy, I can see that. You probably did real well in school. Went to Yale College or somewhere. Me, I didn't, and I ain't all that bright to begin with."

"That's not what I hear."

"Huh?"

"You're clearly a very bright person. They just took away your self-esteem. That's what schools and families do. Besides, Rosalind says you're bright."

"Rosalind says that?"

"She also said you're good with animals. She says you're kind."

"Really? She did? I like animals. Birds too."

"Do you like fish?"

"Fish? Sure. Fish are very interesting creatures."

"I used to know a big barracuda."

"Barracuda are great."

"Would you like to be Environmental Officer when things loosen up? That has nothing to do with whether you decide to go through with this tonight or not."

"Environmental Officer?"

"The wildlife and the environment need protection. You

could test the waters to make sure no one is dumping toxic waste, poaching, or otherwise disturbing the balance of nature."

". . . You want some of this? I grew it myself."

Doom took a toke. . . . Whew. "You're obviously a man in tune with the herbage."

Snack giggled. Doom returned to the Goldilocks bungalow to wait with Rosalind, Longnecker, and the Annes.

Snack was thinking about his uniform—maybe simple khakis with an American flag on the shoulder and his name tag, white letters against a black background, on the front pocket—when headlights flooded the front window. Snack knocked on the wall and listened. Did the cameras come on? Snack couldn't hear them whirring.

Snack opened the door before anyone knocked on it. He froze at the sight of Roger Vespucci.

Roger said, "Step back," and then he barged in. Donny Sikes waited in the car while Roger searched the Baby Bear, looked in the closet, the bathroom, under the bed. "What a shit hole," Roger pronounced. Snack was wearing a Total Immersion T-shirt a size too small and a tight pair of warmup pants, no shoes, so Roger didn't bother to search him for concealed weapons. Roger went out to get Donny Sikes. Guy hadn't had a piña in two days, unless he was sneaking them, but what for? They were his piñas. A sober Donny Sikes made Roger edgy.

What was Snack going to do? He couldn't tell lies on Roger Vespucci while he was in the room.

"Well, Sennacherib Broadnax, how do you do? Donny Sikes here."

Snack shook his hand. Snack's mouth was almost too dry to speak through.

"Sennacherib. Now, there's a name you don't often hear."

Snack tried to say that people called him Snack.

"What?"

"Uh, could we talk in private?"

"This is my associate, Roger Vespucci. I don't have any secrets from Roger."

"Forget it. I talk to you alone or nobody."

"I'll be right outside that door, boss." Roger turned to Snack, paused chillingly, and said, "You try anything cute, I do hideous things to your torso before you die." Then he walked out into the insect night.

Donny sprawled on the bed and folded his hands behind his neck. Snack thought this guy was supposed to be a bigshot. He looked like a little boy, baby flesh with no hair on his arms. Roger Vespucci came off like a true badass, but this Donny Sikes looked like bully bait, and that made Snack feel better. Plus the sativa was riding the curl of a wave between his eyes. Snack sat in a chair. A framed sign on the wall above Donny's head said TO MAKE A HOUSE A HOME—ADD LOVE.

"What do you want? Your note didn't say exactly."

"I want you to leave my father alone. He's an old man. He'll die soon, and you'll get what you want anyhow. You don't need to blow him up."

"Whoa, hang on there, Nellie. Blow him up? What the hell do you mean, blow him up?"

"Blow him up. My old man."

"Somebody blew up your old man?"

"Somebody tried. You."

Donny Sikes was getting hot. Slow it down and take control here. "Let's turn on the air-conditioning."

"It's broke. If you didn't try to blow up my father, how do you explain this—" Snack picked up a paper bag from under the TV and tossed it on the bed beside Donny.

Donny gasped when he saw the bomb in the bag. "I never—!"

"Bullshit! That guy Roger Vespucci told us where it was planted!"

"Roger—?"

"Sure, he said you were down here to ruin my father. He said you were a crazy asshole, and he wanted out. He was sick of making blender drinks for you. Then he told us you planted the bomb on our property, and my father paid Vespucci ten grand to find out where you put it."

A lump of hurt rose in Donny's throat. Any number of

dirtbags would betray Donny Sikes at the drop of a hat, but he never imagined Roger Vespucci would. They'd been together since 1964, when Donny hired Roger to break the Building and Service Employees Union strike by blowing up the union hall—blowing . . . up? Aw, shit. "I don't believe you."

"No?"

"No."

"You want proof? I got proof. I got a picture—" Snack pulled a snapshot from the pages of the Gideon Bible and handed it to Donny.

The picture, apparently a candid, showed Duncan Feeney walking down the front steps of Big Al Broadnax's Greco-Moorish mansion. Donny Sikes peered at it for a long time. Donny Sikes had never had any real friends, only pretenders. He'd never known a warm bosom, except for Gramps's, but Gramps died before he was born, leaving him alone in a chill world, the sound of his own weeping echoing. "It's blurry. Why's it blurry?" Donny demanded. Yet the Broadnax mansion, in fine focus, was for real. Donny had pictures of it back on the boat, so he knew the Greco-Moorish mansion when he saw it.

"You can't miss that big droopy mustache."

That was so. The Fu Manchu loomed large. "Roger!" bellowed Donny Sikes.

The door crashed open, and Roger Vespucci barged in, gun drawn, cocked, ready.

"Roger, will you kill this man, please?"

"Sure, boss—"

Doom and the Annes gasped in the Goldilocks cottage. No one even had time to remove the earphones—

But then Donny Sikes said, "Never mind."

"Never mind?"

Snack thought for a moment he'd peed in his warmups, but it was merely sweat.

"Let's go, Roger."

Roger Vespucci liked Donny better when the piñas were sloshing around in his head, brain bilge. Dry, Donny was growing weird. *Never mind?*

179

GLUB

RIDLY'S ESTRANGED WIFE'S BROTHER USED HIS HOBNAIL motorcycle boot to kick in the door to Ridly's second-floor apartment situated above the abandoned Bijou, which died soon after the Cineplex Twelve opened its doors out at the Spoonbill Mall. Now the cracked and weathered marquee letters said I'M A FOOL FOR JESUS, WHOSE _OOL ARE YOU. This shabby section of Tequesta Key with shell stores and forlorn motels, some from as far back as the tin-can tourist days, was slated for demolition, making way for the proposed Manatee Mall. It would even have a genuine New York deli run by Jews.

Ridly owed four months' worth of child support, three hundred dollars each month. Big deal. Guys with fewer natural gifts than Ridly spent three bills in a single night, on surf-and-turf dinners, tickets to *Cats*.

Ridly's brother-in-law, whom everyone called Wheezer because he smoked four packs of Pall Malls a day, didn't say a word for a long time. He sat on Ridly's rumpled army cot and cracked his knuckles by bending each finger in turn against the point of his chin, three distinct cracks per finger, each finger the size of a pool-cue butt.

"Wanna beer, Wheezer, discuss the matter?"

"Phyllis says I should break both your legs, you scum sucker. I even brought along this bat to make Phyllis happy. But I says to Phyllis, give the scum sucker a chance, he can't pay up he's in traction out to Broadnax General. I says further, Phyllis, look, he don't pay up by next week, *then* I break both his legs. Here you are livin' the lap of

luxury, you ain't got money to support your own little girl.
I mean, what the fuck kinda father are you?"

Ridly knew that Wheezer had about reached the end of
his appeal process on a two-year-old grand theft, auto,
rap. If Ridly could only give him the slip for maybe another
month, this cretin might be off to Raiford, making instead
of switching license plates. Ridly also knew that Wheezer
would make mush of his tibias and never give it a thought,
go out and hot-wire a Lincoln Town Car. "How about a
Colt .45, Wheezer, wet the old whistle?"

Wheezer didn't say yes and he didn't say no. He just
continued cracking his giant digits against his chin. Suddenly Wheezer made an example of Ridly's bedside lamp,
smashed it with a single overhand swing of the Louisville
Slugger. Shards were still ricocheting off the walls when
Wheezer waddled into the john and beat the sink off the
wall. Then he swung away at the commode. It cracked in
half like a coconut. Rusty water sloshed around Wheezer's
size-fifteen-and-a-half hightops you could safely put to sea
in if you didn't bring too many friends along. Wordlessly,
Wheezer laid the bat across his shoulder like an on-deck
hitter and left.

As a direct result of Wheezer's visit, Ridly phoned Lucas
Hogaboom from the corner to ask if he needed a driver
for the killing and what did drivers get these days per trip?
Then Ridly stopped at Binx's hovel to ask if he wanted to
go along. Binx was dropping dead flies into his ant farm.

"Jeez, I better twist one for the road."

Binx and Ridly waited in the car outside Black Caesar's
while Lucas Hogaboom hobbled in on his crutches. His
leg had begun to stink inside the cast like Sheriff Plotner.
That was probably a bad sign. However, the codeine made
his thumping gait feel light, airy, almost balletic. The place
was as dark as a small intestine. Lucas clobbered into the
point of a table and whined in pain. His eyes adjusting,
he saw six white guys wearing greasy baseball caps
crammed into a booth. Except for them and the nigger
behind the bar, the dive was empty. Not counting the

nigger, it looked like Lucas's kind of place. He took a stool.

Black Caesar, hospitable publican, said, "Yeah, what?"

Lucas ordered a beer and placed a twenty on the bar. "Keep the change." Lot of niggers'd do most anything for change of a twenty.

"There ain't no change," said Black Caesar.

"There ain't?"

"Twenty bucks a beer, unless you want imported."

Lucas put another twenty on the Formica. "I'm looking for a old pal of mine name of Loomis."

Black Caesar rubbed his chin musingly. "Loomis, huh? Loomis? . . . Let me see. My memory is sketchy, you know what I mean? Must be because of my combat experiences in Grenada."

Lucas put still another twenty on the bar.

Black Caesar smoothed out the wrinkles, contemplated the bill. "You're a pal of his, huh? Where do you know him from? Upstate? You a legislator? You a man of the people?"

"We was in the navy together. We had some times in the Red Sea, old Loomis and me. Yep, great sea, the Red. He calls hisself Doom." Lucas tried the power of another twenty. "Doom Loomis. You know him or what?"

"Oh. *That* Loomis. Doom Loomis. Sure. He's got his yacht boat tied up out back."

"Now?"

"Out back. Right now. But Doom Loomis has been a big boon to the local economy, and he wouldn't like it if I sent just any fuckhead around to see him." Black Caesar spotted the fake pearl butt of the bad news bulging in Lucas's waistband. "But you're old comrades in arms, shipmates from the big waters, right?"

"Right."

"So you just go on out that back door, turn right on the dock, and there's his yacht boat. You can't miss it. Want another beer? I'll knock off a buck."

Ignoring the nigger, Lucas headed for the back door. Maybe he wouldn't do it this time, maybe he'd just reconnoiter for another time, at night, when he felt better. Lucas had a hard time navigating the rickety dock with the big holes in the planking. He turned right.

Black Caesar removed the wet mop from its bucket and carried it to the dockside window. He pulled open the curtain as Lucas came along. "See it? Right there?"

As Lucas passed the window, Black Caesar placed the mop head against Lucas's cheek and with a flick of the wrist ramrodded him off the dock. The splash was spectacular.

Four of the white guys in greasy baseball caps gathered at the door to watch. Billows of bubbles broke the milky surface. One crutch, then the other, floated up languidly. But not Lucas Hogaboom. His cast was stuck in the mud like a mushroom anchor. The guys in baseball caps watched until their beers began to turn tepid in the sun. The natural light was hurting Black Caesar's eyes, so he returned to his place behind the cash register. The white guys straggled in after him. They didn't give a shit, as long as Black Caesar didn't start charging *them* twenty bucks a Bud.

Binx and Ridly waited in the car, engine running, for twenty minutes, during which Ridly told Binx about his brother-in-law problem.

"Think something's wrong with Lucas?" asked Binx.

"Definitely."

"No, I mean do you think something *went* wrong?"

"Do you want to go see?"

"I'll twist one, then we'll go see. . . . Gee, that's real troubling, Wheezer on your ass like that."

"Thing is, Wheezer's about the size of a Jeep Cherokee. I don't know how he got that big. My wife is a petite person."

"Big knockers, though."

"Don't talk that way about my wife."

A half hour later Binx and Ridly blundered into the darkness to see what had become of Lucas Hogaboom. When their eyes adjusted, Binx asked the black guy behind the bar if he had seen a friend of theirs, large fellow, leg in a cast.

"He's out back."

"Out back where?"

"Swimming," said Black Caesar.

"Swimming? How can he be swimming!"

"Breast stroke?"

"He had about four hundred pounds of plaster on his leg!"

"I told him it wasn't a great idea." Black Caesar walked out back, Binx, Ridly, and the four guys in baseball caps following. "He went in right there." Black Caesar pointed to a spot on the milky green surface.

"And where'd he come out?" asked Ridly reasonably.

"Didn't."

"You mean—he's still down there?"

The white guys stood in a knot like backup singers in a Caucasian doo-wop group and nodded in unison.

"Maybe I ought to go in and get him," suggested Binx.

"I wouldn't do that," said Black Caesar.

"No?"

"I've seen guys dissolve in that water. Come out looking like a turd in a pizza oven."

Binx wasn't interested in dissolving. He looked at Ridly, who was peering into the water. "Well," said Ridly, "we'll stop back later."

"Yeah, he might be up by then," said Black Caesar.

WALTER VALE

MR. R. J. KREELY DROVE HIS JAGUAR FROM HIS SPRAWL-ing split ranch in Poinciana Plantation Estates north on

South Bayshore Drive past the art museum, on whose board he sat, past Deering's eccentric old mansion, Viscaya, where R.J. picked up the Rickenbacker Causeway onto Virginia Key, past Planet Ocean and the Miami Seaquarium, across Bear Cut Bridge onto Key Biscayne. There was scant traffic at 7:30 Sunday morning. By ten the route across the bay would be clogged with picnickers and beachgoers heading for Cranden Park, which was why Mr. Kreely and his cronies teed off at eight. Walter Vale followed him at a discreet distance in a Budget Rent-a-Car.

Walter Vale had never heard of R. J. Kreely before he started following him two days ago. Kreely was just another of those self-made men who thought his wealth and standing in the community made him invulnerable. It didn't matter to him who he pissed off. They were all the same, those self-made men, arrogant and stupid.

Mr. R. J. Kreely turned right onto a narrow lane lined with causerina pines and thick hedges shielding the mansions from rubberneckers. He turned right again at the gate of the Henry Flagler Golf, Tennis, & Bath Club and paused at the security guardhouse. He must have said something funny, because the sun-bleached blond teenage attendant laughed and waved him through. Walter Vale drove two hundred yards past the gate, pulled over and stopped at the side of the lane. He smoked a Kool and watched an ancient black guy edge around the ornamentals with a Weed Buster before he turned around and drove back to the guardhouse, where the teenager eyed him coldly.

"Hello," smiled Walter Vale, "I'm a guest of Mr. R. J. Kreely."

"Oh, yes sir, he just went in. They're teeing off at eight. You can just make it."

Walter Vale sat down on a bench in the shade of an ancient banyan tree near the first tee. He stretched out his legs to admire his new alligator-hide penny loafers, which he wore sockless. With his maroon yachtsman's slacks, white leather belt, and blue knit shirt, a penguin on his tit, Walter felt he fit right in among these self-made chumps.

By the time he'd snubbed out another Kool, R. J. Kreely and the rest of his fat foursome, each member dressed nearly identically to Walter, putt-putted up to the tee on their cart. They got down and waved clubs around, warming up, trying to touch their toes. Not one of them had seen their own dorks without a mirror in twenty years. Walter Vale had positioned himself close enough to the first tee to eavesdrop on the foursome.

R. J. Kreely was bragging about someone named Conchita, who had "the cutest little tits you could ever hope to see. Nice big brown aureoles. The wife's visiting her old lady in Trenton for *one whole week*. It's a time of bliss for old R.J. vis-à-vis Conchita."

But Walter Vale knew that was not true. R. J. Kreely's wife had not gone to Trenton. Walter Vale had followed her to the airport yesterday. There she had met a guy who looked like a forties movie gigolo at the Varig Airlines check-in desk, and arm in arm they boarded a flight to São Paulo. Walter wondered if Kreely knew about that.

The bulbous golfers chose up sides, settled on a cheap wager. The fat guy who hit first knocked one short but straight down the immaculate fairway. Then the second fat guy sliced one into a stand of melalucca trees. It ricocheted off three boles before it plopped into the soggy marsh grass.

"That's one for the snakes, Humphrey."

"Monica Hardcastle got bit in the ass by a snake in the rough just last week. You should have seen the guys line up to suck it out."

The foursome giggled like a clot of frat boys.

Then R. J. Kreely stepped up to the tee and took a couple of wristy backswings, making a big deal about it. Walter Vale noticed that R.J. was left-handed. Good. That alone made the early morning trip out here worth his trouble. Walter didn't even wait to see where R. J. Kreely's ball went.

YOUNG AT HEART

BACK ABOARD THE *KING DON*, DONNY SIKES GAVE HIS
crew the night off. He stood alone on the fantail watching
for shooting stars and listening to the mechanical squeaks
and clanks as the crew ran out the skiff davits. Lowering
away, they cackled about female body parts and what they
intended to do with same. Everything was closed within
twenty miles, except for bucket-of-blood bars and all-nite
chicken carryouts, devoid of female parts, but youth was
ever hopeful. Donny wished he could go with them, perhaps build a beach bonfire, roast hot dogs, tell dirty
jokes—sweet, youthful doings which, if once you missed,
you never got a second chance at.

Lonely and sad, Donny had just downed his third piña
colada. Roger was blending another. Donny could hear
the whir from the wet bar. He had been looking for shooting stars, but he hadn't seen any. He and Gramps used to
look for shooting stars at the sylvan cedar-log Throckmorton Camp in the Adirondacks. Gramps would paddle
him out into the middle of Saranac Lake, where, bobbing,
they would search the summer sky. Gramps said for each
shooting star you see, one wish will come true. Donny
would lie on his back in the bow for the panorama while
Gramps stroked the still surface.

"There's one!" Its tail shed sparks, arcing across the
blue-black sky. "I get one wish!"

"That's not a shooting star," said Gramps. "That's a
comet."

"It is?"

"It's Throckmorton's Comet. Comes right over the camp every August."

"You mean it doesn't count?"

"Doesn't count? Of course it counts. It means we're special. How many people have their own comet flying over their summer place? Keep looking."

Donny kept looking until his neck stiffened and sleep seemed impossible to stave off. But then the entire sky awakened with shooting stars. When one fizzled, three others exploded in its place, crisscrossing, flitting, and popping in the upper atmosphere.

Gramps smiled. "That's enough wishes to last you a lifetime."

Had Donny made that up, imagined it? There really were shooting stars, weren't there? Most of his wishes had come true, hadn't they? He was one of the ten richest. He had property, yachts, jets, lackeys, you name it. People bowed and scraped; he got invited places, inaugural balls, opening nights, auctions. So the shooting stars couldn't have been just fireflies or something, passing airplanes, swamp gas, all puffed up with memory and with longing. Could they?

"It'd be sweet to be that age again, huh, boss?" said Roger Vespucci, delivering the piña, the crew boat cutting a phosphorescent wake shorebound, almost like aquatic shooting stars.

Donny felt blue. Another piña would cut the gloom, might even put Throckmorton's Comet back into the firmament.

"I know what, Roger. Let's go swimming."

"When? Now?"

"Sure, let's go. I used to go swimming every night in the summers after I watched the shooting stars."

"Where was this?"

"Saranac Lake."

"A lake? That's different. This is the middle of the ocean. They got sharks in there which'll bite your spine out just for the hell of it. I've seen pictures. You don't want to go in there." Probably even now fins were cleaving the black surface, waiting for chumps in trunks.

"But I'm hot."

"Maybe a nice cool shower?"

"Come on, get into your suit, Roger." Donny Sikes was already wearing his.

"I'm sorry, boss, but there's no way I go swimming at night. Hell, even daytime I don't swim anywhere I can't touch. I get cold chills just thinking about that black water out there. I'll do a lotta things for you, but swimming at night ain't one of them."

"Uh, would you plant a bomb in the Broadnax mansion?"

Roger decided to humor him, get him into bed, he'd sleep off his snootful, forget all about bombs and suicide swims. The guy was falling into one of his funks. "Is that what you want me to do, boss?"

Donny said he wasn't sure whether or not that was what he wanted to do, but he was considering it. "You still know bombs, right, Roger?"

"Sure. Bombs are just like bicycles. Once you learn, you never forget."

"Well, how about coming down the gangway and watching for sharks while I take a swim?"

"Will you wear a life preserver?"

"You just don't want to have to rescue me."

"You got that right, boss."

The gangway was a complex and ingenious piece of hardware made necessary by the *King Don*'s twenty-five-foot-high topsides. Without a climbable contrivance of some sort, there was no way to board guests from a small boat alongside. Commercial ships solve the boarding problem in spartan fashion—they drop a Jacob's ladder down the side of the hull—but hosts can't ask influential guests and business associates to clamber up a glorified rope ladder in Italian suits and $500 Foot-Joys. The *King Don*'s gangway was engineered like an escalator. When lowered, as now, it formed a civilized flight of stairs down to the water with a secure platform at the bottom. When raised by means of an electric winch, the gangway automatically collapsed to stowable size, each step folding neatly under the one above. Even the boarding platform tucked itself away in three small rectangles.

Roger Vespucci followed Donny Sikes down the steps onto the platform three feet above the shark-infested water, undulating. It was just a matter of moments before the boss would chicken out. Wasn't it? Roger considered asking the boss if he could tie a rope to the life jacket, pull him in if necessary, the richest shark bait in the Atlantic.

"Wait," said Donny, "I forgot my earplugs. I'll be right back." Donny went back up the steps two at a time. Roger didn't even like standing that close to the sea at night.

Aboard, Donny switched on the electric winch, and the big drum began to turn. Donny watched it turn, trying to figure out which way the rope went around it. He'd seen the crew do this dozens of times. . . . Clockwise.

Donny took three turns around the drum and pulled. That was it. The gangway began to rise, collapsing as it did so. If there was any doubt about that—Donny couldn't winch and watch at the same time—the shout from Roger dispelled it:

"Boss! Boss, the fucking stairs—the stairs—going up!"

Heaving on the line, Donny knew what was happening out there over the bulwarks. The steps were turning vertical and tucking away under Roger's skittering feet.

"Boss!" Roger's voice was thin and shrill. "Hellllllp!"

Donny kept the line taut as he looked over the side. Roger was hugging the unit, feet kicking for toeholds. Roger looked up into the boss's face, and a terrible realization momentarily displaced Roger's panic.

Donny Sikes was doing this on purpose.

Then Donny cast off the line. The gangway plummeted. When it reached the end of its rope, it snapped open with a sharp crack, the force of which flipped Roger Vespucci off backward. Donny saw the bottom of Roger's shoes as he hit the boarding platform and bounced into the Atlantic with surprisingly little splash. Donny winched the gangway back up out of Roger's reach.

Roger surfaced, arms flailing. "Boss! What are you doing! Are you nuts!" Roger already knew the answer to that, why'd he waste breath asking?

"You tried to cut an independent deal with Broadnax." Donny leaned his elbows on the cap rail and looked down. Tears streamed. "Did you think I wouldn't find out?"

"Boss, no! I didn't! Why—? Boss, let's talk this over—" Roger swallowed some saltwater, like hot sand in the back of his throat, and began to retch.

"It's no use, Roger. I saw the bomb. That wasn't too bright, Roger."

"Boss! I never! Never! Some—somebody's bullshittin' you! Please pull me up!"

"Don't think it doesn't hurt me to do this, Roger."

Roger splashed to the hull and clawed for a handhold, anything, a rust crack, a rivet head, but there was nothing, a wall of glare ice. "Please, boss! I didn't! . . ." But Roger knew it was no use.

His only hope would be to swim ashore. He'd better get started before he wasted his energy. "Hey, boss, you know why you're always lonely? Because you're a crazy ass-hole!" The sharks were taking numbers, lining up from here to Nassau. "Land ho!" shouted a sailor in Spanish from the masthead. Barefooted seamen slapped across the wooden deck and shinnied up the yardarms to see it— land! They hadn't fallen off the edge of the earth. They were safe! Roger Vespucci stepped stalwartly onto the bowsprit and said, "Listen, Christopher, I don't think that's China at all. I think that's a whole new land, an undiscovered land. You know what I'm saying?"

"No shit?" said Christopher. "Undiscovered? Then we'll call it Rogerland, okay?"

"Okay, great."

Donny Sikes sat on the fantail finishing his piña colada and watching his friend Roger Vespucci drown.

Hearing Gramps approaching from the main salon, Donny Sikes had the quickness of mind to chuck his piña over the side. Gramps wouldn't have understood how Roger's treachery had hurt him and how there was nothing to do but chuck Roger overboard. "I haven't seen any shooting stars yet tonight, Gramps."

"Well, keep looking. Perseverance pays dividends."

"Right you are, Gramps."

Shooting stars could break your heart.

YOUR LOVE

DOOM AND ROSALIND LAY ON THEIR BACKS NAKED IN the V-berth. Droplets of sweat were forming, Doom noticed, in the valley between her breasts. Their lovemaking, now finished, meant only a brief respite from the cloudy depression that hung over Black Caesar's Yacht Club.

The milky creek remained still and airless. Breezes often twittered the topmost mangrove leaves but seemed never to descend to sea level. On occasion, decomposing fish with diseased gills floated by among the plastic six-pack yokes and soda bottles. Even the threadbare egrets patrolling the shallows moved torpidly, as if on their last legs. Only mosquitoes and horseflies flourished. A green scum had formed around *Staggerlee*'s waterline, and she too seemed dispirited, immobilized. Doom feared vaguely that just being here would cause her to give up her watertight integrity and sink in despair. Fine white coral-rock road dust settled deeper on her spars and deck with each passing pickup truck. How different she'd feel in the open ocean, cool and free, with no home port painted on her transom.

"Doom?"

"Huh?"

"Have you noticed how happy everybody is? Duncan,

the professor, Longnecker, Bert. All of them. They're having a ball. Even Marvis is having fun accounting all the crooked money."

"How come we're not?"

". . . I feel sorry for everyone. Even Donny Sikes and Big Al. I never thought I'd feel sorry for Big Al Broadnax."

That was because she was hanging around with Doom Loomis, but he didn't say so for fear she wouldn't contradict him. "Professor Goode told me this can only end badly. He says violently. Are you scared of that?"

"Yes. That too. Are you?"

"Yes."

"If I'm here with you, I'm scared they're hurting my grandmother. With her, I'm scared for you. This place isn't the end of the world, even if it looks like it. They could find you anytime they set their minds to looking. I don't know—"

"What?"

"You're so good at it. . . ."

"Conspiracy?"

"Yes."

Doom was afraid of that. "I didn't want to do it," he said lamely.

"I know it."

"Maybe we should go away by ourselves."

"Just forget the whole thing?"

"Yes."

"Then they'd be free to kill Small Hope Bay."

"Maybe Small Hope Bay isn't worth it."

"What do you mean? Of course it's worth it. . . . Worth what?"

"What we'll have to do to save it."

Rosalind rolled over and hugged him close. Doom nestled his head between her breasts, in that place where children and adult males long to live, nipples plugging their ears against rude sounds.

The phone rang. Doom had had a telephone installed aboard *Staggerlee*. Naked, he padded aft to take the call at his navigation station and conspiratorial nerve center.

"It's me, Plotner. I'm up at the hospital, and I got one Roger Vespucci here. You know, the guy with the droopy mustache. Well, he's half drowned. A widow from Ohio found him washed up on Omnium Beach, gave him artificial respiration. He's been delirious, rantin' about sharks, saying how Donny Sikes tried to murder him. I guess your plan worked right out. I guess that makes you one smart fellow."

"I'll be right there."

ROGER LIVES

ROSALIND DROPPED DOOM UNDER THE PORTICOED entrance to the emergency room, where Sheriff Plotner and the Annes waited, then went in search of a parking spot. How did the Annes always know what was happening? Sheriff Plotner led Doom through the waiting room, past the distraught kin of the cut, clobbered, gouged, and gut-shot into the Authorized Personnel Only elevator. The Annes followed, filming. None of the hospital staff questioned their movements. That would have meant subjecting themselves to the sheriff's stink.

When the aluminum elevator door closed, Sheriff Plotner turned on Doom: "Lemme tell you something, son. I don't give a crap what you got on me, I ain't gonna be your slave. I'm a duly elected peace officer. It don't matter that Big Al rigged the election—I'm still sheriff here. I ain't gonna be nobody's gofer. What we got here is anarchism, people strivin' to kill each other like there ain't no law in Broadnax County. I'm here to tell you there is, and I'm it. You ain't it. I'm gonna start acting like it, and, boy, you best not get beneath my wheels."

"Okay, Sheriff Plotner."

". . . Okay? Just like that?"

"You're the law here. I'd welcome your ideas."

"You would?"

"Yes, I would. What do you think we should do about Roger Vespucci, Sheriff?"

The sheriff clapped Doom on the shoulder. "Watch."

Longnecker stood guard at Roger Vespucci's door. Seeing the sheriff enthusiastically leading the way, Longnecker leapt to attention, clicked his heels, and sarcastically saluted. "Nothing to report, *sir!*"

Sheriff Plotner ignored him.

Doom shook his hand.

"I always wanted to be a screw," Longnecker said.

"Me too," said Doom.

The sheriff flung the door open. Roger Vespucci was sitting up in bed, combing his mustache, smoking a cigarette that burned the back of his salt-scratched throat, and watching pregnant women do aerobics on TV. "Hey, Sheriff, you can't keep me here against my will. It's unconstitutional." Roger saw Doom. "You? What the fuck are you doing here? Hey, get these cameras out of here!"

"You're under arrest for the murders of Ozzie Mertz, Doris Florian, and Dennis Loomis," said the sheriff.

On TV someone said, "There's gotta be a cure for athlete's foot."

"Never heard of them," insisted Roger.

"I know you killed them on orders from Donny Sikes. We'll go easy on you in return for your testimony."

Roger stared resolutely at the ceiling.

"I also know Donny Sikes tried to pop you."

"I tripped on a banana peel and fell overboard. It was an accident. The boss is probably worried about me right now." And damn right he should worry about Roger Vespucci, the great navigator of the undiscovered land from whose bourn no traveler returns. He oughta be quaking in his boots.

"You said so yourself—that he tried to kill you."

"I never said that. When'd I say that?"

"When you was unconscious."

"Unconscious don't mean dick. You got nothing on me, you're peeing into the wind. What's that stink?"

"Could I have a word with you in private, Sheriff?" asked Doom gently. The Annes followed them out into the hall.

Roger Vespucci moaned. What *did* they have on him, and how did they get it? Had that bloat Donny Sikes set him up for the fall? Roger considered bolting for parts unknown right then and there. He got out of bed and tiptoed to the window, his hospital garment falling away from his hairy white cheeks. A jump for it would break both his legs like pretzel sticks, besides which the goddamn windows didn't open. Someone on TV said, "Five hundred dead in renewed shelling."

Sheriff Plotner held the door open for Doom, who said, "Maybe we can work something out, Mr. Vespucci."

"Just who the fuck are you!"

"Agent Armbrister of the FBI." Doom showed him ID to prove it.

"Let me see that, don't just go waving badges at me. I wasn't born yesterday. You could be showing me your Discover Card." Roger clutched Doom's hand for a close gander. Christ, it looked genuine. Then they had him for bopping an agent on the coconut. What else? Illegal possession of a firearm, kidnapping a federal officer, enough to land him in the hard-time house if they chose to press it.

Doom explained that the real Doom Loomis was still cooling his heels in prison. He, Agent Armbrister, had assumed Loomis's identity as part of an extensive sting operation aimed at Donny Sikes. They had substantial evidence against Mr. Sikes, and they were nearly ready to move for indictment. Doom spoke softly, a reasonable man, a stand-up guy. He said: "But, off the record, we have a problem. A smart lawyer might be able to prove entrapment within reasonable doubt. That's just the way our system works. I wouldn't have it any other way, but I mean to protect my case. Call it professional pride. Now, since his attempt on your life, I thought we might be able to work something out."

"I fell off the boat—"

"Bullshit, let's just nail him for kidnapping an agent of the federal gum'ment," said Sheriff Plotner right on cue.

"I appreciate your zeal, Sheriff, but Mr. Sikes is a wealthy man with the finest of legal representation. I'd much rather have Mr. Vespucci's willing testimony. Failing that, of course, we'll have no choice but to press for Mr. Vespucci's indictment as you suggest."

"I guess you're right, Armbrister. Like usual."

Roger Vespucci gave that some thought. On TV a beer drinker said, "It doesn't get any better than this." Roger Vespucci said, "I ain't about to talk for cameras."

"These are official Bureau photographers. Specifically, we'd like you to participate in a new phase of our sting operation as a gesture of your good faith. In return for which I shall move the grand jury to grant you immunity, and we'll keep the fact that you kidnapped me between ourselves."

"Or you can go down with Donny Sikes," said Sheriff Plotner.

". . . What do you want me to do?"

"We want you to play dead," said Doom.

"Play dead?" Roger's head was spinning. He needed time to think. There was a lot here that just didn't wash. This Agent Armbrister, for one, but playing along at least to the extent of playing dead seemed in his own best interests.

DOA

～～～～～～

DONNY SIKES HADN'T EXPECTED THE BODY TO SHOW UP. He paced the fantail, feeling edgy, finishing his second piña, but his piñas weren't nearly as good as Roger's, no tang, and the purser's piñas were worse. Why hadn't the sharks gotten Roger? Did sharks nap at night? And now the coroner wanted him to identify the body. What could he say but yes? That was an oversight, Donny guessed. The sea does cast up its dead. It cast up Dennis Loomis.

What would the authorities want to know? . . . Why he hadn't reported Roger missing? No, Roger had been missing only twelve hours. Actually, as far as Donny was concerned, Roger wasn't missing at all. He was merely away. He'd say Roger went into town to buy a piña blender and never came back. No, they could trace that. Dumb hicks probably wouldn't, but assuming so would be reckless. No, he'd tell them that Roger had a lady friend on Tequesta Key, where he often went to get laid. Nothing unusual in his absence. No, Donny didn't know her name.

Donny told himself to relax, don't volunteer any information, don't act like a guy with an alibi to protect. They had no cause to suspect foul play. After getting laid, Roger must have returned to the boat drunk, tripped over a cleat, and fallen overboard. Accidental drowning. Happens. . . . At least Gramps wasn't there when Plotner called. Gramps was ashore, watching the bulldozers assemble at Omnium Settlement to take out that nest of squatters and put up something the right kind of people would like. Pretty soon the way would be clear, but this Roger Vespucci corpse-viewing could be sticky. He'd have to remain on the ball.

Donny Sikes ordered the skiff run out and had the purser, a sneaky young man, deliver him to the town dock on Tequesta Key, where he hired a Lincoln Town Car in which the purser drove him to the Broadnax County Hospital. During the slow, snarled ride, Donny considered the question of grief. Should he display same? Or would manly stoicism, a slight twitter of the jaw muscles, be more appropriate? He'd see how he felt when he got there.

"Wait!" said Donny. "Stop here!"

"Where, Mr. Sikes?"

"There. The Wreck Bar. See the puce neon sign?"

"The what neon sign?"

"Puce! Puce!" Donny got a couple of piñas in plastic cups to go. "Hold the umbrellas."

Sheriff Plotner met Donny under the portico, called him Mr. Sikes, and thanked him for coming. Then he led Donny down a long white corridor to the morgue.

When, earlier, Doom had taken the morgue trip—with Sheriff Plotner and Roger Vespucci—to set things up, he had thought about his mother's own walk down this long white corridor, through swinging aluminum doors with round portholes, to the periphery, where all pretense of decor expired, to view his father's crab-bitten body, and he had hoped she was happy with Norman Futterman in Wyandanch. Painted walls, acoustic tile ceilings, and indoor/outdoor carpet runners gave way to naked pipes and cement floors, along which Roger had hopped, trying to coax his skimpy hospital garment to cover his ass, while the Annes filmed from astern. Corridors became tunnels. Cellars don't exist in south Florida because seawater lurks a scant six feet down, but this place had all the earmarks of one. Down here they washed the bloody, bile-befouled laundry, stored the cleaning agents, the heavy equipment—and the corpses.

Roger Vespucci had smelled a rat on the way. This was very weird police procedure, even for the FBI, but he figured he'd play along, covering his ass in every sense.

Besides, it might serve his own best interests for that pumped-up sot of a pudgy lunatic to think he was dead. But how did his death serve the interests of the law? Unless of course they were running their own scam for unknown reasons. Roger couldn't wait to see how Donny would play it.

"He don't look dead to me," Sheriff Plotner said about Roger on the aluminum slab with the nasty-looking fluid channels running down each side.

"Maybe some makeup," Anne suggested.

"To make his eyes look sunken," added Anne.

"Yeah," said the sheriff, "he needs to look more hideous, cuts and contusions, like that—"

"Come on," said Roger, sitting up, "I drowned. I didn't go through a windshield. I don't want no makeup—" Roger didn't want to look ridiculous in death. "Here, you want hideous, check this." Roger lay back down on the cold table, stuck the tip of his tongue behind his lower front teeth and made the middle of it protrude grotesquely. He rolled his eyes up and to the side and lolled his head on his shoulder. . . .

"Not bad," observed the sheriff.

"Can you hold that long enough?" Doom asked.

"Hell, he's just gonna look at me, right? He ain't gonna perform an autopsy, is he?"

"Okay," said Doom.

Donny Sikes walked silently down those same halls with Sheriff Plotner, who paused at the morgue door for dramatic effect, then flung it open. Roger Vespucci lay on the table, his face covered with a green sheet. The conspirators had placed an instrument stand, like a breakfast-in-bed table, over his midsection so Donny couldn't see him breathe.

Identity obscured beneath a surgeon's scrubbies and mask, Doom pretended to autopsy another green-sheet-covered body (Longnecker's) while the Annes filmed the operation. When Donny Sikes entered, Anne sneaked her camera up onto his face.

"That there's Professor Armbrister from up to the college. Don't mind him," said Sheriff Plotner. "He's doing a guy got eaten by a alligator. Ain't pretty."

Doom got nervous when the sheriff started ad-libbing, because he tended to get carried away. But it didn't seem to matter. Donny had eyes for nothing but his victim. Sheriff Plotner paused again for effect, then snapped the sheet from Roger Vespucci's face. Roger had added variations to his hideous visage—he had pinched his left eye shut, scrunching that side of his face into a contorted mask, and he had twisted one wing of his Fu Manchu upward at a crazy angle. Not bad touches, Doom thought.

"That him?" the sheriff asked.

Donny Sikes nodded. The sheriff re-covered Roger.

"I—I think I'm going to—" Donny swallowed hard to return the piñas to their appropriate place, but they didn't go. "I'm gonna—"

"Down the hall, first door on the left," said the sheriff, trying to suppress a grin.

Roger Vespucci sat up and glared at the still-swinging morgue door, and the Annes caught on film the violence in his eyes. Doom didn't miss it either. Then Longnecker sat up, and Doom removed his mask. Longnecker looked at Doom as if to say what now, chief?

Sheriff Plotner was surprised at Donny's softness, a bag of feathers, as he poured Donny into the backseat of the idling Lincoln Town Car. He thanked Donny for the performance of his civic duty, and Donny gurgled in reply. Then the sheriff returned to the morgue to escort Roger Vespucci back to his room.

"Look, Sheriff, my ass is hanging out. No dignity. How about some clothes?"

"That's hospital clothes. You're in the hospital."

The Annes filmed Doom, thinking. He said to Longnecker, "Let him escape after dark, okay?"

This Doom Loomis was one devious guy, and Longnecker loved it.

In the hall outside Roger's room, Sheriff Plotner's radio crackled.

"Plotner here, over." Cheap Jap radios, you had to hold them right up to your ear. Sounded like someone was wadding up newspaper on the other end. Sheriff Plotner thought he caught something about bulldozers. "Huh? What do you mean bulldozers? Over." Burning bulldozers? "Did you say burnin'? Over." Fifty bulldozers burning in Omnium Settlement? "Jumpin' Judaica! Over." Nobody's going to burn up bulldozers on his beat and get away with it. Probably Miami drug kingpins. Sheriff Plotner waddled down the hall, heading for his car to nip it in the bud.

Doom decided to follow him.

BATTLE HYMN

CARMINE BLUNCHELLI WANTED TO KNOW WHAT THE flying fuck those five yellow dozers were doing on *his* job site.

"Search me, chief," said Carmine's foreman and brother-in-law, Mario Gepetto.

Carmine's own bulldozers were russet, and there were no yellow ones here yesterday when he trucked in his entire fleet of six from Opa Locka. Carmine Blunchelli glared at the yellows—they must have slunk in under the cover of darkness—and flicked his upper plate with his tongue, a sure sign, Mario knew, that Carmine was pissed.

"Hey, chief, look. Ain't that Frankie O'Mera over there?"

"Over where?"

"By the old motel—"

"Goddamn is! Miami micks! Lower'n snake shit in a wagon rut."

Even as Carmine and Mario squinted at them, spouts of acrid blue exhaust puffed from the capped exhaust pipes on the yellow bulldozers. Frankie O'Mera was getting under way, forming up his charges to push down the squalid remains of Omnium Settlement under the terms of his contract with Big Al Broadnax. O'Mera thought Big Al was a crazy old asshole, but business was business and most clients assholes, anyhow. Frankie O'Mera was a self-made man, like Carmine Blunchelli, and that's why neither trusted the other. Those wops were trying to cut him right out of the picture. They'd have to get up a lot earlier than this to fuck over Frankie O'Mera from County Mayo.

"Saddle up, Mario," said Carmine, who knew his rights. He had a hard-and-fast contract, fifty percent down, with Donald Sikes, the tycoon, and he meant to execute it, even if he had to squash some micks under his treads while he was at it.

Mario Gepetto waved his Red Man Chew cap in circles overhead. Like RAF pilots scrambling to meet the Hun, his operators leapt aboard, fired up their engines, and the humid Florida air filled to bursting with the throaty snarl of eleven D-2 Caterpillar diesels.

"Hey, Carmine," said the cool-headed Mario Gepetto, "maybe you oughta go talk to O'Mera first. You know, try to reason with the worm."

"Reason? What is this reason?"

"Well, I mean try to tell him nice like, get them dozers off our site. Otherwise you might be liable if you don't even try to talk things out."

"Yeah, liable to chop his seeds off." But Mario had a point there, Carmine knew. If he shoved O'Mera's dozers into the bay without a powwow first, slick lawyers could grab onto his ass like a cheap suit. Fuckin' lawyers made this country lousy. Didn't used to be like that back when he was coming up, back when a guy got in your way you ran over his feet with heavy equipment, because if you didn't, then he'd run over yours. That's why, even today, everybody wears steel-toe boots. Survival of the fittest.

Now the government sticks its— "Okay, Mario. I'll reason. You got anything white?"

"I got a napkin in my lunch pail."

Waving Mario's napkin, Carmine walked out into the open area between the lines of snarling bulldozers. Frankie O'Mera walked out to meet him. They stood in the dust facing each other like gunfighters at high noon.

"What say, O'Mera?"

"What say, Blunchelli?"

"Hot."

"Hot? This ain't hot. August's hot."

"What are you doin' here?"

"Workin'. What are you doin' here?"

"Workin'."

"You mean to push down that town?"

"Then haul it away. You?"

"Uh-huh."

"You still fuck sheep?"

"No, your old lady said I should only have eyes for her."

They peered at each other for a time, the sun pounding on their receded hairlines, then each turned and walked back to his respective squadron.

"Did you reason with him?" asked Mario Gepetto.

"Yeah."

"What'd he say?"

"Nothin'."

"Well, he can't say you didn't try to reason with him."

Frankie O'Mera's yellow bulldozers, plows poised for maximum destruction, moved in a phalanx on the forlorn remains of Doom's hometown. The engine noise, it was subsequently reported, could be heard as far afield as High Hat Key. From the glassless windows of Fred's Hobby Shop, uncombed heads peeped out at the armored division heading their way with malice aforethought.

Like Harry on the eve of Agincourt, Carmine Blunchelli exhorted his drivers, stout fellows all, to squeeze the most from their machines, to give it all they had. He scurried back and forth before his line of russet bulldozers, shouting and waving and gesticulating. When they began to move, he leapt aboard the nearest, hanging off the driver's protective cage, calling for speed, more speed, full speed, for he sensed that the initial encounter would determine the day.

Likewise, Frankie O'Mera exhorted his fellows. He saw what the wops were about, a flank attack. Blood up, teeth bared, he signaled for his line to wheel left, meet the wops head-on—yellow and russet closing fast, heat wavering from their hoods.

Nothing could stop it now save orders from generals Sikes and Broadnax, but like many in the history of conflict, these generals were nowhere near the field.

Carmine dropped from his perch, bellowing berserkers' oaths, one of which expelled his upper plate into the sand, but he ran right over it, hurled himself toward Frankie O'Mera, who through the dust and the fumes saw Carmine Blunchelli coming and made ready. Frankie laid his shoulder onto Carmine's shoulder, like a couple of football lummoxes on the line of scrimmage, with a crushing thud. Foreheads met.

Frankie and Carmine were both sixty years old or better, and the impact did instant, irreparable hurt to their spinal discs. Both felt the damage as it happened, but neither gave a shit. This was war, and they were young again; they were yearling wolverines in full rut. After that impact they recoiled, did a dizzy, rubber-legged turn or two, and when their eyes refocused, when each saw his adversary still afoot, they butted heads again hard enough to fold up their ears—

Then their bulldozers met plow to plow.

Raccoons foraging for oysters on the mangrove roots at the sinking side of the battlefield froze, tuning their senses to comprehend the crash. What harm did it mean to them, this human endeavor? Green, reddish, and great blue herons, brown pelicans, snowy egrets, and scarlet ibis took wing over Small Hope Bay. Slider turtles and mangrove terrapins hunkered into the trembling mud. Having for centuries reaped the benefit of human endeavor, turkey vultures circled the battlefield on hot updrafts, waiting aloft for the inevitable.

The center of the line met head-on with steel-buckling impact. Those machines were demolished on the spot, and the sudden stop hurled operators over their control levers onto the accordioned engines, where they too met their opposite numbers head-on.

Events transpired differently on the right and left flanks of the line. Russet outnumbered yellow by one, so the russet right attempted a flanking maneuver against yellow's left. Yellow countered with a parry, and their combat took jousting and shovel-fencing form, but the end result—destruction—was the same as at the center; it only took slightly longer.

New to modern conflict, armor debuted on the Western Front in 1916. Armor met again at Tobruk, El Alamein, and, in the greatest of all tank battles, at Kursk. Twenty-eight years later new, improved tanks fought it out on the Sinai, where the resulting carnage shocked even the combatants. By that measure, the Battle of Omnium Settlement—where no shots were fired, no men actually perished—was a petty skirmish, a mere footnote to the bloody history of mechanized war.

One bulldozer remained running. Its shovel was ripped off, bodywork and driver shorn away, treads clanking. The machine spun in an ever-diminishing gyre like a half-stomped horsefly until it dug itself into its own hole and quit forever. Frankie and Carmine lay supine, staring at the sun. Here and there, crippled drivers crawled away from their machines for fear of explosion, but there were no other stirrings on the field of battle except, as at Waterloo, that of dust, smoke, and buzzards on the wind.

WALTER VALE II

WALTER VALE RETRACED HIS ROUTE BACK ACROSS BIS-cayne Bay on the Rickenbacker Causeway. The outbound traffic was beginning to snarl, but since it was still early morning, his side of the road was almost free of obstruction. Crossing, he watched a fleet of J-35s tacking and jibing around their starting line on a fluky southwesterly breeze. Walter Vale had always wanted to own a sailboat until he realized how slow they were. Probably owned by a bunch of snobby bastards anyway. Maybe one day he'd buy himself a forty-foot Cigarette boat, call it the *Sociopath* or the *Fuck Yourself* and cut a swath through the sailboats at fifty miles an hour. Imagine spending the day on a slow boat to nowhere with guys like R. J. Kreely and his four-some. Same buttholes, they just wore Topsiders instead of cleats.

At the foot of the causeway, he picked up the Dixie Highway south to Le Jeune Road, which led him to Poinciana Plantation. He was getting pretty adept at navigating Miami streets, a good thing, since this seemed to be the land of plenty for the likes of Walter Vale.

The bottoms of billowy cumulus clouds over the western part of the city had flattened and darkened as a rain squall marshaled its forces. Stark sunlight accentuated the darkening clouds and made the impending weather seem more ominous and dangerous than it would be upon arrival. Walter Vale liked south Florida rain, liked watching the fat drops fall and the fingers of steam rise from the hot asphalt like miniature battlefield fires, but he didn't want to get his new alligator shoes wet. Only a few drops can ruin your alligator shoes for good, which seemed odd to Walter, since alligators lived in water to begin with.

R. J. Kreely owned one of the old homes, a Spanish-style split ranch with rows of half-round red tiles on the roof and some kind of ivy with little red flowers growing up the tan stucco walls. Another white Mercedes convertible and a green MG-TD were parked in the open-air carport. A couple of rambunctious blue jays chased each other off the manicured Bermuda-grass yard.

This whole spread on an acre and a half lot'd be a steal at $2.5 mil. Why would a guy like that with everything to lose want to go piss people off? How much does a man need? But from experience Walter Vale knew that when a man reaches a certain financial standing, people tend not to question his actions. The stupid guys take this absence of criticism for the possession of real power, and they piss people off. The next thing they know Walter Vale is motoring up their driveway in a rented Buick.

He knocked on the massive oaken door. A young Hispanic woman in a French maid's uniform answered. Her big black eyes were shy and roving, never lighting directly on Walter's.

"Good morning, I'm Walter Vale. I'm playing golf with R.J. today."

"Ohhh, well, sir, he already left to play golf."

"Already left? Gee, did I get my signals crossed? When did he leave?"

"Maybe two hours ago, sir."

Walter Vale snapped his fingers. "Doggone it. Say, are you Conchita?"

"Yes, sir."

"Conchita, may I come in and phone the club?"

Conchita vacillated for a moment. She really didn't want anyone around while she cleaned, because she was embarrassed by the scanty uniform R.J. had her wear, showing her legs in black spandex and lifting and squeezing her breasts together—but how could she say no? She stepped aside and held the door open.

"Thank you very much, Conchita."

It was almost cold inside. Walter Vale shivered before he adjusted to the thirty-degree plunge. The living room, about the size of a handball court, was sunken three steps, its floor covered by a spotless white shag carpet that Walter thought tacky. Just because you had money didn't mean you had any taste. The telephone sat on a thick plate-glass coffee table surrounded on three sides by an off-white over-stuffed couch. Little intricately carved jade dogs were displayed in a pack on the table, Conchita's feather duster lying among them. Walter Vale made no move toward the telephone, didn't even descend into the living room.

He peered at Conchita in a way that made her nervous, so she excused herself.

"Conchita—"

". . . Yes, sir?"

"My old pal R.J. says you have the cutest little titties."

"Wha—?"

"So I'd like you to take off your uniform."

The man was grinning. Maybe this was some kind of dirty but harmless joke. She wasn't surprised to learn that Mr. Kreely said rude things about her to his friends. "Telephone's over there," she said, and turned down the hall.

"Conchita—"

When she turned back, she saw that the man had a silenced pistol in his hand. She had seen guns like that on "Miami Vice," where only evil came of them. She began to tremble.

"Take off your clothes, Conchita." The man didn't even bother to point the gun at her. "Don't worry, Conchita, I just want to see if old R.J. was right."

Conchita stood staring at him as if he were a bad dream which with time would recede.

"Conchita, I'm a busy man, fully diversified. I can't wait all day for you to shimmy out of that sweet little suit."

"Please, sir—"

"Conchita, I won't ask you again nicely."

She began to cry and to cover herself as if she were already naked in front of this man. "I'm not wearing any underwear," she blubbered.

"Is that the way he wants you?"

"Yes, sir."

The man nodded as if he sympathized, but then he made hurry-up gestures with the gun.

Conchita pulled off her shoes and dropped them. Then she stopped as if that would satisfy the man.

"Conchita, I have pressing engagements."

A single sob escaped from her chest, then she reached behind her back to unzip the uniform. Walter Vale noticed that the white apron was not a separate piece but was attached to the black dress, if something that small qualified as a dress. She pulled it down in front, exposing her breasts, which she quickly covered with her upper arms but not quickly enough to prevent Walter Vale from affirming R.J.'s judgment about them. "Please don't hurt me," she pleaded as she let the dress fall about her ankles.

Walter Vale assumed she wore tights, but she didn't. They were stockings, and they clung to her upper thighs of their own accord. She tried to cover herself in that wonderful way stripped women always did, at least in Walter Vale's experience—moving their hands and arms from top to bottom, trying one means, then another, realizing it was futile, and then giving up, standing with their arms at their sides, heads bowed in humiliation and fear. Walter Vale always enjoyed that process.

"Now we're going to go back to the bedroom—the master bedroom. Lead on."

Conchita whined, then turned, stepping out of her crumpled skirt, and led Walter Vale down the long hall decorated with identically framed Winslow Homer originals. He noticed that Conchita had an allover tan, and he wondered if R.J. Kreely had requested she sunbathe nude. Some men were knocked out by that; however, Walter Vale preferred sallow women. Otherwise they ended up with a lot of unsightly skin cancers. Conchita turned left at the end of the hall into an enormous bedroom. It was obviously decorated by a woman. The walls were peach, and there was a lot of chintz and lace and more jade figurines, busy, like pictures he'd seen of Victorian boudoirs. Conchita had just finished making the bed.

Walter Vale pulled the coverlet away and dropped it on the floor. Cream-colored satin sheets, creaseless as if they'd been ironed right on the bed. "Now, Conchita, what I'd like you to do is get in the bed."

"Oh no, please, don't rape me." She sat on the bed in a ball. Christ, it was a water bed. This guy Kreely was something else. Little Conchita bobbed up and down, enhancing her helplessness. Walter Vale made a mental note not to puncture the bed and get his alligators wet.

"Now I want you to rumple around in it."

". . . What?"

"You know how you make angels in the snow?"

"I've never seen snow."

"No, never?" Patiently, Walter Vale told her how you make angels, and she did it. He told her to wriggle her ass around to make a lot of wrinkles, and she did that too.

When it was done, she sat up with her forearms folded across her breasts, thighs clamped, and looked at the man.

Walter Vale shot her once in the upper chest.

He watched her body bob and roll like a Cigarette boat in a bouncy anchorage.

And then he sat on the living-room couch to wait for R.J. Kreely. Shoving aside the pack of jade dogs, he sprawled his feet out on the coffee table. Excellent shoes, those.

AFTERMATH

SUNLIGHT LENT THE SCENE AN INCONGRUOUSLY CHEERY air. This was vacation light, light meant to be frolicked in, beach balls tossed to toddlers, Frisbees flipped, the kind of morning light in which self-serious surfers bob on gentle swells while zinc-oxided tourists munch potato chips on the beach and brush sand out of the youngsters' suits before it chafes their little butts raw. On Omnium Beach tourists ceased their play, packed up toys, masks, snorkels, fins, food, towels, lotions, unguents, Handi Wipes, and stood solemn-faced at the edge of the road, staring out across the smoking yellow and russet corpses. What had happened here?

Children wept, and the elderly trembled. Some of the latter had seen it before; they knew what war meant. Down the hill, squatters emerged from their hovels into the light to watch, to ask each other *why?* There was simply no sense to it. Surfers in wet suits hotfooted it across the road and gathered in a semicircle at the entrance to upper Main Street.

"Radical," observed one.

"Gnarly," added a second.

"I hope I never get to be an adult."

Emergency vehicles arrived from Tequesta Key, from townships on the mainland side of Small Hope Bay, and from points west. Their strobes pulsed, twinkled, and fluttered; their sirens whooped and cried. White-clad stretcher bearers hustled to and fro. Battle-shocked combatants murmured prayers to their Blessed Savior as they were borne from the field. Their broken limbs flopped at sickening angles. Many of the injured were in shock, babbling.

The Volunteer Firefighters of Tequesta Key careened up in a hook and ladder, six ardent volunteers following in six elevated pickup trucks. Sweating like rubber-wear enthusiasts in their black slickers, the firemen alighted, bustled about with their gear, bellowed at obstructing gawkers, unrolled their six-inch hose—hot to trot, ready to extinguish any conflagration you could come up with. But nothing was burning.

"Aw shit," said a disappointed volunteer.

"It ain't too late. Any one of them things could blow right up."

TV newshounds jogged down the hill for some live closeups, while their colleagues hung out of circling helicopters for the panoramic perspective shots. A rerouted C-130 reconnaissance aircraft from Homestead roared in low over the scene, and a Coast Guard chopper hovered, trying to determine whether the destruction below was drug-related.

Back on the ground, police contingents squabbled over who had jurisdiction. Nobody wanted it. The man who screwed this one up would find himself picking shit with the chickens. The contingents could agree only that the tourists and the surfers ought to get the fuck back on the beach and *play*. The cops hauled out bullhorns and told them so. And since the state troopers had a bilinguist on the scene, they had him repeat the order in Spanish, a language no one else present understood.

Sheriff Plotner skidded to a stop, flasher and siren going, a half mile from Main Street, his path impeded by this clot of emergency vehicles. The heat sapped him upside the head as soon as he opened his door, and the trek to the scene left him gasping against an ambulance fender. Hotter than a fresh-fucked fox in a forest fire.

However, he forgot the heat when he got a look at Omnium Settlement, *his* town. He stared slack-jawed at the smoking dozers cheek by jowl. One, a red one, lay on its side, and a yellow one had been blown upside down, treads pointing skyward like the legs of a dead cockroach. Christ, what force could do that, demolish a fleet of earth-moving machines? Who had that kind of military capability? Castro? Iranian Muslin extremists? What the fuck was there in south Florida for Muslins? Dick. Must be Castro. . . . But then, it might be anti-Castro cadres from Miami. . . .

A medic scurried from cop to cop, trying to establish who was in charge here.

"I am, goddamnit! Right here. Sheriff Lincoln Plotner."

The medic saluted, then said, "I have a casualty report, sir."

"Who the hell are you!"

213

"Steven Schwartz. Medalert Ambulance Service, Inc. We got"—he consulted his notebook—"seven fractures of the outer extremities, four of those compound, nine fractures to the thoracic region, four concussions, three spinal injuries of unknown severity, nine dislocations of major joints, internal injuries also of unknown severity, and just a shitload of cuts and contusions. All in all, I'd say we got off pretty light under the circumstances."

"What circumstances!" Sheriff Plotner wanted to know.

"I saw this before. Up in Quang Tri Province near the DMZ. Only one thing can do this kind of shit, Sheriff."

"What!"

"Incoming."

"Incoming what!"

"Rockets. I'm talking Russian-made SAMs here, Sheriff."

Video cameras whirled on the word "rockets," and reporters converged.

"Rockets? What rockets?"

"Terrorists?"

Boom mikes swung in over the sheriff's head—he knocked the more aggressive away with his hat—and the press began bumping each other for position. "Did you say rockets, Sheriff?" The sheriff was suddenly surrounded.

"Whose rockets, Sheriff?"

"PLO?"

"Hezbollah?"

"Right to Life?"

Just then an injured combatant crested the hill on a stretcher carried by two skinny bearers.

"Step aside, give me room, get the fuck outta here—" The press parted for Sheriff Plotner as he made his way to the casualty. It was time for some answers.

The casualty was a big man. The stretcher bearers strained and wavered under his weight. His clothes were bloody. He whimpered and bleated, muttering prayers to the Holy Mother of Jesus in the Field for delivering him from the jaws of death. He wore only one boot.

"What happened here?" the sheriff demanded.

The man, clearly in shock, slowly rolled his battered head toward the sheriff and came face-to-face with twenty-five ambitious reporters, print and electronic, jabbering inquiries at him. There were prizes, accolades, jobs in New York and Washington awaiting the best coverage of rocket attacks on innocent construction workers. The man's pained eyes went round with terror. His bottom lip quavered. Then he screamed from deep in his soul, as if at another onrushing twelve-cylinder Caterpillar Earthmaster.

The press recoiled a step but quickly recovered and surged inward—hot shit: real-life emotion. Real-life emotion looked fabulous on TV, like that cracker from last week who ran over his infant daughter with his swamp buggy, great stuff all around, real pain. They pursued the casualty in a surging, compressing clot all the way to the ambulance, where they got some terrific ambulance-door-closing material.

That, momentarily, left the sheriff alone, where he could *think*. The other cops waited, smirking, to see Sheriff Lincoln Plotner, Big Al Broadnax's right nut, fuck up and humiliate himself.

The last victim was being carried up the hill. To get a leg up on the press, the sheriff waddled down to meet him. He brought the bearers to a halt.

"What happened here?" the sheriff demanded.

This last victim's left eye was swollen shut, and his front two teeth were missing. "Christ!" he whistled through the gap. "It was hideous!" The victim seemed to have had a mustache, but the left side of it was singed or ripped off. "Hideous, I tell you! I ain't seen nothin' so hideous since Pork Chop Hill!"

"Yes, but what happened?" The sheriff tried the gentle approach, taking the man's hand in his own, patting it.

"They just kept comin' at us, wave after wave of them!"

"Of what?"

"Red bulldozers!"

"Uh, what red bulldozers?"

"Every red dozer in the world!"

Things were not coming clear. "What were all those dozers doing here?" That was more specific.

"We was hired to knock down the town."

"Hired by who?"

"Big Al Broadnax."

Sheriff Plotner studied the battlefield. There were red bulldozers and yellow bulldozers. "You were on a yellow dozer?"

The last victim nodded vigorously.

"Sheriff," said the rear stretcher bearer, a pockmarked kid in his late teens, "we better get this man out of the sun."

"I'm conducting a goddamn investigation here!" The last victim's eyes were rolling around as if at a celestial tennis match. He was about to pass out. "Who hired the red ones?"

"Bikes."

"Bikes?" Was he delirious? Wait! "Sikes? Do you mean Donald Sikes?"

"Whatever."

"Look, Sheriff, we'll lose our job if this guy cashes his check."

"Okay, go."

It was about this time that Doom and Rosalind arrived from the hospital and parked behind the sheriff's black-and-white. Wordlessly, they hiked to the top of Main Street. "Good God," Rosalind muttered.

"Look," said Doom, ducking behind an ambulance fender, "it's Sikes."

"Where?"

"Right there—next to the fire truck."

"The pudgy guy?" Donny Sikes reminded Rosalind of the fat boy from high school who had b.o. and was good in chemistry. "We better get out of here."

The smoke had been plain to see from Big Al Broadnax's Greco-Moorish mansion down the beach. He insisted that Snack load him aboard his specially designed handicap van, with license plates that said BIG AL!, and drive him to the scene. Snack lowered his old man to the hot pavement and wheeled him up for a close look.

"Get the fuck aside!" Big Al bellowed at cops, fire fighters, and gawkers. "Get out of my stinking way! Can't you see I'm an old man!" When Snack had rolled him to Main Street, he began shouting questions. This was his town, and he wanted to know what the stink had happened here, damn it. But nobody would tell him. "Fools! Imbeciles! Where's Frankie O'Mera!" he demanded.

"In the hospital," somebody told him.

"What the hell's he doing there!"

Snack caught a glimpse of Doom and Rosalind hunkering behind an ambulance, but his father didn't seem to notice.

"Where's Lucas Hogaboom!" Big Al wanted to know. Big Al had been asking that question ever since he'd sent Lucas to knock off Doom Loomis. "Get me Lucas Hogaboom!"

"He's not around, Dad."

"Where is he? Is he in the hospital, too?"

"I don't know. Maybe he's in jail," said Snack.

"Then get him out! Where's that nincompoop sheriff of mine!"

"Right here," said Sheriff Plotner, ascending the hill after touring the battlefield. Nincompoop, huh? Sheriff Plotner was glad to be betraying this old coot. He nodded at Snack, who stood behind his father's chair, then said to Big Al, "Did you hire bulldozers, Mr. B.?"

"Yeah, I hired—who the hell did I hire, Sennacherib?"

"I don't know, Dad. You didn't tell me you hired anybody."

"Well, I hired somebody. O'Mera! That's right, Frankie O'Mera, a mick!"

"Did you hire red bulldozers or yellow bulldozers?" asked the sheriff.

"How the hell would I know! Red, blue, pink, who gives a rat's ass!"

"What did you hire them to do, Mr. B.?"

"To tear down the town. Not that's it's any of your stinking business!"

"Well, you can't tear down a town in Broadnax County without a whole raft of clearances and variances. It's the law."

"It's my county, you cunt!"

"Well, no sir, it ain't. It's a county of laws, and the law says you can't just tear down towns whenever you feel like it."

"Have you gone crazy, Plotner?"

"Do you own the land down there, Mr. B.?"

"What! Of course I own it! My father *made* that land! Without my father that land would still be a sinkhole of a sweaty swamp!"

Doom and Rosalind peeked out over the ambulance's hood to see Donny Sikes saunter up to Sheriff Plotner, but they couldn't hear what Donny said when he got there.

What he said was this: "I own the land, Sheriff—in conjunction with my partner, Mr. Broadnax. Good afternoon, Mr. Broadnax."

"Partner?" squinted Big Al.

"Donald Sikes is the name."

Sheriff Plotner studied the soft little man. What was he trying to pull? "I guess you have papers to prove that, Mr. Sikes."

"Indeed I do, Sheriff. I don't of course have those papers on my person, but I would be happy to present them to the proper authorities. You see, Mr. Broadnax and I got our signals crossed. We each hired competing construction firms, and apparently an altercation ensued."

"An altercation? You call this an altercation?" said Sheriff Plotner. "Looks like war to me!" He wished Doom were around to help him.

"I take full responsibility, Sheriff, and I'm prepared to make good any damages to property and person," said Donny Sikes with a smile meant to be charming.

"How is it Mr. Broadnax didn't recognize you, his own partner?"

"It's my eyes," lied Big Al. "Bright sun gets me in the

218

eyes. I got bad eyes. Ain't that right, Sennacherib? I got bad eyes?"

"That's right, Dad." Snack exchanged glances with Sheriff Plotner, but neither knew what to do, except to play along.

"Well," said the sheriff, who was through playing along. "I want all construction—and destruction—to cease and desist right now till we sort things out. See what laws have been violated."

"Are you nuts! Who the fuck do you think you are! You get in my way, you end up directing elementary-school urchins across the street!"

"And another thing. I want these dead bulldozers out of here by tomorrow this time, and I want to see their owners in my office right after that. Otherwise you're all under arrest." With that the sheriff turned snappily on his heel and walked off to complete his investigation. He felt great.

"You slut! Who does the cunt slut think he is!"

"Why don't we have a little chat, Mr. Broadnax?" suggested Donny Sikes. "Don't you think it's time we talked things over before they get out of hand?"

"So talk."

"In private."

"How about in the van?" suggested Snack Broadnax.

A LITTLE CHAT

SNACK PUSHED BIG AL ONTO THE BOARDING PLATFORM, and when he activated the mechanism, his father rose to floorboard level. Big Al rolled himself on into the van. Donny Sikes climbed in behind Big Al and sat on the jump seat while Snack stowed the boarding platform, slid behind the wheel, and started the engine to get the air-conditioning going. He adjusted his rearview mirror onto Donny's face.

"Let's get right down to brass tacks, Mr. Broadnax—"

"To what?"

"Brass tacks."

"Who gives a fuck about tacks!"

"Skip it. This is ridiculous, what happened here. It's going to cost us both real money, and we didn't accomplish a thing except to call a lot of attention to ourselves. Besides which there's some funny business going on here—"

"You tried to blow me up, you whore!"

"No, I did not. A disloyal ex-employee of mine tried to do that. He's been taken care of now. But that's the kind of thing I'm talking about."

"What is?"

"Funny business." Had Donny Sikes known just how stupid this Big Al was, he might have handled things differently. Yet he still needed to be careful, because stupid people were dangerous; they didn't respond predictably to stimuli.

"You sent that punk Loomis to sell me a phony deed!"

Donny said no again, that Doom Loomis did that on his own and that he, Donald Sikes, had nothing to do with it. "Mr. Broadnax, I propose that you and I join forces, that we let bygones be bygones. Let the past die and think about the future. Perfection Park is the future. You see, Mr. Broadnax, we have a common enemy in this punk, as you rightly call him, Doom Loomis. His father bought up Omnium land with our money and siphoned it off into a phony corporation called Palmetto Properties, which he controlled and which upon his death reverted to his son. They were in it together, don't you see? Discovering the attempted swindle, I in good faith encouraged the younger Loomis to sell me his interests in Palmetto Properties for a fair price. He did so. Then he turned around and tried to sell you the same interests."

"The slut's pulling a fast one."

"Ex-actly. When he sold me his interests in Palmetto Properties, he agreed to leave the state. Well, he didn't. In fact, he's right over there."

"What? Where? Lucas didn't—?"

Donny Sikes leaned over the front seat and pointed out the windshield. "There—see him, getting into that truck?"

Big Al wheeled himself up behind the front seat to see— Lucas didn't kill him! What the fuck was taking him so long!

Rosalind started her truck. Doom scrunched down in the passenger seat behind the dashboard. "I was afraid of that," said Doom. "That was always the chink in the plan, that those two would get together one day and compare notes."

"Do you think they saw us?"

"Probably."

"What are we going to do?"

"I think we'd better get back to the boat. Rosalind, I'm afraid I've ruined things by coming here to see the bulldozers."

"It's hard to skip a bulldozer battle in your own hometown."

"Yeah."

"Should we drive right past the van?"

"Otherwise we'll get trapped up at the north end of the island. . . . On the plus side, Snack's in the van. He'll tell us what they're planning."

"Okay, get down."

"I'm down."

"Here goes—"

As Doom and Rosalind drove past, Big Al said, "Look! It's that hag Rosalind, the crone whore! Look at that, Sennacherib, it's your bitch sister-in-law with the pox!"

". . . The turncoat," muttered Snack.

"In short, Mr. Broadnax, we've got to get rid of this Doom Loomis once and for all," said Donny Sikes.

"I already got a man on it," said Big Al, thinking that first they'd eliminate Loomis, then he'd figure a way to cut this Sikes punk right out of the picture. "That punk

DALLAS MURPHY

Loomis kidnapped my own son, didn't he, Sennacherib?"

"Yes, Dad."

"Is he a pro?" Donny wondered.

"Who?"

"The man you have on it."

"A pro what?"

"A professional, uh, eliminator."

"He's a sex offender. But he does what I tell him. Sennacherib, get me Lucas Hogaboom."

"He's gone, Dad. Nobody's seen Lucas for days."

"There's my point," said Donny Sikes. "We need a pro."

Snack pointed out that nobody knew where this punk Loomis was hiding out.

"That's why you need a pro, Sennacherib. Pros find their people. That's part of what they're paid for."

Big Al asked Sennacherib if he knew any professional killers.

"No, Dad."

"Well, I do," said Donny Sikes. "I've used him before, on three separate occasions, and I can recommend him highly."

Donny thought maybe Big Al had died, but he was just thinking. Big Al said, "Sennacherib, would you do me a favor?"

It was always a bad sign when his old man was polite. "Yes, Dad?"

"Would you go over and tell that shit pot of a sheriff he better get in touch with me today? Tell him if he don't, then he's washed up in Broadnax County."

Snack sat rooted in indecision. The old man was clearly trying to get rid of him. Why? Yet he didn't have much choice but to obey. Tears welled up in Snack's eyes. His own father was plotting Doom's murder with another killer. There was no hope now. Only death and sadness would come of this. "Yes, Dad." Snack got out of the car and approached the sheriff, who was himself trying to figure out what to do now.

"He's a nice boy," said Donny Sikes. "Do you know he

222

came to me to plead for your safety when he thought I was trying to blow you up?"

"Aww, he did?"

"That's how I knew Roger Vespucci was a villain."

That warmed the cockles of Big Al's heart. His boy loved him. "Sennacherib's a loyal boy, but he's sensitive. That's why I sent him away."

"Why?"

" 'Cause I got an idea. We don't know where to find this punk Loomis, am I right?"

"Yes."

"Well, I know how to get Loomis out in the open."

"How?"

Sheriff Plotner figured that the first thing to do was get these vehicles off the road. The crowd of gawkers was growing by the minute. Pretty soon Ted Koppel would show up. He had to break this up. "Hello, Snack," said the sheriff, waving at gawkers, emergency vehicles, surfers.

"Hello, Sheriff."

"Hey, you all right, son?"

"No. My father and Sikes are sitting in the van over there, planning to hire a killer to murder Doom."

"Damn! Your old man's goin' too far, Snack."

"I know it. We got to warn Doom. I don't know if I'm gonna be able to get away. Oh, my dad sent me over here to order you to call him today."

"I'm sorry, Snack, but your old man's on the shit list as of now. I ain't callin' him no more."

"Okay, Sheriff. Just don't hurt him."

"Hey, why don't I go over there and arrest them both?"

"That would blow it, Sheriff. We'd never find out anything. That's what I'm doin' spyin' on the old man."

"Yeah. Okay."

"By snatching that bimbo Rosalind Rock," said Big Al Broadnax. "That'll bring Loomis out sure as shootin'."

Maybe old man Broadnax wasn't such a moron after all. In fact, he and Donny had a lot in common. But of course he wouldn't say anything like that to Gramps. "Hmm, maybe you've got something there. Maybe we could make it look like a murder-suicide. Happens every day all over the country. Get rid of them both with no questions asked. Good." Donny Sikes offered his hand. Big Al shook it with his own gnarled hand, which felt to Donny like a bunch of bent pencils.

Snack returned to the van. "He says okay."

"Here's my card. Call any time, night or day." Donny Sikes got out of the van. "I'll be in touch, partner," he said to Big Al. "Nice to see you again, Sennacherib."

"Yeah," said Snack.

Donny walked back to his own car and ordered the purser to return him to the *King Don*, where he could make a private phone call.

"We got this punk Sikes just where we want him," chuckled Big Al Broadnax.

"That's great, Dad."

BAD VIBRATIONS

PROPPED ON PILLOWS IN HIS HOLIDAY INN BED, WALTER Vale watched TV, smoked Kools, and waited for the news to come on. He fed another quarter into the vibrating machine and felt certain erotic tingles, which gratified him, since he had taken the trouble of changing a twenty.

"I'm Biff Champion, and this is 'Live at Five, the Eyes and Ears of South Florida.' Today's top story involves murder and suicide in exclusive Poinciana Estates. We take you live to the scene with Kitty Calhoun. Over to you, Kitty—"

"Thank you, Biff." Holding a microphone to her mouth,

Kitty Calhoun stood on the sidewalk in front of R. J. Kreely's split ranch. She had nice pointy tits, Walter Vale observed, vibrating. "Poinciana Estates was rocked today by another chapter in the seemingly endless book of violence in south Florida—" Behind Kitty, two black guys in white coats lugged a rubber body bag out of the split ranch and loaded it into an ambulance while uniformed and plainclothes cops looked on. "Though Dade County police have refused comment pending investigation, our exclusive sources on the scene tell a sordid story of murder and suicide.

" 'Live at Five' has learned that Mr. R. J. Kreely, the garbage-disposal king, was conducting an illicit affair with his housekeeper, identified as Conchita Castro, twenty-five, of Opa Locka. Ms. Castro's unclothed body was found in the bedroom, shot once in the chest. Mr. Kreely was found in the living room dead of an apparently self-inflicted gunshot wound to the left temple. The same handgun was used in both deaths. A blank sheet of paper and an uncapped pen were found near Mr. Kreely's body, and sources speculate that he was about to write a suicide note, but for reasons unknown he never did. Mrs. Kreely, visiting her mother in Detroit, could not be reached for comment. Mr. Kreely's neighbors are stunned, left with the knowledge that if it can happen here, it can happen anywhere. Kitty Calhoun reporting live from Poinciana Plantation. Back to you at the station, Biff—"

Pretending to be troubled by the story, a real sensitive anchor, Biff Champion shook his head. "In other stories, a rogue alligator—"

Walter Vale punched off the TV with his remote device, stretched in a languorous, self-satisfied way and dropped another quarter into the vibrator box. He fantasized Kitty Calhoun naked, trying to cover herself.

Then the telephone rang. "Walter Freed here," said Walter Vale.

"Hello, Mr. Freed, it's Mr. Shipton," said Donny Sikes. "I'd like to discuss a job with you."

"Always happy to oblige," said Walter Vale, tingling. This guy Shipton was getting to be a regular.

MESSENGER OF DOOM

AS SOON AS HE RETURNED HIS FATHER TO THE GRECO-Moorish mansion and deposited him under the leafy hydrangea in the garden, Snack tried to call Doom at the boat, but Doom hadn't returned yet. Unable to wait, Snack jumped on his Norton, sped across Hurricane Hole Creek and up Route One at ninety plus. Forty minutes later he parked his bike in front of Black Caesar's Yacht Club. He felt a surge of relief to see Doom, Longnecker, Holly, and the Annes sitting in *Staggerlee*'s cockpit.

"They mean to kill you, Doom!"

"Who?"

"Sikes and my old man, they're hiring a hitter."

Holly moaned as much at the news as at the fact that Longnecker was grinning. Holly knew that grin. No good ever came of that grin, and the Annes got it on film.

"They saw you and Rosalind at the bulldozers."

"Is it Lucas Hogaboom?"

"No, a pro. Nobody's seen Lucas for days. They're hiring some killer Donny Sikes knows."

"So let's us hit them first," suggested Longnecker.

"We ain't gonna hit my old man."

"It looks to me like your old man is in true need of a hitting," Longnecker insisted.

"That's true, but we still ain't gonna hit him."

"Okay, Snack," said Doom, who had no inclination to hit.

"Then let's do Donny Sikes," said Longnecker.

"What if we all just split?" Holly wanted to know.

"We could," said Doom, but he knew they wouldn't. "Do they know where I am?"

"No, but Sikes said killers find people. It's their job."

"Could you find out what they know?"

"I think so. The old man trusts me."

"What about Rosalind?"

"What about her?" asked Snack.

"What did they say about her?"

"Just the usual slut stuff. The old man hates her."

"Where's Rosalind now?" asked Holly.

"At the dive shop. She had a lesson scheduled this afternoon," said Doom.

Longnecker went out to his car and returned lugging a duffel bag loaded with heavy objects. No one needed to ask what was in the bag. He went directly below, cleaned and loaded the objects.

As, piece by piece, Longnecker assembled his arsenal on the table, Doom phoned Total Immersion, but no one answered. He then called Bert, Marvis, Duncan, and Professor Goode at the trailer park and told them to stay inside, lock their doors and don't answer for anyone until they hear from him. After that he called Lisa Up-the-Grove, but Rosalind wasn't there either. Doom told Lisa to tell Rosalind to call him immediately if she heard anything. He suggested that Lisa might want to find another place to stay for a while and if she wanted to stay on the boat, she'd be welcome.

"You remember what happened to Jackson soldiers who come into the 'Glades after Seminoles?" she asked.

"No."

"They never come out again."

"I see."

But still no one answered at Total Immersion.

"Snack, would you go back home and try to learn some details?"

"No matter what happens, we ain't gonna hurt him. Right? Say it."

"We won't hurt him."

Snack looked at Longnecker.

"Sure, sure."

"Even if he deserves it."

"He sure deserves it," said Longnecker.

After Snack had left, Doom said, "There's still Roger Vespucci. Maybe he'll do it to Donny before Donny can do it to us."

"He's pretty slow about it."

"For all we know he's in Norway."

"He didn't look bright enough to split."

Doom agreed, but perhaps the same could be said of him.

ROSALIND, MEET WALTER

WALTER VALE STAKED OUT TOTAL IMMERSION DIVING. He sat across the street in his car and watched five students leave. They stowed their gear in their trunks and drove away. He waited awhile longer to be sure before he entered the shop. Finding himself alone, he turned the sign on the door around to say SORRY, WE'RE CLOSED.

He heard sounds, metallic clicks and clunks, from the back room, but no one was visible. He browsed the equipment displays, finding all that rubber clothing, instruments, mouthpieces, and things titillating. He'd seen most of the stuff before on Jacques Cousteau, never in real. Maybe when he had time he'd take up scuba diving, but then he'd have to deal with hammerhead sharks.

She was a lanky brunette, and she was wearing a wet suit, damp hair, nice tits, her thighs didn't touch at the top. He smiled at Rosalind.

"Hi," she said. "What can I do for you?"

"Actually I need you to take off that cute suit."

"Beat it, asshole."

Walter Vale struck her backhanded across the mouth. The blow didn't knock her down, but it stunned her, bloodied her lips, whipped back her head. Instantly, Walter Vale hit her again, this time with his fist, in the solar plexus. She crumpled in a heap, gasping helplessly for breath. He stood over her and said, "What do you do when you close?"

Rosalind didn't know what he was talking about, but she couldn't have answered anyway. Walter waited until she could breathe.

"When you close. What do you do? Do you turn out the lights, do you bar the windows?"

"The shade—I pull down the shade."

Walter did that, then he turned out the lights. Casually, with a practiced hand, he removed his silenced automatic from his waistband, cocked and pointed it at Rosalind.

"Come on, please don't do that," pleaded Rosalind from the floor.

"Either you take off that suit or I shoot some holes in it," grinned Walter Vale.

Rosalind removed her wet suit. She was naked underneath.

Lately Walter Vale had been lucky that way. "Stand up."

Rosalind did so. She made no move to cover herself. Body aching, she stared at him defiantly.

That fascinated Walter Vale. "Do you have any tape? I like that silver kind best."

"In the workroom."

"Show me."

He made Rosalind tear off three-foot-long strips. Then he taped her hands together behind her back. He used another strip to close her mouth, wrapping the tape around and around her head. He ordered her to sit, and he taped her ankles and knees together. "Now, what we're going to do is wait for dark. Then we'll take a little ride."

Rosalind laid her head on the floor and squeezed her eyes shut. Good-bye, Doom.

After dark Walter Vale backed his Budget rental up to the front door and popped open the trunk. He dragged Rosalind by the ankles to the door, made sure the coast was clear, then loaded her into the trunk. Her big black eyes, round with fright, peered up at him. He heard her whimper as he slammed the lid.

Even the toughest whimpered when you slammed the lid on them.

TADPOLES

DAY HAD PASSED TO NIGHT WITH NO INTERVENING DUSK, as if nature were in a rush to get it over with, by the time Snack returned from Black Caesar's to the Greco-Moorish Broadnax mansion. He wished he could hate his old man simply and directly, but he couldn't. Every time he looked upon his father's gnarled, useless legs, anger vanished, and he wanted to hoist him onto his shoulders and carry him safely through what remained of his life. What did the Bible say about sons who betrayed their fathers? Snack couldn't really remember, but it wasn't good. Such sons sure as shit never found their way into the Kingdom of Heaven. Snack sat on a marble bench near his father's chair.

A facial tic had developed. About every fifteen seconds something activated it. Big Al's eye would blink, his lip would curl, and the entire right side of his face would scrunch up in wrinkles. That was something new. What did the Bible say about evil made manifest in the faces of men? Or was that just what happened to you when you got old? Snack missed his big brother. There was still something of Claudius left on Big Al's face, screwed up as it was, and when Big Al went, so would the last of Claudius.

Snack remembered the tadpoles Claudius had found and raised to frogs. Claudius had built a little environment for them, explaining to Snack—who was, what, four?—that frogs were amphibians, which meant that they live both on land and in the water. Snack and Claudius kept records of their growth and transitions, marking an X on the calendar when their legs appeared as indistinct little floppy things. They had changed so fast it was frightening. One day they were tadpoles, next day they were frogs. Then the day after that, they had hopped out of their amphibian environment and vanished. Why'd they do that? There was nothing for them elsewhere but death. Snack remembered Claudius sobbing, and seeing that, Snack sobbed, too, when they found the first of the frogs, stiff, dry, and petrified beneath the chifforobe. You could hold the dead frog by the flipper, and the rest of him stuck straight out. That's what death was—stiff dryness. Dry stiffness. Like his father's face. Regardless what the Bible said.

"I don't want you riding that motorcycle around town, Sennacherib."

"Why, Dad?"

"Only white trash ride on two wheels."

"Okay, Dad, whatever you say." The truth here, Snack knew, was that he *was* white trash, and so was his old man. "So who's Sikes sending after this punk Loomis?"

"I don't ask. Don't you ask neither. We don't want to know. See, if we know, then they can get us as excesses after the fact."

"But don't we already know? I mean, you just discussed it with him, right?"

Big Al frowned at his son, the way he frowned when Snack got picked up for speeding. "Who heard us, son?"

"Nobody. Just you and me, Dad."

"Exactly! See, son, after Sikes gets rid of that punk Loomis, we're going to have that stinking sheriff arrest him for murder. Two birds with one stone, get it?" The rictus grin arrived at the same instant as the tic, a grimace of hideous fear on the face of a man buried prematurely. "That's one thing you've got to learn, son, because someday you're going to inherit all this."

"What's that, Dad?"

"What?"

"What I got to learn."

"I don't know. . . ." Big Al had drifted off somewhere like a frog. "This Sikes is scum. So's his whole family. His grandfather was scum. You remember what his grandfather did to my father. Ruined my father because he was jealous. Throckmorton killed my father as sure as if he'd wrapped a rope around his neck and squeezed. My dad trusted Throckmorton, and look what happened to him. *That's* the thing you need to learn! You can't trust nobody who ain't kin! That's what my father taught me, and now I'm teaching you."

"I get it, Dad. But what are we going to do after we send Sikes up for the murder of that punk Loomis?"

"Then we're going to build Perfection Park, only we ain't going to call it that, and it ain't going to be a hotel for any punk with the price of admission. I been ruminating on this. Sitting here in my chair. Ruminating. We're going to build a museum!"

"A museum?"

"*Yes!*"

"What kind of museum, Dad?"

"A Broadnax museum! You'll be the curator after I'm gone! We—the Broadnaxes—we *are* the history of Florida! The Colonel A. C. Broadnax Memorial Museum. And we're going to use Donald Sikes's money to do it with!" Big Al Broadnax began to cackle, to gasp and cackle again. Chest fluids gurgled as he cackled and gasped and cackled.

"Excuse me, sir—" It was Wing Li, bowing and scraping with a telephone in his hand—

"What do you want!"

"Telephone call, sir. A Mr. Donald Sikes on the line, sir."

"Give it to me." As Wing Li plugged the phone into

the garden jack, Big Al said to Snack, "Son, would you get me a slice of key lime pie?"

Wing Li wondered why the old son of a bitch sent his heir to wait on him while his butler was standing three feet away.

"Sure, Dad, be my pleasure."

Wing Li waited for further orders. "Get out," Big Al ordered.

Snack went directly to the extension in the hall. Wing Li went directly to the extension in the kitchen.

Donald Sikes said, "It's done."

"You got her?" said Big Al.

"Yep, got her. Say, Mr. Broadnax, I understand this Rosalind Rock is your daughter-in-law."

"She used to be. But my son is dead. What's it to you?"

"Nothing. I hear this Rosalind Rock is some looker. My man tells me. He's got her naked. I was going over to have a look. Want to come along?"

"I got other plans. . . . Where do you have her?"

"Safe."

"We got to let Loomis know where you got her. Otherwise, what's the point? How are we going to do that?"

"You let me handle the details, Mr. Broadnax. Besides, we'll want to wait a few days to let Loomis get scared and careless. My man won't mind the delay. He's having a good time. If you change your mind about seeing her, just give me a call." Donny Sikes hung up.

Snack slid down the wall and hugged his knees to his chest. Rosalind! Then he found himself in the garden with a slice of key lime pie in his hand. When he noticed it there, he hurled it at Big Al. Leaves and fronds fluttered as pieces of pie hit them; the plate shattered somewhere.

"Rosalind!"

"Wha—?"

"It was you! It was *your* idea!" Snack screamed at the sky like a gutted animal. He began tearing out plants by the roots. The old man's favorites first. The hydrangea, the orchids—

"You! You!"

He crushed the mangoes, pomegranates, and guavas in his fists, threw their remains at his father—

"I'll never be able to save your ass now!"

The viburnums, pyracanthas, sapodillas went down next. Shreds of silk fluttered like ashes after an eruption.

"He's going to kill her! Rosalind! I tell you what, Dad— If that guy hurts Rosalind, then I turn you in! You'll rot in Raiford!"

Big Al Broadnax couldn't believe his senses. His garden looked like Verdun—his own son, his heir, turning him in.

"Shut up! Don't you speak! If you do, I might kill you myself!"

Snack started in on the various palms. Once he had ripped away the fronds, he jumped up and down on the fiberglass trunks until they were flat—

"You're a dead man anyway. Do you know that? Doom and them, they're going to kill you! Hell, Longnecker's ready to kill you right now!"

"What? You betrayed me! How do you know what they—? You betrayed me! Ahhhh! My only son—!"

"Just shut up! What am I going to do? . . ."

"You been with them all the time!"

"Yeah, that's right. My kidnapping—it was all a fraud. I knew you were doing something crazy! I knew you were doing something to get yourself killed! Now you have! What am I going to do? . . . Where are they keeping her?"

"They didn't even kidnap you, you slut?"

Snack collected himself. He had to. He had to think. How could he find out about Rosalind? He had to be smart. Wily, like Doom. You couldn't ever tell what was going on inside Doom's head. He was calm. Snack had to be calm. "Okay, Dad, you're finished here. I mean, you can go on living in the house if Longnecker doesn't kill you— but otherwise, you're finished. You're—what the fuck do they say?—you're unfit to have affairs. I'm taking over right now."

"Over my dead corpse!"

"Exactly. . . . Wait! I got it!" Calm, calm. . . . "Now I want that card Sikes gave you."

"No!"

Snack advanced on his father, who started spinning his wheels to escape. There was no escape from Snack. He grabbed the handles behind his father's head and shook him out of his chair onto the floor as if he were crumbs on the seat. There Snack searched his father's person until he came up with Donny Sikes's card. It said *King Don* and a phone number. Snack wheeled his father's empty chair out of the ruined garden, leaving the man himself on the floor screaming obscene oaths.

After practicing several times until he got his voice under control, Snack called the number. "Hello, Mr. Sikes, this is Sennacherib Broadnax calling for my father."

"Call me Donny. All my friends do."

"Okay, Donny. Call me Snack."

"Snack?"

"That's what my friends call me. I'm calling to say that Dad changed his mind. He would like to see Rosalind. Like your man's got her. . . . Naked. I guess the old goat wants to gloat." Snack was warming to it. He could hear Doom making a call like this. "Yeah, he'd love to see her tonight. Naked, huh?"

"Naked if I know my man."

Snack and Donny giggled, both shooting for lasciviousness.

Donny Sikes couldn't believe the old man was that stupid, to walk right in on the scene of a crime, but if he wanted to make it easy, why should Donny demur— "Well, I'll just call my man and let him know you're on the way."

"Great, Donny. The old man'll get a kick out of it. Where do you have her?"

"Seventeen fifty Shore Road, on Tequesta Key."

"Uh, will you be there, Donny?"

"No, something's come up."

"Okay, I'll be seeing you, Donny."

"Right, Snack. Bye now." Hanging up, Donny gave a

little whoop of delight—it was almost too easy. He'd have Walter Freed kill both Rosalind and Big Al, make it look like a case of murder-suicide, beautiful to behold. Then he'd take out Doom Loomis, and Donny's way would be clear.

Snack called Doom. "It's Rosalind! Sikes kidnapped Rosalind!"

Doom sagged into the navigator's seat. The Annes were asking what? what? but Doom shushed them. "Tell me, Snack."

"Sikes hired a guy, a professional, to kidnap Rosalind so's to draw you out. I don't know who, but I know where." Snack told him where.

"How do you know this, Snack?"

". . . I heard Sikes say it."

Obviously, he had said it to Big Al. Moreover, Doom thought, how did Sikes know about Rosalind without Big Al telling him?

"There's another thing, Doom. I'm going over there. I set it up. I told Sikes that my father wanted to gloat over Rosalind." Snack thought he best not mention the part about Rosalind being naked. "The professional guy is expecting me. He's going to let me in!"

"That was brilliant."

". . . You really think so?"

"Yes! But don't do anything until we get there, okay?"

"Okay."

"What's that sound I hear? Shouting?"

"Nothing. It's a family matter," said Snack.

"Where should we meet?"

"How about Rosalind's dive shop? That's only fifteen minutes from Shore Road."

"We're leaving now—Snack, thank you."

Snack was flushed with pride. Before he left, he looked in on his father. Wing Li was hoisting Big Al onto the marble bench.

"Wing Li, that will be all for tonight. I want you to go home."

"Great," said Wing Li, who turned on his heel and left.

Snack propped his father up with pillows, comfy, then he tore the phones out of the wall. But after it was done, it seemed to have been unnecessary. Big Al wasn't going to call anybody. He had fallen limp, spent. The life had gone out of his eyes.

SHOES

ROSALIND HAD NO IDEA HOW LONG SHE HAD LAIN LIMP with fear in the dirty trunk. The car moved all the time. Hyperventilating, sweating, at first she had thought she'd smother in there, but she managed to return her breathing to normal. That, however, was small comfort, bound naked in a killer's trunk. By the end of the ride, she found herself hoping that he would shoot or strangle her, something quicker than the agonizing death that would result if he abandoned the car somewhere. She struggled against the tape, but that was hopeless and she knew it.

The car stopped, the engine died. Rosalind forgot her pain, waiting for whatever would happen next. The trunk lid popped open. Rosalind was blinded by the light. She sat up squinting as Walter Vale, grinning, loomed over her. She seemed to be inside a residential garage. Without saying a word, he pulled a black sack over her head and tied the drawstrings around her neck. Then he slit the tape around her knees and ankles and said, "Get out, dearie," but she couldn't, her legs wouldn't work, so he hauled her out. Rosalind dropped to her knees but caught herself before she fell forward on her face.

Walter Vale pulled her upright by the arm and led her into the house. Rosalind could feel carpet beneath her feet, and for a moment she forgot she was naked, Walter

Vale ogling her at will. Then the carpet gave way to a cool, hard surface, where she was left standing. She heard a chain clanking, but blind, she could do nothing except wait. He wrapped the end of the chain twice around her ankle and padlocked it there. She knew the other end would be locked to something implacable. He pulled the hood away. She was in a dark blue tile bathroom with fancy gold fixtures, chained to the base of the toilet with three feet of slack.

Walter Vale snapped open a knife right under her chin, but Rosalind figured he wasn't going to stab her after going to the trouble of chaining her up. He used the knife to cut the tape from her mouth. She gasped and said, "Who are you, what do you want?"

He didn't answer. He looked her up and down, grinning.

"Please untie my hands."

Walter Vale paused and said, "Naw." Then he walked out.

Rosalind looked at herself in the mirror. Her face was puffy, her eyes tear-stained slits. Her mouth and cheeks were raw where the tape had been removed, and blood had dried inside her lip on the left side. Silver tape still stuck to her knees and ankles. She sagged to the cool floor, leaned her back against the tub, and wept quietly.

Hours dragged.

Then something strange passed her Italian tile prison door. It was Walter Vale rolling himself along the hall in a wheelchair. Its tires left two distinct, dusty tracks behind. Walter Vale seemed amused by those tracks. He kept looking over his shoulder at them, giggling. On the way back he paused at the door, spun around in the chair to face Rosalind, who sat in a tight ball in the corner.

"This was my idea," said Walter Vale.

"I don't get it."

"Who drives a wheelchair?"

"Big Al Broadnax."

"Right. I never actually had the pleasure, but as soon as I hear he's in a wheelchair, the idea occurs to me."

"What idea?"

"What are the police going to think when they find wheelchair tracks all over the house?" Walter Vale loved to see their faces at the moment when truth dawned on them—

"Then you're going to kill me."

"Of course, dearie."

The phone rang.

"Excuse me," said Walter Vale. He wheeled himself away.

Rosalind thought about her animals. She'd never see the animals again. And Dragoon's Hammock and Lisa Up-the-Grove. And Doom. She wished that she and Doom had sailed away before it was too late. She hoped that after she'd gone, Doom would get this man, would kill him slowly.

Walter Vale returned to the bathroom, this time without benefit of the wheelchair, and said, "How about that? He's coming over himself. Seems he wants to have a look at you. A man can't get much more stupid than that."

"Who! Big Al?"

"Yeah, it seems he wants to gloat over, uh, your present condition."

"Oh please, no!"

"I was hoping you and me'd have some time to get to know each other, but things don't always work out. Too bad."

"You're going to kill us both?"

"Yeah, only it's going to look like the old man did you. Making it look like murder-suicide. That's kinda my specialty. Then it's this guy Doom Loomis's turn. But I don't give discounts for the family plan."

"Was it you? Did you kill Doom's father?"

"Yep. Also that stupid embezzler, what was his name? Ozzie. Stupid name, stupid guy. His girlfriend too. Don't remember her name. A man can't be expected to remember the names of everybody he did. You know, you look real beautiful sitting there like that. How about begging me to let you go? How about telling me you'll do anything if I let you go?"

"How about I ask you a question?"

"Shoot," grinned Walter.

"Where'd you get those alligator shoes? Nobody but asshole geeks wear alligator shoes."

The smile vanished. He kicked her in the side with his shoes, knocked her against the tub. That's where he left her.

ROGER RUNS

EMERGENCY EXIT ONLY. ALARM WILL SOUND. THIS WAS an emergency if Roger Vespucci ever saw one. So he bolted through the door at full tilt, and the alarm did indeed sound, a whooping Klaxon noise like that in submarine movies. Gown streaming in his own apparent wind, his parts flopping painfully, he sprinted through the parking lot, over a landscaped knoll with stunted cabbage palms, where he tripped over his hem and skidded in the mulch. There he crouched for a while to reconnoiter and to determine the extent of his injuries. They were slight, but he still had two problems—clothes and transport. Well, three, if you counted the gun.

Broadnax County Hospital, like many things in south Florida, was situated next to a shopping center, this one called the Pink Flamingo Plaza. The alarm still whooped. Soon security goons would show up with flashlights and conduct a general search. Roger needed to be elsewhere. He ran around to the rear of the stores and hid behind a rancid yellow dumpster. PEDRO'S CHICKEN EAT-IN OR CARRY-OUT said big white letters on the receptacle's side. So far so good. He sat down for a rest, but when his bare ass touched the still-warm blacktop, he decided to keep moving—

Just then a delivery truck pulled to a stop, its headlights lashing Roger, crouching. He ducked around to the dark side of the dumpster. The truck bore Pedro's emblem—a tap-dancing chicken in a red sombrero. The teenage driver propped his can of Bud Lite on the dash, climbed down with a tray of dead chickens, and kicked open the screen door to Pedro's kitchen. . . . Like wheels from heaven. The kid had left the engine running.

He couldn't go after Donny Sikes in a dancing chicken truck, but he might get far enough to steal something less conspicuous. He leapt aboard, located first gear, and lurched away, a couple hundred fryers behind his head.

But where was he going to go? Full of indecision, Roger drove Pedro's chicken truck along a six-lane boulevard lined with retail establishments, eat-it-and-beat-it joints, their gaudy neon come-ons flickering and flashing, drive-up banks, and gas stations bathed in the halogen yellow of mortal illness beneath two-ton signs sixty feet up in the night sky. He'd have to ditch this chicken truck soon.

He ducked blindly off the boulevard into a gridded subdivision of single-story, pastel-painted cinder-block residences. A person could spit, often did, from his kitchen window into his neighbor's carport, which, like every other carport in the subdivision, overflowed with rusting recreation gear, hibachis, bicycles, deep-sea fishing rods, snow tires, boats. Whimsical sculptures walked on the chinch-bug-infested lawns. Each street was named after an indigenous water bird. Up Sanderling Drive, down Tern Terrace, Roger Vespucci patrolled.

On Bittern Boulevard, he spotted a fat guy working under his 427 turbo-charged four-wheel-drive Dodge pickup truck with enormous knobby, reptilian tires and objects hanging from the rearview mirror. A woman held the light for him. He had an eight ball tattooed on his upper arm; something was behind the eight ball, but Roger couldn't make it out.

Roger pulled right into their driveway. A Doberman

staked out in the patchy lawn barked, snapped and snarled, and leapt against its chain. The fat guy slid out from under his truck and, with his woman, peered coldly at this tap-dancing chicken truck from out of the wild blue yonder. Roger didn't want to alight with his pale ass hanging out of his garment in such a way as to alienate strangers, so he waited until they came to him.

After a while they did, keeping their distance. The man wore greasy cut-off jeans and a Weekeewachie Springs T-shirt under which his hairy pink belly peeked. It was "Mom" behind the eight ball. The woman, who still held the light, was built like a fire hydrant with pendulous breasts, their spread barely repressed beneath a lime-green stretch halter.

"Shuddup, Nestor!" bellowed the man. The Doberman flopped on its side and panted. "You lost, man?"

"Look," said Roger from behind the wheel, "I got at least fifty chickens in this truck. I'll trade you fifty chickens for a shirt, pants, and a pair of shoes."

The man's expression, blank, didn't change. He wiped his hands on a rag and stuck it into his back pocket. Her expression didn't change either, but she turned off the light. "What, you ain't got clothes of yer own?" the man queried.

"No, I don't. I'm talking top-drawer fryers here."

"Cooked or what?" the woman asked.

"Raw. You can do them up any way you like. Have the folks over, freeze the rest."

"Make it sixty chickens," the man said, "you got your-self a deal."

"Sure, sure, sixty. Throw in a jacket and a hat, you can have every chicken in the truck. Wait—what's that there? In the carport."

"That's a Dodge Ram."

"No, that two-wheeled thing—like a motor scooter—"

"That there's a moped."

"Does it run?" Roger wondered.

"Everything I got runs. I'm a master mechanic. I used to be on the Alaska pipeline."

The woman hiked up her halter as affirmation of that.

"Great, great. Is that where you got that swell tattoo?"

"Yeah. I got others."

"Swell, swell. Look, I'll give you this whole truck and everything in it for the clothes and that moped."

The man and the woman slowly circled the truck in opposite directions. When they returned to the driver's window, the man said, "You stole this truck, ditn't you?"

"Of course I stole it," said Roger Vespucci.

KILLER

~~~~~~

LONGNECKER ARRIVED ON ROSALIND'S BOAT. THE NIGHT was calm, enabling Bert to nudge the bow right up to the high-tide line, and Longnecker hopped ashore without even getting his combat boots wet. As Bert backed away, Longnecker crept up the short beach in the dark. He crawled through the tangle of buttonwood and sea grape to the edge of the road. From there he could see the house and could hit anybody in front of it. He hosed himself down with bug spray and assumed the traditional prone position beneath the trees.

Bahamian-style, pastel pink with a white roof and white wooden hurricane shutters, the house was low and over-hung with dark vegetation. Across the street was the At-lantic Ocean, making this modest house worth about two million. The living room was lighted, but the porch was not.

Occasionally headlights passed, but no one slowed down in front of the house. Longnecker flipped the leather cover off his watch face. It was about that time. He cocked his rifle and put the safety on. Something slithered in the bushes. Snakes? He froze. Crawling up his pant leg? He rolled over onto his back and sprayed bug juice all around his position until the can emptied with a hiss. Maybe vipers, as well as insects, hated Off. It was worth a try. Another set of lights came slowly from the north. The brights flashed on and off. Right on the money.

Snack parked his father's van in the driveway, alighted, and activated the machinery that lowered the wheelchair to ground level. But it was Doom, not Big Al, who sat in the chair. His legs—and his sawed-off shotgun, which Longnecker had called an alley sweeper—were covered with a crocheted quilt. He wore a wide-brimmed straw hat slung low over his brows, and on that part of his face still showing, the Annes had done an admirable age makeup job.

Doom had never intentionally injured another person in his life, but now he was filled with resolve to change that. His heart pounded. If this man had hurt Rosalind, so much as a contusion where he gripped her arm too hard, then Doom meant to point his alley sweeper at him and pull the trigger. If that didn't have the desired effect immediately, then he'd pull it again. After that he would do the same thing to Donald Sikes and to Big Al Broadnax, then to anyone else who seemed in need of a good sweeping. Point-blank murder wasn't what he had had in mind when he came down here, and for a moment, as Snack wheeled him up the walk, Doom wondered if there had been another way, or was this simply the natural outcome of events, as Professor Goode had predicted. Perhaps he'd work that out in recollected tranquillity, if there was ever to be such a thing. Sheriff Plotner crouched in the back of the van, ready to make an arrest. He and Rosalind had had their differences, but if this man had hurt her, he'd never make it to jail alive. He would tell Ted Koppel that he had died trying to escape.

Tense and stiff, Snack rang the doorbell. Rosalind heard it from the bathroom and began to tremble. Her life would end with Big Al Broadnax smirking at her crouching naked and helpless on a shower mat.

Walter Vale peeked out under the curtain in the living room. Doom ducked his head. Snack waved at Walter Vale.

It seemed as if two days had passed by the time Walter Vale opened the front door. Doom was soaked in sweat. It ran down under his straw hat into his eyes, but he dared not lift his hand from under the quilt to wipe it away. He had no makeup on his hands.

"Well, come on in. She's waiting," grinned Walter Vale.

Snack was having trouble getting the chair up over the doorstep, so Doom didn't wait. He tore off the quilt and pointed the shotgun at Vale's head. Vale's jaw dropped, looking down the black tunnel.

"Don't move! Don't move at all!" Doom kicked Walter Vale in the shin with the combat boots Longnecker had loaned him: "You can't kill wearing Topsiders."

Vale cried out and dropped to one knee. Doom gripped the hair at the back of his head and jammed the shotgun barrel into Vale's mouth. Two front teeth dribbled down into his open collar. The ragged edge of mad rage brushed across Doom's forehead as he forced the barrel deeper, against the back of Walter Vale's throat, held it there, and ordered Vale to put his hands on top of his head.

"Search him!" Doom shouted at Snack, and the sound reverberated in his ears. "Rosalind!"

"Doom!"

"Are you hurt!"

"No!"

Doom whined with joy. "Where are you!"

"I'm in the bathroom! He's got me chained!"

"I'm coming! Longnecker!"

The kitchen door exploded open, glass jalousies flying in pieces, and there stood Longnecker. He cradled his black automatic weapon in soft hands, ready to spray the opposition in a surgical assault, leaving his friends standing, his enemies wondering where the center of their thoracic regions had gone. But everything seemed under control, and Longnecker felt slightly disappointed at the anticlimax of his kick-ass entrance.

Snack emptied Walter Vale's pockets onto the rug. There was a wallet, a dandruff-flecked comb, keys, the switchblade, and the silenced automatic. Doom still noticed in himself a deep longing to turn this man's head to mush—

Doom removed his shotgun from Walter Vale's mouth, and Vale removed his hands from the top of his head to examine his smashed dentition—

"No!" Longnecker snapped the rifle to firing position, aimed at Walter Vale's temple— "Get 'em on your head, or bid farewell to everything from here up."

Doom picked up the keys and ran into the bathroom. When he saw Rosalind naked on her knees at the end of her tether, he threw down his shotgun, dropped to his knees, and hugged her. Doom pulled at the tape that still held her arms behind her, but he couldn't get it loose. He unlocked her ankle from the toilet.

"He killed your father and he killed Ozzie and Doris. He was going to kill me and make it look like Big Al did it!"

Doom ran back into the living room, barely noticing that Sheriff Plotner had entered, and returned with Vale's knife. When he'd cut her hands free, Doom took off his Big Al jacket and helped Rosalind into it.

Blood was running down Walter Vale's chin, dropping onto the front of his white shirt as Sheriff Plotner was telling him he had the right to remain silent, anything he said could be held—

And no one saw Rosalind pick up his silenced automatic from the floor.

—against him in a court of—

"What's your name?" Doom asked him.

"Fuck you," replied Walter Vale, whistling slightly.

"Oh, this guy's something," said Longnecker.

Doom sat down on the edge of the couch. His legs felt weary and unsure of his own weight as the speeding adrenaline slowed. What were they going to do with this guy now that they had him? This guy was different. Here he was beaten, captured red-handed, and he didn't even look frightened. "Donald Sikes hired you to do this, right?"

"Donald Sikes? I never heard of him."

"You're in the can for the rest of your life," said Sheriff Plotner. "You know that, don't you? You know what happens to punks like you in Florida jails?"

"Lemme ask you something, cop," said Walter Vale. "Do you know you stink like a dead turtle?"

Doom picked up Walter Vale's wallet. It was full of driver's licenses and credit cards, all in different names. Walter Freed. Walter Valley. Walter Honnerside. Walter Simkus. Walter Love. Walter Schot. "So what was the plan?"

Walter Vale showed his bloody gums in something like a grin and said, "There was no plan. I did it because she looked sooo sweet buck naked begging for her life—"

Rosalind shot him in the right collarbone. Pop. Walter Vale spun and hit the wall. She shot him twice more, pop-pop, blood spots exploding on his chest. Either one of these would have been fatal, but Rosalind continued to shoot. Bullets pocked the wall, and one more struck Walter Vale's body. The last hit him in the forehead, causing his entire body to bounce.

"Rosalind! Stop shooting him!"

"Why!"

Silence reverberated.

"Because we'll never be able to make it look like suicide," said Doom.

The hot gun dropped from her hand.

"Forget that, pal, this is war. Out in the sunlight, no more conniving necessary," said Longnecker.

Doom hugged Rosalind, took her out into the night before she had time to look upon what she had done. Snack followed and sat with her in the front seat while Doom returned to the scene, trying to get his mind to work.

Longnecker picked up Walter Vale's gun and put it in his jacket pocket.

"I've seen suicide before," said Sheriff Plotner, "and I'd say this was a open-and-shut case of it."

Bloody froth bubbled in the corner of Walter Vale's

mouth. Even the arms of his white shirt were sodden with blood.

Doom averted his eyes. One couldn't look upon that and think too. "You're still acting coroner, aren't you, Sheriff?"

"Sure. Why?"

Among Walter Vale's phony IDs Doom had seen a blank white business card with a phone number written on it. "Snack, do you have Donald Sikes's number on you?"

"Yeah." He handed it to Doom. It matched that on Vale's card.

"Longnecker—?"

"Yeah, babe?"

"What's the best way to sink a ship?"

"Submarine."

"What's the second best way?"

BOOM

~~~~~~~

ABOARD ROSALIND'S SKIFF THEY MOTORED OUT through Ponce Pass, seaward, into the teeth of a freshening east wind. Bert, Doom, and Rosalind had feared that east wind; Longnecker, a landsman, hadn't given it a thought. At dawn it was blowing fifteen knots, eighteen with higher gusts by noon, more than enough time to rile the ocean. Now the wind held steady at eighteen knots, and because of its unobstructed fetch all the way from the Bahamas, conditions could only deteriorate. This would have been a glorious night's sail aboard a seaboat like *Staggerlee*, but Doom and Rosalind wouldn't be on the water, they'd be in it. Even in the absence of moonlight, whitecaps glowered, plain to see.

Off the starboard bow the lights of the *King Don* twinkled like a nighttime encampment in the desert. Everyone
was tense and silent except for Longnecker, who was simply silent, seasickness clawing at his lower face. His head
lolled. Someone might have suggested he concentrate on
the horizon, but there was none. A black and belligerent
cold front, gathering force, marching westward, had
obliterated it.

Bert added some speed, but Rosalind's boat immediately began to pound—he could feel the hull flex beneath
his feet—so he throttled back, giving the foul weather
further opportunity to overtake them. In a wet suit, on
her hands and knees, Rosalind checked the equipment still
again. Doom never tired of seeing her body strain at the
rubber, but tonight he didn't even notice. She strapped a
big luminous-dial compass to her left wrist and test-
breathed each of the four tanks for about the tenth time.
What if she got killed or caught and he didn't? There'd be
no way to live with that, suicide the only alternative. Was
Small Hope Bay, or revenge, or justice, or whatever he
was doing this for, worth the risk of her life? He put his
back to the apparent wind and considered aborting the
madness, but he was still angry, and he knew that if he
did, he'd never be able to suit up and go again. . . . Forget
next time, could he drop into that black ocean this time?

"I'm a professional," began Rosalind after they had
made love twenty-four hours earlier. "This is my job, and
I don't want you out there getting in my way."

"I won't get in your way, because I'm going alone."

"Absolutely not. You're my student and I've never lost
one yet. You stay in the boat."

"You stay in the boat."

"How many night dives have you done?"

". . . None."

"There's my point. I've done over two hundred."

"What about right now?"

"What do you mean?"

"It's night now."

Doom reveled in the nighttime reef. He had been anxious on the outbound boat ride, but anxiety vanished as soon as warm, still water covered his head. The coral bottom was only thirty feet down, and the powerful light in his hand felt secure, like personal, portable, on-demand daylight. But it was when Rosalind signaled him to kill his light that the wonder of the marine night revealed itself.

Coral is a living thing, a tight colony of tiny animals called polyps. Only in daylight does coral appear to be inert, if colorful, stone. Indeed, beneath the upper, living layer it *is* stone, the protective limestone secretions from thousands of generations of now-dead polyps. But at night living polyps by the millions protrude from their stony niches in the upper layer to feed, casting minute poisonous tentacles for microorganisms in the water, and the blackness comes alive. Polyps flash blue and red and green like points of gaudy neon against black water.

Other, bigger creatures make nighttime appearances. By day only the toothy snouts of moray eels protrude from their holes in the reef, but at night they swim free, undulating, some six feet long and weighing eighty pounds. Octopi slither in the open. Colors shimmer as creatures move by every imaginable means of propulsion. Night after night it goes on, this extravagant sea show, as it has since the last Ice Age.

It felt to Doom a privilege to be down there with Rosalind, the darker purpose of the practice dive forgotten. She took his hand in hers and drew him gently down to the sandy bottom. She had seen something beneath the arching base of an elkhorn coral tree, and she wanted to share it. Seeing it, Doom forgot to breathe. A stoplight parrot fish slept. Red belly and caudal fin, green on top, the two-foot-long fish floated motionlessly in a bubble of mucus secreted to repel predators while the parrot fish dozed in peace and safety. Gently, Doom held it in his hands. Its black eye moved languidly. . . .

But tonight was entirely different. There had been no wind last night, the sea flat, calm, benign. The reef was life-rich, warm, and welcoming. Tonight's sea was dark and deathly. There was no coral close below. Here at the northern extreme of coral's range, few polyps can survive in the diffuse sunlight and cool water fifty feet down; the depth sounder was showing 92. (Christ, Bert was thinking, how much anchor rode would it take to hold the *King Don* in these conditions?) Last night's ocean beckoned; tonight's warned the foolish to stay the fuck on the hill. Longnecker leaned over the side and barfed.

"Come on, Bert, give us some speed," Rosalind snapped.

"She's gonna pound like mighty Jesus."

"Then let her pound."

Longnecker had curled into a helpless ball.

"Better go out and drop you to windward of her," said Bert. "You won't make it otherwise."

Rosalind nodded. The boat dropped off a crest and slammed into the trough with a tooth-splitting crack.

Preparations had been carefully laid. Longnecker had built a simple, artistic time bomb, but the means of housing it—watertight—had proved a thornier technical problem. They considered welding it into a metal box but discarded the idea, since the resulting ensemble would have weighed over a hundred pounds. They considered stout plastic freezer bags, but experiments showed that the bags leaked under less than one atmosphere of pressure. Then Rosalind hit upon the solution: an underwater-camera housing. Size and weight were practical, and watertight integrity was guaranteed by the manufacturer. That solved, they had debated how best to attach the bomb to the *King Don*'s hull. Longnecker had suggested taping a strong magnet to the housing and sticking it to the bottom of her keel. With that, technically, at least, they were ready. Emotionally, they were all atwitter.

Rosalind took the helm while Bert rigged twin fishing rods, their cover, and stuck them in holders on the stern. Rosalind slowed to a credible trolling speed. Longnecker threw up and lay in it. The *King Don* was abeam of them now, several hundred yards away. Bert recovered the helm, and he and Rosalind discussed their course. Seaward of the target, they would turn south and pass as close aboard as they dared, slowing to a stop momentarily while Doom and Rosalind dropped into the black water, then continuing on the phony fishing trip.

Grimly, Rosalind began to gear up, and Doom followed suit. She strapped a heavy knife to her shin, slid an extra snorkel into her weight belt, clipped two underwater lights to the belt, and stuffed a pair of emergency flares into the Velcroed pocket on her buoyancy compensator. Then she stopped to think, consulting her checklist. The *King Don*'s lights would bedazzle the night vision of all aboard her, and that was good—they'd probably never even see the boat that bombed them. But the weather was bad and getting worse.

Her beam to the wind and seas, Rosalind's boat rolled violently. Doom sat on the sole to pull on his tank straps. Then he steadied another tank for Rosalind to don. Damn! He should have fetched the bomb from the cuddy before he put his tank on. Should he take it off? Could he get it back on? No. Timing his trek to the top of a roll, Doom crawled through Longnecker's vomit to get the bomb, which he placed in a nylon net bag. He tied a knot in the bag and strapped it to his belt, but he tied it too low—the bomb bounced against his thighs. He shortened up on it.

Some piece of his consciousness stood apart from himself, slightly above the jouncing deck, watching critically. Only madmen did this kind of shit, it seemed to contend. But there he was, tugging, adjusting, yanking at his gear. Everything chafed, and, sweating in his wet suit, he began to smell himself in offensive waves with each movement. Rosalind was doing the same. Did she stink too? Doom looked over his shoulder, dreading the sight. The *King Don* was abeam of them again, bow-on to the wind. Something—what the hell was it?—was bouncing against his shoulder.

This guy's going to panic on me. Rosalind knew it. He had totally checked out, another hemisphere. She stopped tapping his shoulder and considered leaving him. "Doom!"

"Huh! What!"

"Time to go."

"Okay. I'm ready—"

"Sit up on the gunwale with your back to the water."

Damn fool, contended the floating part of Doom's consciousness as he did so. Rosalind sat beside him and clipped the eight-foot-long tether to him with a snap shackle. The rolling threatened to throw them over the side.

"Good luck," mouthed Bert as he throttled back to neutral. Longnecker gurgled something similar.

And Rosalind rolled over backward. The snarling sea took her without a splash. Doom clutched his mask and regulator and rolled—

The water throbbed as the boat motored off. Surfacing, Doom watched the phony fishing rods waving wildly. He was face-to-face with Rosalind for a moment, then a wave enveloped her. She bobbed up again. She was signaling something. What? *Concentrate!* His eyes were blurry. She was signaling him to submerge. His eyes were blurry because it was dark and his mask was wet. That all made perfect sense. He submerged.

Fifteen feet down the blackness was total, but the motion was easier, as if this were a different ocean. How deep was the blackness below him? Best not to dwell on that. . . . The plan was this: Rosalind would take a bearing on the *King Don* before submerging, and maintaining a depth of fifteen feet would swim that bearing down until they came upon the ship. If they didn't find the ship, if sea or the current set them off course, Rosalind would poke her eyes up and take another bearing. Had Rosalind taken the initial bearing? Doom didn't remember seeing her sight across her compass. . . . The tether between them jerked tight—

Rosalind flashed her penlight in his eyes. He flashed his back, the okay signal. His job was to follow her fins, keeping some slack in the line so as not to pull her off course, but he wasn't doing it, he was lagging, fucking up. Concentrate! He felt the turbulence from her fins on his face. Just keep it there, right there on the forehead, no more, no less turbulence than this. They were swimming in harmony now. . . . Was his father down there somewhere?

What was swimming in the wake of his own fins? Some maw? Any second now he'd feel the bayonet teeth tear through his thighs, hot billows of his own blood, Rosalind reeling in his legless torso. . . . Keep the cadence, kick, kick. Christ! The bomb! Where was the bomb! He should have felt it against his thighs! Was it gone? Or were his thighs gone?

Rosalind stopped, and Doom swam into her fins. A black wall surged, plunged, rose and plunged again an arm's length from their faces, a hundred tons of bucking steel. How could they attach a thing to the bottom of that without getting themselves crushed? Doom was sucking air like a diesel engine, but he had the presence of mind to check his pressure gauge. It showed fewer than a thousand pounds remaining. Rosalind dropped another fifteen feet and swam beneath the keel. Doom followed, telling himself to think about the task at hand, not about the reality of the pitching and plunging keel of a hundred-and-twenty-foot-long ship above their heads.

Rosalind shone her big light on the bottom of the hull. It was red, not black, encrusted with barnacles and green, mossy growth like fringe on a plate-steel cocktail dress. The entire hull climbed slowly up ten feet as each wave cleared the bow, but it came back down three times faster in a killing dive before the frightful process repeated itself. Doom switched on his own light and shone it on the same spot while Rosalind unstrapped the bomb from his belt and cut it out of the net bag, which she cast adrift. Then she unclipped the tether from her own belt. She'd need complete freedom of movement for what she was about to do. She lay in the water, neutrally buoyant, watching the bounding steel plate, timing her attempt.

She waited until the hull dove down to its deepest point. Then it began its upward surge. Rosalind ascended three feet and waited for it to come back to her. And it did. She stuck the bomb in place, then deftly bolted toward the sea bottom. The ship bucked the next wave, and when it dropped again, the bomb broke free, began to sink.

Doom caught it in his light but immediately lost it. He

dove, no time to equalize the stabbing pressure in his ears. Finning hard, thighs tightening, knotting, he waved his light at black nothing. His light seemed absurd in its puniness. The bomb was gone. Doom slid into sea-dark despair.

Something hard hit his fins, and panic squeezed out despair. A Gulf Stream of adrenaline pumped. Once the shark tore off his legs at the crotch, perhaps death would be mercifully swift, and he'd be spared the actual perception of the teeth that tore his person to bloody tatters. But his blood would alert others, and finding Doom slim pickings by then, they'd head for Rosalind. But it wasn't a shark that had struck his fins—it was the bomb.

Upside down he caught it against his belly, and suddenly he was exhausted, nothing left, not even a firm idea of which way was up. "This is the stuff of panic right here, boy. You know what follows panic, don't you, boy?" said that part of his consciousness that remained separate, critical. "You better get hold of yourself, because this is how fools like you *die!*" But that part didn't have any idea which way was up either. Thinking ponderously through the mucus of panic, Doom hit upon an idea. He'd blow some air into his buoyancy compensator—it could only lead him up. Physics.

The trip up seemed to take two days, after which the pounding steel hull—and Rosalind's "okay" light—hove into view. . . . What was she doing? And what was that noise? It sounded steely, a scraping sound. He shone his big light on Rosalind. Christ, look at her!

She chased the hull upward, then when it began its plunge, she braced her feet flat, crouched upside down, and, as if straddling it, rode the *King Don* toward the bottom. But why? Another in the welter of emotions he'd undergone in the last five minutes washed over him—admiration and love for Rosalind—when he realized what she was doing. The magnet hadn't gotten a good grip because of the marine growth on the bottom. Rosalind was scraping it off with a big knife!

Doom hovered, holding the light for her. She rode the

ship twice more before she took the bomb from Doom's arms and stuck it in place. Doom and Rosalind swam aside and watched several bucks and plunges while the bomb stuck as securely as a mussel colony. Then Rosalind sighted across her compass and pointed due west. She hooked the tether back onto Doom's belt before, side by side, they swam toward the pickup point. Doom took Rosalind's hand and squeezed it, not too hard, he hoped. Escape death only to have her digits crushed by an overstimulated lover.

They swam underwater for several hundred yards before Doom felt breathing resistance. A calm, a sense of well-being just short of euphoria had set in, and Doom felt he could go on like this forever, alone with Rosalind, swimming through three-dimensional darkness—except for the fact that Doom was running out of air. Was Rosalind? he wondered. Probably not, what with her professionally disciplined air consumption. Gently Doom pulled on the tether, and Rosalind stopped swimming. Doom held his pressure gauge before her mask. The luminous dial said Doom was down to two hundred pounds per square inch. Rosalind pointed at the surface and headed there.

Fifteen feet down, they felt the tug and toss of the seas, but that was lullaby rocking compared to the chaos at the surface. Waves broke everywhere in white swirls. In their troughs the night seemed still, but on the crests wind whined maliciously. Here in shallower water, thirty feet deep, there was none of the predictable rolling Doom and Rosalind had experienced beneath the *King Don*. Here there was no order to the steep seas. Waves butted and tripped over each other, crashed together at oblique angles, a horde without sense or mercy. Spume flew in snaking ridges across the sea. Visibility from the decks of *Staggerlee* would have been strained; from the surface it was nearly nil.

This was the part of her plan—the pickup—that she feared most. She had never tried anything like this—ship killing on nasty nights didn't often come up in sport diving sessions. She kicked hard, trying to propel herself far enough out of the water to see. Doom imitated her.

Rosalind gasped into her mouthpiece when finally she found the lights of the *King Don*. It was far to the south. These inshore currents were another source of fear. They were unpredictable in force and direction, "set" and "drift" in marine parlance. That night a strong eddy had set them over a mile to the north, even though Rosalind had aimed due west. Bert would be searching for them well south of their actual position, unless he noticed the current and put two and two together, but by then it might be too late. She popped out of a crest waist-high and waved her big light at the southern darkness, but no light answered her. She dropped her weight belt and wriggled out of her backpack harness. A wave swept the tank from her grasp and carried it shoreward before it sank. Doom did the same.

She shouted instructions at him: They'd have to swim for shore. Doom was afraid of that. She told him to fully inflate his flotation vest, leave his mask on, swim on his back, easily, conserving energy, letting the wind and sea help them home, never mind the waves breaking over his head. How far was home? They could see shoreside lights, what, a mile and a half away? Add to that the current's northerly set, and call it two miles even.

"Don't worry, Doom, we'll make it. It won't be comfortable, but we won't sink." What if he did? What if her sloppy plans got Doom killed, later to wash up, bloated like his father, on Omnium Beach? No, she would get him in no matter what.

Would the *King Don* go up while they were still in the water? Would they feel the concussion? Doom wished they could talk, discuss what they had shared, but conditions prohibited chitchat. Sometimes waves would heave and break directly under their legs, pitch-poling them, fins in the air, and the swimmers would come up entangled in their tether and each other. They swam in the chaos for nearly two hours. Then Doom recoiled at the feel of something hard beneath his fins.

"Rocks!" shouted Rosalind, and to keep her draft as shallow as possible, she began to body-surf. Doom followed. The last wave buried him, pulled and yanked at his arms and legs, bounced him off the sandy bottom inshore of the rocks and left him in a heap on the beach. He crawled away from the sea. . . .

Rosalind! Where was Rosalind! She was on her knees nearby, framed against the relatively bright western sky. Doom crawled to her and hugged her. They were safe on Omnium Beach, not fifty feet from where his father had washed up. Doom let out a yelp of joy, and Rosalind was giggling. Then, knees drawn up, they sat like tourists watching the sea on a sunny afternoon.

"My suit's full of sand," said Doom, chafing.

"Mine too."

"Then perhaps we ought to remove them."

"Not now," grinned Rosalind. "Later."

"Where do you think Bert is?"

"God knows. What time is it?"

Doom looked at his watch. "Oh. It's about that time."

"Let's watch the lights go out."

And there they sat waiting for the *King Don* to go down. Doom held Rosalind's hand. . . . The time came. And went. Neither spoke. Doom looked at his watch again. They waited.

Nothing.

Rosalind flopped back in the sand. "It must have fallen off. It's my fault."

"Naw, it's my fault. It was a crazy idea in the first place. We should have just lured him ashore and ambushed him. Or something."

"It's all my fault," said Captain Bert to Longnecker, disregarding the fact that Longnecker had lost the capacity to respond. He had curled into a ball against the base of the control pedestal. Occasionally he whimpered. Doom and Rosalind were gone, swept away, just like the poor tourists aboard the *Amberjack*. Bert would never forget the feel of the bow plunging into the trough, the stern tripping over the bow, all control lost. He could do nothing but hang on as the sixty-foot boat was heaved onto the jetty, smashing her starboard bilge, sinking in minutes. He'd never forget the disdainful looks on the faces of the investigating officers as they administered the drug and alcohol tests, but Bert hadn't been drinking. He had simply made a mistake, and six people drowned. He'd never forget the emptiness in his heart and the confusion in his head, the same emptiness he felt now as he searched the black surface of the violent sea, without hope. He urged himself to think, think like a seaman. . . .

Captain Bert pulled the throttle lever back to neutral. His line of position placed him on a range between the lights of the *King Don* and the lights of the Broadnax mansion. By stopping, drifting, he'd gain some reference to the set and drift of the current, but visually he would have to separate drift from leeway, particularly hard to do at night in an unfamiliar boat. It would take a born seaman's instinct. Dead in the water, Rosalind's boat pitched and rolled wildly. Longnecker moaned. Bert waited, pinching out the panic with maritime logic.

Yes, he was being set well north of his range marks. Like a corpse, Longnecker rolled from port to starboard and back again. Bert shoved the boat into gear and pointed the bow at zero degrees. He plugged in Rosalind's handheld searchlight and waved it around his course, but there was nothing to see, only rampant whitecaps.

Back on the beach, tingling excitement had turned to barren disappointment. The sand chafed inside their suits. Rosalind had flopped on her back, staring at the sky. Doom sat clutching his shins, still hoping to see the *King Don*'s lights shake, then sink, but it didn't happen. Nothing happened. The lights twinkled on.

"Damn it!" said Rosalind, sitting up.

"What?"

"Tar! I laid in a glop of tar! Feel it—it's in my hair! Fucking oil companies! Look—" She pointed seaward.

A light beam poked at the sea.

"It's Bert." She switched on her own light, blinked it on and off.

Bert saw it and whooped with delight. "Longnecker! I found them, Longnecker! They're on the beach!"

Longnecker was glad to hear that, but the only sign he could manage was an ill-formed "okay" gesture.

Fifteen minutes later Bert was circling slowly off the beach. He couldn't go in any farther or the breakers would drop him on the rocks.

"He can't come in any closer," said Rosalind. "We're going to have to swim for it."

"Swim?"

"Yeah, it does sound like a drag, all right. Would you rather walk?"

"Yes."

"We could have him pick us up at the Flamingo Tongue. We should have planned it that way in the first place. Shit. It's all my fault."

"No, it's my fault."

It took a while, shouting back and forth in the wind, but finally Rosalind got her message across the breakers. Bert motored off toward Bird Cut, which would be a nasty place, especially if the tide had turned. Lugging their remaining gear, Doom and Rosalind trudged up the beach toward the Flamingo Tongue.

On the way Doom said, "Rosalind, I hope you don't feel guilty about shooting that guy Walter. We didn't get to discuss that yet."

"Guilty? I don't feel guilty. He killed your father. He was a scumbag."

"Okay. Just checking."

"You know, I love you."

"You do?"

"Yeah."

Longnecker crawled out of the boat and flopped facedown on the dock. The restaurant was closed for the night, the docks dark. They couldn't see the pain and shame on his face as Longnecker said, "I'm sorry, sorry, sorry. It was my fault."

But Doom had another idea, a crazy idea, not as crazy as trying to bomb the *King Don* at sea, but still crazy.

READY ABOUT

〜〜〜〜

DONALD SIKES PACED THE FANTAIL. HE HADN'T SLEPT since the night it had allegedly happened. When was that precisely? Night before last? Why hadn't he heard from Mr. Freed? And now the wind was blowing so hard, Donny was getting seasick. Perhaps it was all those piñas. And what's more, Gramps was beginning to notice his anxious drinking. . . . Maybe Mr. Freed had gypped him. He'd already paid for the murders. Maybe Mr. Freed absconded. But that didn't sound like Mr. Freed; he had an impeccable reputation for honesty. Donny Sikes decided to have a shower and go to bed. His breath stank of tropical fruits.

The telephone rang.

"Mr. Sikes, please," said a gravelly voice on the other end.

"Who are you? Where'd you get this number?"

"You can call me Mr. DeSoto. I'm an associate—a kind of agent—of the man you hired to perform a certain task on the evening before last. Do you follow me?"

". . . Yes." Even professional killers had agents?

"I've been asked by that man to tell you the job is complete. The old man, the scuba diving woman, and the old man's son. Do you follow me?"

"The old man's son too?"

"Yes, and that is the problem. You neglected to tell my client that the son would be coming as well. So the original plan will not work. My client has, therefore, disposed of the, uh—need I spell it out for you, Mr. Sikes?"

Yes! Donny would have loved to have had it spelled out for him. What had happened in that house? "Uh, Mr. DeSoto?"

"Yes?"

"Let me ask you this. Will we read about them in the newspapers?"

"Let me put it to you like this, Mr. Sikes. We might read about their absence, but not their discovery. Do you follow me?"

"Yes . . . what about the other matter?"

"What other matter is that?" asked Mr. DeSoto.

"Uh, the other gentleman?"

"Mr. Loomis?"

"Yes."

"He just left. Do you follow me?"

"Tonight?"

"Tonight."

"Will he be coming back?"

"No. There will be a nominal additional charge for the son and the inconvenience his presence caused my client, and I'll be in touch with you about that. On behalf of Mr. Freed, it was a pleasure doing business with you. Good-bye, Mr. Sikes."

"Wait just one minute there, Mr. DeSoto. How come you're calling me Sikes? That isn't how Mr. Freed knew me. He knew me as Mr. Shipton." Donny smelled a rat.

"It's in Mr. Freed's interests to know the true identity of his clients. For security reasons. Learning his clients' true identity is one of the services I perform for him. Do I need to spell it out for you, Mr. Sikes?"

"No, but I'll bet you I don't know *his* true identity."

"I wouldn't take that bet, Mr. Sikes."

Donald Sikes smiled, then giggled, his seasickness forgotten. He went below to tell Gramps that the way was clear for construction to proceed apace.

Mr. DeSoto's gravelly voice hurt Doom's throat.

THE DELEGATION

EARLY NEXT MORNING ROSALIND'S BOAT APPROACHED the *King Don* through sloppy swells. The wind had dropped to below ten knots and veered to the southeast, but it would take all day and most of the night for the sea to settle.

Professor Goode, wearing a new suit, gripped the steering pedestal with white knuckles. "I'm going to upchuck," he said.

"Concentrate on the horizon," offered Captain Bert, who wore a freshly starched khaki captain's uniform. A little rectangle of darker cloth remained over the left breast pocket from where Bert had removed the name patch of his last command: the *Amberjack*.

Sheriff Plotner in his best dress uniform with the Mountie hat wasn't feeling so chipper himself. Breakfast bacon grease was creeping up the back of his gullet.

The Annes, filming, felt all right, delighted to be in the thick of things.

"Think about something else," Bert suggested. "Think about the rodeo."

The rodeo? Professor Goode was frightened that he'd be unable to speak and thereby ruin everything. He considered calf roping, bronc busting. "I—I can't . . . talk!"

"Hmm," mused Bert. "How 'bout you, Plotner? Can you talk?"

"Gak," said the sheriff.

"Maybe you'll feel better when we get aboard. The motion on that thing'll be a lot different, won't be this bounc-

ing slap-slap. It'll be more like uuuuup then dowwwwn—
so you might feel better."

Professor Goode threw up over the starboard bow, Sheriff Plotner the port.

"You guys always want to throw up downwind. Listen.
I'll give them a jingle." Bert snapped up the VHF trans-
mitter. "This is whiskey, able, bravo, two-niner approaching the *King Don* from the west-northwest." That was a
lot of unnecessary bullshit under the circumstances, but
Jesus, the words felt good in his mouth. "Come in, *King
Don*, over."

Donald Sikes hadn't been to bed. He had dozed fitfully
on the fantail, suffering little boy's nightmares, and now
the sun knifed him in the eyes. He stood up. "Roger—"
he called, wanting coffee brewed the way he liked it. Then
he remembered. He had murdered Roger. That's when he
saw Rosalind's boat approaching his starboard stern
quarter. Christ, there was a Mountie aboard. Those bastards always got their man. Maybe they'd caught Mr. Freed
in Canada, and he talked. . . . Then Donald Sikes recognized the uniform as that of the local law. There was a
civilian aboard in addition to the boat driver. And two
women were taking pictures. . . . Why were the civilian
and the cop staring down into the ocean like that?

The purser summoned Donald Sikes onto the bridge
because the approaching boat was hailing him on the radio.

"What do you want?" asked Donny. "I'm in international waters."

"Roger that, *King Don*. I got Professor Armbrister with
the Florida Historical Society aboard here. Him and Sheriff
Plotner, representin' the town council, would like to invite
you to a celebration they're having, over."

The fear stopped churning in the half-digested piña
juice. They weren't coming to arrest him. They had camera
people aboard to take his picture. Local news hicks, probably. "What kind of celebration?"

"Well, it's Founder's Day on Omnium Key. We want
to honor the pioneerin' efforts of Prentiss Throckmorton.
Professor Armbrister researched up the fact you and him

was related, so they'd like you to be guest of honor, over."

Donny Sikes couldn't help laughing out loud. You just can't ever tell how things will go down here, and Donny found that kind of charming. "Did you hear that, Gramps? Founder's Day!"

The Annes panned the *King Don* from bow to stern before they went aboard.

Sheriff Plotner and Professor Goode were pale and panting by the time they climbed up to the main deck. The Annes were amazed at the bad taste topside. It looked like network TV's notion of a New Orleans whorehouse. Chandeliers on a boat? A wet bar? At first they thought it was a joke. Everyone introduced themselves in the main saloon, then they repaired to the fantail. The Annes got a covert shot of the ridiculous fluffy carpet on the way out.

"Who'd like a piña colada?" asked Donny with a clap of his hands, the hale host. It was 8:45 in the morning.

The very thought of a cloying rum libation caused the professor's gorge to rise like a dead bird in his throat.

"Sounds good to me," said Captain Bert. "I could use the vitamin C."

Donny gave last night's pitcher a good shake to get the layers of rum and fruit-juice pulp to mingle before he poured out two big ones. "Founder's Day, huh?" Donny giggled.

"Yes, sir," said Bert.

"Bottoms up," said Donny.

"Yes sir."

"Uh, tell me, will Mr. Broadnax be attending? I understand his father was involved in this region's past." Donald Sikes kept wiping his cheek as if something wet and gooey had landed on it. Anne zoomed in on it. Nothing was visible on his cheek. "You folks must be making a moving picture."

"Oh yes," said Bert, "we have movies of Founder's Days back, oh, fifty years? Wouldn't you say, Professor Armbrister?"

"Yes."

Was Bert going to have to fly this entire show solo?

Sheriff Plotner was regaining himself now that he was aboard the larger vessel, and he had his end to uphold as an elected official of Broadnax County, so he said, "It's funny you should mention ol' Big Al—that's what we folks call him around here, fondly, you know. Thing is, we been trying to get hold of him for a couple of days now, but he must be away. Van's gone. His young son Sennacherib's gone, too. Funny, though, the servants didn't know anything about it—them leavin', I mean. Big Al hasn't missed a Founder's Day in a coon's age, but he's an independent one, ole Big Al. Can't ever tell what he'll do or not do."

"Actually"—the professor took a series of deep breaths—"his father and your grandfather were partners here in south Florida. Did you know that, Mr. Sikes?"

"Please call me Donny," said Donny, wiping his cheek.

"Why, thank you, Donny, and may I say what an honor it is to meet you. I'm a fan of yours, of your deals."

"Are you really?"

"Oh, yes." Professor Goode couldn't wait to see himself flattering Donald Sikes on film. "Yes, Throckmorton and Broadnax made this region great. Why, before them it was a putrid swamp utterly hostile to the desires of man."

"You don't say—"

"Yes, indeed I do. They collaborated on the construction of a hotel, but more spectacularly, those two managed to make land where there was only water and wildlife. Isn't that astonishing? It's man's desire to change his environment for the better that separates him from the beasts of the fields—swamps, as it were. Ha-ha. Yes, these men were giants of the old mold. Being related to such men must have proved a benefit to you in your deals."

"Why, Professor," said Donny, delighted, "you sound like my biographer."

"I have been the biographer of great men of the past."

"No kidding? Who?"

"Crashaw, Herrick, Herbert, and Vaughn."

"A law firm? Little joke there."

"They are the Metaphysicals."

266

"What kind of money did they pay you? I mean what do you charge for a biography? Ballpark."

"It's never the money, Donny, it's the subject. Without a worthy subject a biography is nothing. A worthy subject makes it priceless, but in your case I'd say about point one percent of your next deal." Professor Goode was feeling great now. "That should set me up handsomely for my remaining years."

Donny chuckled. He liked this Professor Whatshisname. A biography would please Gramps. Perhaps as a Christmas present—

"I just hope you get to meet Big Al," interjected Sheriff Plotner toward the camera. "Yes, we'd sure like to have pictures of that meeting."

Now Donald Sikes seemed to be batting invisible mosquitoes from his face.

"In fact," continued the sheriff, "the parade route leads right to the site of the old Oseola Hotel. We'll take you to the very spot."

"Parade?"

"Oh well, now you can't go expecting no Macy's parade like the one in Chicago. We're just a little community, but we'd be tickled pink to have you in our celebration."

"Perhaps you'd care to say a few words to the local residents assembled at the site?" suggested the professor.

"About my grandfather?"

"Just anything at all," said the sheriff. "Folks'd love to hear about some of your deals. Professor tells me you have some big ones. Deals."

"Piña colada?" asked Donny.

"Sure," said Bert.

"Gentlemen, my anchorage here isn't entirely a coincidence. My next deal, as the professor puts it, will be local." Donny twisted in his seat to present his profile to the camera. A powerful profile ran in the family. "I was putting you fellows on a bit. The fact is, I know my family history intimately. And that's why, now, I intend to build on that very site of the old Oseola Hotel a new and grander facility. Certain changes to the in situ geography which I have in mind will require the creation of over two thousand new jobs."

Bert, Sheriff Plotner, and Professor Goode exchanged bowled-over glances.

"Yes, gentlemen, prosperity beyond this county's wildest dreams. Perfection Park, I call it, for that's what I mean to create. Perhaps Founder's Day is an appropriate day to present my main stipulation."

"Stipulation?" smiled Professor Goode.

"Are you taking notes, Professor?"

"Always."

"I want the name of the county changed from Broadnax to Throckmorton, and wherever the Broadnax name appears within the county—on roads, municipal buildings— I will want those, too, changed to Throckmorton. I would be pleased if retail establishments complied as well with the name change, but I shan't insist. It's private enterprise, after all." Donny Sikes brushed a swarm of invisible arachnids from his cheek.

"Sounds good to me," said Sheriff Plotner. "Ole Big Al'll be disappointed, but what the hell, what's he done for us lately?"

"That's the spirit that made this land great," said Donny.

"But I don't have that authority. Wish I did. It'd have to be put to a vote by the Town Fathers."

"Why don't we let the constituents decide?" suggested Professor Goode.

"How so, Professor?" asked Donny.

"Why don't you present your proposal in broad outline form to the people who gather for Founder's Day. It suggests to me the old New England town meeting. The seedbeds of democracy."

"You mean today?"

"Sounds most appropriate to me."

Bert and the sheriff nodded vigorous support of the idea.

"I guarantee they'll be interested," said Sheriff Plotner.

"Hmmm," mused Donny, pretending reluctance. He'd let them encourage him some more.

And they did.

"By the way," said Sheriff Plotner, "why don't you come on in and use the docks at Bird Cut. We got enough water, and it'd sure be more comfortable than bouncin' butt out here. By the way, how many crew do you have? So we can make arrangements."

"I'm down to four, since the death of my friend Roger Vespucci, which of course you know about."

"Well, your crew's more'n welcome at the party."

"I'd offer you gentlemen a ride back in this boat, but I'll need some time to perfect my speech."

Bert, the sheriff, and the professor giggled like boys on the way ashore. They replayed their bullshit, taking turns assuming the role of Donny Sikes, and they laughed and clapped each other on the backs. That Doom Loomis was a genius, and they were his trusted bullshit artists. So excited, so mirthful were they that they forgot to get seasick again.

DEBARKATION

THE TEQUESTA KEY REGIONAL HIGH SCHOOL PEP BAND, hired by Doom, played Bobby Goldsboro's greatest hits as the hired captain of the *King Don*, a sun-bleached blond young man who when Donny's back was turned used the ship to smuggle pornography into Nicaragua, maneuvered her into her berth at the end of the dock where before the recent unpleasantness *Staggerlee* used to live. His crew smartly swung out the boarding ramp for Donny Sikes, who wore his blue blazer with the fouled anchor on the breast, neatly creased blue tropical slacks and a captain's hat with gold braid on the brim. He paused at the top of the ramp and waved to the assembled throng.

It was a pretty raggedy-assed throng. A knot of barefoot tourists in polyester Bermudas had assembled on the dock to get an early spot from which to view the sunset. Smoking cigarettes, they didn't seem to have any clear idea who was aboard this huge white yacht that had just blocked out any hope of a sunset view. Professor Whatshisname was down on the dock wearing a red and green academic sash like a bandolier across his chest. The dykey chicks were there filming his arrival. The smelly sheriff was there. And the other guy, the one who drove the boat. Bart, or something. They were smiling in welcome. But everyone else had blank looks on their faces.

Donny's crewmen had misrigged the boarding ramp. When Donny stepped slightly off its centerline, the narrow plank flipped out from under him. Only the rope railing catching him around the ass, burning it, prevented a plunge into the bay he meant to drain. He clawed and kicked for purchase and tried to boost himself onto the upturned edge of the ramp.

"Cut, cut!" he shouted, but of course the Annes never cut.

The tourists had now been joined by a gaggle of locals and the folks from the Flamingo Tongue. The swelling crowd pressed in close to watch this puffed-up little fuck in the sailor suit fall off his own gangplank.

Rosalind, Doom, Marvis, and Longnecker watched through binoculars from the south jetty of Bird Cut as Donny's crewmen tried to right the ramp from the onboard side, while the Flamingo Tongue skippers shouted conflicting shoreside directions to Donny, who hung fluttering and flailing, squeezing a railing stanchion in a love grip. It was an ignominious position for the guest of honor at the Founder's Day festivities to find himself in. "Get me off this goddamn thing, you bulletheads!"

This did little to ingratiate Donny to his would-be rescuers, and they began to disperse. His crew, however, finally managed to square away the ramp, and Donny, visibly shaken, low-walked ashore.

Bert, Sheriff Plotner, and Professor Goode all helped to brush him off.

"I'm all right." His left lapel hung by a thread. He'd lost his red paisley breast-pocket handkerchief and his captain's hat with the yellow braid on the brim. His crew was trying to fish these items out of the water, but, bursting with the giggles, the crew couldn't hold the boat hook steady. Bert, Plotner, and Professor Goode, also fighting the giggles, continued to brush Donny off. "I'm all right! Christ!"

Donny whirled on his crew lining the bulwarks: "You're through! You're finished! Get off my ship or I'll have the sheriff arrest you! As pirates!"

Ironically, that's exactly what Doom had planned— Sheriff Plotner would arrest the crew on some trumped-up charge and hold them for a couple of hours, thereby isolating Donald Sikes, but this was better still.

"You heard the man, boys," the sheriff said. "Get on out of here now. Don't you worry none, Donny. Bert and me, we'll get you a new crew. Crews are a dime a dozen in these parts. Come on, we'll get the parade started—"

"That place"—the Flamingo Tongue—"does that place serve drinks?"

"No, sir, that's like a coffee shop. But I've taken precautions—in my car."

They all four climbed into the sheriff's squad car, and he broke out a gallon cooler full of fresh piña coladas. He poured generous portions into clear plastic glasses from the picnic section of the Winn Dixie. "Hell, bad start there, Donny, but that'll just make the festivities seem all the sweeter."

"Hear hear!" said Professor Goode.

"I'll drink to that," said Bert.

FOUNDER'S NIGHT

SHERIFF PLOTNER WONDERED WHY THERE WERE SO many dumpsters. Didn't there used to be just one dumpster, a green dumpster? Or blue? Now there was a whole family of dumpsters cavorting and frolicking like cartoon elephants. His eyes kept slipping in and out of focus, and the palms of his hands perspired profusely. In order to get to Founder's Day, he would have to drive through all those unruly dumpsters. . . . Professor Goode, also in the front seat, couldn't feel his feet. Visually they were present; neurologically they were absent. Another piña colada might retrieve sensation. Donny and Bert giggled together in the backseat.

As soon as the squad car departed, Doom slid into the water to execute Phase Two, while Duncan, Marvis, and Longnecker set in motion Phase Three of the plan.

"How about coming to work for me, Bert?" Donny asked.

"As what, Donny?"

"As captain of the *King Don.*"

"Sure, Donny. Great."

They drank on it.

Why was it so dark? Professor Goode thought his vision must be following the way of his feet. That's what old age was, a gradual diminution of faculties and parts. "Why is it so dark?" he asked Sheriff Plotner.

" 'Cause the sun went down."

That explained it. . . . Yet the view from cars at night was often brighter than this due to headlamps. "Excuse me, Sheriff, but might I inquire as to whether or not your headlamps are alight?"

"I think so. . . . Sure, see the white line—right there."

Professor Goode did not. "Oh yes," he said. Thank Jesu his job was nearly done, since he was approaching absolute incapacitation. Must be all that citrus juice, he surmised. Grapefruit juice was insidious, and pineapple juice, you just couldn't trust pineapple juice. Many a stout fellow has been laid low by the curse of citric acid.

"But why are there so many dumpsters?"

"I beg your pardon?"

"Dumpsters, dumpsters. They're creating a public nuisance."

This being a parade, Donny figured a string of cars, perhaps even floats sponsored by the Rotary and assembled by wholesome high school students up all night stuffing colored tissue paper into chicken wire palm trees and indigenous waterfowl, followed behind the squad car, but in fact they did not. Only two vehicles followed: the Annes' production vehicle and the Big Al Broadnax van. Anyway, Donny was too drunk to swivel his head astern for a look. He'd see them all when the parade arrived at its destination, when he nailed down his stipulation.

Bert, new captain of the *King Don*, was telling Donny a truncated story he could barely follow about a fellow with three testicles, who, when asked, "How you hangin'?" replied, "One behind the other, for speed," and Bert cackled knee-slappingly. Then he poured Donny another piña, after which he held the Igloo Cooler up beside his ear and shook it. Emptiness approached.

After an initial overshoot, the sheriff retreated and successfully negotiated the right-hand turn into the ex-town of Omnium Settlement. He flipped on his siren and flasher and managed to maintain control down the hill to the flat land beside the bay, where a crowd was gathering, not a huge crowd, but it was beginning to swell respectably; at least in the dark it seemed that way. Sheriff Plotner parked beside the stage.

The stage, a hurried affair made from part of the rear

wall of Fred's Hobby Shop set horizontally atop a bulldozer
corpse braced up with wires, faced west out across the
sinking town, moonlight shimmering on the encroaching
bay. A makeshift podium stood center stage, and from it
orange streamers arced to the corners of the stage. Across
the front, colored plastic flags, which Longnecker had stolen from a used car lot on Cormorant Key, fluttered in the
soft west wind. And the ruins of Omnium Settlement were
hung with Japanese lanterns gently jouncing in the breeze.

Very festive, Donny observed, though he wondered why
they held Founder's Day at night. Crackers just didn't do
things the way normal people do them, yet wasn't there a
sweet innocence about observed traditions in hick towns
throughout this land of ours? The Annes filmed him as he
and Sheriff Plotner unsteadily ascended the steps to the
stage. After his encounter with the gangplank, Donny was
leery of all means of elevated egress and ingress.

Captain Bert never made it to the stage steps. He
stepped in a hole and fell on his side. It was kind of comfy
down there in the warm sand, so he elected to remain for
a brief nap. Professor Goode, who was supposed to appear
behind Donny on the dais, couldn't get the car door open.

Anne's Electro-pak lighting unit flooded the stage.

Sheriff Plotner raised his hands to the audience, calling
for quiet as if before a restive capacity crowd at the Orange
Bowl. He thumped the microphone. It worked, but he
liked the sound, so he thumped it again. "Ladies and
gentlemen of Omnium Settlement"—feedback pierced the
night—"we're gonna get this Founder's Day party in full
swing here, but first a couple announcements—" Sheriff
Plotner was ad-libbing now, getting in shape for Ted Koppel. "Be sure you all buy your raffle tickets for the new
Evenrude outboard motor. Remember, if you ain't in it,
you can't win it. Also if yer drinkin' out there, remember,
you gotta keep yer bottles in brown paper bags; it's the
law of the land. Now, without further doo—ado—let me
introduce our guest of honor, who come all the way from
New York City to grace us with his presence. Weren't for
this man's gran'daddy, why, there wouldn't be no Omnium

Settlement. We'd all be living in cheekees, wrestlin' alligators, and holdin' bingo games. Our guest of honor took
off from his busy schedule of makin' deals to help us keep
the memory alive, so let's give him a big round of applause,
let's give a big southern welcome to one o' the best of the
good ole boys! Ladies and gentlemen, Mr. Donald Throckmorton Sikes!''

Stage right and left, twin 400,000-candlepower halogen
boat spots snapped on, and beams of yellowish light, like
solid things, struck Donny in the temples.

Donald Sikes wobbled at the podium and peered out
across the land. The site. The unit. The lot. The waxing
moon danced on the dark surface of Small Hope Bay, soon
to become new land. Gramps would be proud, and that
made Donald Sikes feel warm inside. After all these years,
Gramps's vision was to be vindicated, and he, Donny
Sikes, was the agent of vindication. And soon the entire
county would carry Gramps's name. The town fathers
would cave in to his demands. He had no doubt of that.
Why wouldn't they? They had all to gain, and nothing to
lose. With Big Al gone the way of Jimmy Hoffa, who was
there to block his vision? And now he wished to stand
here for a moment in the limelight, as it were, and watch
the audience watching him, savor the festive feel of it,
lanterns bobbing, moonlight shimmering, soft breezes ca-
ressing, the tropical splendor of victory—

And look! The audience was lighting candles. How
quaintly charming an effect. They were lighting candles to
honor him, holding them beneath their chins, illuminating
their faces. . . .

The realization came slowly at first, eyes adjusting to
what seemed like a thousand points of light, then focusing
on the faces themselves, but when realization finally
struck, the force of it knocked Donny back a pace from
the microphone. Bums! These were the faces of bums.
Victims! These faces were beat to shit! What did it mean?

Indeed the effect was powerful. The Annes had made
up the squatters of Omnium Settlement to look like the
Beggars of London in *The Threepenny Opera*. Hideous

skin eruptions, goiters, scars, pus, red festering wounds, wreckage of humanity, stunted children and hopeless adults—

Donny whimpered in shock at the sight, but this was nothing compared to the next: the sight of Big Al Broadnax, house center, his son Sennacherib holding a candle before his face!

Ghosts of Founder's *Nacht!*

Was he going insane? Donny Sikes brushed at the winged insects alighting on his cheek. He turned upstage away from the dreadful audience, and then he saw her, sitting on the stage beside the stinking sheriff—the scuba diving woman, with the tits! Alive! Grinning at him!

Donny stumbled stage left, then right. The boat spots followed him from side to side, then settled, soaking him in the harsh light of confusion as he regained his balance. Grinning at him! After brushing off the last insect, he began to collect himself at least enough to ask himself some questions. For example, what the fuck was going on here in the dark! These weren't ghosts, these were people, living people, whom Mr. Freed *did not kill!*

Donald Sikes grabbed the podium, tilted it, and hurled it at Rosalind. Sheriff Plotner went over backward in his chair, but Rosalind dodged the rolling podium. But she didn't stop grinning! As if they had him dead to rights. Donny Sikes dead to rights! They had nothing! They couldn't prove a thing! What could they prove?

"I'll get you for this!" he screamed in a choked, boyish voice before he leapt off the upstage edge and ran for the road. He smashed into a stand of wild sea grape, and the world turned dark. He tore wildly at their leaves and batted at their branches, but he was getting nowhere. He dropped in the sand and belly-crawled around their boles. The trees tore at his clothes and scratched his face, but he continued to crawl until he came out on the road, where he began to run for the *King Don*.

He'd never make it on foot. He halted, panting. He needed transport. Bad. What was this? A moped. Donald Sikes didn't know much about motor vehicles, since someone else always drove him around, but he knew mopeds, having rented one once in Bermuda. He mounted up and kicked at the starter. Pudgy knees akimbo, he twisted the throttle for full speed.

"What the fuck is going on here!" Big Al Broadnax demanded of his son. "Who the fuck was that guy!"

"He's a comedian, Dad. They hired him for the celebration," said Snack.

"What celebration!"

"Why, the celebration for the Colonel A. C. Broadnax Memorial Museum. These folks here, they're the ones going to build it."

"Oh. Really? . . . They could use a bath."

EMBARKATION

TEETH BARED, DONALD SIKES SPED DOWN THE DOCK past *Staggerlee*'s late berth and careened the moped deftly up the gangplank right to the bulwark above the *King Don*'s main deck, but he slammed his balls on the seat prong as he dismounted. The moped fell into the water, sizzling as it sank. Shit! Donny forgot the dock lines. His balls throbbed. Moving hurt, so he decided to skip the dock lines, let the ship tear them off.

But could he operate the *King Don*? He'd watched his crooked captain do it numerous times. There was nothing that pothead could do that a man of Donny's caliber couldn't. Donny hobbled up the companionway into the wheelhouse. He'd flee full speed ahead to international waters, then decide what all this meant, this Founder's Day. It was some kind of setup, but what kind? What was the point? He fumbled for the light switch on the after bulkhead. The light came on. He screamed—

Donny Sikes was not alone in the wheelhouse. There was a man wearing a bathing suit in there with him, and it didn't take an M.D. to know that that man was dead as a hammer. There was a corpse sitting in the helmsman's seat! Not exactly sitting. This dead man was as stiff as a plate-glass window. Why was he stiff like that? Donny approached. . . . The stiff wasn't wearing a bathing suit; he was wearing a pair of blood-encrusted Jockey shorts! The bugs were bouncing off Donny's cheeks now. Panic welled. . . . Mr. Freed!

Donny tapped Mr. Freed's forearm with his fingernail. Mr. Freed's forearm was frozen. In fact, *all* of Mr. Freed was frozen! That's why he wasn't exactly sitting in the helmsman's seat. There was a blue-black hole in his forehead ringed with cold gray ooze. Donny Sikes clutched his face and bellowed. The pep band played Chuck Berry's greatest hits.

He glanced out the shoreside window. The sheriff was roaring up the road. Others—the halt, lame, mutilated— were making their way on foot down the dock toward the *King Don*. Marchers still carried twinkling candles. The parade was coming after him! He should have known killers didn't have agents! Gramps would call him a fool for that. Later. He'd worry about that later. First priority was speed. Maybe he didn't need to make it all the way to international water. Maybe he could find a nice swampy hole where he could dump this frozen hitter, whose pupils were milky discs like the eyes of a dead barracuda.

Donny punched the starter button, and his three MTU 16V396TB94's roared to life. There was hope in that sound, sea room in that sound. The green lights and gauges on the instrument panel cast a cozy glow. Needles jumped. Maybe everything would be all right. But how did Walter Freed get—! Donny shoved the throttles to their stops.

Small Hope Bay frothed and boiled under the stern. The bow line fell slack as the stern line twanged taut. It stretched to its limit. The dock creaked and groaned. The dock gave up first. The plank to which the cleat was bolted pulled through its fasteners, and like a slingshot the recoiling line hurled plank and cleat through the panoramic smoked windows of the main salon. The same thing happened with the bow line. It tore out a large section of dock and trolled the boards against the side.

Just then, when escape seemed possible, Donny spotted Doom Loomis. Legs crossed, he was sitting on a dock piling like a nasty fucking leprechaun. He was wearing a wet suit. And he was wet. Why was he wet?

The *King Don* didn't steam ten feet over the bottom before the new, improved Longnecker special detonated under her keel. Concussion tore through the ship in waves. The sound of things breaking followed each wave. Marble cracked, steel snapped, glass shattered. Donny found himself on his ass. But that was minor compared to the damage below the waterline. The bomb had buckled a steel plate and flattened the engine room's forward bulkhead. Almost instantly the power plants, flooded, died with a violated hiss. And the *King Don* came to a stop. Chlorine gas from the batteries coursed through her insides.

Donny whimpered like a little boy abandoned in a shopping mall. . . . He couldn't hear! Doom Loomis did it! Defeated and deafened by some geek, some nobody! Donny screamed at the outrage of it all. Then he began to kick things. He drove his fist through the radar screen. He moved in the smoke of disbelief. Doom Loomis! A small-timer's son! A depressed *sailor!*

Mr. Freed! He had to get Mr. Freed over the side. Mr. Freed's presence would be hard to explain. Walter Vale, a.k.a. Mr. Freed, had been frozen at the morgue in a recumbent posture, arms at his sides, bare feet falling outboard, fish eyes staring at the ceiling. Donny clutched Walter Vale's head under his armpit, dragged the stiff's heels along the wheelhouse floor and out the door on the starboard side, the side away from the dock.

Groaning, balls and brains throbbing, Donald Sikes hefted Walter Vale up against the bulwark and leaned him there like a shovel. Donny didn't mean to look Walter

Vale in the face, but he did. There was the stuff of insanity in the sight. Little icicles hung from his eyelashes. His blue-black lips formed an O as if the bullet that made the mouth-like hole in his forehead had come as something of a surprise. And that wasn't the only hole in Mr. Freed. His torso seemed riddled with hideous puckers. Donald Sikes squatted, clutched the icy thighs, and lifted the corpse's lower region up to the bulwark rail. Donald Sikes shoved Walter Vale over the side.

No splash? . . . Why was there no—? Donny peeked over the side. He moaned at the sight: Walter Vale hung upside down by a 500-pound test fishing line tied around his ankles. Only his head bobbed in the water. Where was the other end of the line! Donald Sikes crawled along the line until he got to the knot. It was tied to the base of the helmsman's seat. He clawed at it. He bit at it, but he couldn't break the knot under that load.

The lights went out aboard the *King Don*.

"Gramps! Gramps!" keened Donald Sikes to the darkness as he scurried in tight circles on his hands and knees. He peeked out the dockside window. The crowd had assembled there, candles flickering. There was that bitch Rosalind, the stinking sheriff, and Doom Loomis!

Doom waved at Donny.

Donny ducked out of sight and resumed his confused circular crawling. He had to get off this boat! With its life sentence hanging dead to rights off the starboard side. On the next lap he noticed something strange—not as strange as Mr. Freed hanging over the side, but still strange. The crowd was now looking straight into the wheelhouse window, directly at Donny circling. When Donny had boarded his boat, her bridge deck floated twenty feet above the dock. Now dock and wheelhouse were level. That could mean only one thing! Either they were pumping up the dock or—

Donald Sikes ducked under Walter's tether, hurled himself out the door and over the rail. His feet hit something hard before they hit the water, something that might have been Mr. Freed.

Light beams from the Annes' movie cameras were pawing the black water, searching for him. He ducked underwater and swam for his life. Roger Vespucci was among the first to see him surface, but Roger did not point out his position to the crowd. He wanted Donny Sikes alone. He was swimming south out around the parking lot. A thicket of red mangroves lined the shore in that direction all the way down to Omnium Settlement. It looked to Roger Vespucci that the man who had tried to murder him in cold blood was heading for the cover of that thicket. Roger cocked his spear gun—the best gun he could come up with under the circumstances—and ran across the lighted lot to vanish among the mangrove roots, to wait where no light penetrated.

Doom Loomis felt sorry for Donald Sikes in his wild-eyed flight and for the *King Don* sinking pathetically in the shallow water of Small Hope Bay. Soon she would come to rest on the oozy bottom with only the bridge deck protruding. She hissed and boiled as if protesting the waste of it all. Doom averted his eyes. Rosalind put her arm around his shoulder.

Tears ran down Rosalind's cheeks. Doom put his face in her hair. "I guess this is it," Rosalind muttered.

"I knew we wouldn't feel good when it was over," said Doom.

The Flamingo Tongue skippers discussed the intricacies of marine salvage law without moving their lips.

But it wasn't over yet.

Donald Sikes crawled ashore in the mangroves. Flaying his ankles on the root oysters, he clambered into the thicket. Through the chinks, he could see the crowd heading his way, lights licking at the trees. Then a flashlight beam hit him flush in the eyes and knocked him to his knees—

"Come on, Donny, give yourself up!" It was the smelly sheriff calling. "You'll only get hurt in there—" But it wasn't the sheriff's light that struck him in the face.

"It's me, Donny," said the man with the light, a voice full of glee.

"Who? Who are you?"

"I'll give you a hint: Want a piña colada, you crazy lush?"

"Roger!"

All the dead were coming back to haunt him! "Half a mil, Roger. All yours. Just help me get out of here!"

"You aren't going to get out of here," said Roger flatly.

"What?"

"This is where you're going to die. Not a very nice place, huh? Tough shit." Squinting, Roger Vespucci peered down the shaft of the spear, lined it up with Donny's heart, and he would have pulled the trigger, he intended to pull the trigger, but—

A gun fired a single shot. It struck Donald Sikes in the right temple. In the beam of his own flashlight Roger saw Donny's head jerk violently left, then back to its normal attitude. Donny Sikes was dead before he hit the ground. He sagged straight down into the mud. His body wanted to fall over, but the mangrove roots prevented it. Instead, he sat there, hands in his lap, head lolling.

Roger cringed, waiting for the impact against his own head. . . . When it didn't happen, he slowly turned the light to his left, where the shot had come from.

It was an old lady! An old lady with a leather face! Maybe it was a mask, a disguise. Maybe it was a transvestite. Roger threw down his spear gun. "Don't shoot, don't shoot! I didn't like him either!"

Lisa Up-the-Grove examined Donny's head. It didn't take long to assure herself that Donny was dead. "This man kidnapped my granddaughter. Had her stripped, scared. He was going to kill her. You do that to my granddaughter, you get shot in the skull. The tide goes in, the tide goes out. That's the way things work."

"Sure, lady, absolutely. I don't blame you," said Roger. Did she mean to shoot *him* now? "He tried to kill me. That's why, uh, I was going to spear him—" Roger was backpedaling in the mud. "We better get out of here, you know what I mean? Don't wanna be caught hanging around your victims— You take care now—" Roger Vespucci turned and crashed out of the thicket, taking a terrible beating on the way, but that was better than a bullet in the brain pan.

Lisa Up-the-Grove silently dematerialized.

Sheriff Plotner shone his light on Donny Sikes after he had cordoned off the area.

The Annes filmed the body.

"He's dead," said the sheriff when Doom arrived on the scene alone, having convinced Rosalind to spare herself the sight.

"And I bet I know who done it," said Sheriff Plotner, who was crowded shoulder to shoulder next to Doom in the thicket.

"Who?" said Doom, in the excitement barely noticing the stink.

"That joker Roger Vespucci. That was your idea, right? I mean that's why you let him go, ain't it?"

"Yes."

"He'll be here somewhere. I'll block off the bridge. He ain't got a prayer of escape—" The sheriff started to slog off, tripping over roots.

"Ahh, Sheriff—"

"Yeah, what?"

"I think we ought to let him go again."

"What? Why!"

"Because if we catch him there will be a trial. We don't want there to be a trial."

No trial, no publicity. No publicity, no Ted Koppel. Shit.

"A lot of things might come out in the trial. Some of the things could land you and me and our friends in jail. It's just like the Annes' film. It can't ever see the light of day. The Annes know that. We've discussed it, haven't we?"

The Annes nodded. . . .

But that still wasn't the end of it. That night Duncan Feeney stole a rough cut of the *Doom Documentary* and disappeared.

SHOW BIZ

Duncan didn't wait until he got into Manhattan. He phoned his ex-agent from the baggage claim area at La Guardia. "Shelly, Shelly baby, it is I, Duncan Feeney, and I have gold in my grip."

"Who is this?"

"Feeney, Duncan Feeney!"

"Oh yeah. Listen, I don't handle prison memoirs."

"Prison? I was never in prison! They'll never get me!"

"Do you know what time it is?"

"Okay, forget it, Shelly. Big-timers, forward-lookers, they'd kill for what I got. But forget it, sorry I imposed. Take dork in hand and go back to sleep. I'll find a man of vision who'll know what to do with what I got."

"What have you got?"

Duncan Feeney told Shelly what he had in the six film cans he was waiting to claim.

"Jesus. . . . Dennis Loomis? The guy who wrote *Splendor?*"

"*Splendor* was my idea! My fucking idea! Why does no one remember that?"

"This is all true? It actually *happened?*"

"I thought this might get your attention."

"It said on TV that Donald Sikes drowned while swimming off his own boat."

"Well, he didn't. Do you want it or do you not want it?"

"Do I want it? What, are you nuts! It's gold."

Duncan grinned. He could see it now—acclaim, celebrity, money. Especially money. The offers would pour in.

284

He still might become spokesman for a Japanese auto manufacturer, get his picture on an American Express ad, or one of those scotch ads where they tell the drinker's profession (conceiver), interests (Spandex), and last book read (*Splendor*).

In a plushly private screening room on Broadway and Forty-ninth Street, Duncan Feeney, Shelly, and his associates viewed the Annes' rough footage. It took five hours, and it left everyone speechless. A true crime story, on-the-scene footage of a criminal conspiracy in the making. Murder, arson, sun-baked intrigue, Oedipal stuff, you name it. *As it happened!* Could have been more about drugs, spics from Columbia with pinky rings, but what the hell, we have the downfall of heavyweights, everybody loves that, the sins of the father. This thing had themes, big themes, you know, like *Equus*. Christ, Florida's hot right now, still riding the wake of "Miami Vice." Now you mention it, we could get Don Johnson to narrate, or if he's not available, the other guy, the lieutenant who never moves his mouth when he acts, the fuck's his name? We're looking at an Oscar for best documentary, at least a Pulitzer, points, video subsids, the Jap rights alone would set us up for life.

"Would you pardon us for a moment, Duncan? Let my associates and I discuss this matter?" asked Shelly. "Can I have my girl get you something?"

"No, but can I have your girl?" said Duncan.

"Ha, good one, Duncan. Have my girl, great." Shelly's associates grinned without mirth.

"He's right, this *is* gold," said Morty Goss after Duncan had left. Morty Goss was hot just now because he'd made a ninja version of *Beowulf* starring Brigitte Nielsen as Grendel, which lost twelve million dollars.

"Oh, big bucks, *pan grande*," predicted Kink Frazier.

"I'm deeply moved by it," said Mick Mercy.

"Only thing is, this Feeney guy—" added Taylor Crasswell.

"Yeah," said the others too junior to express any other opinion.

"But what do we need this Feeney guy for anyway, a fugitive? So what he was there? Nobody cares. He didn't make the movie, did he? He doesn't own the rights, does he? Doom Loomis—and this Rosemary chick—they're the ones we care about," Kink pointed out. Kink was the literary man, the man in charge of structure, characterization, and verisimilitude. His job was to get to the artistic meat of things.

"So what do we do, buy him off?"

"Yeah, cheap."

"I mean, fugitives hanging around a project—poison. Majors won't touch it with fugitives. I mean, also the guy's got no class."

"So maybe he won't want classy money."

"How much you figure? Ballpark."

"I got a better idea," said Shelly. He shouted up to his girl in the projection booth, "Janice, get me the FBI."

"Pardon me, Mr. Klepton?"

"Get me the FBI, please."

"Did you say FBI, Mr. Klepton?"

"Yes, I did, Janice." To his associates, Shelly said, "I'll bring the poor bastard a fruitcake one of these years," which cracked up his associates.

That very evening in the screening room, Shelly and his associates decided to get aggressive on this thing. They had to find out who actually made the movie, and secure rights, sure, but that could wait. For the immediate future, they scheduled test screenings before a strictly invited audience.

The audiences, over cheap champagne, Brie, and crudités served by out-of-work SAG members in mime whiteface, agreed that this was indeed a gold mine. No one in the audience could recall ever seeing anything like it.

"I've never seen anything like it!"

"And it's actually *true!*"

"No—"

"Yes! It actually happened. Conceptually, that's the whole *point*."

"What is?"

286

"That it's true!"

"Who told you it was true?"

"Shelly Klepton."

"Klepton wouldn't know true if it nipped him in the bud."

"Nevertheless. Do you know who made it? The Annes made it."

"Who?"

"Big-time dyke documentarians. Artist types. Sincere. Don't you read the trades?"

"Oh yeah, they made *Mom,* sure."

"*Mom?* What was *Mom* about?"

"Uterine cancer."

"Who was in it?"

"You know what I hear? I hear Shelly hasn't got the rights. Might be time for a trip to the sunny South. Have checkbook, will travel. Even to Florida."

"Yeah, but documentaries don't do shit in Dubuque. Do you think we could release it as a theatrical film?"

"Come on, get with the program on this."

". . . Would you consider a docudrama?"

Word spread quickly from Broadway to Beverly Hills, and that New York heard about it first struck fear into the hearts of Californians.

"Why didn't you hear about this *Doom* thing first? What? I got to hear about it from that dickup Klepton? Not even Klepton! Klepton's girl!"

"We heard about it first."

"You did?"

"Didn't you get our memo?"

"It's New York pretending like they mean something."

"Yeah, New York's pulling a fast one."

"Amazing anybody still lives in that filth."

Underlings lied to their bosses and their bosses lied to the majors. Seventy-two hours after Duncan's arrest, the origins of the *Doom Documentary* were hopelessly obscured, tangled in power-breakfast lies and parent-company myth. The majors decided to see for themselves, scope it out, have an on-site look-see to blow the smoke away, figure out whether this thing had wings, and they hired special charter flights from LAX straight to Miami. There fleets of stretch limos waited, drivers studying maps to learn exactly how the fuck you get to this hick town, Omnium.

Duncan, in custody, wasn't silent during those hours.

He sang like a mockingbird in the hopes of sneaking by with probation and a suspended sentence. "We're talking murder here! Three, no four, capital crimes. Donald Sikes murdered! His boat sunk. Hell, you can still see it sitting on the bottom! I'm ready to cooperate with you guys. I'm a friendly witness!" That fucking Shelly. One day, one day he'd get that fucking Shelly. Shelly will never work in this town again.

"Hey, boss," said Agent Deeds to the director at a urinal, "we got some funny business going down on Omnium Key, Florida."

"Bullshit, Deeds, you're just trying to cadge a cheap vacation."

"No, sir, I think this is the real thing." Agent Deeds peed on his hand by accident, but he didn't let on in front of the director. "About the death of Donald Sikes."

"The tycoon? He drowned, didn't he?"

"I got a guy says he was murdered as part of a conspiracy. Guy says he's got it on film."

"So let's see the film."

"The guy ain't got the film."

"I thought you just said—"

"I mean he's got it on film, but he don't have the film. He says some associates stole it from him."

"Sounds pretty murky to me, Deeds."

"Yes, sir."

"Okay, check it out, but I don't want to see a lot of funny business appear on the expense account. The Bureau ain't paying for fellatio."

"Oh, no sir."

"Yeah, bullshit."

THE MAJOR PLAYERS

A MOROSE CREW GATHERED ABOARD *STAGGERLEE* IN THE dying light of dusk. It had felt sweet to Doom and Rosalind to emerge from Black Caesar's sordid backwater into the soft light at the Flamingo Tongue docks, where the *King Don* sat on the bottom, brown pelicans and cormorants homemaking in her superstructure. Marvis was working on a deal to sell the salvage rights. Marvis and Bert were aboard *Staggerlee*; so were Longnecker and Holly and Professor Goode, who felt particularly guilty, since he and Duncan Feeney had come to Florida together.

When the Annes arrived, Rosalind cast off the dock lines and Doom got *Staggerlee* under way. He realized this was the first time he'd ever seen the Annes without the tools of their art in front of their faces. The Annes were limp, befuddled.

In a soft, moist west wind Doom and Bert set the main and the light number one genoa, which for the hell of it, Bert barberhauled out to the toe rail to improve sail shape, and they beam-reached down Small Hope Bay at under five knots. It was dark by the time Bert and Doom trimmed up the sails and joined the others in the cockpit.

Shortly after dawn that morning, the Annes had received the first of a string of disturbing phone calls from their agent, Agnes Steel. The night before, Agnes Steel had crashed one of Shelly Klepton's screenings after rumor reached her that Shelly was showing her clients' work as if he owned it. "I felt like I'd been raped," said Agnes Steel.

At first the Annes were disbelieving. He wouldn't dare! But they knew that was nonsense; of course he would dare. This was the worst that could happen. The Annes blamed themselves. Agnes would bring heavy clout down on Klepton's skull and the Annes would eventually recover their film, but what would happen to them? They could all land in jail, but it would go worse for Doom, the ringleader, as their own footage established. He already had a record. It would be hard time for Doom Loomis.

Agnes called again before noon. She told them that the FBI had arrested Duncan Feeney on an outstanding warrant for fraud, conspiracy to defraud, mail fraud, and literary mischief.

She called again at 6:30. "It's public knowledge now, the whole ball of wax is out of the closet." A story about the *Doom Documentary* and its sensational contents had just appeared on "Eyewitness News."

Shortly before *Staggerlee* got under way, Agnes phoned a fourth time to tell them that Ted Koppel's people at "Nightline" had called. They wanted an interview with the Annes, and they wanted to meet Doom Loomis. They wanted to devote an entire show to the *Doom Documentary*. "What do you want me to do?" Agnes Steel had asked. And that's where it stood when they boarded *Staggerlee* to make some decisions. Doom was sick of making decisions.

"There's at least three limos parked in front of every motel on Tequesta Key," said Rosalind.

"We know those people," said Anne, "they're ruthless."

"They'll stop at nothing."

"What they can't buy, they'll steal."

"It's all my fault," said Professor Goode. "I brought him."

"Don't worry about blame," said Doom. "Anyway, it was my fault. I agreed to let us be filmed. I feel like Richard Nixon."

"We shouldn't have done it," said Anne. "As soon as it turned illegal, we should have backed off."

"Who knew it would get this big?" added Anne.

"But we were excited."

"Titillated."

"We let our feelings get in the way."

Doom bore off slightly to port in order to stay in the channel, and Bert eased the sheets. Doom knew it wasn't merely the show-biz sharks that had arrived. A couple of guys in blue pin-striped suits had been spotted hanging around the Flamingo Tongue. They'd arrest him anytime now, and all the publicity around the case would make them even more ardent. That's how careers got made.

Rosalind sighed.

No one spoke. Small Hope Bay, safe now, gurgled beneath the hull.

The Annes had to do it. Politically it was the only correct course of action. They knew that Doom knew it, too—they could see it on his face—but he was too polite to bring it up. The Annes exchanged glances. Anne began: "The problem for us is that this movie is *true*—"

"It's a documentary," Anne clarified.

"Right," said Anne, "but suppose it wasn't?"

The concept began to dawn on the others.

Anne continued: "Suppose we accepted the invitation to appear on 'Nightline' and told Ted, what's all the fuss about? This is"—the word stuck in Anne's throat—"fic-shun?"

"A theatrical film."

"All acting."

"Who's left to contradict us?"

"Nobody."

Doom knew how much it would hurt the Annes to call cinéma vérité fic-shun on network TV, and the offer to do so touched him. It was the only alternative to hard time. But would Ted believe them? Probably not. There were too many loose ends.

Rosalind put her arms around the Annes and hugged them. They stroked Rosalind's hair.

Staggerlee's crew felt close, connected, familial. They

sailed along in silence until the bridge over Hurricane Hole Creek loomed.

"Ready about?" Doom asked.

Captain Bert eased the barberhaul and took two turns off the portside primary winch. "Ready," he muttered.

"Helm's alee," muttered Doom.

After completing the tack and retrimming the sails, Doom said, "We still have to decide what to do with Omnium Settlement."

After a brief discussion they concluded that they had no choice. They had to let it sink. Back to its pre–Broadnax/ Throckmorton shoreline. As nature intended and history demanded. And then use the money they had stolen to keep it that way.

"But what are you going to do?" Holly, speaking for everyone aboard, asked Doom and Rosalind.

Doom and Rosalind looked at each other. . . . Good question.

MUSEUM QUALITY

SNACK BROADNAX OPENED THE SLIDING DOOR AND lowered the platform to its horizontal boarding position. Then he wheeled his father's chair onto the platform, lowering him to the ground.

"Son?"

"Yes, Dad?"

"Where are we?"

"We're at the future site, Dad."

"Future?"

"The future site of the Colonel A. C. Broadnax Memorial Museum. It'll be very grand when it's done."

That made Big Al happy, Snack could tell. His father's fingers began to tap the armrests.

Snack wheeled Big Al into the shade of the causerina pines at the crest of the hill from which, six feet up, he could look down on the work already under way in Omnium Settlement. Snack sat on the cool, fallen pine needles beside his father and pointed out to him the features of the Broadnax Museum, its shape, contents, and future location. A Bahama longtail lizard scurried from under Big Al's chair into the deep cover of sea grape and buttonwood along the road.

There was in fact work going on down in Omnium Settlement, but it had nothing to do with the Broadnax Museum. There would be no museum. The workers—squatters whom Marvis had hired at a generous wage—were disassembling the remains of the settlement board by board, brick by brick, and loading it into huge rented dumpsters. Marvis had made a sweet deal with the carting company. While the work progressed, Snack was housing the squatters in outbuildings, most opulently appointed for guests who had never been invited, on the Broadnax compound. His father, who now seldom left his canopied bed, never saw them. In, say, five years, when Small Hope Bay had reclaimed its bottom and Omnium Key had returned to its primeval shape, there would be no sign that Omnium Settlement had ever existed. Time passes, all things die.

"Well, son, it sounds grand, a grand museum for a grand man."

Gone, dead, just like his father, before too long. Big Al seldom ate, seldom even raised his voice these days. Big Al had passed away; it's just that he hadn't died yet.

"Oh, yes," said Snack, "I forgot to tell you about the Claudius wing."

"The Claudius wing?"

"I talked it over with the architects and engineers, those type guys. It's all set. We'll have his diving gear on display, pictures of him under the ice in the Antarctica, all the great dives he made."

"It sounds grand."

The last of the dead bulldozers had been removed, but the earth still retained deep white scars. The scars would probably remain until Small Hope Bay covered them with brown water. Snack knew his father would be dead by then. Snack and his father sat watching while those squatters who had earth-moving experience pushed down Fred's Hobby Shop with a rented backhoe. Fred's squeaked in protest as it fell.

Watching, Big Al fell asleep. His lips vibrated with each exhalation. Snack stood up to take him home, but before he turned the chair around, Snack leaned down and kissed the top of his father's head.

"Huh?" murmured Big Al.

"Nothing, Dad."

"Son?"

"Yes, Dad?"

"What happened to Lucas Hogaboom?"

"I don't know."

"He didn't even say good-bye. . . . He was like a son to me."

FORCE-7

THE FLAMINGO TONGUE SKIPPERS AND OTHER KIBITZERS urged Doom and Rosalind to delay departure. Miami marine weather warned of a fast-approaching Arctic Maritime cold front bringing sustained winds of thirty knots and severe localized depressions, miniature hurricanes spawned by unusually warm Gulf Stream water, spinning off the leading edge of the front. Winds in excess of fifty knots had been recorded in the depressions. Twelve- to fifteen-foot seas were expected to follow the front. Even now swirling dark clouds had gathered in the northeast, and the sea had turned an ominous green. Waves broke constantly over the jetties at Bird Cut.

"*Staggerlee* can take it," Doom said.

"We ain't worried about the boat," said Arnie.

"We're worried about the crew," said Bobby.

But this was precisely the weather Doom and Rosalind had been waiting for. The media were pressing in. Network news was calling for interviews, and camera crews had already begun to gather at Miami International, clogging car-rental desks. The Annes' denial, scheduled for airing tomorrow night—the Annes had already left for New York—wouldn't get the press and show-biz sharks off their backs, even if it temporarily deflected the law from the path of justice. Maybe it wouldn't do that either. It was time to go.

Rosalind and Lisa Up-the-Grove loaded stores and gear aboard *Staggerlee*. With help from Bert, Marvis, Sheriff Plotner, and the Flamingo Tongue skippers, Doom inspected sheets and halyards for signs of wear, checked that reefing lines were correctly led and that the hanks on the storm jib were in working order, oiled the stiff ones, and saw to it that the hatches could be effectively closed and dogged. Then they inspected the standing rigging. Bert examined the shroud tangs through binoculars. There was a grim mood around the preparations that morning, as if departure, planned for 1500 hours, might be the last any of them would see of Doom and Rosalind.

They ran and cleated jack lines, attachment points for safety harnesses, the length of the deck. They unflaked the mainsail and inspected its headboard, its tack, clew, and reefing grommets. They repeated the process on the numbers one and two genoas, the working jib, and the storm trysail. They tugged and yanked on the winches, the leads, and the cleats to test their mountings.

Helping, the Flamingo Tongue skippers discussed sabotage among themselves, noting that Doom had only one mainsail. All they'd need to do was cut a six- or seven-inch slit along a stress point to render the sail useless, immediate departure untenable, but none of them had the heart to draw a knife. Hell, Doom might just go anyway, even if they holed the boat. He appeared blindly determined to depart come hell or high water, both of which were forecast, and that seemed out of character for him. Rosalind went about her preparations with cold resolve, like a prospective suicide.

"You got an EPIRB?" Arnie demanded.

"What's that?" Doom asked.

"Emergency position-indicating radio beacon."

"Oh, yes, I have one of those."

"Let's see it."

Doom pretended he was too distracted to show it to them.

The Flamingo Tongue skippers cornered Bert. "Look, Bert, what do you think about this voyage?"

"Bad weather. I think they ought to put it off."

"That's what we're sayin'."

"Guy's tryin' to get himself killed."

"Rosalind too."

"Yeah."

"Well, can't you do anything? Hell, you're the captain."

"I already tried. What more can I do? Besides, Doom's the captain now."

They stood around in a knot, talking about the state of the sea without moving their lips. You could feel twenty knots of true wind on your face—right down here in the harbor. Imagine what it was gonna be like *out there* beyond a thousand fathoms.

"He ain't got the skills yet," said Arnie. "Two weeks ago he didn't know how to take a shit on a boat."

"Takes years."

"He's a smart guy, sure, but he ain't got the skills."

"Even if you got the skills you don't go out in *this*."

"Talk to him, Bert."

"I did. I told you."

"Look, let's all go talk to him at once."

"Okay, let's."

But it was no use. Doom and Rosalind were adamant.

A glum group gathered on the dock to see them off. Billy, Bobby, Arnie, and Arnie Jr. felt frustrated, angry that their advice was going unheeded, but that wasn't their true feeling. They were, frankly, sad to see Doom and Rosalind go and afraid they'd never be seen again. Doom and Rosalind and the rest of them had done some funny business, though no one knew clearly just what. Some people said they had sunk the *King Don* and killed Donald Sikes, but that was all for the good as far as the Flamingo Tongue skippers were concerned. Sure, there were a lot of suspicious Yankees hanging around, but they could be dealt with. You could always bullshit Yankees, get them so confused they'd go home. Doom and Rosalind didn't need to bolt in panic like this.

Dawn and Archie waved white dish cloths.

Captain Bert, Sheriff Plotner, Longnecker, Holly, Marvis, the professor, and Lisa Up-the-Grove stood silently watching *Staggerlee* back out of her berth, motor around the breakwater past the sunken hulk of the *King Don* and into the swift ebb tide blowing through Bird Cut.

"It's suicide, goddamnit," said Arnie. His compatriots concurred.

And it was, in a sense.

Doom and Rosalind were shocked by the state of the sea outside the Cut, even though they knew it would be bad. Great green hulkers in endless ranks broke spectacularly against the north jetty. Spray, sometimes solid water, flew clear across the Cut onto the south jetty. Between the jetties, visibility was nil. Outside the jetties chaos reigned.

In full foul-weather gear, Doom sat at the wheel with his back to weather. There was a smile on his face. They were going to sea together. They were going to die together. There was a wonderful kind of intimacy in that. Rosalind moved from the relative shelter under the canvas dodger and came aft to sit beside Doom. He put his arm around her, but he quickly removed it when he found he was unable to maintain control with one hand on the wheel.

When they presented their beam to the wind, waves broke over it. Doom turned his bow quarter to weather. Rosalind took the helm while Doom crawled forward to the mast, clipped his safety harness to the spinnaker pole fitting, and set the trysail. He then went forward to the bow to set the number three jib. It was bulletproof, but Doom decided it was too big, so he hauled it aft and set the storm jib instead. He had never been on the bow of a boat in these conditions. Things were different up there.

Extreme motion is most violent in the ends of a boat. When the bow dropped off the backs of the waves, Doom found himself momentarily airborne, following the bow down to where it disappeared underwater. It took him twenty minutes to set the jib, attach the tack and halyard, and tie on the sheets, a task which in fair weather he could have done in five. He spent most of the time hanging on.

Rosalind, tight-lipped, fought the wheel. Doom came aft to help. He clipped Rosalind's safety harness around the steering pedestal, and then his own. He had never seen the Florida sky look so bellicose before. The darkness in the northeast obliterated the horizon as if that part of the ocean and the sky had joined forces, become one, and attacked.

The sullen bon voyage party climbed up to the road where, shielding their eyes against driven sand, they watched *Staggerlee* diminish into the spindrift. They could see the tip of her mast snapping back and forth, spray exploding around her bows.

"Goners," pronounced Arnie with a slow shake of his head.

They watched until *Staggerlee* vanished, then Archie said, "Well, come on back to the Tongue. I'll close up, and we'll all have a stiff drink."

The storm blew all night. Passing over the Middle Keys, it eroded beaches, blew down palm trees, wrecked several boats at a marina on Upper Matacumbe Key, and lifted the roof off a grade school on Vaca Key. Up and down the string of islands, wherever salty locals gathered to discuss fish, boats, and the ocean, old men said that short of a hurricane, they'd never seen a storm so prolonged and violent. "Rough as a cob out there." Back up at Bird Cut, a tourist family of three from Manitoba, ignorant of the power of the sea, was swept from the south jetty and never seen again.

The next morning, winds down to the high teens, seas still wild and confused, Bert, Marvis, Longnecker, and Holly walked the beach. That's when they came upon the wreckage of *Staggerlee*. They carried her remains back to the Flamingo Tongue, since that was the nearest phone from which to call the Coast Guard at Miami. They piled the wreckage on a table near the door. Silently, the skippers, Archie, and Dawn gathered around as if it were the corpse of a drowned friend.

Dawn began to cry. Holly held her.

There was the horseshoe life ring with her name on the yellow cover, the broken man-overboard pole, some plastic drinking glasses also bearing *Staggerlee*'s name, her number one genoa in its torn and sodden bag.

Arnie Jr. began to weep silently.

Archie phoned the Coast Guard. He put Bert on the phone to describe the boat more precisely. Bert felt guilty talking to the officer, but it had to be done. He just hoped none of their people got hurt in the search.

There were also cockpit seat cushions and a dropleaf from *Staggerlee*'s table. There was the wooden frame of a hatch cover and the cracked toilet seat from her head.

The skippers sadly shook their heads. Billy wiped a tear from his cheek with a paper napkin and pretended he had something in his eye.

"Who's gonna tell Mrs. Up-the-Grove?" Dawn wondered.

A giggling tourist family from Moline, Illinois, wandered in, but Archie told them he was closed, sorry.

Holly and Longnecker, Bert and Marvis, Professor Goode and Sheriff Plotner all felt guilty.

"Wait a minute," said Arnie, "I got a question. How come *you* all happened to find this wreckage, and how come you found it all in one place? You know what I mean? I mean, don't that seem a little unusual from what we know about shipwrecks?"

"Yeah," said Bobby, "now you mention it."

"Yeah. And how come nobody else found any wreckage?"

The conspirators looked at each other, hesitated. They simply had to tell these good people the truth about their friends' death.

SEA STRUCK

DOOM LIKED TO GO DEEP. HE LIKED THAT HIT OF nitrogen narcosis and its accompanying feeling of fluidity, of tranquillity. Something happens to air under pressure. Its component gases mutate. Beyond 250 feet our friend oxygen turns toxic. At much lesser depths, nitrogen takes on narcotic qualities. Jacques-Yves Cousteau, Emile Gagnan, and Frederic Dumas "discovered" nitrogen narcosis in the pioneering days, called it "rapture of the deep" and described the wild, deadly antics of a pixillated diver who thought he didn't really need all that air and genially offered his mouthpiece to a passing grouper. Doom had never experienced anything that extreme, and when he asked Rosalind if she had, she hesitated, then said only, "Claudius liked to go deep, too."

At depth Doom generally experienced a happy sense of unity with the ocean and its animals. They ignored him, but sometimes Doom felt he and Rosalind could live a blissful life among the indigo hamlets, harlequin bass, fairy basslets, glassy sweepers, mutton snappers, schoolmasters, tomtates, sailors choice, French anglefish, threespot damselfish, beaugregorys, Creole wrasse, slippery dicks, and puddingwives. Intellectually, of course, he knew they could not. He wasn't besotted with the nitrogen. He was besotted with Rosalind.

Here at Doom and Rosalind's newly discovered favorite site an enormous rock plate, a piece of the continent's underpinnings the size of a small shopping center parking lot, had undergone titanic fracturing and uplift. The rock had cracked evenly in half as the outer edges folded upward, perhaps during Jurassic times, to form a steep-walled canyon with a narrow sandy channel at the bottom. Now the nearly vertical rock faces were decorated with soft corals, sponges, plumrose anemones, feather stars, Christmas tree worms, purple sea fans, and other crynoids and gorgonians.

Staggerlee had not gone to sea in the strict sense of the term. Doom and Rosalind had sailed east out into the fringe of the storm where seas towered and the wind clawed at Doom and Rosalind's weak points. They agreed that conditions in the brunt of the storm must have been terrifying, far beyond their experience and perhaps beyond their ability to survive. It was easy to understand how even seaworthy boats like *Staggerlee* could be enveloped by those breakers, broached or pitch-poled, and dismasted. Perhaps even overwhelmed and driven under. But Doom and Rosalind turned south and ran before the blow. The apparent wind dropped radically, but still it had been a wild, white-knuckled ride.

They ducked into Meridian Passage Bay through Farewell Pass below Cormorant Key. In the lee of the islands, where the seas were short and steep, *Staggerlee* sailed fast all night and most of the following day when, near dusk, they found a quiet anchorage between Stirrup and Russel keys. They set a Danforth anchor and a big CQR, both with heavy chain and hundred-foot rodes, and they lay low for two days while the storm died.

During that time they painted out the name *Staggerlee* on the stern. *Staggerlee* had ceased to exist.

They couldn't stay long in one place. They bounced from anchorage to anchorage, heading southwest as far as Big

Pine Key. There were problems. For instance, what were they going to do now? They talked about crossing to remote parts of the Bahamas, then dismissed the idea because they couldn't clear customs without proper boat papers. The authorities by now would have given up the search for *Staggerlee*, but someone would remember her name. They could repaint the boat, rename her, but she'd still have *Staggerlee*'s papers. So they decided to stay in American waters. But where would they be safe from persistent members of the FBI, the media, and the major studios? Where could they remain obscure, nameless? And how long would it take before the heat was off, before they were forgotten? Everyone dead is forgotten eventually.

Rosalind joined Doom at the bottom of the canyon. Doom could tell she was being a diving instructor, peering deeply into his eyes. Were they spinning like slot machine cherries? Was he about to eschew air? He gave her the okay sign, and she seemed to relax. He reached up and squeezed her left breast under her stretchy suit. Coyly, she knocked his hand aside.

Doom and Rosalind disturbed an eagle ray, an old one with a five-foot wingspan, grazing for mollusks in the sand. After an initial blast of escape speed, the eagle ray slowed and flew languidly along the canyon, banking and jinking like Hollywood's notion of a spacecraft, and then glided softly to a landing on the sand, where it continued to graze. Doom envied the creature its several million years of adaptation to the ocean environment. This was an animal that fit in. That was the trouble with mankind. Mankind controlled the earth, but he never fit in. His gifts allowed him, finally forced him, to stand apart and envy the peace that must accompany perfect adaptation to a specific environment, while he remained anxious, frightened, maladjusted, and, therefore, destructive.

Was that a profound thought? Doom wondered. Naw, probably just the nitrogen talking. The reality of the ocean is depth, and Doom wondered what the nitrogen would say beyond 200 feet. Would it be the source of profound

insight at that pressure, or would it render one a helpless gob of stupidity with the mental acuity of a gooseneck barnacle? Finally, Doom supposed, it would render one a drowning victim, and as one's body sank, the weight of the water above would crush it like a Dixie cup. Was that the ocean's means of protection from mankind? But then, Doom and Rosalind had already died at sea, and that wasn't too bad. Wet, cold, rough, but nothing one couldn't survive.